The Spider Gem

www.lovesey.net

To order additional copies, please contact us.
BookSurge, LLC
www.booksurge.com
1-866-308-6235
orders@booksurge.com

TAFF
LOVESEY

THE
SPIDER GEM

Book One of the Portal
Chronicles

2005

The Spider Gem

CONTENTS

For Bridget, Jamie and Ceri

CHAPTER ONE
Recovery

P ush harder my warriors! Drive for the centre of the chamber!" The warlock shouted his orders and the Graav strained at the stone slabs that formed a solid wall, blocking their progress further along the ornately carved corridors of the deserted temple. As the creatures pushed against the slabs, the large blocks began to slide backwards. The Graav increased their effort in an attempt to bring down the obstruction and, eventually, the lower blocks of the wall began to slide inwards. As the first block of stone fell from it's place in the wall, long slim grooves were revealed on either side of the corridor exhibiting racks of sharp, metal tipped arrows aimed directly at the Graav, their points coated green with poison. The Graav hardly paused in their efforts to move forward. Turning their heads as one to look through the flame red slits that formed their eyes, they momentarily glanced at the arrows, before returning to their demolition of the obstructive wall.

With a loud twang, forty arrows shot from their housing, making a swishing noise through the air as they were released. The poisoned tips struck the Graav but merely bounced off their hard stone exteriors. The Graav hardly seemed aware of the arrows as they continued their task. A second rack of arrows was automatically released but met with the same lack of success as the first volley, once again failing to puncture the lava rock skin of the Graav. Those that had built the defences for this temple had expected to be protecting it from creatures made of flesh and bone, not fire and stone.

The Graav had now formed a large hole in the wall and suddenly, the weight of the remaining slabs could no longer support the barrier and the wall fell in on itself.

"Forward! Forward, my Graav! We are almost there!" screamed the warlock and the creatures blindly obeyed, climbing over the rubble. As they stepped over the threshold and entered this new chamber, jets of flame erupted from the grooves cut into the ceiling. The dwarf that was accompanying the warlock recoiled from the heat and turned to flee, but his retreat was prevented by the grasping arm of the warlock as he grabbed the dwarf's collar and jerked him back. "And where do you think you're going Zarn?" demanded the warlock.

The dwarf flinched, "Um, uh, nowhere master," he replied fearing to invoke his master's wrath. "I was merely shielding my eyes from the heat."

Ahead of them, the Graav poured into the chamber, they stretched their limbs in the flame and writhed in pleasure, soaking up the energy of the fires that danced around them. The warlock and the dwarf waited and watched as the flames burned strongly, fed by some form of fuel source hidden in the ceiling of this central chamber. Finally, the fuel source was exhausted and the sheet of flames died down allowing them to follow the Graav and into the new chamber.

The chamber continued for twenty yards or so and was terminated by an alabaster wall, which housed a large central, dark wood door. The door itself had been embossed with a gold representation of a spider and, to the right, a handle of solid gold, also shaped in the from of a spider. An intricate locking device had been installed directly under the door handle. The warlock smiled broadly as he looked at the door and reached into his robes to withdraw an equally intricate gold key. He spoke as he handed the key to the dwarf, "We'll now find out how reliable your sources were. Dwarf, unlock the chamber!"

Zarn hesitated before taking the key with a shaking hand, "But master, there may be more traps, can't we use the Graav to do this?"

The warlock shook his head, "This task is far too intricate for the Graav, it needs the touch of flesh and blood," replied the warlock.

Zarn's lip quivered and he quickly attempted to hand the key back to the warlock, "It sounds like this task is much too intricate for my hand too master, surely you would be better to do this yourself."

As Zarn stood with hand outstretched, offering the key back to the warlock, his master glared at him with a thunderous look on his face. The warlock raised his hand, palm outwards and uttered words of incantation. Blinding pain shot through the brain of the dwarf and he grabbed his head and screamed, "No! No! Not again master! Please stop! I'll do it! I'll do it! Please stop the pain!"

The warlock lowered his hand, "Now, that's what I like to see," he smirked, "Loyal subjects that are willing to do anything I ask." He threw his head back and laughed.

The dwarf reluctantly turned and made his way to the door. He tentatively touched the golden handle and when nothing untoward occurred, he attempted to open the door. He was not surprised when the door refused to move, it was firmly locked. Nervously he looked at the ornate key in his hand and slowly inserted it into the key hole, shutting his eyes as he did so, fearing the worst. Again nothing happened and so, with confidence growing, he turned the key anticlockwise.

There were three loud clicks but when he tried the handle, the door remained closed. Zarn swallowed and turned the key another rotation, three more loud clicks resulted. He tried the handle once more and watched in awe as the door slid back into the wall to reveal a small room. This inner sanctum was peppered with weapons of silver and gold with suits of golden armour hung around the walls. At the centre of the room was a marble dais and on this sat a staff. The staff itself was about four feet long and was tipped with a large red gem. This was the object for which they searched, the Spider Gem, a magical gemstone that would allow the holder to command a great army of arachnids.

The warlock grinned when he saw his goal and shouted his orders, commanding Zarn to pass the staff to him. The dwarf leapt to obey and reached for the staff. As his fingers clutched the shaft, a force of white energy exploded from the dais and threw him across the room. The staff fell to the floor with a clatter, right at the feet of the warlock.

He picked it up and the gem began to glow and throb as he did so. The warlock lifted the staff into the air and shouted in triumph, "At last! Now Portalia will be mine!" As he spoke, thousands of spiders appeared from cracks and crevices and soon filled the chamber and corridor, painting the walls and ceiling black with their dark hairy bodies. All of the arachnids then sat, comatose, awaiting the orders of the holder of the Spider Gem. The warlock looked at his new army and his grin broadened. He began to laugh and turned to look across at the dwarf. When he saw his minion he suddenly stopped laughing and, for a fraction of a second, he even felt the tiniest touch of remorse. This was soon shrugged away though and as the dwarf looked up at his master, the warlock began to laugh again, this time even more hysterically, pointing at the dwarf and unable to talk through his laughter. Zarn raised himself to his feet painfully and wondered at his master's reaction. Turning to look at the spider army, he caught sight of his reflection in one of the gold shields. He stopped in horror as a stranger stared back from the mirror like surface of the shield. Zarn raised his hand to check that what he was seeing was indeed his own image. He gaped as his reflection mimicked his every move. Initial horror turned to fascination as he looked at his image. He raised his hand to his hair which was now bleached white. He looked from the image directly at his skin, it had changed from the dark skin of a mountain dwarf, to a pale and pallid hue. Worst of all though were the eyes that stared back at him from the depths of the shield. Each of his pupils had been turned a deathly shade of white.

Behind him, the warlock continued to laugh.

CHAPTER TWO
Rhys

Rhys Morgens hated spiders and had done for as long as he could remember, probably all thirteen years of his life! He especially hated them in his bedroom. After all this was his bedroom, his sanctity, and spiders had no right to be there without his permission.

He watched as a rather large one crawled across his ceiling and left his bedroom via the window. Rhys always slept with his bedroom window open whilst at his Auntie Glenys' house so he could smell and feel the fresh sea air.

"Curious," thought Rhys, "that is the tenth spider in the past hour to crawl across my ceiling and leave by the same route. It must be some form of spider's night out." He smiled at this thought.

His curiosity now piqued; Rhys turned on his reading light and stood on his bed to look closer at the ceiling. He waited a while for his eyes to adjust but failed to see anything unusual in the dim light. He decided to wait a few minutes but no more spiders appeared. Eventually, yawning and stretching he realised that he had closed his eyes a number of times. He lay back on his bed, snuggled up in his quilt and settled down to sleep, hoping that he would not dream about spiders.

As Rhys closed his eyes, two more spiders scuttled across the ceiling.

***

Rhys awoke the next morning, he stood up and walked to the window. The sun had risen and was shining brightly and he could hear the surf breaking on the sandy beach as the seagulls wailed over the cliffs. Rhys loved staying here during the summer holidays. As they had done for the previous two years, his parents had dropped him off at his Auntie's just a few days before and would return in four weeks. This gave Rhys ample time to explore the local Pembrokeshire coast, to meet old local friends as well as tourists enjoying their summer vacations on the Welsh coast.

His Auntie's house stood at the edge of a grassy field, now full of summer flowers waving their colours in the light sea breeze; pinks, whites, purples, reds and yellows. A well worn path led across the small field to a stile that broke the line of a wooden fence surrounding the field. Over the stile a narrow path snaked down to a secluded sandy beach, forty feet below.

Rhys picked up his watch, it was 8am. He knew that high tide had just passed and that soon, the beach, currently a thin sandy line, would expand as the water subsided to reveal a rocky shoreline potted with a myriad rock-pools teeming with sea life. Rhys would spend hours searching the rock-pools and walking along the exposed shoreline. A short distance away was Salty's Cave, inaccessible at high tide but open to entry from the beachside when the tide had dropped a little. He made up his mind that today he would call for Michael Evans, a local boy who he'd made friends with the previous year, to see if he wanted to explore the cave together. After all he was now a teenager and knew how to look after himself and was well aware of the need to keep an eye on the tides. In previous visits to his Auntie's home he had been prevented from visiting the cave and, despite promises that an adult would take him, he had never been inside more that a few yards and was itching to explore deeper. This year he was sure that he would be allowed to explore the cave on his own, especially as Michael would be with him. With thoughts of cave exploration in his head it was little wonder that Rhys had forgotten about the strange spiders of the previous night.

Rhys washed and dressed and ran downstairs. Auntie Glenys was making breakfast, hot croissants and marmalade with a pot of English breakfast tea. His Auntie Glenys was his mother's older sister. She was in her early 50's still fit and healthy, a fact that she put down to the sea air. Rhys loved his Auntie, even though she could be strict at times. He had to say that she was fair though and she rarely got cross with him. For his own part, Rhys, fearful that he may not be allowed to visit the next year if he annoyed her too much, ensured that he was on his best behaviour. On top of this, Auntie Glenys was a superb cook and Rhys enjoyed every meal he ate there, or was that too the effect of the sea air?

"Here you are my crimbol, hot croissants and home made marmalade," said Auntie Glenys who had referred to Rhys as 'her crimbol' ever since he was a baby. Rhys didn't mind. He liked the pet-name and his Auntie never used it in front of any of his friends. When he had asked about it, his mother had explained that when his Auntie had first set eyes on him she had claimed that he was so perfect that the fairies must have swapped the human baby for a fairy baby, or as it is known in Wales, a crimbol.

Rhys looked at his Auntie. She was so much like his mother, fair skinned with dark brown curly shoulder length hair, blue eyes and an elfin chin. Both women possessed a Celtic beauty, although his Auntie Glenys' had been slightly flawed by a large scar on her left cheek, the remnants of a deep cut from a fall on the rocky shore many years before.

"So what are you planning today then?", asked his Auntie.

Rhys bit into a marmalade coated croissant, "I thought I might call on Michael and see if he wants to explore Salty's Cave?" replied Rhys hoping that his Auntie would not throw a fit and give him one of her lectures.

She looked at him and smiled. She knew that he was eager to explore the cave and had already spoken with his parents about allowing him to do so. Rhys' father had agreed and had left two powerful walkie-talkie radio handsets with his sister-in-law for Rhys to use whilst exploring. She pulled these out of the kitchen drawer and handed one to Rhys, "You'll be needing this then. Your Dad assures me that these are powerful so we should be able to communicate with each other for most of the time, although we may lose the signal when you are deep in the cavern. The cave goes back a fair way under the cliff face, I explored all the way to the back once when I was younger."

Rhys took the handset from his Auntie and looked at the buttons. "Dad's right, these are powerful, he's brought them home before and allowed me to play with them with some friends. I don't know what their range is but they worked from our house to my friend Tom's house and that's about 2 miles."

His Auntie nodded in approval, "Good, I've used walkie-talkies before too so we shouldn't have any trouble with these. We'll test them after breakfast before you leave. You can call me on the radio every hour or so. If you enter the cave as the tide turns you'll have a good eight hours to explore before the water cuts it off again. Even so I'll feel more comfortable knowing that you can contact me in an emergency. I'll make you a packed lunch for yourself and Michael. When you've finished breakfast I'll give his parents a call to check if they will allow him to go. You can go up to the attic. I have some large torches stored up there as well as some old miner's hats fitted with miner's lamps that would be ideal for exploring the cave. They are stored in one of your uncle's old sea chests."

Auntie Glenys rarely spoke of her husband. Rhys knew that his uncle, Liam Sagot, had been a sailor and that he had been lost at sea long before Rhys was born. There was an old picture of him in his Auntie's bedroom and mementos of his sea faring life scattered around the house. An ancient ship's wheel hung on the living room wall, various glass bottles and floats adorned shelves and cupboards throughout the house, lobster pots still hung in the shed outside and there were various brass instruments spread around. Evident too were numerous artefacts brought back from the places that his uncle had visited. A large wooden mask that looked like it had come from the South Pacific, a tom-tom drum, a set of wooden boxes from the US West Coast with bears and whales carved on them, porcelain from the Orient and bright coloured native clothes made of feathers and colour dyed animal fur. Most macabre of all a dried and shrivelled shrunken head from South America. His Auntie had told him that the articles on show were some of her favourites but that his uncle had brought back many other things from his travels and these were stored in the attic. "There must be twenty or so sea chests up there. He salvaged them from the wreck of an old Welsh trading ship, sunk whilst in the Indian Ocean," added Auntie Glenys.

After Rhys had finished his food she handed him a large set of padlock keys painted in various banded colours, "The chest that you want is directly beneath the attic window. It'll be easy to spot as it has a large padlock and a picture of a daffodil on the lid. All of the chests are decorated in a different way and all have some form of representation of Wales, either through a symbol or a depiction of a tale from Welsh folk lore. The key that you need is the one with the green and yellow band, easy to remember as it matches the colours of the daffodil. You should find the torches and the hats inside, call me if you can't find them."

Rhys looked at the bunch and picked out the green and yellow key.

"Oh, one other thing. Please do not disturb the other chests as they contain some old and delicate objects," commanded his Auntie.

Rhys nodded and thanked his Auntie for breakfast he made his way up the stairs to the wooden attic door that led off the upper landing. The door, originally gloss white, had now yellowed with age. A large bolt and latch secured it and Rhys reached up to release these. Directly behind the door, twelve more steep wooden stairs led up to the attic itself.

The attic was dimly lit by two small windows located in each of the end walls, the two side walls of the main cottage building. Rhys closed his eyes tightly and counted to fifty to help his eyes adjust to the dim light. He walked over to the window on the left where the daffodil sea chest sat. Taking the green and yellow banded key, he unlocked the chest and pulled up the lid which came open with a loud creak. Inside Rhys saw various pieces of equipment for use in the outdoors. The hats, Miner's lamps and torches were all on top and hence were quickly found. Rhys removed two of each and placed them to one side. Underneath the torches, Rhys found a large battery for use with the torches and, having found one, he began to search for a second. Rummaging amongst old canvas, camping equipment and waterproof clothing, Rhys saw a second battery sticking out of a large pencil box with a sliding lid partially closed. He picked up the box and slid the lid completely off. Inside, next to the battery, was a metal pendant on a silver chain. The pendant itself was round with worn edges. It was adorned with an engraving of a Celtic knot and, in the centre of this motif, a small triangular slot had been cut. Rhys reached in to pick it up. As he touched the pendant it seemed that it gave off a shimmer of light which made Rhys jump and drop it back into the box. He looked at the pendant again and plucking up courage picked it up for a second time. This time nothing remarkable occurred and Rhys told himself that somehow the pendant must have reflected the sunlight through the open window, although, in his own mind he knew that this could not be true. The window was facing north and that the sun was in the south east at the time. Slipping the pendant over his head, Rhys picked up the second battery and placed it with the other items. He continued to search the chest but he could see nothing else that would be of use on the trip to Salty's Cave.

After closing the lid and re-fitting the padlock, Rhys stood up and scanned the rest of the attic. Sea chests of varying sizes were everywhere, most covered in dust and cobwebs and had clearly not been opened in some time. Rhys started to look around at the other chests, brushing them clear so that he could see the painted lids. As his Auntie had told him, each chest was decorated with some form of Welsh symbol or scene, he recognised most but not all, a red dragon, numerous castles, a crown, a scene of Conway Bay, St David's Cathedral, Anglesey Island, Celtic knots and various runic symbols which Rhys could only assume were Welsh. The largest chest was made from a dark rich red wood. On the lid of the chest was painted the towering peak of Mount Snowdon, the highest mountain in Wales. This chest stood almost as tall as Rhys' and was three meters long and two wide. It was sealed with an enormous padlock, rimmed with two gold bands. Rhys wondered what treasures were contained within but when he checked his key ring, there was no matching key.

Linked to this enormous chest by a small silver chain was the smallest chest of all, it was made from dark wood and it's lid was secured with a black padlock. The small chest was about the size of a lunch box and on the lid was a drawing of a coastal cave. The picture itself was etched in black and difficult to make out on the dark wood, but Rhys was able to discern the detail by squinting and concentrating hard. He stared at the box. There was something familiar about that picture and yet, at the same time, it made him feel uneasy. A shiver went down his back and he turned away from the box.

Rhys had now lost all enthusiasm for examining the remaining chests. Gathering up his things he went to make his way back to the kitchen, but as he moved towards the wooden stairs his face brushed into some cobwebs, clinging to his cheeks and hair. Rhys' brushed them off and suddenly remember the spiders of the night before. He traced the line of the attic and guessed the point where his bedroom was directly below. Getting down on his hands and knees he examined the floor but did not find anything unusual, not a spider to be seen. "In fact," he whispered to himself, "I haven't seen a single spider since I came up here, lots of webs but no spiders." Rhys looked around and started to search the webs fruitlessly for the creatures. He found none. The goose-bumps came back again, something strange was happening. Gathering up his things, Rhys made his way back down the wooden stairs and closed the attic door.

When he got back to the kitchen his Auntie had just finished her phone call with Michael's parents, "Everything is arranged," she said, "Michael will get ready and then he'll make his way over here to meet you." His Auntie noted the bundle that Rhys carried, "I see you managed to find everything, those torch batteries have hardly been used so they should be fine but we'd better check them out." His Auntie took the torches and batteries from Rhys and flicking up the locking mechanism, she slid the batteries into place and closed the cover once more. She then turned on both torches, both shone brightly. Looking up at Rhys she noticed the pendant that he wore around his neck. "Oh, I see you found your uncle's old pendant." Rhys noticed that she said this with some sadness in her voice and he immediately went red with embarrassment.

"I'm terribly sorry Auntie Glenys, I didn't mean to pry. I didn't mean to upset you." His Auntie waved away his apology, "No need to apologise Rhys," she continued, "the pendant just reminds me of your Uncle. He used to wear it as a lucky charm. I'm sure that if your Uncle had known you he would have liked you to have it. I'd be honoured if you would keep it as your own keep sake and wear it for luck."

"But Auntie Glenys, if it means that much to you I couldn't possibly take it!" exclaimed Rhys.

"Of course you can," responded his Auntie, "I put it away in the sea chest a year or so after your Uncle disappeared, I found that it made me sad when I wore it but, seeing you wear it makes me happy. A beautiful token such as that should not be shut away in a box," she said, "Please take it. It would make me very happy."

Rhys accepted and hugged his Auntie although he still felt bad that he had intruded on his Auntie's memories. He made her promise that she would ask for the pendant back if she ever changed her mind and found she couldn't be without it. As he tucked the pendant safely inside his shirt he braced himself for the cold touch of the metal against his bare chest, curiously though, the pendant felt warm to the touch and rested against his breastbone as if it had been made for him.

CHAPTER THREE
Ashley

Ashley Rees-Jenkins raised her arms in the air in celebration of her third goal. Yet another hatrick for her High School soccer team, her fourth this season. At fourteen Ashley was eligible to play with the under-sixteen squad and, even though she was the youngest on the team, she had made a permanent place for herself. Whilst not tall, she was a solid athlete and it was this that allowed her to compete with the older girls. She also possessed blinding pace and used balls skills that dazzled many a defender. Soccer was her main sport, although she was good in a variety of other sports too, especially tennis and badminton. She also represented the school swimming team but refused point blank to try out for the diving team, she just could not bring herself to dive into water from a height greater than the lowest diving board in the school pool.

As the referee's whistle blew for full time, Ashley jogged off the field with a huge smile on her face. This victory made it five wins out of five for her team and they were looking good to make the Oregon High School play-offs this year and then, hopefully, on to the Inter-State Championships.

After showering and changing into her street clothes Ashley made her way to the car park where her parents were waiting.

"Great game today Ash," said her Dad with a smile as wide as a four lane freeway.

"Thanks Dad," she replied, "I love playing with this team. The girls pass the ball a lot and that makes it even easier for me to score goals."

"That's true, but I think you made a couple of goals for yourself today. You had those defenders turning inside out trying to stop you." Ashley beamed with pride at her father's words.

Ashley's father laughed, "It must be that British blood you have from your grandparents. When he was alive your Bamper always played soccer with you in the yard, mind you he used to chastise us when we called the game soccer and said that this was the real football, not the American Football version. Of course, I think he was quite mad." He winked at Ashley. "Being Welsh your Bamper was also a great rugby fan and used to think our American Footballers over protected in their padding and helmets. If I hadn't put my foot down I'm sure he would have had you playing rugby too. I've seen what British rugby players look like after a few tough seasons and there was no way I was having my beautiful daughter ending up looking like a chewed up sweet potato."

Ashley climbed into the back seat of the car. Whilst not part of the High School Cheer Leader brigade, where looks were everything, Ashley was still very attractive with fair complexion, dark brown shoulder length hair and bright blue eyes. Although she had dated a few boys in the past, she'd rather spend time on her sports, as well as playing computer games and listening to music. Ashley also found that many of the boys found it difficult to compete with her athletic ability and enthusiasm and seemed to feel a little threatened by it. This didn't bother her though. If those boys were so stupid as to need to be bigger and better than her then they were not worth bothering with anyway.

Her father pulled the car into the drive and pressed the remote to open the garage door. Ashley ran into the house, threw her kit bag into the family room where it landed with a solid thump. She then ran upstairs to find Sam, her pet Labrador puppy. As she suspected he was sat in his basket in the corner of her bedroom. The puppy ran to the door to meet Ashley, his tale wagging furiously from left to right as he skipped and jumped up her legs. She bent down to give him a big hug and to stroked his fur energetically. Picking up a chewed and gnarled tennis ball, Ashley rolled it to the pup who pawed and gnawed at it enthusiastically before pushing it back to Ashley with his over sized paws.

"We won again today Sam and I got another hatrick." Said Ashley to the dog. Sam looked at her and yelped excitedly, she was sure that he understood everything she said, even if he was just a pup. She wrestled the ball from the jaws of the puppy and rolled it for him to chase once more.

Turning her attention to her dressing table, Ashley turned on her radio, which was tuned to a local popular station. Lifting the lid off an ornate jewellery box, decorated with scenes of Oregon and made from Maplewood, Ashley removed her lucky pendant and hung it around her neck. The pendant nestled against her breast bone, warm to the touch even though it looked as though it were made of cold steel.

The pendant had been sent to her grandmother by a friend of hers who lived in South Wales. Ashley had taken an interest in the pendant when she saw it hanging in her grandmothers bedroom and, when she asked about it, her grandmother had told her that it was supposed to be a lucky charm and that Ashley could keep it for herself. The very next day Ashley had scored her first goal in a local soccer match and had cherished the pendant as her lucky charm ever since. She looked at the pendant and traced the outline of the flat metal with her finger. The pendant itself was circular with worn edges and was attached to an old silver chain. In the middle was a looping design which her grandmother had told her was a Celtic knot. Above the knot was a curious little triangular hole that Ashley tended to rub with her index finger when she was concentrating on homework, or whilst she read. Unfortunately her grandmother had not known the origin of the pendant and, despite searching the internet, Ashley had not been able to learn anything about it herself either. However, she had promised herself that one day she would visit her grandparents homeland to find out a little more about the country and, if possible, the pendant.

Calling Sam to her, Ashley made her way back downstairs, the little puppy followed behind, carefully leaping down each stair whilst avoiding the heels of his mistress. The pair entered the kitchen together where her mother was cooking dinner. "What have we got today Mom?" asked Ashley.

"Chicken casserole with sweet potato and beans," came the reply. "Could you set the table for me please Ash."

"Sure Mom," responded Ashley, opening the drawer and taking out the table cloth and silverware for the evening meal. She carefully shook the red and white chequered cloth and spread it out neatly on the table top. "Mom, have we decided where we are going on vacation this year?"

Her mother replied while she busily stirred the casserole, "Not yet honey. We had thought about heading down to Southern Utah and spending some time in the Canyonlands."

Ashley looked disappointed, her mother looked at her sympathetically. "I'm sorry Ash. I know you have your heart set on going to Europe and visiting Wales but your father won't allow it. He hates flying himself and is still concerned that commercial aircraft may be a target for terrorism. As a result your father does not want us to fly together as a family, not until things have settled down a little anyway. I'm sure they will soon though. We can visit Europe another year."

Ashley's mood changed from disappointment to annoyance, "This is silly Mom. Everyone knows that since the attack, airport security has been increased and the airlines have all sorts of rules to make things safe. Can't you talk to Dad and get him to change his mind? Why is he so scared?"

Her mother sighed, "I'm sorry Ashley, your father won't be moved on this. He's not exactly scared but he feels that the risk is too high. He continues to fly for his work but he is not willing to let us fly together as a family on a long haul trip, not yet anyway."

During this last exchange Ashley's father had entered the kitchen and added his comment,. "I'm sorry Ash but I am not yet ready to change my mind on this. I believe that the risk is still too high. There are strong rumours that the terrorists will strike again, most likely against aircraft bound for the USA from Europe, or vice versa. I promise that we'll make the trip as soon as things settle down." Her father frowned as he spoke. Ashley understood but also felt that her father's attitude was like giving way to the terrorism. She had raised this before and her father had been furious, she knew better than to bring it up again.

"I tell you what," continued her father, "How about I make it up to you a little by splitting our vacation this year. We can spend a first week in Canyonlands and the second in Southern California and do the 'theme park' run. How does that sound?"

Ashley however was not to be appeased, "It sounds OK but not as exciting as going to Europe Dad. Lots of the other kids from schools are going despite the terrorist threats."

Her father scowled, "I'm sorry Ash, we've been over this before. I've made my decision and I do not intend to change it. If others choose to take that risk then that is their choice. I do not feel that it is too much to ask to suspend the trip for a year or so until things calm down in the Middle East and Europe. Now I will hear no more on the subject!"

Ashley fell silent at this point knowing through experience when not to push her father too far on a subject.

Dinner was eaten in relative silence that night. When Ashley had finished she quickly excused herself to her bedroom to listen to music and to generally feel sorry for herself. She so wanted to go to Europe this year and she quietly cursed the terrorists for ruining her chance. It took her an hour or so to calm down but eventually the lively music changed her mood and she was soon back on her computer playing games. Her favourite were role playing games based on swords and sorcery. She had a number of games of this genre and she enjoyed most of them. She generally chose her character to be a female warrior type but also a magic user. Wherever the game allowed she chose her character to be a paladin and gave her a Welsh name such as Ceredwen or Rhiannon. She had tried a number of times to chose a character on the side of evil but could never bring herself to be ruthless enough to play these well. Others that she played with on the internet often chose characters that were totally opposite to their real life personalities. Ashley was different though, she most enjoyed playing characters that mirrored herself.

The rest of that evening was spent in a land of dragons and wizards, saving creatures in distress, finding treasure and fending off evil characters. As usual; she became totally involved and was surprised when her mother entered her room to tell her that it was time to turn off the computer and go to bed. They then went through the usual ritual;

"Aw Mom, I just have to......."

"It's too late, time to finish..."

"Please Mom it will only take me 15 minutes...."

"Ashley, you are already like a bear with a sore head in the mornings and even worse when you are over-tired. Now turn the computer off and go to bed...."

"Well just ten minutes then Mom! I promise I'll then go straight to bed."

"OK five minutes and not a minute more. I'll be back to say goodnight and I expect to find you tucked up in bed."

Neither Ashley, nor her Mom, were sure why they went through this ritual but this occurred almost every night. One day she'd have to agree with her mother that they just start at the five minutes extra play time and save themselves the negotiation.

True to her word though, she powered down her computer five minutes later. Pulling on her night shirt she climbed into bed and hung her pendant over the bed post, it's usual night-time location. A few minutes later her mother came in to say goodnight, "Ash, I'm not making any promises but I'll talk to your father one more time about the vacation. I'm fairly sure that he won't change his mind though so don't get your hopes up."

Ashley beamed, "Thanks Mom, I know we'll wear him down and get our way. We generally do."

Her mother laughed, "Yes, but don't tell him that, he hasn't worked it out yet." Her mother raised her right palm, "Give me five for woman power!". Ashley slapped her mother's palm with her own and laughed. "Thanks Mom. I love you. Goodnight."

"I love you too Ash, goodnight sweetheart," replied her Mom, kissing her lightly on the forehead.

Ashley snuggled down, wrapping the cosy bedclothes around her and shouted at the top of her voice, "Goodnight Dad, I love you!"

Downstairs her father responded, "Night Ash, love you too. Sleep tight, don't let the bed bugs bite!" He sat back in his favourite chair to relax in front of the TV for a few hours. As he did his thoughts returned to the earlier conversation with Ashley about their vacation. He smiled to himself, as despite his fears, he knew that the continued nagging of his wife and daughter on the subject would probably mean he'd eventually give in and agree to a European trip. He shook his head, "Why do I always lose the argument when the females of this house gang up on me!" he said to himself. It was a question to which he already knew the answer. It was because he loved them both dearly.

CHAPTER FOUR
Escort to Fortown

The sun was rising over Portalia, painting the countryside in wonderful shades of colour. The green of the forest, the vibrant amber rock of the Red Hills, the Snake River meandering through the valley reflecting the colour of the landscape around. Beyond, to the North, the tall peaks of the Pinnacles, purple in hue and with only a vague sign of summertime snow on the highest peaks.

Gorlan looked out from his vantage point in the Red Hills towards the west, where the River of Yew met the Snake River, and decided this would be where he and his men would camp tonight. Food would be plentiful there with fish in abundance at the river junction. Wildlife too could be hunted in the Halfman Forest to the south. His band of thirty Pinn warriors would be able to relax for a while on the banks of the river and refresh their spirits before they continued their long ride west. This point also offered an easy crossing of the river Yew. Here the waters were shallow and could be easily traversed by man and horse.

They had left Pinnhome three days earlier on instructions from the Overlord. Already Gorlan had sensed disheartened spirits in his men. Softened by three generations of peace and by the tranquillity of the city of the Pinns, his men were not hardened to swift travel. The Pinn city, once a formidable citadel, was nestled at the foot of the Pinnacle Mountains in the

Valley of Heroes. Over the years it expanded from it's fortress foundations to become a large and ornate city, rich in art and culture and greatly loved by it's residents. In generations past the city was rarely visited by travellers, but now the city was seen as one of the wonders of Portalia and welcomed visitors from near and far. Some came for trade and others simply to discover the delights that the city had to offer, tourists searching out the wonders of their world.

Gorlan, Warlord of Pinnhome, contemplated the instructions that he had received from Toran, OverLord of Pinnhome. He wished that he could provide better information to his men as to what they may face at the end of their journey but this was very much a voyage of discovery and certainly, Gorlan did not want to alarm his warriors with rumours that may yet prove false.

The Overlord had looked grey and troubled when Gorlan had been brought before him just a few days before. The Warlord recalled the scene;

Toran, Overlord of Pinnhome looked worried as he addressed his Warlord.

"Gorlan, you must listen well for I have an important task for you to undertake,"

"Of course my lord, your wishes will be honoured as always" Gorlan replied.

The Overlord looked at him and smiled, "Earlier today a messenger arrived from Fortown. As you know, this is an outpost town that sits on the borders of the Dargoth Mountains. It was founded generations ago by the combined troops of the Legion of Portalia following the defeat of the hordes of Shangorth the Warlock. Since those days the town has grown from a fort into a larger farming community.

The messenger was one of seven sent throughout Portalia to request assistance to investigate some curious happenings. It is reported that black eagles have been seen in the skies above Dargoth once more."

"*Black Eagles!*" exclaimed Gorlan, "*There has not been any such sightings in years, I assumed they were all killed in the Warlock Wars*".

"*As did we all Gorlan, but now it appears that they are back. We need to know if there is dark magic behind this. I want you to take a squad of your best men and accompany the messenger back to Fortown to investigate.*"

The Overlord gestured to a young man stood to his right before continuing.

"*Gorlan, this is Molt who carried the message to us. He will accompany you on your journey to Fortown.*"

Molt stepped forward. He was a youth of around 17 years. He had an untidy crop of blond hair and striking blue grey eyes. "*It is an honour to meet you Warlord Gorlan. I look forward to our journey back and to introducing you to our town and to leader, TownMaster Cortrain. It was he that dispatched the messengers throughout the land.*"

Gorlan looked the youth up and down and, making his usual quick assessment of folk, he determined the lad to be trustworthy, honest and true. "*Greetings Molt, it is good to make your acquaintance. I believe my lord mentioned that seven messengers were sent?*"

"*That is correct Warlord, Seven of us were sent, obviously I travelled northeast from Fortown to yourselves here at Pinnhome.*

Two rode north. The first to the dwarves in Drenda, the second to the centaurs in Eumor City.

Two rode east, one to call for the help of the Elves from Forest of Lorewood, the other to request an audience with the Dark Elves of Rusinor."

"*Rusinor!*" exclaimed Gorlan, "*That indeed is an ambitious mission, for it is many years since anyone has made contact with the Dark Elves. It is rumoured that some may even have tried and failed to return from the ancient forest, I fear for the messenger who had to make that journey. Please continue.*"

"I fear for that rider too Warlord, although thankfully my brother, Meld, was the messenger chosen to ride to Eumor to request an audience with the centaur council.

Another of my family, a cousin, was instructed to travel west to the water-elves of Seahome on the island of Llan, so hopefully his journey will not be too dangerous either. The last was sent north-west to The Gates, the human twin towns of Northgate & Southgate at the mouth of the Snake River. All carried the same request for assistance."

OverLord Toran turned to his warlord once more, " TownMaster Cortrain made a wise decision to send for our help. I am sure that the humans of Pinnhome and the Gates will answer the call as likely will the Elves of Lorewood and the dwarves of Drenda. The other races are more likely to wait before committing to such a venture, I doubt whether the elves of Llan or Rusinor will intervene, both races tend to keep to their own business. It is anyone's guess how the centaur's will respond. The council is not as decisive as it once was."

A short silence ensued as each thought on the Overlord's words.

"WarLord Gorlan, prepare your men for the journey, you will leave at first light tomorrow morning. Be advised that we should keep this story quiet until we know more. I do not want rumours of the Black Eagles to cause panic amongst the people. I would also ask that you keep this information from your troops too, at least until you arrive and can substantiate or dispel the rumours."

As commanded they departed the next day for the journey to Fortown. The troop rode for three days without breaking for camp, surviving on short rests to take in water and food. Now both the men and the horses were in much need of a rest. The river junction would offer an ideal location for this.

Gorlan rode back to his troop. The travelling party consisted of thirty warriors, Molt and himself. Each warrior was accompanied by his *Fire Eagle*, an ancient warbird which had been magically forged by the crossing of a phoenix and an eagle. The birds possessed a wing span of over twenty feet from tip to tip. Their wings carried the markings and colouration of a golden eagle whilst their heads bore the bright red and yellow feathers of the phoenix with a large orangey-red hooked beak. Their legs were strong and powerful, ending in two large clawed feet possessing vicious tearing talons. When closed tight, their tails resembled that of an eagle but once opened and spread, the dark brown feathers were augmented by feathers of flame red, yellow and orange. The Fire Eagles made the Pinn warriors a fearsome force, for, as well as being impervious to the cut and thrust of normal weapons of battle, the creatures possessed the strength and agility of a giant eagle and the fire magic powers of a phoenix. Carrying their Pinn riders on their backs during battle, the eagles were offered protection by the soldiers whilst they fought enemies with beak and claw. Their talons offered a particular threat as, once an enemy was within their grasp, the birds were able to use fire magic to engulf their prey in flames, incinerating flesh within seconds. Even those foe immune to death by fire were not safe, still susceptible to the powerful ripping and tearing abilities that the giant birds possessed.

Sadly, following the Warlock Wars, when the wizards were slain, the knowledge of how the birds had been created was lost. However, the birds enjoyed a longevity of life via the Ceremony of Choosing where individual birds would select a new and younger Pinn warrior as their partner. Many of the warbirds had been kept this way for generation after generation.

Although, through this ceremony, the birds did not age, they were not immortal. Fire eagles could still be killed by the use of magical spells and by certain creatures with knowledge of the magics. Many had been lost in previous battles to warlocks, witches and warriors with enchanted weapons. Fire Eagles had also been lost through the death of their Pinn rider. The pairing of the rider and Fire Eagle, undertaken at the Ceremony of Choosing, forms an inseparable bond between the two. If the Fire Eagle's soul partner is lost in battle, then the bond is broken and the lone Fire Eagle immediately flies to the west and is never seen again. What happens to the eagle is unknown but legend tells that they continue to fly west, gradually fading in form until they no longer exist.

The only way that this soul link can be broken, without the loss of the eagle, is through a change of bonding at the Ceremony of Choosing. The outgoing warrior rides his warbird into the ceremony and takes his place at the centre of a large circle formed by the new recruits. As the sun sets the Fire Eagle soars high into the sky bursting into flames as it rises. It is believed that the birds then use a magic of their own to choose their new partner by sensing the quality and honesty of the recruit by touching the very soul of the individual. The ashes of the burning eagle fall to the feet of this chosen warrior. Once selected the new rider makes a cut in their palm, allowing the blood to flow and drip into the ashes at their feet. From these ashes arises a newly reborn Fire Eagle, ready to fly and serve its chosen soul partner. After this choosing the warbird remains with the chosen warrior until death or succession at another Ceremony of Choosing.

Once the Pinns had boasted over five thousand Fire Eagles but now, through the death of Fire Eagles or riders, only a little over one hundred remained. As a result of this decline, previous Overlords had ruled that the use of the birds should be strictly controlled and they were now rarely ridden other than for training or very occasionally, into battle.

Gorlan was therefore both honoured and extremely happy

that the Overlord had given permission for the Fire Eagles to be used on this mission. If the reports were true and Black Eagles flew the skies again, then the Fire Eagles would be more than a match in any direct combat.

Gorlan approached his band of warriors, "Warriors of Pinn," he shouted, "You have ridden well and we make good time on our journey to Fortown. We are approaching the mouth of the Yew and there we will make camp. There should be plenty of fish to catch and the forest will offer game. We will camp this evening and rest until the morning."

No-one cheered, or offered any comment, but Gorlan could sense the relief amongst his men. They were good soldiers, if a little inexperienced, and he had pushed them hard over the last few days. They had responded well but it was clear that his men were tired and needed this break. Gorlan was most surprised by the youth, Molt who, despite Gorlan's fears, had kept pace with the warriors and had not faltered. He rode over to the Fortown youth.

"Well ridden Molt, you have coped well with the pace".

"Thank you WarLord, the ride from Fortown to Pinnhome had toughened me and the rest and refreshment that I enjoyed in your city was enough to revitalise me. That said, I am sure that my rear is the colour of a monkey's backside and I will welcome a swim in the cooling waters of the River Yew."

Gorlan laughed and slapped Molt on the shoulder, "Well in that case, I think I'd better tell my men to bathe before you as I wouldn't want your backside to turn the waters to steam before they'd had a chance to freshen up themselves!" Both laughed.

They arrived at the river junction by early evening. Apart from the benefits of abundant food, the setting for their camp offered a natural beauty that helped to raise the spirits. The shallow waters of the Yew danced across large pebbles worn smooth over the years. Grasslands to the north gave way on the south bank to the luscious green Halfman Forest, whilst the river waters themselves deepened and churned as they dropped sharply to join the Snake River. Gorlan spoke with his captains and the soldiers were split into various groups, some to hunt game, some to fish and others to set-up the camp for the evening on the grassy north shore. Molt wanted to help the soldiers hunt game but Gorlan insisted that he rest and allow his troops to carry out their designated activities. Molt reluctantly agreed but insisted on setting up his own tent.

Within a few hours the camp had been prepared, fish had been cleaned and the hunting band had returned with deer, rabbit and game birds. Campfires were lit as the sun set beyond the White Peaks to the west. Everyone seemed in good spirits and Molt sensed a keen camaraderie that is often felt by those sharing a particular hardship. Molt made his way to one of the campfires, pulled off a chunk of venison, spooned a large portion of freshly dug wild vegetables into his dish and filled his tin mug with cool drinking water. He turned to his right and saw two warriors sat on a log, the light of the campfire illuminating their faces. Molt was surprised to note that they were twins. The brothers were almost identical and Molt estimated them to be only a few years older than himself. Large in stature, dark hair, prominent noses and with rustic bronzed skin they were indeed formidable warriors standing at over six foot six inches. Despite their similarity, their eyes offered the key to their identities. Whilst the first possessed dark brown eyes, the other looked through eyes of bright blue. Both were blessed with laughter wrinkles though which foretold of a friendly demeanour.

The blue eyed twin noticed Molt and raised his right fist

in the traditional greeting of Pinn folk. "Well ridden Molt, that venison was truly earned. My name is Carl and this is my brother Stern. Please, won't you join us?"

Molt raised his right fist in return. "Thank you. Other than Gorlan I have had little time to meet anyone in the past few days. I also feel that eating alone brings little pleasure so I doubly appreciate your offer." Propping a cut log upright to form a third seat, Molt took his position next to the twins.

Stern turned to Molt, "This venison tastes so good after the dried rations of the last few days. My brother is strange though as he actually likes dried rations. Look at him now."

Carl had taken two dried oatmeal biscuits and was making a venison sandwich with them. He bit into his creation. "Now that is what I call food! The best of both worlds, the dry of the biscuit and the succulent juice of the meat."

Stern stared at his brother and laughed, "Carl, sometimes you are a very strange person," he said jovially.

Molt talked with the brothers and found out more about them. They had lived with their parents, brothers and sisters on a farm in the Valley of the Heroes, a few hours west of Pinnhome. Their parents were originally from one of the hamlets in the Pinnacle Mountains. Molt knew that the mountain folk were hardy people, born tough to live in the inhospitable climate, where a glorious summer day could quickly turn to fog and freezing temperatures. There were only a handful of hamlets in the mountains as, like the twin's parents, most had moved to the more temperate climate of the Valley. A few families decided to remain though and Stern estimated that there was still a hundred or so folk living in the four hamlets. Their parents had lived in the northernmost hamlet, which was also the highest of the four. Stern and Carl could not remember much about their lives in the mountains as they had been only three years old when their parents had made the journey south. At that time there had been a number of severe winters and the Overlord, concerned for his mountain citizens, made arrangements for additional land to be cleared in the Valley to accommodate farms. He then offered these farms to the folk of the north. Many argued against the move, as the mountain folk had lived in the Pinnacles for countless generations. Those that felt strongly decided to stay, but the vast majority gratefully accepted the Overlords offer, driven by too many years of hardship and family bereavements in the frozen northern winters.

The mountain folk settled in their new valley homes and were surprised at the hospitality accorded to them by the Pinnhome people. Each year more families came down out of the mountains and, true to his word, the Overlord set each up in small farmsteads.

Carl looked thoughtful, "It is good to see so many of our folk settling into their new homes but, at the same time, it is sad to think that many of our customs and traditions are to disappear. Of the folk that remain in the hamlets most are old and very few have children. It is true that we can visit our old homes in the summer but, although we are offered hospitality by our old friends and colleagues, a divide has been created between us. Those that remain feel that we have turned our backs on our heritage and our ancestors. I know what was done was right, otherwise many would have died over the years, but sometimes I cannot help wondering if those that criticise us are correct. Some say that when the winters grow mild again we will return to the mountains. Stern and myself agree that this is unlikely though, as all that have made the move have settled and their farms are thriving. There is also more opportunity for children in the valley. Some stay and work the farm, others obtain work in Pinnhome. Many of the boys take up training with the Pinn army although we are honoured to be the first to be accepted by the warbirds as part of a Fire Eagle unit."

The mention of Fire Eagles reminded Molt that earlier, when the camp was set, he had witnessed the birds fly off to the west in a large single flock. He asked the brothers the reason for this.

Stern replied, "At the end of each day in Pinnhome and when camp is set on a journey, the Fire Eagles all fly west. They return at first light the next morning."

Molt looked worried, "But why?"

Carl and Stern shrugged, "No-one knows."

Molt continued, "And what if a unit is attacked at night? Do you then have to fight without your war birds?"

The brothers shook their heads, "Ah, now that is another magical thing about the beasts. Pinn warriors have the advantage of knowing when they can get a good night's rest during battle as the birds instinctively know if trouble is in the air. If the flock doesn't leave at night, then it is time to beware as the unit is in danger. When this occurs the number of guards are increased and everyone sleeps lightly, if at all. However, sometimes the very fact that the eagles remain with us, and that extra guards are posted, is enough to ward off any attack."

Molt thought on this and frowned, "But if no-one has attacked during this time, how do you know that there was danger and it was not just that the birds had got it wrong?"

The brothers looked shocked, "We've never even considered it! To question a Fire Eagle's instincts would be to insult the bird and damage the bond that we have. No, there is no question about it, if a Fire Eagle stays with you during the night, you'd better be on your toes."

"Has your bird ever remained with you at night?" Molt asked Stern.

"No never. I have been fortunate enough not to have had to do battle, either day or night. My fighting has been limited to the training arena."

Molt looked at Carl, "How about you Carl, has your bird ever sensed danger and stayed with you at night?"

Carl nodded in affirmation, "Just the once. We were on a training trip in the Red Hills. There were ten of us. On our fifth night our Fire Eagles stayed and sure enough we were attacked by a band of forty or so brigands. They were no match for us. Thirty were killed in a matter of minutes and the rest ran off. It was my first and only taste of combat. The power of the Fire Eagle during that fight was incredible, my beast had clearly gained a bloodlust and wanted more, it took all of my strength and skill to subdue the bird to prevent it flying after the survivors and completing the rout. They are incredibly fearsome when they are in battle."

Molt tried to imagine the scene and thought he had a sense of how it must feel to fight against a foe with such power. This was something he hoped never to have to face, or indeed observe.

Stern smiled, aware of Molt's musings, "Don't worry Molt. A Fire Eagle has never been known to harm a comrade in arms, no matter how strong the blood lust during the fight.". Stern picked up some wood and stoked the fire , his brown eyes looked even darker in the dim light.

Fuelled by the openness of the twins, Molt asked another question, " I notice that the Warlord is not accompanied by a Fire Eagle. Does he not possess a warbird?"

Stern looked at his brother and grinned, "Our Warlord, as with Warlords before him does not need a Fire Eagle. He has his own beast to call upon. Have you noticed the horn that Gorlan carries around his neck?"

"I have," replied Molt, "I presumed it was a horn to call troops to battle."

"Well you were right about calling something to battle, but it is not for our troops. Many years ago a Warlord saved the life of a red dragon who had been cornered by a fire demon. Even in those days red dragons were rare and the Warlord was not going to stand by and see another be killed needlessly, even though there was no great love between the folk of the Pinnacles and the red dragons. The Warlord ordered his men to attack the fire demon which fled, thus sparing the life of the dragon. In thanks the dragon gave the Warlord the Horn of Summoning. When any Warlord enters battle he may blow the Horn and a red dragon will appear to accompany the Warlord into combat."

Molt looked amazed, "I have never seen a dragon but I have heard rumours that they no longer exist."

Molt continued dreamily, "Imagine how things must have looked during the Warlock Wars. To see a dragon carrying a Warlord into battle must have been an incredible sight. That alone would be enough to strike terror into the hearts of the enemy, let alone seeing this man and beast being followed by a band of Fire Eagles warriors!"

"I have not seen a dragon either Molt. Gorlan has not had a need to use the Horn in his lifetime. Legend has it that the Warlord must not use the Horn unless the strength of the dragon is essential to win the battle. It is said that if a dragon is summoned by a Warlord when there is no need for it's strength, then the power of the Horn is spent and red dragons will no longer answer it's call.

Some also argue that it has been so long since the Horn

was sounded that the dragons will no longer respond anyway and many have called for the Horn to be blown to call forth a red dragon to ensure that the power still exists. Overlord and Warlord agree that this should never happen and the original pact to summon only during battle be honoured for all time.

But now to other things, tell us, what brought you to Pinnhome and what do you know of our mission? Our Warlord has told us that we are to escort you back to Fortown and that the TownMaster has asked for help but has said little else. Are you able to share anymore information than this?".

Molt felt uneasy and shuffled on his log. "I'm afraid that I am not at liberty to say. I have promised your Overlord and Warlord Gorlan that I will not speak of our mission. However, what I can say is that the need is great and the request for assistance was not made lightly. My heart hopes that on your arrival in Fortown we will require nothing more of you, other than to enjoy our hospitality. Alas though, my head tells me that we may well have need for the skills and strengths of yourselves and your great war birds."

Stern turned to his brother, "You see, it is as I said, you will be seeing battle for the first time my brother." Carl nodded and placed a firm grip on Molt's shoulder, "Do not worry friend, we will not ask any further and would not request that you break your word to our leaders. My brother was sure that there would be battle at the end of this journey but I was not. I am no coward and one day I hope my training will be put to good use, but I do not relish the thought of conflict. Some men fight for the love of the battle but I am not one, I will fight for necessity to protect my family, homeland and kinfolk, but I do not expect to take any enjoyment from it."

Molt fully understood this attitude as he too felt this way and he acknowledged this to the two brothers. He pointed to the Halfman Forest, "If all goes well on our journey through the forest then we have less than two days ride to Fortown. Over the years there have been many stories of people disappearing in these woods and once they were teeming with villains and robbers. These days they seem to offer little hostility. In fact I have ridden through them many time myself without incident. Even so I still follow the advice given to me by my father and I always stay to the well trodden track, even though it winds it's way through the forest and makes for a longer journey. It is thought that many of the stories of monsters and evil creatures have been created through the exaggeration of rumours of folk who have stupidly tried to take short cuts through the trees, losing their way and dying of starvation rather than more sinister means. I myself have also seen large wild boar amongst the trees and I can imagine that these creatures would make short work of anyone that they came across weakened, vulnerable and lost in the woods."

Carl shrugged, "I'm sure that we will not have any problems travelling through the forest and even if we did, I feel that we are a match for anything it cares to throw at us. I agree with your philosophy though, why court trouble by leaving the beaten path. I'm sure that Gorlan would not take any unnecessary risks and that you'll be back in your own soft bed before two days are out my friend."

Molt spent the rest of the meal chatting idly with the brothers. When he had finished his meal and drunk the last of the water he bade them goodnight and made his way to his tent. It had been erected close to the river, a short distance from that of Gorlan's. Molt walked along the riverbank, the moon was almost full and it's light was reflected in the babbling waters of the Yew. Suddenly out of the corner of his eye Molt caught a glimmer of moonlight amongst the trees on the other side of the river. He peered into the darkness of the forest but could see nothing at first, then another glimmer and movement amongst the trees. At first Molt was startled but then realised that there would probably be guards posted on both sides of the river. Laughing at himself for being so stupid he continued to his tent to retire for the evening.

Meanwhile, across the river, two small creatures watched Molt's progress. The creatures stood only three foot tall, their skin was as black as the night. They possessed long gangly arms that swung close to their knees and walked with a stoop on short hairy legs. They wore nothing but a leather loincloth and into this was tucked a crude short sword. Their eyes were small and pig like and were coloured blood red. They grew no hair on their heads and their ears were merely two small holes. From the centre of their foreheads protruded a rhinoceros like horn, dark grey and leathery. The larger of the two creatures grabbed his colleague who had stumbled through the undergrowth just as Molt had looked across the river. "Fool," he hissed, "You were almost seen. Stycich must punish you now." The larger creature curled back thin dark blue lips to reveal sharp yellow teeth. Lifting the left hand of the smaller creature, Stycich bit off the middle of seven fingers. Blood ran down his chin as Stycich chewed and swallowed the morsel. The smaller creature held it's hand painfully but dared not cry out for fear of attracting more attention and further punishment. Stycich used his own hand to mop up his bloody chin and licked his fingers clean ravenously. Moving with little sound, the two creatures melted deeper into the forest so that they would not be found if anyone chose to investigate. When they were sure that no-one was coming, they moved back a little closer to the river so that they could observe the camp more closely.

Stycich glared evilly, "For now we merely watch humans, but our Lord will have his moment soon and we will be rewarded for our service to him. Sleep well while you can."

CHAPTER FIVE
Two Boys and a Cave

Michael looked up at the blue cloudless sky as he and Rhys walked across the field towards the beach. He watched the gulls over head as they called to each other. Occasionally one would dive towards the beach to lift out a shell fish, before climbing swiftly up again to drop it on the solid rocks below. The shell would shatter, releasing the juicy interior, and the gull would swoop down once more to feast on the tasty morsels.

The boys wore their backpacks, filled with food, drink and the equipment needed for exploring Salty's Cave. The radio, which they had tested with Auntie Glenys before they left, was hooked to the belt on Rhys' jeans. They both chose to wear tee shirts as the day was warm. They also donned training shoes to help them clamber across the rocks, rather than the light beach shoes they normally wore on the sands.

Michael was pleased to have his friend back for the summer, "I'm glad your parents let you come and stay again," he said. "There aren't many kids living in the village these days, most have moved off to bigger towns."

Rhys smiled, "It's good to be back Mike. I was glad to hear that you were still living here. When I left last year your parents were talking about moving to Milford as their business wasn't doing so good."

"Well it was touch and go there for a while. Then a

friend of my mother's suggested that we put the business on the internet. Dad looked into this, contacted a company who helped him set up his web page and things started to pick up from there. Now he's receiving orders from all over the world. It seems that there are lots of people out there interested in buying his Welsh troll sculptures. I don't think we're going to get rich but at least my Dad should now be able to pay off the mortgage on the house. I'm glad we didn't have to move, I would have hated living in Milford. Mam is really happy too as she can now carry on with her teaching job at the local primary school."

Rhys turned up his nose, "No offence, but who would have thought that there were so many people out there interested in buying those weird creatures that your Dad makes."

"I know," laughed Michael, "They are hideous, but some people find them cute. Dad also signs and numbers every one so that they appeal to collectors too. He's received loads of orders from the USA. The Yanks seem to collect anything. He also now includes a small 'biography' for each of the figures which makes each one more unique. Each troll has a Welsh or Irish background, and this appeals even more to the Americans, as so many have Celtic ancestors."

The boys paused as they reached the beach and removed their socks and shoes. Rolling up their jeans to their knees they both ran onto the warm sand. Rhys in particular was happy to feel the grains between his toes again and laughed brightly. "You are so lucky to live here. I love the coast. I wish my Dad and Mam would move here."

"Do you think they would?" asked Michael

"No, not really. There is no work here for them. They need to live close to the larger cities. That's why we moved to Birmingham."

"Never mind," replied Michael, "Hopefully they'll keep leaving you with your auntie for a few years to come. Come on, I'll race you to the sea."

The boys broke into a sprint, sand flying up behind them and their toes making a comical squeaking sound as they pushed through the dry sand. Rhys was the faster runner and quickly moved ahead. They soon reached the wet sand and raced on, splashing into the water.

The boys started to kick water at each other playfully but then thought better of this, remembering the torches and the radio that they had with them. They started to head for the outcrop of rocks to the north, wading through the shallows for a few minutes before heading back to the dry. They chatted idly about what they had been doing through the year before turning the conversation on to the more immediate task of cave exploration.

Rhys asked Michael if he had ever visited the cave before.

"Yep, a few times with my parents. We've been quite a way into the cave but never right to the back as we have never had torches with us and it really is too deep to explore without some form of light. Dad has said a few times that we'll go exploring it properly one day, but he's always too busy when I ask. In fact, when I asked him if I could come with you today I think he was too embarrassed to say no. I love Dad and he's really good to us all, but I sometimes wish he'd work less and spend more time with me and Sarah."

Rhys looked up at the mention of Michael's sister, "Gosh, I had forgotten all about Sarah, how is she?"

"As much as a pain as ever," replied Michael, "She had her fifth birthday party last month and I swear she gets more evil and crafty by the year. She seems to want to join in with everything that I do and just won't leave me alone, especially when I have friends around. Sometimes Mam intervenes to give me a little peace, but Sarah is usually back bugging us again within a few minutes. I've asked Dad if he will move the handle on my bedroom door so she can't reach it. He said he would but it's another of those jobs that he is too busy to get around to doing."

Rhys slapped his friend on the back, "Never mind Mike, it could be worse, I'm not sure how, but I know it could be! At least your parents didn't ask you to bring her today!"

"I know but that didn't stop her trying. Dad had to give her a lecture and send her to her bedroom as she tried to follow me twice."

The boys had now reached the rocks. Brushing the dry sand from their feet they put their socks and shoes back on.

"Yeuch!", moaned Rhys, "I love walking on the sand but I hate putting my shoes back on afterwards. All that loose sand rubs in between your toes."

"Mmm, me too," replied Michael, "but we have to wear the training shoes or we'd never get to Salty's Cave. The rock is fairly smooth here but further up they are jagged and difficult to walk on in bare feet. We should be careful of the seaweed though and try to keep off it. It's very slippery and tends to coat the bottom of your shoes. This is usually when you are trying to cross a particularly tricky bit. You skip and leap your way through the hazards and triumphantly make the last leap. Then, your seaweed coated shoes touch smoother rock and you find yourself flat on your bum! Not cool and not funny, except for everyone else watching you."

The boys made there way across the rocks, pausing to search the fresh rock pools for crabs and fish. This part of the coast was off the tourist track, although the occasional hiker could be seen using the coastal path. Today though, the boys seemed to have the beach to themselves. Rhys stopped at a particularly large rockpool and bent to lift a large stone. A crab scuttled out from under it. Sprinting across the bottom of the pool it searched amongst the greens, yellows and oranges for a new hiding place. Eventually it found a suitable rocky overhang at the edge of the pool and climbed up inside.

"He was a good one Mike," said Rhys.

"He was," replied Michael, "but you often get even bigger ones than that. I one saw one twice the size of a rugby ball crawling over the rocks near the cave. Mostly I don't mind picking them up, but the pincers on that one could have taken your arm off. I stayed well clear!"

"Well if you had caught him he wouldn't have had to worry 'cos you'd be 'armless!" joked Rhys.

Michael smiled and groaned, "That's a terrible one Rhys, I hope your jokes are going to get better than that."

Despite stopping numerous times to check out larger pools, the boys made good progress and soon approached the point of the headland where Salty's Cave sat nestled at the foot of the cliff.

Near the cave was an isolated arch of land that had broken away through years of erosion. The boys made a slight detour to pass through the arch to approach the cave. As they left the shade of the arch Rhys stopped with a sharp intake of breath.

"What's up?" asked Michael.

"Now that is spooky. It's the same cave as painted on the sea chest in my Auntie's attic," replied Rhys. He told Michael about the strange small box and the curious painting that adorned the lid. He then explained about the other sea chests and showed Michael the pendant that he had found. "I guess I've never approached the cave from this angle so I didn't recognise it when I saw the painting on the box. Quite a coincidence though."

Michael looked thoughtful, "Maybe your Auntie or Uncle used to paint as a hobby or something. Lots of people do when they come here because the scenery is so fantastic. Salty's Cave is a well known local feature so I guess it's no surprise that they chose it as a subject for a painting. I wish you hadn't told me about the shadows though, gives me the spooks."

Rhys smiled, "I wouldn't worry. I've read that some artists use light in their painting to give the illusion of movement. You know what I mean. Like old paintings of people that you see in galleries, the eyes seem to follow you around everywhere. I think it was the same thing with the painting on the sea chest. As I moved my head the angle of the light would change making the shadows appear to be moving. C'mon, I'm sure we're quite safe and there are no sea monsters lurking in the dark to eat us, not today anyway."

"There you go with that weird humour again. I'm going to buy you a new joke book for your birthday!"

The boys walked up to Salty's Cave. The rocks leading up to the cave were covered in seaweed so they had to tread extra carefully. When they reached the entrance the boys stopped and peered in. The sun was almost directly overhead and only broke into the cave a little way. The boys could make out the first fifty feet or so before it gave way to darkness. The entrance itself stood some forty foot high at it's peak and was shaped in an almost perfect half circle. "Mike, let's radio Auntie Glenys and have some thing to eat before we go exploring." With this Rhys took the radio off his belt and pressed the transmit button,

"Rhys and Mike to Auntie Glenys, come in Auntie Glenys, over"

Michael started to laugh and said, "That's weird, it sounds just like in films. Next thing you know you'll be calling for an air-strike!"

Rhys giggled, there was no reply so he pressed the transmit button again, "Rhys and Mike to Auntie Glenys, come in Auntie Glenys, over."

The radio chirped into life, "Auntie Glenys here, how are you doing boys?"

Rhys waited a short while and replied, "We're fine Auntie Glenys, we've just arrived at the cave and we're going to have a bite to eat before we explore, over."

"That's a good idea."

Another pause.

Rhys pressed his transmit button again, "Auntie Glenys you are supposed to say over at the end of your sentences, over."

"Why"

…a longer pause,………. "..over", the boys could here the amusement in her voice.

"You say over to let the other person know that you've finished what you wanted to say. If you don't say over then we may both try to talk at the same time and we'd miss what we were trying to say."

..another pause, Michael laughed out loud, "Rhys, you forgot to say over!"

Rhys looked annoyed, "…oh sorry, over!"

Auntie Glenys reply came back loud and clear, "OK, I've got it now. You boys have fun down there but be careful of the rocks and keep in touch, over".

"We will Auntie Glenys, over and out."

The boys took out their packed lunches. Auntie Glenys had packed a fair amount of food for them, some pork pies, ham rolls, peanut butter sandwiches, tea cakes, a large packet of crisps each (family size as she knew what they were like), a large bar of milk chocolate and a bottle of water and lemonade each. Eager to start exploring the cave the boys decided to eat a single roll and a few crisps each before they continued. They would keep the rest for later and eat it in the cave.

The boys quickly finished their snack and removed the torches and helmets from the backpack, storing the remainder of their food. They tested the torches once more and checked that the Miner's Lamps were working and secured firmly to their helmets. "OK, let's go!" Michael said as he entered the cave, closely followed by Rhys who was still struggling with his backpack and had one strap on and one off, "Hold up a minute Mike," he shouted and with that flicked his shoulders to adjust the weight evenly across his back. Now more balanced he strode forward, "OK, let's rock and roll!"

At the entrance the floor was formed from soft wet sand, surrounded by damp dark rock on either side. The occasional rock bed broke through the sand and sometimes formed a small rock pool. The walls were worn smooth on both sides by the tide. Michael and Rhys looked in the rock pools that lined the sides of the cave where the sandy floor met the rock wall. Here the sea had formed overhangs and clinging beneath they saw numerous starfish; yellows, oranges and even the odd purple one. Michael managed to gently prise one off the rock and the boys both looked closely at it, fascinated by thousands of tiny legs. Rhys, who had picked up a starfish before, was always amazed by how hard they felt. After looking at it a while, he gently placed it back under the ledge and the boys continued into the cave. Fifty yards or so further in, the sandy floor gave way to solid rock, rising gently in a soft inclination towards the rear of the cave. The going here was a little trickier due to the damp rock which was almost as smooth as glass in places. As the boys made their way into the cave the rocky floor continued to rise slowly and light became less and less. Their eyes adjusted however and there was still enough glow to allow them to continue their progress without the use of any of their artificial light.

When the rocky floor had climbed three feet or so above the original sandy floor of the cave the boys stopped.

Michael looked at Rhys and said, "Listen to this," and with that he put his hands to his mouth and gave a short sharp shout "HELLO!"

Hello! Hello! Hello! Hello! Hello! Ello! Llo! Lo! o!.... Michael's voice came back to them in a multitude of echoes.

"COOL!" shouted Rhys, grinning from ear to ear as the sound reverberated around the cavern.

The boys spent the next ten minutes shouting various exclamations, as well as the occasional obscenity, and the cave dutifully cloned their words and shouted them back a hundred times.

Rhys turned to Michael, "The light is getting really low now so we should use our torches from this point on." The boys flicked the switches on their handheld torches and on their helmets. Once more, started to make their way across the rock. They walked another thirty yards or so and came to a step in the floor. The step ran the entire width of the cave and was around ten feet high. It was riddled with foot holds though so the boys had no difficulties in clambering their way up. When they were on top the boys looked back towards the entrance. Michael spoke first, "It looks like the rocky floor had given way at some point and dropped to form this higher ledge. I don't remember seeing this with Dad when we came in here so we must be further in than I've been before."

"That would make sense. I don't think you could have come this far in without light." Rhys replied. "Let's turn off our torches and see how dark it is." Michael agreed and on the count of three they turned off all of their lights.

Although they could still make out the entrance of the cave, a beam of sunlight in the distance, the cave suddenly seemed a large, dark and ominous place. Without light their hearing became more acute and the sounds of the cave and the wind whistling through the passage made goose-bumps rise on their skin. Michael spoke, his voice quivering slightly, "Yep, I think that's pretty dark, dark enough for me anyway, how about you Rhys?"

"Oh, I'd agree that this is just about dark enough," And with that they both turned on their torches, flooding the cavern with artificial light once more.

They smiled at each other, "Excellent!" they both exclaimed in school-boy bravado, although neither of them offered up the suggestion of turning the lights off again.

They made their way further into the cavern, coming across another step, this time only six feet high, they scampered up it and paused for breath. Rhys shivered, "Gosh, it's getting really cold now." He removed the backpack and took out a red woollen sweater that his Auntie had insisted he take with him, despite his objections. Michael did likewise and started to slip a dark green woollen sweater over his head, trying to lay his backpack down gently at the same time, Michael dropped his sweater, he cursed under his breath and picked it up, "Hey Rhys look. The ground is dry above this ledge, the tide must not come higher than this."

Rhys bent down to look, "You're right, that should make it easier to walk, no slippery rock to worry about."

Now clothed a little warmer, the boys continued into the

cave, "I must admit that I'm a little disappointed," said Rhys, "I hoped that we'd see stalagmites and stalactites but the cave walls and roof are all featureless."

Michael looked, "I think it's because of sea erosion, although now that we are above the high tide point we may see more interesting shapes. Also, since that last ledge have you noticed how the floor is sloping upwards? If you look back you can no longer see the cave entrance. The walls and roof have closed in too." Rhys looked and saw that the roof was now only some ten feet tall at this point "It's almost like we're in a tunnel, I wonder how much further it goes, we must hit the end soon," he said, peering into the darkness.

The fact that they could no longer see the cave entrance made Rhys a little nervous and he clutched his torch a little tighter. Feeling a sudden need for something sweet to take his mind of the uneasy feeling Rhys asked, "Do you fancy some chocolate? I took some out when we put or sweaters on back there."

Michael smacked his lips, "Mmmm, yes please. I'll share my bar with you later."

Rhys took out the chocolate bar and broke it in half. Nibbling on the treat the boys continued into the cave, somehow, things never seemed so bad when you were munching chocolate and the cave didn't seem so frightening anymore. The footing on the dry rock face was much easier now but, a few minutes later Rhys, who had taken the lead, stopped dead in his tracks. Michael not noticing bumped into him, "What's up, why have you stopped?"

"I think we've made it," Rhys pointed towards the back of the cave where a large rock wall rose all the way to the roof.

Michael walked to the wall and tapped it. "I think you're right. This is solid, we've reached the end of the cavern."

Rhys turned back towards the entrance but could only see darkness. "How far in do you think it is Mike?" he asked.

"I'm not sure. We must have walked close to a mile though. Mind you I've read that distances can seem further in the dark so it may not be as far as we think."

Rhys smiled, "No I reckon you are just about right. I know what you mean about walking in the dark though. It feels like we've come more like five miles. I'm starving again too. Let's eat the rest of our lunch."

Once again the two boys unpacked their lunch. They sat and ate the peanut butter sandwiches and cake and finished off their lemonade drinks.

Rhys looked at Mike thoughtfully, "Mike, you know back there, when we turned off the torches? Were you scared just a little bit?"

"Well maybe just a little, how about you?" Michael replied sheepishly.

"Yea, me too, just a little bit. Even so, do you know what I was thinking?"

Michael looked worried, "No, but I think I can guess. Does it have to do with trying it again?"

Rhys gave a wicked grin, "Well when we did it back there we could still see the entrance so it wasn't really completely dark. Now that the entrance is obscured from our view it would be. I know it is going to scare us stiff but shall we give it a try and turn off our lights again?"

Michael looked uncomfortable but did not want to be the one to back down on this dare, "Well OK, we'll turn them off, count to thirty and then turn them back on again. Will that do?"

Rhys agreed and they both turned off their lamps and reached for their torches.

"OK Mike, on the count of three we'll turn off the torches, One-Two-Three!"

The cave was plunged into utter darkness. Both boys could hear their hearts pounding as they counted to thirty in their heads. Michael strained his eyes fruitlessly trying to make out anything in the gloom. Without the lights, the temperature appeared to drop even further, he shivered and goose bumps appeared once again on his skin and the hairs on the back of his neck stood up in fear. When he reached twenty five seconds he started to count out loud, "twenty-six, twenty-seven, twenty-eight, twenty-nine...."

"WAIT!" Rhys shouted, "Do you see that?"

Michael suddenly realised that he had his eyes tight shut, he opened them but could see nothing in the darkness. "Do I see what? I can't *see* a thing!"

"There above our heads on the back wall of the cave. Can you see that dull glow?"

Michael turned and looked up. At first he saw nothing, but as he moved his head he noticed something out of the corner of his eye. Turning towards it he saw precisely what Rhys referred to. A few feet above their heads, slightly to the right of where they sat, a pale blue glow emanated from the cave wall.

"What on earth is it?" exclaimed Michael.

"I have no idea, but let's find out. The glow is very weak so I don't think we'd see it with the torches turned on. You keep an eye on it and point to where it's coming from and I'll get us some illumination. "

Michael squinted into the gloom at the strange glow, raised his arm and pointed his finger at it. Rhys reached for his torch and after checking that Michael was ready, he turned it back on. He followed the line from Michael's arm to the rock face and in his mind marked the spot. "OK, I've got it, you can take your arm down now."

Michael lowered his arm and reached for his torch too.

Rhys had already made his way closer to the base of the wall, directly under the point where they had seen the glow. "I can't quite make it out from here. It looks like there may be a ledge up there. I'd have to climb up to be sure though. It's a bit further up than I first thought but still reachable if you give me a bunk up!"

The boys packed their things away again, including Rhys' torch which would be too cumbersome to carry as he climbed. "OK, I'll go first," said Rhys.

Michael held his hands out and Rhys placed his foot in them so that Michael could lift him. Rhys grabbed the edge of the ledge and was able to pull himself up until he was safely seated on the edge.

Before him, at the back of the ledge, was a tunnel. Now that he was close to it he could just make out the dull blue glow, even with his torches burning bright. The tunnel was about five feet high and three feet wide and appeared to continue to slope upwards. Rhys squinted into the tunnel but could not see the end so had no way of knowing how deep it was. He alerted Michael of his find. "You see, I knew that the climb up here would be worth it. The tunnel continues into the cave so we've still got some exploring to do."

Rhys peered into the darkness and could easily make out the blue glow emanating from deeper within the tunnel. His thoughts returned to the strange small box that he had found in the attic. There was something about this scene that reminded him of that picture on the box lid.

"Oi Rhys, you gonna pull me up or what?"

Rhys looked down at Michael, then at the cavern floor

below and then back at the tunnel. The dull glow seemed to pulse brighter for a moment, refuelling the adventurer in Rhys. He shrugged off his sudden fear and stretched down to pull Michael up next to him on the ledge.

Rhys raised a finger to point behind Michael, "Look the tunnel is that way and is large enough for us to walk through if we lower our heads a little."

Michael turned and looked down the tunnel. There was a definite bluish glow, *this must be from sunlight,* Michael thought to himself and his spirits picked up considerably suspecting that they had discovered another way in and out of the cave. He unhooked the radio from his belt and handed back to Rhys. "Come on then let's explore!"

Rhys picked up his backpack, turned on his torch and helmet light and followed Michael down the tunnel.

They had covered about thirty yards when Michael stopped, "Listen! Can you hear something?"

Rhys stood still and listened. At first nothing, but then a soft rustling sound much like the wind blowing through dried leaves, very faint but clearly coming from the direction they were walking.

"What the heck is that?" Rhys asked.

"I'm not sure. Maybe it's the wind blowing through cracks in the cave. Just in case though I think we should move quietly until we can make out what it is."

The boys continued along the passage, moving stealthily. The bluish glow was getting brighter and brighter and the passage was starting to angle steeply upwards, getting smaller and narrower until they could only move in single file and had to drop almost to all fours to continue. Michael was ready to suggest they turn around when he noticed that a short way ahead the passage changed shape.

"Look! Up there! It looks like the tunnel is going to open out again," he said.

Rhys nodded, "It does. Also, have you noticed how bright it is. I don't think we even need the torches on anymore."

Rhys was right, the boys turned off their torches and they could still see clearly enough to make their way. The tunnel opened out ahead of them, the light intensified and they noticed that the rustling sound was getting louder and louder and was accompanied by a strange clicking.

Rhys whispered a command to his friend, "Mike, let's crawl quietly to the end of the tunnel, I have a bad feeling about this. I'm not sure what that noise is but I know I don't like it and I want to be sure of what we're walking into before we go blundering into someone, or something, that may not like us snooping around."

The boys dropped to the ground and leopard-crawled up the last few yards. The tunnel opened out high up the wall of a large natural amphitheatre with a dome roof forty feet above their heads. A path led off to the left and wound it's way around the wall to the floor, some twenty feet below. Michael and Rhys looked over the edge, both took a sharp intake of breath in fascination and shock at the sight which met their gaze.

In the centre of this amphitheatre stood a small creature next to a large arch of light. This was the source of the blue glow. The arch itself seemed to be made of liquid, changing hue and tone as if it was flowing but retaining it's arched shape as it did so. From all around the cavern, through a multitude of cracks and crevasses, emerged a mass of spiders, forming a carpet of black. Rhys' thoughts were immediately drawn back to the strange happenings in his bedroom the night before, "My god, look at all those spiders!" he whispered more to himself than to Michael.

Michael opened his eyes wide, he wanted to run but was frozen to the spot. "Sp-sp-sp-spiders?" his voice trembled, "but there must be thousands of them!"

The spiders were scurrying and running to the archway and as they entered the light they appeared to disappear into thin air. There were spiders of all types; small, large, fat, thin, hairy, black, brown, red, every variety of spider that you could think of. Rhys turned his attention to the strange creature that stood next to the archway. This creature stood about four feet tall. His skin was pallid, pale, almost white and looked sickly. He wore a large white beard and crop of untidy white hair. His eyes were the most unnerving. The white of his eyes seemed almost yellow punctuated by glistening white pupils with dark black centres. The creature wore white leather clothes and carried a large black axe tucked into a white belt. Rhys was reminded of albinos that he had seen on TV. He could not help but shiver as he looked into the eyes of this creature.

Michael spoke, "It's a bloody dwarf! An albino dwarf."

Rhys looked at Michael and then back at the dwarf, Michael was right, it definitely resembled a dwarf. Around his neck the creature wore a metal pendant. In his left hand, he held a staff made of a dark wood. On the top of the staff was a large red gem in the shape of a spider which pulsated with a red light.

"Rhys," said Michael, "Do you think that the staff is what is drawing the spiders?"

"Maybe, but this is just too weird to put any logic too, it's like we're living in a fairy tale or something. What do you think is happening to the spiders? Do you think he is killing them?"

Michael shuffled his position to get closer to the edge, "The spiders are coming from everywhere and heading straight

for the light. I don't think they're dying though, I think that
the archway is a portal of some kind and this dwarf is sending
the spiders somewhere. Goodness only knows where and why."

Rhys shuffled to get a closer look and moved towards the
edge of the ledge on which they sat. As he shifted his weight
the earth below his hands gave way and Rhys toppled over
sliding down the slope towards the creatures below.

Rhys screamed as he fell and heard Michael shouting
his name as he grabbed to try to save him. The shout from
Michael and the scream that Rhys let out reverberated around
the cavern walls, echoes sounding like the voices of a hundred
people.

Rhys hit the cavern floor with a jar, rolling to prevent any
serious damage. He looked down and saw that he had crushed
a significant amount of spiders in his fall. Standing, he turned
towards the albino dwarf who by now was screaming and
shouting at him. The sight of the dwarf ranting and raving,
red in the face and jumping up and down on the spot was so
comical that Rhys soon lost any fear that he felt. He decided
to throw caution to the winds, drew himself up tall, looked
directly at the dwarf and spoke, "Who are you and what are
you doing with these spiders?".

The dwarf stopped shouting stood still and stared at
Rhys. He glanced up the slope at Michael, let out one high
pitched scream and jumped into the archway. He immediately
disappeared and the portal closed behind him with a small
popping sound. The cavern was thrown into darkness.

Rhys stood still, unable to see. He had dropped his torch
and helmet as he fell. He began to shake, wondering what the
spiders were doing in the darkness. It seemed like he had been
there for a long time before a beam of light lit the cavern and
he heard Michael calling his name. "Rhys, are you OK? Rhys!
Rhys!"

"Yea! I'm here! I'm OK! But I've lost my torch and helmet, can you point the light down here please so I can find them."

Michael did as he was asked and Rhys easily found the dropped items. Both had suffered from the fall and would never be used again. Rhys surveyed the chamber. There were now only a few spiders scuttling around and no sign of the dwarf, other than a few footprints left in the sand. It appeared that with the vanishing of the dwarf the spiders had returned to normal behaviour and were probably already returning to their webs through the cracks and crevasses in the cave wall.

Michael was making his way down the path to the cavern floor.

"So what the heck have we stumbled onto here then Mike?" Rhys asked, looking around the cavern. A quick survey confirmed that there was no other way out of here. The domed cavern was completely sealed, other than the tunnel by which they had entered. Apart from the size of the cavern it was fairly unremarkable.

Michael shouted back, "Well making an educated guess I'd say it was an 'evil albino spider stealing dwarf from another dimension'! Sort of an everyday occurrence in Wales this time of year!" The boys both laughed, grateful for some humour to lighten the moment.

"It looks like you were right with your gateway theory,' Rhys observed.

"Maybe," replied Michael. "I wonder where the gateway led, not that I'd want to find out first hand mind you. Do you think that the dwarf will come back again? He didn't look to happy when we disturbed him."

Rhys had walked over to where the dwarf had stood. He shrugged his shoulder, "Dunno! Maybe we should get out of here just in case he does. If he can go to and fro as he wants then he may come back with help. There doesn't appear to be another exit so we'll have to retrace our path back out of the cave. We won't be able to call for any help or advice either, the radio's bust!" Rhys pointed to the broken radio on the floor.

"Come on then, replied Michael, "let's go!!" Michael turned, eager to be away from this place. As he started back up the path , his foot caught against something in the sand and he almost tripped. Swearing in frustration he looked down expecting to see a stone. Instead, poking out of the sand, he saw a small wooden box.

"What the heck is this!" Michael scrabbled at the sand holding the box and picked it up. It was made from a plain light wood with no exterior decoration. The lid was hinged at the rear and was secured by a small bronze hook and eye. Michael flicked the hook and lifted the lid. Inside was a small handwritten note and another smaller box. Michael took the note and read out loud.

Portalia south, north, east and west,
To ease the travel on any quest,
The knot, the peaks and the old oak tree,
Servant chains amount to three.
A ring to trigger a call to home,
Returns all three to their Runestone.
A stone-made key makes up the set,
Unlocking the paths of the portal net.

Rhys and Michael looked at each other and shrugged.

"Check out the small box," prompted Rhys.

Michael removed his miner's hat and placed it on the floor to offer better illumination before he leant to open the smaller box. Inside was a gold ring. Ornate decoration had been etched around the band of the ring. The gold had been flattened on one end to form a small round area. In the centre of this area was a raised equilateral triangle with the same etched pattern once again adorning the face of the triangle.

Rhys stared and suddenly recognised what he was looking at, "Mike, that pattern is a Celtic knot, the same one as on my pendant." He reached inside his sweater to pull out the pendant. The boys compared the two and confirmed Rhys' belief.

Michael observed something else too. The raised triangle of the ring was exactly the same size and shape as the indent in Rhys' pendant. "It looks as though the ring would fit almost perfectly into the pendant," he said.

Michael held the ring next to the pendant and showed Rhys so he could compare the indentation and the raised triangle of the ring. Rhys inserted the ring into the pendant. There was a soft popping sound.

***

Rhys was confused and frightened. One minute he was in the cave, the next he was engulfed in a blue haze which oozed and flowed all around him. None of his senses gave him any clue as to where he was. He could not hear, smell or taste anything. All he could see was the blue haze and all he could feel was a slight pressure all around him as if he was underwater. He felt panic rising! Had the cave filled with water? Was he drowning? Rhys was suddenly aware of the pendant around his neck, it felt warm and tingly against his body and somehow it reassured him. The fear and panic subsided, lulled by the comfort of the pendant.

His fear now gone Rhys began to think straight and he realised that he was breathing normally. This could not be water. He tried to call out for Michael but no sound came from his mouth. He tried to move but it seemed that for every effort that he made, the force exerted on his body increased, pinning him to where he was. Was he dead? Would he be trapped here for-ever? Had the evil looking albino dwarf caused this? Once again he felt the panic rising only for the warmth of the pendant to ease it once more. He tried to call out again but to no avail. He floated there, his thoughts on Michael and whether his friend was also in this predicament. After a few minutes Rhys noticed that the blue glow was beginning to fade and that the pressure on his body was decreasing. With another popping sound he suddenly felt solid ground beneath his feet again, the blue haze vanished and he was free to move.

He was stood on a large triangular platform in the centre of some form of chamber. Beneath his feet the platform had been adorned with a large Celtic knot. In front of him at the centre of the platform stood a pedestal about three feet tall. The only light emanating from the chamber was from this pedestal, which gave off a dull bluish white glow. The only other source of illumination was from the beams of his helmet and torch. Rhys remembered the dwarf and looked around to see if he was present, but the chamber appeared to be completely empty.

Rhys heard another popping sound to his right and two more to his left, all three in quick succession. The two to his left were accompanied by a loud scream as first Michael, and then a teenage girl, appeared out of thin air. To his right a third figure appeared but quickly hustled off into the darkness. In the short time that the figure was in the light, Rhys caught a glimpse of an old bedraggled man, dressed in rags, unshaven and unkempt. Rhys' nostrils suddenly burst into awareness as from the direction of the old man came the fetid odour of sweat and decay. He wrinkled his nose in disgust and turned to Michael and the girl. Michael stood completely still staring at Rhys and the surroundings. The girl looked frightened when she saw the boys and she immediately withdrew from them her back pushed against the central pedestal.

"Are you OK?" Rhys asked Michael, concern clear in his voice.

"Uh, yes, I guess so. What happened? Where are we?" replied Michael shakily.

"Your guess is as good as mine. I wonder who the girl is? She looks as surprised and confused as us so I presume that she knows as little about what is going on as we do."

At the sound of the boys talking the girl had stopped whimpering. Michael and Rhys walked over to her.

"Are you OK?" Rhys asked.

The girl looked puzzled but clearly relaxed as she sensed that the boys were friendly. "I'm fine, just a little confused. Where are we and how did we get here and what was that blue stuff?"

Rhys smiled at her trying to reassure her despite his own fears, "We're not sure ourselves but we don't seem to be in any real danger." He chose not to mention the appearance of the old man, not knowing if he would turn out to be friendly or otherwise and Rhys did not want to alarm the girl further. "Here, let me help you up, there is no need to be afraid. I'm Rhys and this is Mike, what's your name?"

The girl was annoyed with herself that she had shown her fear to these two younger boys. She took a deep breath and looked Rhys straight in the eyes, "My name is Ashley Rees-Jenkins. You can call me Ash."

CHAPTER SIX
Halfman Forest

Molt awoke to the sound of activity all around the camp. The sun had risen to the east and it looked like it was going to be another glorious summer day. Molt dressed quickly and pushing the canvas door flap aside, left his tent. A night of rest had clearly lifted the spirits and refreshed the whole party. Pinn warriors whistled and sang as they went about their business of breaking camp, preparing for the journey through the Halfman Forest and on to Fortown.

Molt made his way to the river, nodding a good morning to Carl and Stern as he passed. He washed and shaved in the cool water. Overhead he saw that the Fire Eagles had returned to the camp and were hovering over the river. Every now and then one would drop from the sky, plunging through the surface of the water. A few seconds later they would emerge, clutching a fish in their beaks. They would then beat their wings, climbing back into the heights to digest their food as the water was shaken from their feathers in a fine spray..

"Majestic creatures aren't they?" Molt jumped a little, he had not realised that whilst he was observing the birds, Gorlan had approached.

"They most certainly are," he replied. "Although I doubt that any enemy would think of them that way."

Gorlan nodded, "Sometimes I wish I had been chosen to ride. What must it be like to soar the airways on the back of those great creatures. You know, no Warlord has ever been chosen as a bonding partner. The birds sense that destiny holds a different path for those recruits destined for this rank. Of course, the benefit ~~of that~~ is that those unsuccessful at a Ceremony of Choosing can still hope that they are destined to be a great WarLord. This can soften the disappointment a little."

Molt stood and watched the birds. Gorlan spoke again, "You know, sometimes I cannot help feeling sorry for the Fire Eagles. Did you know that truly, they do not like to be ridden? That is why we do so as little as possible, limiting carriage for training purposes and in times of need."

Molt was surprised he had assumed the birds enjoyed the experience, "If that is so then why do the birds allow themselves to be ridden?"

"Because it is their very reason for existence. They were magically created for this sole purpose. The eagles are bound to man, to serve us as warbirds for as long as we require them to do so. It seems such a sad existence though, maybe not so bad in times of peace such as we have enjoyed these past generations, but think of their lives in time of war. Born to serve with their riders, they have little life outside that of battle."

Molt sensed the sadness that Gorlan felt, "I had not thought of it that way. Is it not possible to release the birds from this bonding?"

Gorlan shook his head, "Unfortunately not, the Ceremony of Choosing and the bonding with their rider is all that keeps the birds alive. Many years ago a Fire Eagle was allowed to bond with a rider and remain with him until that rider died naturally, no attempt was made to allow the creature to choose a new bonding partner. It was hoped that when the rider passed away, the fire eagle would be free to live on. Unfortunately, this did not happen, as the rider sucked in his last breath, his eagle took to the skies and began it's westward journey into oblivion," a short silence followed before Gorlan continued, "But enough of this! My men have all but finished breaking camp and it's time we made tracks through the Halfman Forest," with this Gorlan turned and walked away to rejoin his men.

Molt followed and found his tent already dismantled by the Pinns. His belongings were piled neatly on the ground and he loaded them into the saddlebags on his horse.

***

Across the river, Stycich watched and listened with interest, "So the humans are making their way to Fortown. What a surprise they'll have when they reach their destination." He turned to the halfman that accompanied him and slapped him hard on the back of his head, "You! Keep tracking them and watch everything. I'll go to report to our master. I will find you in the forest later, when I will expect you to report precisely what you have learned."

Stycich travelled quickly and silently through the woods, familiar with the hidden pathways that dotted the thick undergrowth. He travelled confidently, aware that nothing would dare attack him in his woods. Even the wild boar had learned to keep well away from the fierce halfmen. His forest enclave was a few hours from the junction of the river, hidden deep amongst the trees where human eyes did not pry. Halfmen were mostly stupid creatures but even so, their ability to hide and remain unseen in the Halfman Forest was unrivalled and human kind thought the creatures were merely a myth.

Stycich had forged himself as leader of the halfmen. Not only was he one of the largest in the clan, but he possessed more of a brain than most and was able to plot his way to

the leadership, murdering others who held any such ambitions.
His clan consisted of some three hundred halfmen but only
thirty halfwomen, with each women enjoying the company of
many mates. Each generation saw the ratio of men to women
increase. Stycich worried at this, even the most stupid of
halfmen realised that more females were needed to continue
the survival of their species.

In an effort to correct this, Stycich had formed a deal with
a new master, the warlock who had appeared to him out of thin
air at the holy place. In return for the service and obedience of
the halfmen clan, their new master had promised to eradicate
human men from Portalia and to deliver hundreds of captured
human women into the custody of the halfmen. This restocking
of females would allow the halfmen to mate and create new
generations of the halfmen horde. The warlock had told Stycich
that he had knowledge of herbs that would ensure that hybrid
offspring would possess the halfmen gene line, rather than the
repulsive, soft human characteristics. Stycich snickered, saliva
dripping from his mouth as he thought about how many wives
he would be able to have in the future. He yearned for the
day when his master's plans would be fulfilled. He wondered
whether his master would reward him today for the news he
brought of the humans. Maybe he could ask for the delivery of
a human woman. That would show his clan that he was a great
leader. He would keep this first woman for his use alone, to be
enjoyed by him and no other. She would bear the first of the
new halfman breed.

With these thoughts in his head, he redoubled his efforts
to reach his camp and to report the latest news to his master.

***

Gorlan's troupe had entered the forest. The Warlord, on

advisory words from Molt, had briefed his men to stay together on the main track. A short while after they entered the forest the woods began to thicken and light faded as a vast canopy of green shaded the riders. The group slowed their pace as they approached a fork in the trail. Molt confirmed that the road to the left led to Fortown, whilst the trail to the right ran parallel with the river leading east towards the elven forests. The band continued south-west, the direction indicated by the Fortownian youth. The fire eagles flew high overhead, the canopy of the trees and the narrowness of the trail preventing them from flying closer to their bonded warriors. The further they rode along the trail, the deeper and denser the forest became, until not even a bird fluttered amongst the lower dark growth. The silence of the forest was eerie. Molt had experienced this before but, to the men of Pinn, it was unnatural and put them on edge. They rode in silence, senses alert looking around them as if they expected to be attacked at any moment.

Gorlan rode at the head of the band accompanied by Molt, he turned to the messenger, "This silence is racking my nerves and I am sure that something watches from the trees. Do you feel it?"

Molt stopped and catalogued their surroundings. He could see nothing unusual and the forest felt the same way as it always had. He reassured Gorlan that everything seemed normal and that there did not appear to be any danger. Gorlan nodded but was less than convinced.

***

Stycich reached his enclave and made his way to the sacred place, a series of stones laid in a circle and used as a shrine to worship the halfman gods. Once they had sacrificed their own to appease these gods but, since the coming of the new master, this practice was no longer needed and all that was asked of them was to make regular offerings of food, gold and gems. Stycich himself had added that the halfmen were duty bound by their new lord to increase their numbers and to spread their race across Portalia.

Stycich sat on the rocks and waited, his clan stood around watching nervously. When the sun was directly overhead and shadows diminished, the master would open the gateway and would send his messenger, the White Dwarf. Stycich planned to tell the White Dwarf that he had urgent news and to demand that he be taken to the master. He would then convey the news of the Pinn's progress and be rewarded.

Stycich glanced up at the sun as it reached it's apex. A glowing blue archway formed amongst the rocks of the sacred place. The White Dwarf appeared as he had done so many times before. He looked at the gathering and raised his hand in acknowledgement as the halfmen fell to their knees. He then made his way forward to collect the offerings . There was an abundance of fruit and numerous gems, mined from the rocks near the enclave. The White Dwarf gathered up the items and put them into a large sack that he carried over his shoulder.

"Shangorth the Warlock is pleased with your offerings!" he shouted to the halfmen. "He continues to build his strength and his army is growing. Soon the time to destroy humankind will be upon us and Shangorth and his armies will once again rule Portalia."

The White Dwarf paused and drew out his axe as Stycich approached. "Stop, why do you approach the Messenger of Shangorth, halfman?"

Stycich stopped, confidence draining from him as he stared at the black axe. "I have news for our master. News of the human kind that he will find of interest."

The White Dwarf relaxed, "You can give that news to me, I am Shangorth's eyes and ears."

Stycich hesitated, he did not want to give this news to the White Dwarf, he wanted to talk to the master himself and receive his female reward. Thoughts of a female brought new courage to him, "I feel that this news is too important to give to a messenger. It must be delivered to the master himself.!"

The White Dwarf screamed in rage, "You DARE to question the Messenger of Shangorth.," and in so saying he stepped toward Stycich, raised his axe and brought it down on a rock that stood inches to the left of the halfman leader. The rock exploded into fragments with a thunderous sound and Stycich backed off cowering. He turned to his clan for support but all had fled, not waiting to see what would become of their leader. Stycich used his brain again and decided that now may be a good time to back down. He lowered his head to the ground and asked for forgiveness. He then proceeded to inform the White Dwarf of the arrival in the forest of the humans and of their journey to Fortown. The dwarf listened intently before replying, "You have done well halfman, I will take this message back to Shangorth and will return shortly. Wait here for my return."

The White Dwarf turned and walked back through the portal which disappeared behind him.

***

Gorlan and his men had been travelling for five hours when they came to a widening of the trail. A stream ran alongside their route at this point and offered an excellent place to allow the horses to drink and for the men to take on dry rations.

Molt decided to search out Stern and Carl for company. He found them towards the back of the group. Once again

Molt found Carl munching on his dry rations smacking his lips as if they were the finest meat.

Molt stared at Carl who acknowledged him with a grunt. "How the heck can you eat so much of that stuff Carl?", Molt asked watching in amazement.

"Cosch itsch schcrummy" mumbled Carl with mouth full to bursting. Stern stood next to his brother, shaking his head in resignation. "It looks like we'll make Fortown in good time my friend," said Stern addressing Molt, "I presume that you are looking forward to getting back home to your own people."

Molt thought about his home. He lived with his parents in Fortown with Meld, his elder brother by one year and their two younger sisters, Jade and Amber. His father owned a small farm on the outskirts of the town, where he grew fruit and vegetables. He sold his produce to the local market traders who, in turn, sold it at the local town market. As well as helping on the farm, the boys would also offer their services to the market traders, helping to sell the produce and restock the stalls. When they weren't working with their father on the stall, the boys practiced soldiery with other volunteers. In their spare time they loved to fish and play clayball, a popular sport played on a triangular pitch with hard clay balls and three bases. Molt had played the sport with other boys and girls for years and one of his closest rivals was a neighbour's daughter, a girl called Brianna. She could pitch a solid clay and strike a ball as far as any of them.

When he thought about Brianna, Molt's heart began to race. For years they had treated each other as rivals, but over the past few months they had passed into a new stage of friendship. Molt suddenly found that he wanted to be with her as much as possible. Brianna, on her part, was only too happy to comply. He smiled as he pictured her face, her soft brown eyes and her short cropped brown hair. He closed his eyes as he imagined the smell of her perfume.

A sharp prod in his ribs brought him back to reality. He looked into the face of a smiling Stern, "I'll take that as a yes!", he said, "and if I'm not much mistaken there is a certain young lady that will be looking forward to your return too."

Molt blushed visibly. Carl, now able to speak clearly, his latest portion of dry rations now nestling in his belly playfully chastised his brother for teasing the young man. Molt felt uncomfortable and a little annoyed at the teasing. The brothers sensed this and apologized.

Molt managed to gain some revenge though. As Stern turned to leave to gather his mount, Molt took his chance. Watching the pattern of Stern's feet as he walked away, Molt waited for Stern's left foot to trail, then, as the Pinn lifted this foot and brought it forward, Molt, with perfect timing, gave it a quick flick. Stern's left leg crossed his right leg. His own momentum caused him to trip and fell flat on his face. Many of the warriors had witnessed what had happened and bellowed with laughter as Stern regained his feet, dusting himself off to the teasing gibes of his colleagues. Molt felt pleased with himself and walked back to his horse with a spring in his step. He couldn't wait to tell Brianna about that one. A fully trained Pinn Warrior brought down by one of the oldest schoolboy tricks in the book.

***

Stycich lingered impatiently at the sacred place for the White Dwarf's return. He was not happy that the dwarf had insisted on taking the message to the master himself. He wondered whether the dwarf would steal the glory and take a gift from the warlock for himself. Time seemed to drag as he sat by the rocks. Eventually though, the gate was reopened and he heard the familiar popping sound as the White Dwarf returned.

"Shangorth has considered the news that you bring and he thanks you for this information. He would like to give you some reward for this but first asks that you carry out one more task." Stycich's mouth stretched into a big ugly grin, exposing his yellowed fangs.

"The mighty Shangorth demands that you gather your clan together to attack the humans as they pass through the forest. Shangorth believes that this is a chance for glory for the halfmen and an opportunity for the halfmen to strengthen their allegiance to the great warlock. The canopy and depth of the trees provides a great advantage to your clan. The Pinn fire eagles will be greatly hindered and will not be able to respond to any attack. If your clan uses the cover of the forest you should be able to slaughter the humans without risk to yourselves. The warriors will have to fight from their horses or on foot. Shangorth orders that you use a short swift attack. This will kill many and the others can then be lured into the woods where they can be easily dispatched by your halfmen. Shangorth knows that the halfmen are fierce fighters and are capable of winning this battle. He asks that you kill all of the Pinn warriors and prevent their progress to Fortown."

Stycich was very unhappy and hissed his disapproval at the White Dwarf. "What madness is this! Halfmen have remained hidden in the woods for generations. If we were to attack the humans then they would know of our existence and they would come with many soldiers and kill my clan."

The White Dwarf lifted his black axe high into the air and brought it down with a thump on the ground. "Shangorth thought that you may object. Here is his choice. Fight the humans as commanded or suffer a long and lingering death with your body racked in pain. Also, to show that Shangorth values loyal subjects, if you succeed in stopping the Pinns he has promised to double the number of human women for the halfmen clan breeding stock. Further, Shangorth foretells that the humans will have more important things to occupy their armies than to take time to wreak revenge on the halfmen."

Stycich hesitated, his mind full of frustration and uncertainty. He was now faced with possible death at the hands of the Pinns, or certain death if he disobeyed the warlock.

The White Dwarf looked at him through his pale eyes in utter contempt, "One last thing. Once the task is complete, your loyalty in this will also be rewarded with the delivery of the first batch of human women."

Stycich stopped rocking and smiled once more. "Now why didn't you say so," he hissed, "Consider the task done."

"A wise choice halfman, return here once you have completed your task. I will return to hear news of your battle. Now go and gather your clan, the humans make haste through the forest even as we speak." The White Dwarf stepped back into the gateway which once again disappeared behind him.

Stycich stood, he had hardly heard the last words of the dwarf, his mind now flooded with thoughts of how he would enjoy the human women. He pondered how he would be able to use them to bear halfman offspring. Then, when they could no longer bear children, how they could be used to replenish the clan food supply. He dribbled as his mouth watered. It had been so long since he had tasted human flesh.

Running back to his clan, Stycich summoned the men and ordered them to ready themselves for battle. He was surprised to find that his halfmen seemed excited at the prospect of attacking the humans. He had expected them to be frightened at the prospect. Driven by the promise of more sexual partners and of taste of human meat, the halfmen rushed to gather their bows and knives and formed a band around Stycich. As he led them through the woods, his clan began howling out their bloodlust.

CHAPTER SEVEN
A Fight in the Forest

Gorlan looked up at the fire eagles, they appeared agitated and were flying as close to the warriors as the trees allowed, taking it in turns to swoop down to glide above the leafy canopy. Gorlan sent the word around the men that something appeared amiss and to be wary.

The trail ahead was narrowing so that only three riders could ride side by side, Gorlan and Molt rode at the head and, behind them, the warriors rearranged themselves into rows of three. Concerned by the agitation shown by the fire eagles, Gorlan picked two of his men to ride ahead as scout. He then ordered his men to be especially vigilant. With scouts dispatched, the riders resumed their course, following a few hundred yards behind the two men.

The forest suddenly seemed especially quiet and forbidding. The men looked into the dark dense interior with uncertainty in their eyes and trepidation in their hearts. Numerous times the shadows seemed to hold the mocking faces of enemies, intent on doing them harm. A second nervous look would reveal that the hidden enemy was merely a strangely shaped tree trunk or branch. The buoyant mood of earlier was now left behind as they moved slowly forward.

It happened suddenly! A deluge of arrows flew from the forest felling the two scouts. Their comrades drew their weapons and charged forward to meet their hidden enemy.

In the woods Stycich cursed to himself. His clan had been too swift to attack and the element of surprise was lost. Even so, they had the advantage of numbers and he knew that the war birds were unable to assist, trapped high above the forest floor by the density of the trees.

Before the front rank of the riders reached the point of attack, the halfmen were able to let off more volleys of arrows, striking down four more Pinn warriors and wounding others. Foolishly, numerous halfmen archers held their positions close to the trail, only partly sheltered by the forest. They continued to fire arrows wildly but were soon met by the first of the Pinn warriors and were dispatched with ease. The swiftness and simplicity in which the archers had been slain caused uncertainty among the other halfmen. The creatures now retreated in fear deeper into the woods. In doing so they had stumbled onto the very tactic which would offer them greater chance of victory.

The Pinn warriors dismounted and pushed after their enemy on either side of the path, hacking and slashing their swords into halfman flesh as they progressed. Above their heads they could hear the screeches of their fire eagle companions, frantically trying to find a way through the dense foliage. Driven on by the sound and the madness of battle, the warriors advanced deeper into the woods in chase of their quarry. Gorlan shouted a warning and ordered his men to hold. Some obeyed but others continued their advance, the Warlord's order lost in the howling and screeching of the halfmen horde.

Molt, sword drawn, held his ground instinctively, along with six other warriors. The retreat of the halfmen into the older growth had negated the effectiveness of their archers, who could no longer fire accurately through the dense cover. As a result, the threat of projectiles was removed for Molt and the remaining warriors. Their efforts were now focussed on dispatching sporadic halfmen who burst out of the woods wildly to attack with their knives. These were slain swiftly and efficiently, particularly by Stern and Carl, who fought together, back to back, dispatching halfmen to the left and right.

Deeper in the forest things were very different. The old growth restricted the swing of the warrior's swords and it did not take long for the halfmen to realise that they now held the advantage. The creatures rallied and, using their short knives, fell on the Pinn warriors in numbers. The men fought bravely. They drew their own short fighting knives and used their training to hold off and beat back many of the halfmen. Eventually, the sheer number of their foe overcame them and they fell, sliced and hacked to death by tens of halfman blades, teeth and nails. Once their foe was slain, many of the halfmen lost interest in the fight and instead, turned to satisfy their bloodlust for fresh human meat. The Pinns were horrified by this obscenity and the sight drove them to an even greater battle rage, as they fought for their lives and the lives of their comrades. The numbers against them were too great though and the dense forest provided too much of an advantage to the halfmen. Still fighting bravely, almost all met their deaths in the forest, providing meals for greedy halfman stomachs.

Gorlan, still fighting on the trail, realised that they were facing a massacre. He screamed loudly for the remaining warriors to fall back to the path. Momentarily he contemplated sounding the Horn of Summoning but he quickly dismissed this. Even if the dragon did respond, his own men were fighting hand to hand with the enemy, any dragon fire attack would deliver as much damage to his own forces as that of the accursed halfmen. Surveying the battle scene, Gorlan realised that the natural cover that had worked against the Pinns earlier, would now work for his men by negating the effectiveness of the halfmen archers. This time his order to retreat was heard and passed from man to man, the remaining warriors began to return back to the trail, fighting off the savage halfmen as they did so.

As his troops re-appeared out of the forest, Gorlan ran forward protecting as many of them as possible, whilst ordering them to their horses. The Warlord raced for his own mount as the remaining warriors kicked their animals and galloped down the trail. By the time the halfmen archers realised what was happening, their enemy was well out of the range of their short bows.

Gorlan led his men on through the forest, galloping swiftly under the canopy of trees. They soared on until the tree canopy began to thin and eventually opened enough to see the sky. Molt, riding alongside Gorlan shouted to the WarLord that they were close to the edge of the forest. He nodded and the band continued their flight, trees a blur, as they reached for the safety of the open of the Portalia Meadows. During their retreat, Gorlan glanced at the skies. Crestfallen he realised that only ten fire eagles followed, the others he suspected had now made their westward flight to oblivion. He had lost two thirds of his warriors already and he had not yet reached Fortown. Tears welled in his eyes at the loss of his troops.

Eventually the fleeing riders reached the promised sanctity of open ground as they burst out of the forest onto the Meadows. Gorlan led them a safe way from the woods, out of the range of any following enemy archers and then called his group to a stop. They came to a halt on the open ground of the Meadows, the remaining eagles swooped down to join their riders. At this point Molt also observed that the other fire eagles, their bonded riders slain, had made their final flight to the west. The remaining eagles held their heads down, their body language clearly expressing their own sense of loss. Molt suddenly felt a deep compassion and sadness for the birds. In the heat of battle, he had not even considered their plight as their bonded warriors fought and died amongst the trees below, unassisted by their warbird partners.

Gorlan did a quick survey and confirmed what he had feared earlier, only ten warriors remained. He examined his men, they looked tired and shocked and all wore the bloody marks of battle. Fortunately none were seriously injured and a brief rest would allow them to continue their journey. Gorlan struggled to find the right words, he turned to his men, expression grave and said, "You fought well men and our fallen comrades will not be forgotten. I know that it is difficult to bear that we had to leave our dead to those beasts, but the path chosen was the right one. I regret having to order the retreat but we could not win amongst the trees and I chose to have you live to fight another day. We will return to avenge their deaths but, for now, we will make camp and rest. In the morning we will push on to Fortown to determine what help is needed there. Evil walks in our lands again. Not only do we find ourselves face to face with the ferocious halfmen, who we believed to be nothing but an ancient myth, but my orders from the Overlord were to ride to Fortown to investigate reports of Black Eagles flying over Dargoth once more. I had reason to doubt this report but after today I think differently. We will send for reinforcements when we reach Fortown and we will provide solutions to both problems, whether that threat be in the air or in the forests. Pinn will prevail and will drive evil from our lands."

Despite fatigue and their sorrow, Gorlan's speech roused his men and they raised their swords in salute. Later that evening a great feeling of relief swept over the camp when the fire eagles flew west towards the sunset. Despite this indication of a peaceful night, the Pinn men ensured that a watch was put in place. After the events of the day they no longer trusted their lives to common myths and legends.

***

Stycich waited triumphantly at the sacred place. He had lost a little over one hundred of his clan in the fight but his people revelled in the glory of their victory. They had killed twenty of the cursed humans, a magnificent triumph. His people would also eat well for weeks as no meat would go to waste, human or halfman, all would be used to feed his clan.

The White Dwarf reappeared through the archway as promised and Stycich made his report. The dwarf grinned and proceeded to thank and congratulate Stycich for a job well done. He informed him that his master was very pleased and had a reward for the him. The dwarf turned and stepped back through the archway. As Stycich watched in eager anticipation a body was thrown through the gateway to land in a heap at his feet. He looked down at a white skinned dark haired human woman scantily clad in torn rags. She had clearly been beaten and her body exhibited numerous bruises but no bones appeared broken. Any human that looked upon her would have seen how lifeless her eyes looked, no sparkle, no twinkle, just a vacant stare. Stycich looked at her but saw none of this, all he saw was a woman all for himself. She would be the first to bear him a child, the first to deliver an heir to continue his bloodline and to grow his clan. She would be the first of many.

CHAPTER EIGHT
Eumor City

Rhys, Ashley and Michael stood in the centre of the triangular platform, their faces lit by the glow of the pedestal. They had turned off their torches to preserve battery power. Earlier they had explored the chamber and to their dismay had found the only exit out of the stone room had been firmly sealed. They had inspected the rock that blocked the doorway and were unable to move it. Whoever had sealed that doorway had intended for it never to be used again. During their exploration they had come across the ragged old man and Rhys had explained to the others about his appearance. The strange character stayed well away from them though. Each time they approached his position he would swiftly back away into the darkness, shielding his eyes from the light of their torches. He did not appear to offer any threat and indeed, seemed more afraid of them than they of him.

The chamber itself was elliptical in shape. The stone plinth, on which they had appeared, stood in the centre of this ellipse. The sealed doorway was installed in a wall at one end of the ellipse. All around the chamber their torches had revealed intricate artwork, hand painted directly on to the walls. Each mural depicted a scene and all included centaurs of varying size and ages. The creatures were shown in different poses, most carrying out normal every day activities; looking after their young, teaching, cooking, hunting and eating. The rest of the artwork brought to life centaurs battling with other creatures; eagles, dragons, dwarves, wizards and humans. From the central pedestal the soft glow was not enough to illuminate the outer walls, so the teenagers were surprised when their torches revealed the vivid colours.

Halfway along the chamber a bust of a strange cat-like creature protruded from the wall. It's large mouth was open wide and, inside the mouth, a small flow of water ran out of the wall from the right, over the stone tongue and then back into the wall on the left. A small stone plug had been placed under the tongue to stop any water spilling. With a little difficulty, Rhys had managed to remove the plug and water poured out of the hole and onto the floor. He tasted it cautiously before reinserting the stone plug. The water was cool and fresh so at least they would not die of thirst.

At one time, it seemed that the chamber had been lit by sunlight that would have flooded through windows high up in the domed roof of the chamber. Now these too had been sealed and no longer offered any illumination.

At the far end of the chamber, directly opposite the sealed doorway, the teenagers had found items that seemed out of place in this dark and bare room. A mattress, a small table and a wooden cabinet sat on the floor. Inside the cabinet were a number of long pipe-like wooden tubes with holes cut into them at regular intervals. Some were straight, whilst others curved in on themselves to form a spiral. They were clearly musical instruments of some kind. Ashley, who had learned to play the clarinet in high school, tested out the instruments and found that they offered good crisp and clear tones. Unfortunately though, her ignorance of these particular instruments resulted in the notes sounding particularly off key.

On the bottom shelf of the cabinet Ashley found some

colourful blankets and a striped red, green and yellow poncho. She pulled it over her head, it was a bit big for her but the expanse of it immediately warmed her and she wondered what animal fur it had been made from, it looked like wool but felt much softer. She was extremely grateful for this as, dressed only in her pyjamas, she had started to feel the chill of the chamber.

Further inspection of the cabinet offered up a small notebook and pen. Most of the book contained text which they were unable to interpret and indeed, did not recognise, however, there were a few small drawings, mostly depicting musical instruments of varying kinds. One sketch showed the triangular platform on which they had arrived, complete with a glowing archway, the pedestal and three figures stood in the gateway in silhouette. On two of the figures the artists had depicted a magical glow around their necks, whilst the third figure possessed a glow around the neck and the right hand. On the pedestal itself was shown a small octagonal shaped object, again depicted glowing.

The teenagers had now returned to the platform to compare the pedestal to the drawing in the note book. The top of the pedestal was round, like a table top, and the familiar Celtic knot adorned the centre. Above the knot they saw that a octagonal hole had been cut. There was no sign of the corresponding object as illustrated in the book. The octagonal slot itself was able to rotate and offered twenty-four positions over the full three hundred and sixty degrees. There were small markings on each of the positions, a large closed eye at the top, a Celtic knot to the right, a tree to the left, a mountain at the bottom and twenty small open eyes, four between each of the larger symbols spread around the octagon. Rhys was able to turn the octagonal slot with his fingers but nothing happened.

Ashley traced the shape of the Celtic knot with her finger and said, "This is the same shape as the knot on the pendant given to me by my grandmother." She reached into her pyjama pocket and pulled out her pendant. Seeing Ashley's pendant Rhys reached into his tee shirt and pulled out his own, they were identical. They then showed her the Celtic knot ring that Michael had found.

Ashley looked at the boys with excitement, "These must be the key to how we got here," she said, excitedly. "Before I found myself in the blue ooze I was asleep in bed. I woke and saw the pendant glowing, I had no choice, I had to reach out and touch it. As soon as I did I was transported through the blue ooze to here." She looked at the boys, "Tell me the last thing you remember before you arrived here."

Rhys gave an account of how they had been exploring the cave and had observed the albino dwarf. He then explained how Michael had found the verse and the ring and had inserted the ring into the pendant. The next thing they knew they were in the blue ooze and then in this chamber.

Ashley asked Michael for the ring. He removed it and gave it to her. She examined it closely and observed the patterns and raised triangle, looking thoughtful as she did so. "The silhouettes drawn in the book all possess a magic glow around their necks. That must represent the pendants. One of those silhouettes also has a glow around the hand. This must represent the ring. The only thing I don't understand is that there are four of us here but only three shown in the book."

They pondered this a while and then Michael offered, "Maybe the old guy has a pendant too. It could be around his neck, under his rags."

Ashley and Rhys both agreed that this sounded logical.

Ashley toyed with the ring in her fingers, "So what will happen if we insert the ring into the pendant a second time?".

"Maybe it will take us back to Salty's Cave," Rhys suggested excitedly.

"Or maybe it will take us some other place," offered Michael, frowning.

"Or maybe nothing will happen at all," added Ashley. "We can't get out of this place though so we may as well give it a try. Are we all agreed?"

The boys nodded their heads in confirmation. Ashley gave the ring back to Michael. He slipped it over his finger and then, rather nervously, inserted it into the slot in Rhys pendant.

There was but the faintest glimmer to the senses of the blue ooze but they remained where they stood, next to the pedestal. The ragged man however did not. As usual he had been lurking in the shadows muttering to himself insanely. At the moment the ring had been inserted into the pendant, he had been spirited back onto the platform. He immediately let out a howl, pointed his fingers irritably at the children and ran back into the shadows.

Ashley smiled and said, "Well he wasn't very happy about that was he? I guess we can safely say that the old fella has a pendant hidden about his person somewhere. Did you both feel the tingling sensation for a brief moment?"

They both nodded, Ashley continued her analysis, "The picture in the note book shows three people, rather than four, but one of them is wearing the ring and the pendant so all four must make up a set. We know that the combination of Rhys' pendant and the ring brings us here, but what about my pendant and the ring."

They agreed that this would be worth a try. Michael lined up the ring with the pendant and gently inserted once more. The result was identical. A feint tingling and the transportation of the old man back onto the platform. This time he seemed even angrier. He clutched at his neck, pulled a chain over his head and threw an object onto the floor before running back into the shadows. Rhys made towards the pendant. A loud scream from the old man stopped him in his tracks. Emerging from the shadows, he waved a fist at Rhys before grabbing the pendant from the floor and placed it back around his neck.

Rhys turned to Ashley and Michael, "Well I guess that confirms our theory about him owning a pendant. It seems precious to him doesn't it. He was happy to throw it down but did not want me anywhere near it. Poor guy, I wondered what happened to him." Rhys peered into the shadows but could not see anything in the gloom.

Ashley spoke to Michael, "Do you remember the words of that verse you found?" she asked.

"I can do better than that," he replied. He put his hand into his pocket and drew out the piece of paper that he had removed from the box earlier. He gave it to Ashley and she read it to herself.

After a moments thought she said, "This is telling us something about the pendants and ring." She paused and looked at the verse again, "*The knot, the peaks and the old oak tree, Servant chains amount to three.* I think the servant chains are a reference to the three pendants. The knot must be the pattern on our pendants and ring but I don't understand the reference to the peaks and the oak tree." she read the next piece then continued, "*A ring to trigger a call to home, Returns all three to their Runestone.* That is obviously the ring that Michael found. The return to the Runestone must be what we experienced when the ring 'triggered' our journey here. This platform that we are standing on must be the Runestone. Doesn't tell us where the heck we are though does it?" The boys stood in amazement, Rhys looked at her with admiration and said, "Excellent stuff Ash, what about the rest?"

She read the verse again. "It starts, *Portalia south, north, east and west, To ease the travel on any quest.* Could that be a reference to where we are? A place called Portalia. Ever heard of it?" Both of the boys replied in the negative. Ashley read out the last piece of the rhyme, "*A stone-made key makes up the set, Unlocking the paths of the portal net.* " She pondered on this for a little while with furrowed brow but offered up no explanation.

Michael looking about him contemplating the last few lines of the verse. His eyes fell on the pedestal and the octagonal cut out. An idea formed in his head, "Maybe the 'stone-made key' refers to that glowing object that we saw in the drawing. It must be some kind of controlling device for the pedestal. The rhyme states that it unlocks the paths of the portal net. I'm only guessing but perhaps the pedestal is some kind of control device for the Runestone. The octagonal stone key is the trigger mechanism, you know, like the ignition key for a car. Once the key is inserted, the dial on the pedestal could allow the selection of different paths to travel to different places in the same manner that we travelled here. A network of portals. Instant gateways to travel long distances."

Ashley and Rhys agreed that this sounded like a reasonable explanation. Without the stone key though they had no way of proving this theory. Discussing their next action they finally agreed to split up and search the chamber again, this time looking for places where the octagonal Runestone key may be hidden.

Thirty minutes or so later, Rhys had been just about had enough of the search and so decided to see if he could find out more about the old man. He found him easily and spoke softly and gently as he approached. Removing some chocolate from his rucksack, Rhys held it out as an offering, the old man backed away nervously.

Rhys persevered though and, after three or four attempts, finally managed to get close to him. The smell of decay and body odour was overpowering and Rhys tried not to breath in through his nose as he eased forward. The old man was now only a few feet away, staring at the chocolate with fear in his eyes. Rhys wondered if the old man did not recognise the offering as food, or maybe he did, but was simply afraid to take it. Given the state of the man and his fear of any illumination, Rhys wondered if he had been a prisoner, locked away in the dark somewhere, or maybe a patient who had been shut up in an uncaring lunatic asylum. Rhys doubted that the man was merely down on his luck, his demeanour was far worst than that of the street people that Rhys had seen in the cities back home. Pondering this, Rhys wondered if the old man had thought the chocolate poisoned. To try to reassure him, Rhys took a nibble of the bar, making a clear show of it so the old man could see that all was well.

It worked. With a sudden movement the man leapt forward and grabbed the chocolate out of Rhys' hand. He jumped back away and stuffed the lot in his mouth, chewing ravenously, Rhys edged a little closer, another piece of chocolate between his fingers. He continued to talk quietly to the man, trying to reassure him. The old man looked into Rhys eyes, confusion was painted all over his face, then, as if making a decision his expression softened and he stepped forward and gently took the offered chocolate. Rhys smiled at him and the old man grinned back, nodding feverishly. Rhys spoke gently again, pointing to himself he said, "Rhys, I am Rhys." The old man mumbled something to Rhys but it sounded like gibberish to the boy's ears. He repeated his name and on the fourth attempt the man responded pointing to himself and said, "Lan". Rhys wasn't sure if that was really the old man's name but he thought it was good as any, he turned to the old man and said, "Good, well done Lan," he emphasised the man's name, "Now don't worry we'll find a way out of here and we'll take you with us." Rhys tried to sound confident but inside he was filled with trepidation. Although they had water there was not much food to go around.

Whilst Rhys was with Lan, Michael and Ashley had returned to the Runestone, their search for the octagonal key stone had also been fruitless. Rhys told them about Lan and suggested that they all eat something. The boys emptied their backpacks. They found a handful of sandwiches, four pork pies, some crisps and one bar of chocolate. The lemonade was gone but the bottles remained, they would be handy for collecting water to supplement the two bottles of water given to them by Auntie Glenys.

Rhys broke one of the ham sandwiches into four, "We need to save the food as much as possible as we don't know how long we'll be stuck here. What we have here will only be enough to last a couple of days, after that we will have water but nothing else to eat."

Michael frowned, "I remember reading once about some guys that crashed an aeroplane in the mountains. They survived by eating one of the men. Can you imagine that? No matter how hungry I get, I just can't see myself turning to human meat."

Ashley put her hand on his shoulder, "I think you'd be surprised what you'd actually eat if you were starving. Don't worry though, *you* won't have to eat human meat because you're the first on the menu!" Ashley pushed Michael playfully and smacked her lips in mock anticipation.

Rhys took one of the sandwich quarters to give to Lan. Once again he had to go through the ritual of tasting the food before Lan would accept, but at least the old man no longer ran from him.

Hours passed, the teenagers sat together, talking about their homes and promising to appreciate their friends and families a little more in the future. Gradually, they fell silent and before long all three fell asleep.

Rhys dreamed.

Rhys was standing on a large runestone. At first the runestone held the Celtic knot pattern, then it changed to a tree before melding into the shape of a mountain. Images of places flashed through his dream state. The elliptical chamber, a desert scene, Salty's Cave, a snow capped mountain, a tropical forest, a ruined temple, image after image appeared to him, ever changing, faster and faster. Suddenly the images stopped and the face of the albino dwarf appeared to him. The yellow and white eyes staring at Rhys. Rhys saw the lips moving but could hear nothing, the dwarf raised his axe and sneered at Rhys but just as he was about to strike the face faded and was replaced with the blue ooze. Rhys tried to move but felt himself trapped. A new figure now appeared, it was thin and drawn and dressed in a black flowing cloak. The figure had long grey hair and a skull like face, the skin a deathly pale jaundiced yellow. The eyes glowed a blood red and the lips were thin and grey. Rhys saw that the figure was saying something. He tried to concentrate and break away from the blue ooze to hear what was being said. Finally, a faint sound reached his ears. Once focussed the sound became louder and louder until Rhys ears rang painfully, "DEATH, DEATH, DEATH, DEATH!"

Rhys woke with a start, the words still echoing in his brain. Rhys remembered the face that he had seen and felt a cold shiver run down his spine. He shook his head vigorously and told himself that this was just a dream. Deep inside though, he knew that there was more to it than that and that somewhere, somehow, this figure existed and seemed intent on bringing death to this world. He looked across at Ashley and Michael, both still sleeping soundly, he refused to close his eyes however, frightened that his mind would take him back to the dream. He lay there in the light of the pedestal contemplating everything that had happened in the past day. He became aware of the sounds of the chamber, the tinkling of the water as it flowed through the cat creature's head, the steady breathing of Ashley and Michael as they slept, and the mumbling of Lan still awake and hidden in the shadows. Slowly. He started to feel drowsy.

All of sudden he started awake! A new sound had joined those of the chamber, a feint rattling and scratching noise emanated from the far end of the room, near to where they had found the musical instruments. Rhys realised that it must have been the subtle change in sound that had alerted his senses. He quietly shuffled across to Michael and Ashley and woke them, indicating them to be silent and whispering for them to listen. The rattling sound had now become louder and even Lan had gone silent, clearly listening too. Rhys gestured to Michael and Ashley to follow him and he entered the shadows, working his way down the wall towards the source of the sound. As they approached the area where the mattress and other objects sat, there was a loud rumbling sound and a section of rock slid sideways in the chamber wall. Light emanated from the opening and the teenagers retreated a little into the shadows so as not to be seen. Rhys noticed that the eyes of both his friends were wide with suspense and realised that he too held his breath as his heart pounded.

The light became brighter and lit up half of the chamber as something entered from the secret passage. The teenagers backed away even further into the shadows. At first the light seemed so intense that Rhys could make nothing out in the brightness, his eyes having become accustomed to the dark of the cave and the chamber, but his eyes and brain quickly remedied this and adjusted. As his vision cleared Rhys stared in amazement at the creature that had entered the chamber. The top half of the body was female human, possessing head, chest and arms. At the waist the figure transformed into animal form similar in shape to a horse, with four hoofed legs, a long straight back, sexual organs and buttocks, all covered in a thick coarse brown hair and with a long black horse tail. From toe to top of head the creature stood about seven feet tall. Rhys knew he was looking upon a centaur, a creature of earthly myth and legend. He looked at her head and torso again. The centaur wore her dark brown human hair page boy style. The eyes were brown, the skin bronzed. The nose largish and the lips full. She did not wear any covering on her human form and the boys reddened as they looked upon a muscular back and large full breasts. Rhys was reminded of the women that he had seen on the beaches when on holiday in Italy.

The companions watched and held their breath as the centaur went to her cabinet. She paused a moment as if in thought, then proceeded to pick up a blanket which she wrapped around her shoulders. Next she stooped to take one of the musical pipes and lowered her hind quarters down onto the mattress. As she prepared herself to play.

The centaur shuffled to make herself comfortable and began to play. The sound that emanated from the instrument transfixed the teenagers. They looked at each other in wonder as they listened to the intricate melody. They were mesmerised by the tune, and it seemed that the music itself called to them to join with it as it ebbed and flowed, painting patterns, soothing their being and relaxing their senses. Rhys shook his head to clear it and whispered a warning to Ashley and Michael not to be drawn by the enchantment of the music, they nodded their assent but found they had to concentrate hard to combat the desire to get closer to the music.

Ashley whispered to the other two, "We have no way of knowing if this creature is friendly. I do not think we should reveal ourselves as we do not know for sure what she will do. We now know that there is a way out of here so we need to plan what we do next. The way I see it we have two options. The first is to wait until she leaves and to see if we can find a way of opening the passage ourselves. The second is for one of us to follow her through the passage as she leaves and to watch what she does to close the doorway. They could then hide on the other side until she left and then reopen it for us so we can get out of here. Neither option is what I'd call cool as they both have risks."

Rhys pondered this before replying, "I would prefer the second as we have already searched this side and we didn't find anything that looked like it would open the doorway."

Michael nodded, "I think that's the best option too. If we go with the first and cannot find a way out we have no way of knowing when she'll be back. We need to decide who should try to follow her. I think Rhys, or yourself Ash, as you are both more athletic than me and lighter on your feet."

As Ashley and Rhys looked at each other to decide which of them should follow the centaur, they heard Lan mumbling out loud. They turned to look in his direction and he had left the shadows and was reluctantly approaching the light and the centaur, drawn by the music just as the teenagers were earlier.

The female centaur became aware of Lan at almost the same time. Her eyes popped open in astonishment and she immediately dropped her instrument. With no music to draw him forward Lan immediately recoiled from the light and returned back into the shadows. The centaur stood and stared to where Lan had retreated, uncertainty spread across her face. She was clearly deep in thought and unsure what to do. Eventually she moved towards Lan who, in turn, instantly backed away, mumbling in fright. Every time she approached he retreated until finally, clearly frustrated by this, the centaur galloped hard to him with incredible speed and pinned him against the wall, towering over him.

"Who are you? What are you doing here?" she shouted at him.

Lan was now petrified and curled himself into a ball, mumbling and groaning as he did so. Rhys was concerned that the centaur intended harm to the old man. Lan lay below her, perilously close to her hooves, which were banging heavily on the floor near his unprotected head.

Rhys shouted at the centaur, "Leave him alone you bully! He means no harm and is helpless!"

The centaur was clearly startled and turned to face Rhys, anger clear in her face and demeanour. "Another human! What goes on here?" The centaur turned her attention away from Lan and speedily galloped over to the boy. Rhys felt himself trembling but pride made him stand his ground. "I think we should be asking you that'" he said to the centaur rather cockily.

Ashley and Michael watched in amazement as all confidence and aggression suddenly disappeared from the centaur. "What do you mean," she replied, "I was merely playing music, there is nothing wrong with that if done in private is there?".

Rhys, who had intended on accusing the centaur of having brought them to this place against their will, realised that he had hit upon a sensitive subject. For some reason the centaur was nervous about the fact her music had been overheard. He decided to use this to his advantage. "That may be so but you are not playing in private are you. We are here."

The centaur paused before answering, "But I did not know you were here and no-one has used this Runestone hall for many years. Anyway, you are not SUPPOSED to be here even if this was once a public place it is now forbidden to all."

Rhys continued to play his game, "If it is forbidden then why are you here?"

The centaur looked lost and was now very uncertain of herself, she did not answer. Rhys decided to go on, "Well let's look at it this way. We are not meant to be here but we are. You are not meant to be here but you are AND you were playing music." Rhys still had no idea why playing music was a factor but he continued to play that card, "Therefore, why don't we help you and you help us. We mean you no harm and, hopefully, you mean us no harm either."

The centaur looked at Rhys and contemplated his words, "Very well little man, but before I agree to trust you I need to know how you came to be here and what you intend to do. I will not make pacts with any creature that plans to do harm to my people, no matter how serious a crime I have committed."

Rhys accepted this offer. He waved Michael and Ashley out of the shadows and introduced them. The centaur looked a little startled when they at first appeared but when she realised she was in no danger, accepted their presence. She invited the teenagers to join her on her mattress and introduced herself as Kyrie.

They all sat down and Rhys spoke, "Before I tell you of how we arrived here Kyrie, can you tell us where we are?"

Kyrie looked surprised, she had assumed that they knew precisely where they were, "Why, you are in Eumor City, home of the centaurs in the northern province of Portalia. Did you not already know this?"

Rhys replied that they did not, "What about this building, what is it and why is it forbidden to be here and why do you come here to play your music?"

Kyrie looked down rather ashamedly, "Once, centaur pipe music was renowned across Portalia. The citizens of Portalia would travel miles to hear the best pipe players practice their art. Alas, it was not to stay that way. During the Warlock Wars a skilful centaur called Orran fell in with the Warlocks. He used his pipe music, and it's ability to enchant humans, to entice thousands to their deaths. When the elders of the council heard about the atrocities they banned the playing of pipe music for all time. A thing of beauty had been misused and all suffered as a result, the players and the audiences that enjoyed this art form. At first all obeyed the council's decree but, over time, a few who missed the music intensely returned to their instruments in secret, passing their music skills down from generation to generation. These days there are not too many that practice the art but our numbers are growing. The council are aware of our existence but choose to turn a blind eye, however, anyone who is caught playing the music publicly is dealt with severely, usually with a term of imprisonment."

Ashley sympathised with the loss that the centaurs must feel. The music had indeed been enchantingly beautiful and to make such a decree seemed an over-reaction. After all it was the actions of one centaur that had caused the deaths, not the music itself.

Kyrie looked up at Rhys and Ashley, "So that explains why I come here in hiding. I practice the art here in the chamber where none can hear my music. It is a skill taught to me by mother and grand-mother. I knew of the secret entrance to the chamber as one of my ancestors was involved in building this chamber and the secrets of the chamber have also been passed down, from parent to offspring for many years."

Rhys interrupted, "So what is this place?"

"I will tell you more of this place soon but first I would like to hear your reasons for being here."

It was clear that Kyrie was not going to offer anymore information until she had heard their story. Rhys made himself comfortable and began to explain. Kyrie listened intently.

"So what of your other companion?" she pointed to Lan in the shadows. Rhys explained that he had no idea who the old man was and that he appeared to be quite insane and very frightened. "I see," she replied thoughtfully.

When Rhys fell silent, his story now up to date, Kyrie asked if she could examine the pendants and the ring. The teenagers complied, handing over the items to Kyrie. She examined them carefully before returning them. "Now I understand a little more. You have in your possession some extremely rare and valuable items, thought lost long ago by my kin." She held the ring up in two fingers, "This is the Runegate Ring and these," she indicated the pendants, "are two of the Servant of the Runegate Pendants that belong to the Eumor Runestone. I suspect that the old man possesses the third and final pendant. These were lost many years ago and many thought them destroyed" Kyrie paused. "Legend has it that one other item makes up that set, the Runestone Key, an octagonal stone. Do you also have this?"

They replied that they did not. Kyrie continued, "The Runestones were created by pure magic long ago when the wizards walked the world. During those days the various species of Portalia lived together in peace. To improve trade and communication the wizards created three Runestones, this one in Eumor City, the second in the Dargoth Mountains and the third in the Old Forest at Rusinor. They also gave the Runestones the ability to open portals into various locations, both on this world and into others. To use this ability you needed possession of a Runestone key. Initially the Runestone portals served the world well. The improved trading and communication brought peace and prosperity to all. In honour of this achievement our land was renamed Portalia.

Sadly things did not remain that way and one year, a group of wizards formed a warlock sect and started to utilise dark magic. These warlocks were gradually corrupted by the dark arts and succumbed to evil ways. They took control of a Runestone and used the portals to plunder and attack others. They used dark magic to disguise themselves as differing races, gradually driving the world into chaos and forging mistrust between the species. The good wizards soon lost control and were over-thrown by the warlocks. Many of their powers were stripped from them in fierce magical confrontations and they fled to seek refuge in the Pinn mountains. The races of Portalia split and withdrew to their own domains. The centaurs stayed here in Eumor City and banished all other races except the dwarves. Fearing attack via the Runestones the centaurs set about sealing this chamber so that no-one could enter the city via the Runestone.

The warlocks soon dominated Portalia but then started to fight amongst themselves. Eventually the warlocks called all out war with each other, destroying much of the land as they fought across the face of Portalia. From the sea in the west to the vast forests of the east. From the hot desert south to the impassable northern mountains. Chaos reigned throughout. Finally one emerged as most powerful and he led the remaining warlocks utilising an army of Black Eagles. His name was Shangorth and he ruled with an iron fist over all Portalia from his tower city domain in Dargoth.

Things remained this way for many generations until

gradually, in their mountain retreat, the wizards of Pinn were able to regain many of their old powers. They formed alliances with the other species of Portalia, centaurs, the sea elves, the wood elves and the dwarves and created their own giant war birds, Fire Eagles, to battle the Black Eagle army. The combined might of the alliance, backed by the Pinn army of warbirds, eventually defeated Shangorth. The allied races also suffered heavy losses and by the end of the fighting only two wizards remained alive, Weldrock and Farspell. Peace returned to Portalia although some of the mistrust between species still exists to this day. Exhausted by the battle, Weldrock and Farspell left Portalia never to return. Some believe they still live even today and reside in the most northern of the Pinnacle mountains with the Red Dragons."

Kyrie paused and sighed, turning the ring in her hand as she spoke, "I have given this situation much thought. Given the importance of the objects that you carry I feel that I should take you to meet with the Eumor Council. Let them decide on what should be done."

This last comment worried Ashley, "If you did take us to the council, what do you think they would do?"

Kyrie frowned, a grave expression came over her, "I do not know. The use of portals was greatly feared back in olden times but it has been so long since those days that there is no way of knowing how they'd react. There are rumours that trouble is once again stirring in Dargoth."

Ashley turned to the boys, "Guys, I am really worried about what the council would do to us if Kyrie takes us before them. They're bound to take our pendants and ring away from us and they may even punish us!"

"Or something even worse," added Michael.

Rhys however, ever the optimist, took up a contrary

position, "On the other hand," he said, "the council may be understanding of our plight and able to help us get back home. From what Kyrie has told us I don't believe that the centaurs would harm us unless they believed we were a danger to them."

Ashley turned to Kyrie once more, "Please Kyrie, you have to help us. All we want to do is to get back home. We'll have to trust you to do what's best."

Kyrie moved from hoof to hoof, clearly agitated and uncertain, "Oh, I can't decide what would be best. I believe your tale of how you came here and I truly do want to help you get home. Unfortunately the only way I can see of getting you back to your world is via the portal web. For this you would need the Runestone key. Up until today I had believed that this was not possible. However, now I am not so sure. The dwarf that you saw in the cave was clearly using a portal to get to your world, he therefore must have possessed a Runestone key to open that portal. If that is true then he would also possess the ability to open one here in Eumor City. Please, give me silence to let me think a moment."

Kyrie turned her back on them and paced up and down, lost deep in thought. No-one spoke, honouring her wish for silence. After a few minutes she stopped and announced her decision, "I must seek advice on this matter, however, I believe that I should not yet take it before the council as I am uncertain how they would react. We lost the beauty of open pipe music due to a hastily made council ruling, I will talk with my parents before I decide what must be done. They can be trusted. They know that I secretly play the pipes, although they will not be happy that I have used the secret entrance to this chamber." Kyrie smiled to reassure them.

"My father will not be home until later this evening as he

is hunting with the others. I would ask that you please remain here tonight, the evening already grows late. I will return in the morning with food and a decision on what we must do. You need not fear my parents. I know that once they have heard your story they would not want any harm to befall you."

Although they did not relish the thought of remaining in the chamber, the teenagers agreed to do so. Kyrie promised that she would return at sunrise and with this she made her way back out through the secret passageway, sealing the doorway behind her.

Michael shivered as the door closed, "I hope we can trust her. That may have been the last chance we had of getting out of here if she decides not to return."

"I'm sure she'll return," replied Ashley, "but it's not Kyrie I'm worried about, it is what her parents and the council decide to do with us that frightens me. I don't think this world is quite as safe and cosy as our own."

Rhys had walked back to the Runestone and was examining the pedestal. "Hey you two, come over here and take a look."

Ashley and Michael walked over to join him, "We pretty much worked out ourselves from Kyrie's drawing that we needed a key to put in here." Rhys pointed to the octagonal slot, "there are twenty-four positions around the octagon. I think the top position marked with a large closed eye means 'off', mainly because all of the eye symbols are open, except this one."

"Sounds logical," responded Ashley.

Rhys continued, " The three large symbols represent the Runestones, the Celtic knot for here at Eumor, the mountain for Dargoth and the tree for the Forest of Old. My guess is that the twenty small open eye symbols are the various portals that can be selected and one of these would take us to Salty's Cave." The other two nodded their agreement. Rhys continued, "The open eyes aren't numbered or marked in any way other than their background colour," he pointed to the shading around the octagon. "Ten are shown silhouetted on green, five on purple and five on blue. All of the Runestone symbols are shown on a green background. I'm not sure what that signifies. Any ideas?" The other two remained silent and then shrugged their shoulders, Rhys went on, "The good news is that if my theory is correct, we have a way to get home as one of the portals will open to Salty's Cave. Of course the bad news is that we don't have Runestone Key and we have no way of knowing which one of these positions will take us back to there."

Ashley added excitedly, "True, but we do know that there is a Runestone key somewhere in Portalia. All we need to do is find out where we can find that albino dwarf and ask if he will return us home. Hey, that would be cool, I've always wanted to go to Wales and my Dad wouldn't take me. Gosh, what a shock he'd get if I called him in the States from Wales to come and get me!" Ashley then went silent, a little ashamed at her comment and wishing that her Dad was to help them out of this mess.

Rhys and Michael frowned at each other, "Asking the dwarf for help may not be as good an idea as you think," responded Michael, "that dwarf was not happy to see us and was clearly up to no good. I have no idea what he was doing with those spiders but I can't believe it was anything friendly."

"Mike's right, I have a feeling that if we can find this dwarf then it won't be a case of just asking for his help and using his portal to get home. Even so, locating that dwarf and finding out how he manipulates the portals may be the only way back."

Ashley ran her fingers through her hair, "Well, presuming that the dwarf is using a portal then he must be in one of the locations that Kyrie mentioned, in the mountains of Dargoth or in the Old Forest. Of course that assumes a couple of things."

"Like what?" asked Rhys

"Well, that the white dwarf is actually in Portalia and that he is using a known Runestone key to open the portals. For all we know he may come from yet another place entirely and he may have found another method of opening portals."

This was just too much for Michael, his eyes filled with tears, "You know, I don't think we're ever going to get back home. I miss my Mam and Dad already."

Ashley put her arm around him and held him and squeezed him gently, "Don't think that way OK Mike, we'll find a way, I just know it."

In the dark they heard LAN giggling.

CHAPTER NINE
Rendezvous at Fortown

Gorlan and his remaining warriors rose with the sun to another glorious summer's day. All wore fixed expressions, lost in thoughts of fallen comrades in arms. Gorlan carried out a roll call that morning. Each time a warrior failed to answer his name the soldiers raised their swords in the air and shouted "Gone With Honour!" to the skies. Whilst saddened by their loss, the mood of the warriors had changed from the previous day. All knew that Gorlan had made the correct decision and realised what it had cost him to leave his dead and dying men behind. Rather than destroy their morale it was improved, strengthening the esprit de corps. Every last one would now follow Gorlan without question, even to death. They trusted him and knew that one day he would lead them back to take their revenge.

When the ritual of honouring those fallen was complete, the band mounted their horses and set off for Fortown. As usual Molt rode alongside Gorlan, five ranks of two warriors in their wake. Molt thought that Gorlan had aged in the past day, clearly the loss of his soldiers had taken it's toll. Molt saw something else too, a subtle change had occurred in the Warlord. Before the massacre in the forest, Gorlan was an efficient professional soldier with a soft-hearted human centre. He was clearly well trained and a dangerous opponent but also he was an amicable man with a ready smile, easy to befriend.

The loss of his men had changed him. He no longer wore a smile and those that looked into his eyes would think twice before approaching. Molt also noticed an increased alertness in the Warlord.

They rode in silence for an hour or so before Gorlan spoke. "Molt, tell me more of the black eagle sightings. I must admit that I was very sceptical before. I now have reason to believe. Who was it that spotted the birds and where?"

Molt adjusted himself in his saddle, "It was a shepherd called Ramsey. He had been trailing some lost sheep in the foothills above Fortown. The trail led into the Dargoth mountains and, in his desire to return the beasts to the flock, he continued to follow the trail. He travelled south-west for a day and came to the peak of a small mountain, a little below the snow line. Here the trail was lost. He searched for an hour but could find no further clues as to the whereabouts of the sheep. It was as if they had disappeared off the mountain itself. Finally, giving up the search, he pitched his tent for the night.

As twilight approached Ramsey was settling down for the evening and was about to light the campfire. when he heard the screeching call of an eagle. This cry was answered by three other calls and they seemed to be getting nearer. This was followed by the sound of huge wings beating the air and brought back to the shepherd tales of the black eagles. Fearing for his life, he hid behind some rocks and watched as four enormous black eagles glided over the mountain top. They hovered over the camp, clearly looking for sign of any prey. Ramsey slid himself down even deeper between the rocks and prayed that they would not notice him. Suddenly, the largest of the group, a huge bird with a wing span the size of a three grown men, dropped from the sky and tore the tent to shreds.

Finding nothing it screeched in frustration and perched itself next to the tent, huge wings thumping the air, black and yellow eyes searching the surroundings for any sign of movement. The others continued to hover overhead, they called to each other occasionally in loud and terrifying screeching calls. Ramsey believes that he lay still for hours hardly daring to breathe. Eventually the eagle gave up the wait and launched itself back into the sky. Ramsey was not sure exactly which direction they flew, but he believed it was due west, towards the coast and the town of Dargoth Sands."

Gorlan raised his eyebrows, "Dargoth Sands! Now there is a place that I have no desire to visit. From what I have heard it is home to every cut-throat, pirate and villain in Portalia."

Molt nodded his agreement, "You're right on the mark there. Not a place that you'd want to go sightseeing. However, if Ramsey's story is true I suspect that even the black eagles keep well away from Dargoth Sands, it is rumoured that they do not like to be around men. Shangorth Towers was their old home during the time of the Warlock Wars, maybe the eagles have made a home there once more. The Towers are at the edge of the mountains directly east of Dargoth Sands. They are long deserted now, no-one has lived there since the defeat of Shangorth but they may still offer shelter to a flock of birds, even birds the size of the black eagles."

Gorlan's voice dropped to almost a whisper, he spoke to himself as much as to Molt. "If a flock of black eagles is all that we face then I shall be glad, alas though, I feel there is more to this. Black eagles were eradicated during the Warlock Wars, for them to once again fly over our land, someone, or something, must have drawn them to the mountains through the use of dark magic. Now, with our own eyes, we have witnessed the rising of the Halfmen, another vicious creature thought to be long extinct. No my friend, I fear that there is an intelligence behind this, the question is who or what and what is their ultimate aim?"

The band continued to ride west. Through the day they had passed a few isolated farms off to either side of the trail, but had not observed anyone working in the fields. By early afternoon the farmsteads were getting more regular as the troupe made progress to Fortown. A couple of hours from their destination, they came to a group of farm houses that were closely packed, a settlement that was just starting to show signs of expanding into a village. Here the trail cut straight through the centre of the buildings and the riders slowed their mounts as they entered the farm-ship, not wanting to cause alarm.

Gorlan called the group to a halt next to one of the largest buildings. He turned to Molt, "Do you hear that?"

Molt cocked his head to listen, "Hear what Warlord? All I hear is the songs of the birds and the livestock on the Meadows."

Gorlan nodded, "Precisely my point. Where are the usual sights and sounds of a working farm? There has to be at least half a dozen large farms here and there is no-one around, not a single farmhand at work."

Molt listened again, the peaceful setting that had seemed so calm suddenly seemed oppressive and threatening. Gorlan ordered his men to dismount, "Stern and Carl, you come with me. The rest of you stay here and be on your guard, something is amiss here."

The brothers followed Gorlan to the door of the nearest farmhouse, although uninvited Molt followed closely behind. Gorlan knocked twice at the door but there was no reply. He tried the latch and the door opened and swung inwards.

The home was a typical Meadows farmhouse. The front door opened into a shared living and dining area, an open kitchen was evident through a stone archway at the rear. The table had been set ready for a meal with crockery and cutlery laid out for twelve. Stairs led to the upper floors from the left of the entrance way. Gorlan shouted a greeting but there was no reply. He gestured to Stern and Carl to carry out a search of the upper two floors.

Gorlan and Molt walked through to the dining area. They looked around but could see nothing that offered any explanation as to the whereabouts of the occupants. They continued to the kitchen, taking in the surroundings as they did so. The kitchen showed clear signs that a meal was being readied. Vegetables lay half prepared on the worktops, the cutting knives still sat next to them. A large pot sat on the stove and had been boiled dry, clearly it had once contained a stew of some kind.

Gorlan picked up a knife and cut through a potato. The outside had dis-coloured but the inside was still fresh. "It looks like they left in a hurry and probably within the last few days. The vegetables have not started to rot yet."

A shout from Stern caught their attention and they rushed to the staircase, "Here, on the upper floor, come and see this."

They rushed up the stairs to the large attic on the third floor. The door had been shut and barred, Stern had needed considerable force to gain entry. They entered the attic which was clearly used as a storage area for grain. On the front wall a large swing door had been installed and on the floor near this door were seven skeletons, all partly wrapped in a soft downy substance. There was no sign of struggle but laying next to each skeleton was a weapon of some kind, three swords, two large knives and two axes. Stern looked at the Warlord, "I've examined the skeletons and there appears to be five men and two young boys. I'd guess both were around ten years old. By the lack of flesh on the bones I would say that they had been here for some time, strange though as this is clearly a working farm and this area would have been used regularly. Also, it is unusual for farmers to carry swords. Their clothes were missing too, except for the metal buckles and fasteners that had secured them, those were laying amongst their bones."

Gorlan ran his hand along the nearest skeleton, the downy covering was soft but sticky, "What on Portalia is this stuff," said Gorlan, pulling off a chunk of the covering. He touched the skeleton bone beneath, "Not a sign of any flesh but I warrant that these people have not been dead long. That meal below was being prepared for these men, whatever killed them has picked them clean of all their flesh."

Carl looked horrified at this thought, "But what in the name of all that is sacred would have done that to them. Could the Halfmen have left the forest and attacked them here?"

Gorlan shook his head, "No, this is not the work of the Halfmen, there would be more of a mess than this and they would more likely have taken their kill back to the forest."

"Then perhaps the black eagles have spread beyond the mountain realms and hunt for prey on the Meadows?".

Gorlan shrugged, "Perhaps, although I do not see how a black eagle would have found it's way into a loft. The substance that covers the skeletons is key too, it looks like it may have been secreted by some form of insect."

Molt reached down and examined the downy covering, He played with the tacky material between his fingers and then examined the strands. There were thousands of them all tightly inter-twined. He pulled out his knife and used it to split off a few strands, suddenly he realised what it was, "It's a spider's web!" The others turned to him with inquiring looks, "Look, if you divide it up it's definitely a spider's web. There are thousands of strands here. It would have taken one spider a very long time to weave this."

"Or a lot of spiders a very short time!" added Stern with a look of distaste.

Nervously they scanned the loft. Apart from the web wrapped bodies there were no other signs of spider infestation. There were a few webs around but nothing unusual and no more than would normally been found in a room used for corn storage.

Carl climbed on a box to examine some of the webs, "Have you noticed something else?" he asked, "there are no spiders left in this attic, not a single one that I can see." The others looked and confirmed the statement. Gorlan shrugged, removed his helm and scratched his hair, "Ugh! Makes me itch," he said. They all turned to leave the attic but as they did Gorlan paused at the doorway, "You know, something had been gnawing away at the back of my mind and I have just realised what it is. The table downstairs is laid for twelve, yet here we have seven male skeletons. So where are the other five? Where are the females? What has become of the wives and daughters of these men?" A deathly hush fell across the quartet, each man trying not to imagine the horrors of what had occurred here.

They made their way back down the stairs and Gorlan ordered his men to the other homes. After a thorough search, no other skeletons were found but neither was there any sign of human life. The barns were empty and tools lay where they had been dropped. Livestock still grazed in the fields, undisturbed by whatever had occurred at the farm houses.

They buried the seven skeletons at the rear of the house, marking their graves with stones before they mounted their steeds once more and continued their journey. They had travelled but a short distance when they came across two skeletons laying in the road, both had been web wrapped and picked clean in a fashion similar to those they had found earlier. Gorlan felt a knot of trepidation deep in the pit of his stomach. He called once more to Stern and Carl. "Leave your horses with us and mount your fire eagles. I want you to fly ahead and report back to us what you find. We will bury these two and continue directly to Fortown. Be as swift as you can, but be cautious."

The twins dismounted. Their fire eagles swooped from the sky to land next to them, sensing that they were needed. Carl stroked the neck feathers of his fire eagle and spoke to it gently. "Time to fly together again my friend." The birds lowered themselves to the ground, wings outstretched, allowing the brothers to mount up. The riders wore no saddles but sat perched on the backs of the giant birds, their mind connection allowed them to stay mounted even during the heat of battle when direction changes were severe. Once the brothers were firmly seated, the birds and their riders took to the skies and flew west, keeping low to scout the countryside ahead. Molt watched them as they flew into the distance, the majestic beauty of the fire eagles and the skill of their warrior riders held him in awe.

Gorlan and the remaining soldiers took time out to dig two more graves. As they lifted the skeletons, a large belt buckle fell from the ribs of one onto the floor. Molt stooped to pick it up and let in a sharp intake of breath, "This buckle carries the crest of the Cortrain family. The TownMaster is a Cortrain, as are many of the nobles, it is a long and distinguished family line. I will return this to the TownMaster as he may know who this poor fellow was." Molt slipped the buckle into his pocket and then stopped, head lowered. Gorlan watched him, "What ails you Molt?"

Molt looked up, "I fear for the people of Fortown. Something terrible came through here, something that they were powerless to stop. I wonder whether the same fate has befallen those in the town."

Gorlan looked sympathetically, "I wish I could reassure you my friend, but since we found these two additional skeletons the same thoughts have troubled me. Also, it now seems strange that we did not see any farm workers or travelling folk along the road from the forest." Gorlan placed his hand on Molt's shoulder sympathetically, "My hope is that we fear needlessly and that Stern and Carl will return soon to allay our fears."

The ten remaining riders set off once more for Fortown. They passed numerous farms and buildings but, ominously, observed no other person along the trail. Finally they crested a hill and Fortown appeared in the distance, nestled against the foothills. Gorlan pulled up his mount and signalled for his men to halt. "Stern and Carl should have returned to us by now. The town is just a short sky journey away. We stayed on the road so they could not have missed us as we travelled." All eyes turned upwards, searching the skies between this point and the town. There was no sign of the warriors or their warbirds. Gorlan announced that they should dismount and wait on this hill. He would give the brothers a few hours to find them, reluctant to ride into the town with no idea of what may face them there. The men sat in a circle, the fire eagles descended, their mighty wings thumping the air as they slowed their descent to land next to the men.

A stocky warrior, who Molt knew was called Kraven, made his way to the centre of the circle. The others clapped encouragingly as he did so. Molt was about to ask what was happening when Kraven pulled out a small musical mouth instrument. Kraven turned to his audience and announced,

"I'll entertain you all a while with a tale of heroism in the Warlock Wars." He began to tap his foot and started to play a tune. The others joined in with the tune, clapping to the rhythm. The music came to a natural pause and Kraven began to sing his story;

In days of old when wizards ruled,
Across the land and sea.
When creatures mixed as if as one,
And roamed the world in glee.

A web was drawn, across our realm,
Spun with magic charm.
To serve us all, for trade to grow,
And to keep us safe from harm.

In honour of, this mighty task,
Our kingdom was renamed.
Portalia! was sung by all,
In jubilant proclaim.

But evil lived, in mountains dark,
Awaiting chance to rise.
It used the web, for warring ways,
Spreading fear, hate and lies.

The wizards fled, to fair Pinnhome,
Whilst evil ruled supreme.
The world cried out, scarred with pain,
A sad depressing scream.

THE SPIDER GEM

The years rolled by, a plan was formed,
The wizards stood elated.
From phoenix stock and eagle nest,
An ally was created.

The Warlock Wars now took a turn,
A chance for man to fight.
They called the dwarves, the hoofed foot clan,
The Elves and all their might.

They marched to war, against the foe,
To fight or die as one.
Above them flew, the fire eagle flock,
Soaring in the sun.

A skirmish here, a scuffle there,
Never flinching from attack.
Death rained down, spirits rose,
The enemy falling back.

Relentless on, to the mountain realm,
Where evil reigned supreme.
A final stand, against the horde.
Blood ran as if a stream.

Eagles aflame, fought eagles black,
And won the day for good.
The warlocks fell, all put to sword,
Or burned on a pyre like wood.

So peace returned, her glory days,
Portalia knew once more.

The Warbirds stayed, protectors now,
From woods to sandy shore.

The web was sealed, the risk too great,
If evil came again.
A calm enwrapped, centaurs and elves,
Dwarves and the race of men.

When he had finished his song Kraven's audience burst into applause. Molt noticed that Gorlan had wandered away from the gathering and was stood on the crest of the hill, back to his men staring out across the Meadows to Fortown. Molt decided to join him as Kraven started another story-song, this time a little raunchier than his previous rendition. Molt heard the men laughing as he turned to go. It was the first laughter he had heard since their battle in the woods.

He made his way over to Gorlan, who stepped away and turned his back on him as he approached. Molt hesitated at this reaction believing that he had intruded, he made his apologies and turned to leave. Gorlan spoke, "No apology is needed. The ill manners were mine not yours. I was lost in thought of my fallen men, wondering whether I should have chosen a path that avoided the woods. Also, I now regret sending Stern and Carl ahead. I hope I have not sent them to their deaths also." Molt noted that the Warlords eyes had reddened and were puffy, with much embarrassment he realised that the Warlord had been shedding tears for his lost warriors. He dared to speak his mind, "Sir, if I may, I would like to give my opinion?"

Gorlan nodded his assent so Molt continued. "The paths through the woods were the fastest and most logical route. No-one could have known about the Halfmen breed. Your actions during the battle saved the lives of all who are left with you today. As for Stern and Carl, it was wise to send out a scout and even wiser to send a pair to help protect each other. It is clear that something has occurred here but, even though I have only recently met Stern and Carl, I perceive them to be intelligent warriors and made even stronger by their kindred spirit. I feel sure that they are still alive and that we shall see them soon. However, despite the horrors that we may find, my heart aches to be in Fortown rather than sat here waiting for their return. I fear the worst but I need to know what has occurred in my hometown."

Gorlan looked at the young man and smiled, "Molt my friend, you are wiser than your years. Let us listen to that heart of yours and make our way." He turned to his men, "Come men, mount up! We ride to Fortown!" Gorlan's men stood and made for their horses, a command from Gorlan stopped them, "No, not today men, today you fly! Molt you will ride with Kraven, I will ride with my sergeant, Tosh.

Molt shook, although he marvelled at the war birds he had never believed he would ride on the back of one. Doubts and questions shot through his head, "But will the birds allow two riders on their backs and how will I stay on? What about the horses, shouldn't I stay with them to lead them to Fortown?"

Kraven replied, "The horses are trained to follow the birds when we fly. We will leave them to follow by land and meet up with us in the town. As for how you stay on board, my suggestion is that you hold on to me as tight as possible. There is risk in riding, but we will fly carefully and I will put you to the ground should we encounter a fight."

Kraven's comments did nothing to settle Molt's nerves. He walked by Kraven's side approaching the giant fire eagle cautiously. Kraven spoke softly to the fire eagle as Molt had heard Carl and Stern do so earlier, Kraven then surprised Molt by asking the giant bird for permission to carry Molt. The bird looked from Kraven to Molt and the young man felt his heart pounding in his chest. Kraven spoke to him, "You too must ask permission to ride. Speak gently for their ears are sensitive and they do not like loud noise so close to them."

Molt turned to the bird and quietly sought permission to ride, part of him wanted the bird to reject this request but, in response to his words, the fire eagle lowered itself to allow Kraven and Molt to climb on it's back.

Once aboard Molt grabbed onto Kraven's bindings with all his strength. The bird stood and Molt felt very insecure as he wobbled from side to side. Then, with a slight hop, the fire eagle leapt into the sky. Molt's stomach seemed to be left on the ground. He had to swallow hard a few times to prevent vomiting, as the world lurched and they soared into the sky. As they ascended Molt felt sure he would fall but, when the bird levelled its flight, his fears subsided as the flight became smooth and his motion sickness lessened. He relaxed a little, although he still kept a tight grip around Kraven. Now feeling more secure he dared to look around.

The view from up high was spectacular in itself, but viewed from amongst the other fire eagles it seemed even grander. He looked east, across the halfman forest towards the River of Yew and the Meadows beyond. To the north he could make out the snake river beyond the Meadows, the Plains of Eumor leading to the snow capped Pinnacle Mountains that spread from the Northwest to the Northeast. Molt turned his head to the south where the Meadows seemed to roll forever, he could not make out the Blistering Desert but could see a haze in the distance and knew that this was the heat from the sands. To the west lay Fortown, comprised of single and double storey grey-stone buildings built from wood and stone and with slate roofs. Beyond the town lay the dark mountains of Dargoth. He could make out a storm over the mountains towards the coast. Given all that had happened he felt this was strangely appropriate. Molt turned to look back at the hillock that they had just left and saw the horses galloping below, following the path of the birds. Kraven saw where Molt's attention had been drawn and spoke, "They are well trained. They will continue to follow at full speed until they meet up with us again. They travel much quicker without a rider too. Even when we fly out of their sight the horses will continue in the direction that they last saw the birds. Some say that if they lose the trail the horses will just keep riding until they die. I'd rather believe that our horses are much wiser than that. I'm fairly sure that they would realise when the trail was lost. I've never tested this theory though and hope that I never will."

Molt turned his attention to Fortown again. They were approaching fast, the birds travelling at a speed much faster than their horses could ever hope to achieve. Within minutes they had reached the town and were hovering over head.

What they saw from their vantage point brought a chill to all. The town was bereft of life. No-one walked the streets or shouted challenges or greetings to the warriors. The streets were deserted but on each could be seen what looked to be the remains of the former inhabitants. Molt shivered. Where were his people? Five thousand lived in the town, surely they could not all be dead?

Molt's thought turned to his family and to Brianna and his heart sank as he feared for them all. He closed his eyes and imagined he was with Brianna now, he could see her face clearly, her brown eyes and her sweet red lips. If anything had happened to her then he would wreak his revenge on those that had harmed her. He suddenly understood the look that he had seen on the face of the Warlord earlier that day.

After encircling the town for what seemed an age, the fire eagles, led by Gorlan and Tosh, began to spiral down to the city below. With no sign of any enemy or threat of conflict, Tosh directed his eagle to land in the central square of the town. His fire eagle came to a gentle halt as it's feet found the hard surface, closely followed by the remaining seven fire eagles. The warriors climbed off their birds and formed a line in front of Gorlan awaiting his orders. "Molt, the three storey domed building behind us at the top of the square, it looks important, what is it?"

Molt did not need to turn around to know that it was the town hall, he informed Gorlan of it's purpose.

Gorlan addressed his men, "Form into pairs. Search the immediate area for two blocks in all directions and then return here. Molt and myself will search the Town Hall, if you meet any resistance sound a warning and retreat back to here."

Tosh quickly organized the men into pairs and gave them their search areas. Molt and Gorlan turned and walked to the Town Hall as the Pinn warriors started to spread out in all directions around them. The Fire Eagles took to the air once more.

Gorlan spoke quietly to Molt, "Stay close to me. I want you to stay safe, not only as a friend, but because we need your knowledge of the town to find out what has occurred here."

Gorlan and Molt made there way to the large wooden doors of the town hall, both were closed and seemed to have been barred from within. There were large gouges on the door where someone, or something had tried to gain access. Molt hammered on the doors hoping that someone was within. There was no response. Gorlan put his shoulder to the doors and pushed but it was clear that they would not gain entry this way.

Molt tapped Gorlan on the shoulder and made a suggestion, "Let's try the office buildings. If we can get into them then we can work our way around to the main hall from the inside, there is a corridor on the second floor that allows public access to the upper floors of the town hall."

He made towards the buildings to the left of the square, closely followed by Gorlan. The pair approached the two-storey office buildings that led off the main town hall on either side of the square, similar in fashion to the wings of a large mansion house. The main door of the office block had also been shut and barred and even working together the pair could not force their way in via that route. The bottom set of windows had been closed and shuttered from the inside. They were not built as solidly as the doorways though and the combined efforts of Gorlan and Molt were enough to force one of the shutters inwards until there was sufficient space for them to squeeze through.

Inside the offices were deserted. A quick perusal of the work areas suggested that the occupants had not been at their desks when disaster struck the town. Gorlan indicated silence and the two men listened intently. There was no sound inside the building. Also, with the windows and doors barred shut, no fresh air could gain access and hence inside was hot and humid, the men could already feel the sweat forming on their heads and bodies. Molt pointed to the staircase that led off the far corner of the lower floor, "That's the way to the main hall. We go up one floor and follow the main building. At the end of the upper floor there is an arch that leads through to a small L-shaped room, then under another arch and out onto a balcony above the main hall."

Gorlan looked across at a large open staircase fashioned from dark brown wood. Halfway up, the stairs switched back on themselves one hundred and eighty degrees, turning back to reach the upper floor. Molt led the way, skipping up two stairs at a time, Gorlan hesitated before following, he looked around evaluating all that he saw. When he had caught up with Molt he said, "Do you notice that, just like the farmhouse earlier, there is no damage to any property. We have the same evidence of web wrapped skeletons laying in the streets but no other sign of damage. It's as if the plan was to purge the town and farms of human life, but to ensure that the buildings were kept whole and intact. I wonder to what ends?"

Molt had already considered this in his own thoughts, "I too have noticed this. My first presumption was that it was some form of invasion and that the plan was to take over these buildings for the enemy troops. If that was the case though, where are the troops? One thing is clear to me, the people killed here were not killed by men. Maybe the only reason the buildings have been left is because our foe has no need for the cover of roof and stone. The corpses that we have found show signs of being killed by spiders or insects of some kind. Perhaps our foe moves mindlessly on to their next quarry with no interest in conquest."

Gorlan thought on that before responding, "You may well be right, but my gut tells me that there is more to this. Something drove the halfmen to leave their hiding place and attack us in the woods, I feel there is a plan at the heart of these occurrences. Maybe you're right about there being a need for these buildings. My theory is that we are witnessing the aftermath of some form of extermination, a clearing of the town for those that follow."

Molt swallowed back hard, tears welled up in his eyes at

the suggestion that his love ones had been 'exterminated', "If that is the case Warlord, then we need to send for reinforcements before our enemy arrives to take residence in the town. We must act quickly!"

Gorlan suddenly realized the emotions that Molt was feeling and cursed himself for not considering the implications of their findings to the young man, even so, he knew that there was no real way of softening this blow and so he continued, "Molt, I am sorry but I fear that we may already be too late to save Fortown. If our enemy considers this town as purged then that occupation may follow sooner than we would like. However, let us not consider that for now, we need to determine what has happened here and whether anyone still remains alive. Let's push on."

They made there way along the building towards the main hall. This floor of the office was deserted, much as the floor below. As they walked under the archway and turned right onto the main hall balcony, Molt caught a whiff of a strange scent in the air. "Do you smell that?" he asked Gorlan.

Gorlan sniffed and nodded, "Yes, it smells," he paused to choose the right word but struggled, "...umm, hot, almost like the smell of linen being scorched."

They entered onto the balcony and looked down to the ground floor. Below then was the first true signs that they had seen of any struggle. Thirty or so bodies lay dead in the atrium, ten were web wrapped but the others clearly slain by sword or axe. Around the bodies lay pieces of smouldering rock of various sizes, from small pieces the size of a thumbnail, to larger chunks the size of a man's head. The smell was clearly emanating from this rock.

Gorlan looked for any signs of life around the main hall and then turned his attention to the large wooden balcony. A staircase led to the third floor in each of the northern corners of the balcony, whilst there was only one stairway down to the ground floor, located in the southern corner, opposite to where they had entered from the office building. An identical arch led out of the balcony to the office buildings in the opposite wing to which they had entered.

"Let's look upstairs before we drop to the lower floor" suggested Gorlan. They worked around the balcony to the far staircase leading upwards, making a quick detour to check the upper floor of the opposite office block. Finding nothing unusual they continued upwards to the third floor.

The upper floor of the town hall housed a vast circular library of books and documents. The domed roof was evident above their heads, formed in stone and ornate glass which let light stream in. This room was cooler due to large air ducts that had been cut in the wall, allowing ice cooled air to flow through the room to protect the books. Here were the first real signs of pillage. Books had been scattered everywhere and hardly a volume was left on the shelves. Gorlan and Molt split up and walked in opposite directions around the library, Molt stopped near a set of empty shelves where the contents had clearly been removed and not just thrown on the floor. He raised his voice so Gorlan could hear clearly across the library, "The section on magic has been gutted." His voice sounded louder than he had intended, amplified by the dome shaped roof. Gorlan made his way over to the empty shelves and examined the area that Molt had indicated. He ran his hands over the empty shelves, "Well I guess this supports my theory of their being some form of intelligence behind all this. The fact that every book on magic has been taken does not bode well, someone is either searching for something in particular or seeking to increase their knowledge. Given the manner in which they have gone about this, even a fool could deduce that the searcher is involved in the black arts. How well stocked was this library?"

Molt replied, "Moderately so, although most of the volumes contained here dealt with simple magic and contained information that even children knew through stories told to them by their parents and grand-parents. My understanding is that the more powerful and dangerous books and tomes and indeed, all books relating to the black arts, were moved to Pinnhome many years ago."

Gorlan nodded, "That is good news and thank the heavens that our ancestors had the sense not to leave such power out here in isolation."

They continued their search of the library but found nothing further of interest so made their way back to the ground floor where they had observed the bodies. The scorching smell of the hot rocks was even stronger down here amongst the dead. Thankfully the odour was not too disarming but even so they were glad to open the main doors to the hall and let fresh air flow around the room.

Gorlan knelt to examine some of the smoking rock, he touched it with his sword, tested the heat level with his fingers just above the surface, and picked a piece up to examine it closer. "It looks a lot like the lava rock that you find around volcanoes. I have seen formations like this in the White Peaks where volcanoes once erupted before they fell dormant or extinct. It's cool enough to pick up now but has clearly been super-heated at some point."

Molt had been looking at the bodies of the fallen. "The dead bodies are all of the town guard, they were of the Cortrain section, the Townmaster's personal regiment. I knew some of them as they helped with the training for myself and my brother." Molt pointed to a body with a head that was partly severed and spoke slowly and with difficulty, "This is Chot. I knew him quite well as we often played clayball against each other." Molt walked to one of the web wrapped bodies and was not surprised to find the dry bones of a skeleton when he tore off the covering. "I do not see TownMaster Cortrain here, unless of course, he is one of these poor souls."

Gorlan placed his hand around Molt shoulders, "I am sorry Molt, I know that these were your people and it must be hard. Do not give up hope yet though, some may have escaped."

Molt bowed his head, "I hope you are right Gorlan, but I fear the worst. I would like your permission to leave here and return to my home to look for my kin. Living here I have my parents, two sisters and a dear friend, Brianna, who I love dearly and I need to know if they are still alive or what fate has befallen them. Our home is near the outskirts of the main town. My father owns a small fruit and vegetable farm there." Molt paused before continuing gravely his speech had become hesitant, "........at least, he did."

Gorlan looked at Molt sympathetically, "I am sorry Molt but I must ask you stay with us for the present. I promise that as soon as we are able, we will make haste to your home to search for your family, but for the present I forbid you to travel alone and I cannot yet spare the soldiers to accompany you."

Molt reddened but held back his anger, he knew that the Warlord was right but he ached to return to his home, despite any horrors he may find there.

Their attention was suddenly drawn back to the entrance as the first two warriors returned to the town hall. Soon all the men were back and all reported a similar story. The town seemed bereft of life, most of the citizens that they had found were web wrapped and picked clean but many were killed more conventionally, via sword or axe fight. From the survey of the local businesses the men agreed that the attack must have taken place at night. Most clerical businesses were empty, whilst businesses such as the dairy and the bakers were in advanced preparation for the next day. Once the last of Gorlan's men had finished his report, the Warlord gave an account of what Molt and himself had discovered. He pointed to the smouldering rock and asked if any of the others had seen anything like it around the town. One pair of warriors responded to the affirmative and apologised for not reporting the fact earlier. They had not understood the significance of what they had seen. The smouldering rock had been on the floor of the blacksmith shop and they had believed it to be coals from the smithy's fire.

Through this exchange Kraven had been deep in thought, he stepped forward, "You say that the door was bolted tight from within?" Molt and Gorlan nodded, Kraven continued, "Well if that is the case, how did our enemy get the books out of the library? If these doors were barred then they must either have left by another exit or the doors were barred AFTER they left."

Gorlan mused on this, "It doesn't seem possible that whoever barred these doors is still in here so they must have left by another exit. Molt, we know that both office buildings were barred up too, do you know of another way out of here?"

Molt shook his head, "No, they are the only entrances, most people use the main entrance here, even the office entrances are hardly used. Generally people......" Molt stopped short, "Wait! The hill tunnels! How could I have been so stupid."

"Explain!" ordered Gorlan.

"Sorry, of course. The town was originally built as a fort, hence it's name. During that time the town planners built escape tunnels into the hills. The tunnels have never been used but the Town Masters have always budgeted to maintain them in case there was a need at any time. I should have thought of this earlier, I am a fool!"

"Where are these tunnels and to where do they lead?" prompted Kraven.

Molt pointed to a doorway at the far end of the main hall. "There are entrances to the tunnels spread around the town, I do not remember the location of them all even though we were taught them in school. Behind that doorway is a staircase leading to a wine cellar. I know that you access the tunnels from the cellar but I am not sure how." Molt slapped his head in frustration, "Argh! I wish I'd paid more attention to this topic in school."

Gorlan ordered two of his men to remain at the door to the cellar. They opened the door and saw a dark and narrow spiral stairway leading downwards. Gorlan lit one of the torches that were deposited in a container next to the door. Leading the way he descended to the cellar below.

The cool of the wine cellar was welcoming after the humidity of the floors above. Gorlan surveyed his surroundings. On each side of the cellar stood large wine racks full of bottles. Most of the bottles to his left were shiny and fairly dust free. The rack on his right however contained bottles that were covered heavily in dust and cobwebs. A handful of bottles had at some time been removed from this rack.

The torches on the walls were burned out, Gorlan called up the staircase to have two new torches brought to him. He placed these in the wall holders and set them afire to illuminate the wine cellar. The additional light revealed that at the far end of the cellar there were two enormous wine barrels laid on their sides and balanced on trestles. Each was the height of a tall man and both possessed a small tap at the base for accessing the wine.

Gorlan scanned the cellar for signs of an entrance to the tunnels but his visual search revealed nothing. He ordered his men to search the walls for an entrance of some kind. Molt stood, deep in thought trying to recall those old school lessons, racking his brain for that lost memory. Unfortunately all that came back to him was how he had spent those lessons teasing the girls in his class by flicking chewed up paper at them.

Tosh was at the far end of the wine cellar looking up above the huge wine barrels. A barred grating had been installed in the ceiling. Tosh asked a colleague to help him climb onto the top of one of the barrels to take a closer look. The curve of the barrel made it awkward for Tosh to keep his balance and the position of the grating was such that he had to move to the very edge of the barrel to gain access. Tosh looked in behind the bars but it was too dark to make out what lay beyond. The grating itself was hinged on one side, Tosh took a knife from his belt, inserted it into the gap of the grating and levered it open. The barred door opened with a loud creek and swung downwards. Tosh looked into the opening but was disappointed to find that it was nothing but an air duct, not near big enough to allow entry for a man. Disappointed he grabbed the air duct door and angrily forced it back into position. The momentum of his swing caused the warrior to lose his balance, his left foot slipped on the round edging of the barrel. He grabbed for the grating as he fell, but his weight was far too heavy for the small hinges and, as he dangled in mid air, they snapped. Tosh and fell to the floor in a heap. The grating fell behind him until it hit the edge of the first barrel with a resounding bang before bouncing onto the second barrel which it struck with a dull thump. Tosh looked up at the faces of smiling colleagues, all trying to suppress their laughter as they enquired as to his state of health. Tosh mumbled curses under his breath and dusted himself off as he stood. One of the soldiers quipped, "Hey Tosh, I've never seen you fall off a barrel BEFORE you've drunk the contents." The others sniggered as Tosh scowled at the wise crack.

Molt however did not laugh, he was busy examining the barrels. He turned to the others and said, "Listen." He tapped on the left barrel and then the right. "Do you hear that. The one on the right sounds hollow compared to the one on the left. I noticed it when Tosh fell and the grating hit both barrels." Molt turned the tap of the left barrel and wine poured out, he quickly turned it off again but not before cupping his hand underneath and sampling the contents. "Mmmm, good wine," he commented. He then turned the tap of the right hand barrel. No wine poured out of this time. He looked at the tap and then pulled it upwards.

There was a loud thud followed by a metallic scraping sound. Molt had to step back as the front of the barrel slowly swung inwards, revealing a tunnel beyond which declined sharply as it disappeared into darkness.

Gorlan congratulated the Fortownian, "Well done Molt, and you too Tosh, falling from the barrels like that was a brilliant tactic," he smiled at Tosh before continuing. "I hope to everything that is holy that this tunnel was used as an escape route by the people of the town," he turned back to Molt, "and I hope with all I have that your loved ones were amongst them Molt."

Molt's mood visibly brightened at the finding of the escape route and he was ready to explore further into the tunnel. Once again Gorlan forbade him to pursue this path. "We will explore these tunnels Molt, but not until we have made other preparations and formed a plan. We have but ten of us here in the city and we do not yet understand what occurred here, I want to check out the town for more clues. Further, we do not know what has happened to Carl and Stern. Have patience my young friend."

Molt once again resigned himself to Gorlan's will but feelings of annoyance and frustrations were growing within him, he was a little tired of being ordered around by the Warlord, after all, he was a free citizen and not a soldier of Pinn.

Gorlan ordered that the barrel entrance be closed again, "Kraven, can you go with Molt and search the library on the top floor. There may be some maps or reference to the escape tunnels that will give us a clue as to where any survivors may be hiding. I'd rather enter these tunnels with a map to guide us as I do not know how intricate the paths may be. If I was building an escape route of tunnels I would make sure that there were a myriad of dead ends and circular loops to confuse any pursuers."

Kraven and Molt headed back upstairs, Molt was glad to be doing something positive towards finding his family and Brianna. The rest of the warriors returned to the main hall and Gorlan ordered that the room be cleared for use as a base. The smouldering rock was gathered up and placed in pile outside in the square, Gorlan wanted to preserve this until they understood more about the substance.

Even though the afternoon sun blazed and Gorlan felt that it may be better to rest, he took his men to the outskirts of town where they dug a large open grave to accommodate all of the bodies of the fallen Fortownians. The bodies from the main hall were the first to be taken to the pit. Each warrior took a few moments to utter words of blessing for each as they placed the bodies in the ground. The men cleared away all of the corpses that could be found that had died in more conventional combat. These took priority in order to prevent any disease occurring as the flesh rotted. The web wrapped bodies were left as a secondary task, being picked clean of any flesh, they offered no health risk to the men. By the time the warriors had cleared an area of five blocks square around the central town hall, they had buried one hundred and seventy-five bodies that had been slain by sword, axe or knife. These were a mix of men, women and even a few children. However, this amounted to only a fraction of the total dead in this area. The warriors estimated that there were over fifteen hundred web wrapped skeletons littering the streets and within buildings. Gorlan believed that this figure was high due to their proximity to the centre of the town and the entrance to the escape tunnels. His hope being that the numbers were bolstered due to the people fleeing towards the town hall and to the safety of the tunnels.

As evening approached Gorlan asked Tosh to get two men to collect food and to tell the rest of the men to return to the hall. He then returned to the library to check on the progress of Molt and Kraven. He found the pair busy reviewing a large book. Next to them, on the desk, was a pile of volumes that had been separated from the rest. "Any luck?" asked Gorlan.

The pair shook their heads in unison, "A little. Lots of references to the tunnels but, unfortunately, no useable map. You were right about needing a guide to follow though. By all accounts it is a veritable maze down there."

Gorlan took the next book of the top of the pile, *The Fortownian Yearbook—Places and History*. He scanned the pages but found only fleeting mention of the escape tunnels. He worked his way through three more titles, the last of which offered up at least a hint of where the main tunnel exited.

From the text in a volume entitled *Military Tactics*, a section discussed the use of the tunnels and mentioned that they joined an old mine in the foothills to the north of Fortown. Unfortunately the text did not mention how far to the north or the name of the mine. Gorlan pointed this fact out to the other two and they made a mental note to check for any books relating to mines. The book also made reference to the fact that the tunnels could house thousands of people and that they had been stocked with necessary supplies to keep the residents of the town alive for months. Molt was unable to confirm that this practice had been maintained to the present day. Gorlan checked for the age of the book but it did not carry any publication date. They guessed it to be some forty or fifty years old, so given the population growth of the town since then, they guessed that any citizens that had escaped to the tunnels could remain there for four weeks or so, depending on how many had made it to the tunnels and whether the practice of restocking the supplies had been maintained.

Gorlan told the two to make their way back downstairs to eat and rest. Molt was starving but did not want to stop his search, he gathered up an armful of scrolls that had been found in the 'ancients' section, determined to review these whilst he ate. The three men then made there way back downstairs to join the others.

At least food was not a problem to them in the town. The enemy had killed and destroyed whoever they could find but the only thing taken had been the books, they had not shown the slightest interest in ransacking the town of food and supplies. Even the weapon shops and armouries were untouched. So that evening they dined well on beef and vegetables, washed down with local beer and cool well water. Molt listened intently as he quizzed the men about what they had found in the town. He gasped at the numbers of bodies that they had found but, in many ways he was already prepared for this and, like Gorlan, felt that the numbers would be less as they moved away from the centre. Despite the news about the losses, Molt actually cheered up even more as he now believed that many thousands of his people may have escaped. He hoped that Brianna and his family were amongst them.

The door of the hall opened suddenly and Kraven walked in. Gorlan had placed two sentries on watch outside the main hall, Kraven had just finished his shift. He reported to Gorlan but spoke loud enough for the others to hear, "Sir, whilst I was on my sentry duty I examined a number of the skeletons that lay around the square. It is as at the farmhouse, all of the dead are male but I did not find a single female amongst the web wrapped dead."

Gorlan thanked Kraven for this information but had no idea what it could mean. Given that they had found female dead amongst the corpses earlier he had not considered that the web wrapped bodies were, once again, all male. Once all had eaten Gorlan waited for the change of shifts and then spoke to his men.

"We must get word back to Pinnhome to reinforce this town. I have a feeling that our enemy will be back and may look to populate these buildings with their own folk. I need two warriors to fly back to Pinnhome to request reinforcements." Gorlan pointed to two of his men, "Lloyd and Pinnel, I want you to make that flight. You should make Pinn in a day and a half by flying directly there and, if haste is made, we could have fire eagle reinforcements here within three days and a ground force within five."

This would leave just six warriors, Tosh, Kraven, Flare, Green, Tor and Folken plus himself and Molt to guard the town and to gather any additional information that they could. He still hoped for the return of Stern and Carl but, as each hour went by, it seemed less likely that they were still alive and able to return to them.

Gorlan looked at his remaining warriors. "This leaves the eight of us to stay and try to find out as much as we can about the events and our enemy. We will continue to use this hall as our base. Molt and myself will join the sentry shifts so that we are all able to get enough rest. I pray that our enemy does not return before we receive reinforcements as I think it unlikely that our small band would be able to hold them off. Tomorrow we will explore the outer sectors of the town. Whilst there we will accompany Molt to his home so that he can look for clues as to the status of his family. We will also need to dig another mass grave to bury any corpses that we may find but, once again I regret that we will have to leave the skeletal remains where they lay."

Gorlan turned back to Lloyd and Pinnel. "Make haste, fly like you have never flown before." The two riders turned to leave, their fire eagles had already landed near the doorway anticipating the requirement. They packed some light rations and mounted their warbirds. All watched as they set off northeast, direct to Pinnhome.

Later that same evening Molt let out a shout of triumph. One of the scrolls that he had removed from the library contained a map of the tunnels. The scroll itself was very old so there was no way of knowing if the tunnels had been altered in any way, but the map that it contained was very detailed and should suffice to help them when below ground. Gorlan smiled as Molt showed him the map. "Well done Molt, maybe our luck changes at last." Gorlan examined the map, "It looks like the tunnels continue for quite a way along the hills before they join the old mine. It would take a good day of travel underground to get to the exit but that doesn't stop us exploring the tunnels and caverns at this end of the maze. We will start to search the tunnels later tomorrow after we have explored the outer town."

***

Stern removed the bandages from his brother's shoulder and examined the wound. With relief he saw that the bleeding had stopped. The flesh, punctured where the knife had entered Carl's body, was beginning to close over. Carl had lost consciousness when Stern removed the blade but was now awake and enjoying a hot tea and dry rations that his brother had given to him. Stern tore a small piece of cloth from his undershirt and carefully wiped the wound and wished for some herbal remedies to help the healing. Fortunately the wound looked clean, with no sign of infection. He dropped the used cloth onto the rock ledge where they had landed before rewrapping Carl's shoulder in the bandage.

"How do you feel?" he asked.

"A little light headed but at least the pain in my shoulder has numbed somewhat," replied Carl.

"That's good, the feyberry tea will help you too. It will keep that pain at bay and aid recovery."

Every Pinn warrior was equipped with a small first aid pack containing field dressings and a small amount of dried and crushed feyberries. The feyberry grew all over Portalia, even in some of the more inhospitable places. It was a robust plant that possessed remarkable healing and pain killing properties. It had a bitter taste and was best taken with sugar, indeed many folk drank it laced with sugar for pleasure rather than medicinal purposes. Stern handed him some of the oat biscuits that Carl loved so much and he tucked into them, washing them down with the feyberry tea, the biscuits helping to take away some of the bitterness of the feyberry brew.

Stern sat down and relaxed for the first time in many hours. He contemplated the day's events.

After they had left the others at the farmhouses, the flight to Fortown had been uneventful. On reaching the town they circled the town surveying everything they could. They espied the web wrapped corpses but also those killed by blade. After they had covered the whole town by air, Stern had signalled to Carl for them to land. They chose a spot just on the outskirts of town where they had seen a small group that contained bodies and skeletons.

Both brothers had been examining the dead when a warning cry from their fire eagles drew their attention. They looked up to see a dozen black eagles flying towards where they stood. They swiftly jumped to their warbirds and took to the skies, their powerful mounts beating the air furiously with their wings to gain height. Even carrying their riders the fire eagles, slightly bigger in stature, were faster than the black eagles and they were able to avoid the first assault as the black raptors came in for the kill. Stern and Carl reacted as one, both instructed their mounts to ascend steeply to gain height on their foe. Once the advantage of altitude had been gained, they turned their warbirds into an attacking dive, talons and swords at the ready. They met the front of the black eagle pack with an incredible momentum. Stern took out two of them with sword swinging from left to right like lightning. Carl removed the head of another as they rode through the centre of the black mass. The enemy eagles broke into confused flight, losing their pack formation. The two lowest birds in the pack were not fast enough to avoid the talons of the fire eagles and the claws of the warbirds stabbed deep into their necks. Almost immediately the two black eagles burst into flames, falling to the ground as charred remains.

The brothers broke the dive of their mounts and once again commanded their mounts to soar for height. The black eagles had scattered in all directions and it was now difficult to keep track of all of their foe. Stern ducked as a shadow suddenly blocked the sun. Talons caught his back and bounced off the thick armour plating, his warbird changed direction to take the momentum of the blow and to prevent Stern falling. Stern recovered his balance and composure and warbird and rider gave chase, quickly running down and dispatching the eagle. Stern then turned to check the whereabouts of his brother and the other birds. Carl had slain two more of the black eagles with his sword and his mount held a third, a flaming ball between it's claws as it tore at it's enemy with its beak.

The three remaining black eagles had retreated and Stern could see them in the distance, heading back toward the Dargoth mountains. He shouted to Carl and the brothers gave chase. Their quarry, once their hunters, were now far in the distance but the twins continued relentless.

As they reached the higher, snow capped mountains, the black eagles turned and dived into a high valley between the peaks. The brothers followed, gaining by the minute. As they entered this valley the hair stood up on Stern's neck, he sensed the danger before he saw it. At the foot of the ravine stood a group of fifty or so strange creatures that he could not place. They were shaped as men but smaller, standing at around five feet tall and armed with swords and knives. They were dark grey in colour but possessed fiery red glowing eyes. They wore no clothing, other than a pair of leathery shorts that were used more for carrying their weapons than for warmth or modesty. Stern acted quickly and turned his bird to leave the ravine. Carl was a little slower and a flurry of knives filled the air around him. Stern had watched as his brother tried to avoid the sharp steel, skilfully turning his mount at an acute angle. Unfortunately it wasn't enough and one of the blades had caught him deep in the shoulder. Stern had watched as his brother slumped forward, just managing to cling to his bird. He made haste to his brother and kept one eye on him whilst he searched for a safe place to land. After a few minutes of flight they had eventually found this rocky ledge. This possessed an overhang that would hide them from any that may be searching for them. They had waited a short while to ensure that they were indeed safe before they had dismounted to tend Carl's wound and they were now safely encamped on the ledge. Carl was laid back on the ledge, eyes closed and with a grimace of pain on his face.

Stern stood and turned to his brother, "At least we have answered the question of whether black eagles fly the skies again. Mind you, I think I would have preferred to find that out from a safer distance than two inches."

His brother laughed at this. "Never have you spoken a truer word brother of mine! Did you see the creatures that accompanied the black eagles though? What on all of Portalia were they?"

Stern shook his head, "I have no idea. They obviously weren't looking to welcome us though and I warrant that they were at least partly responsible for the deaths in the town. We will need to get back to the others to let them know what we have found. Do you think you will be able to fly?"

Carl propped himself up a little and let out a groan as pain shot through his shoulder, he managed to get himself sat upright again though, the Pinnacle Mountain men were a tough breed. He stood but wobbled a little, his brother spoke, "Maybe we should rest here for the night. The mountains already grow dark as the sun has dropped below the peaks and evening approaches out on the Meadows."

Carl shook his head, "No, we must get back to the others this evening. Gorlan has to know what we face. The others will have reached Fortown by now and we have alerted the enemy to our presence, they may choose to return to the town to investigate. We fly this evening."

Stern nodded and helped his brother to his eagle. He checked the bandages once more and strapped Carl's right arm to his body. Carl confirmed that he was ready and took to the air, wobbling a little as the bird took off. His vision blurred, his thoughts in a mist, Carl was clinging on for dear life, his entire concentration focussed on remaining seated on the great bird. Later he would realise that he remembered nothing of their flight from the mountains. Stern followed close behind, watching his brother all the time in case he lost his balance. They finally reached sufficient altitude to clear the mountain peaks and headed back to Fortown.

***

It was Tosh who saw them first. The light of the evening had been all but spent when the brothers got their first sight of the town. Tosh shouted to the others and they all rushed outside to stand in the square. Gorlan sent four of the warriors back to get torches so that the brothers could see where to land. Stern saw them and shouted to Carl but received no acknowledgement. He urged his mount to take the lead, knowing that his brother's eagle would follow his own. This would mean that, if his brother lost his balance, he would not be able to catch him.

The two fire eagles swooped down to land close to the other warriors. Stern leapt from his mount and rushed over to his brother. The other men realised that something was amiss and came to their aid swiftly. They carried Carl inside. Despite being tired and dazed he had sufficient wits about him to smile and mumble greeting at his colleagues before collapsing in their arms.

They all embraced Stern whilst Gorlan ushered him inside, eager to hear their story. They gave food and water to Stern and properly bathed and dressed Carls' shoulder before laying him in one of the beds that they had acquisitioned and installed on the first floor balcony.

When he was refreshed Stern told the others all that had occurred. When they had finished Kraven spoke first, "Stern, could you come with me and look at something." Stern nodded his assent and Kraven led him outside to the pile of smouldering rocks. He indicated the rocks to Stern and said, "The creatures you saw, were they this colour?"

Stern frowned, the light was fading and he had to use a torch to get a closer look at the rock pile, "I believe so, but I will be able to tell better by the light of day. Why is this relevant?"

Gorlan had stood at Kraven's shoulder and noticed the look of surprise and consternation on his face at Stern's response to his question, "Kraven, what is it?"

Kraven looked at the Warlord and then at the others, "I cannot be sure but I have heard of a story told through song. I first heard it long ago when I visited the Gate towns on the Snake River. It told the tale of a ship called the Sea Star that had set out to explore the seas to the west of Portalia."

"But why would anyone do that," offered Tor, "everyone knows that the Never Ending Mists lay far to the west of our shores. Once caught in the Mists very few return to tell the tale."

"Many songs are based on story-telling and fiction, so it is not unusual for them to sound like tall tales, but often these stories have an element of fact about them that gets exaggerated in the telling over the years. Well this particular song tells of how the Sea Star broke through the mists and found a string of islands. There are many verses and I cannot remember them all, or indeed the tune itself, but I do remember one set of verses in particular. It portrayed the journey to the third island. Here the sailors came across a large volcano that had erupted out of the sea to form an island. They approached the island and landed but were attacked by strange stone grey creatures, inhabitants of this island. The sailors branded them as the Graav, men, or rather creatures in the shape of man, made from the volcanic stone. The weapons of the men bounced off the rocky hides of the Graav and many of the adventurers lost their lives on the shore. It seemed that the only way of slaying these creatures was to remove their heads. The song tells of the ferocity of the Graav and how they seemed not to feel any pain from the blows of the weapons, or indeed, show emotion of any kind."

Tor started to laugh, "Oh come on now Kraven, are you suggesting that our foe are these men made of stone! That story is an old wives tale and bears little credence in the real world." A few of the others started to laugh too.

Gorlan raised his hand to stop them, "Hold men, I agree that it seems unlikely but I will not discount this. We have seen so many strange things today and I will not ignore the possibility that there is some semblance of truth in this story-song. After all, we have a mound of unexplained lava rock that was laid amongst the bodies. We also have eye witnesses to strange stone shaped creatures marching in the mountains. If anyone else has a better explanation than that of Kraven's then I will hear it now."

The men stopped laughing and fell silent. Tor apologised to the bard-warrior. Gorlan continued, "Very well, let's not talk anymore of this tonight. It is our turn to tell Stern of what we have found today before we rest."

The warriors returned to the comfort of the main hall. They watched as their fire eagles took to the skies and flew west as the last ray of sunlight left the world for the night.

CHAPTER TEN
Dreams and Crystals

R hys was awoken by a high pitched scream, he jumped up and called to Ashley, "Ash, calm down, it's just a nightmare, you're here with us and safe."

Ashley stopped screaming and looked around, her wits gradually returning to her. She took a tissue out of Rhys rucksack and blew her nose. "I'm sorry about that guys. I had this terrible dream."

Michael looked at her sympathetically, "Would it help if you told us about it?"

Ashley paused, uncertain, but then decided that it might.

"I dreamed of a city. It was built in a large open green valley at the foot of snow capped mountains. It was a wonderful place, a bit like those pictures of Switzerland that you see on postcards and chocolate boxes. We were all there in the city and we were amongst friends, human friends." She paused to recall the details. "I was with some soldiers and you were in a large crowd. Everyone was clapping and cheering and I felt happy. The dream then changed, I was still amongst the soldiers but I was flying high on the back of a giant bird. We soared and dived on the air currents in a blue sky above the peaks. Suddenly the sky darkened and hundreds of dark birds attacked us. I felt the claws of one dig in my back and was knocked from the giant bird that I rode. I remember falling and started to scream......which is when I woke up." Ashley shivered, "I hate heights they give me the creeps."

Michael smiled, "I don't think it's the heights that you hate really. It's the falling from them that really gets you." He winked at her.

Rhys sat upright and spoke, "I've been having dreams too, it must be this place and all the weird stuff that has happened to us."

"Tell us about your dream Rhys, was it a nightmare too?" asked Ashley, hoping that listening to Rhys' dream would take her mind off her own.

"It was a bit like yours really, part good and then turning into a nightmare. I've dreamed it a couple of times since we've been here. It's a bit jumbled. It starts with the Runestones. I am standing on the Runestone at Eumor when it suddenly changes from the Celtic knot, to the tree, then to the mountain symbol and finally to a Runestone that bears no inscription. I then see images of different places flashing through my mind, going over and over. That part doesn't frighten me though."

Ashley interrupted, "Well it seems obvious really, it's your brain using the information that you have about the Runestones and going over and over it in your mind. It's because you're worried."

Rhys frowned, "Hmmm, maybe, but here's the thing you don't know, the first time I had this dream was *before* we met Kyrie. I had no idea what the Runestones were back then and certainly did not know that others existed."

Some of the colour had returned to Ashley's cheeks, "Cool! Spooky, but cool! Maybe the Runestone is interacting with your brain in some way." She nodded and looked satisfied, "Yes, that's it, the Runestone is sending out energy and your brain must be susceptible to it."

Rhys frowned again, "Perhaps but let me finish, I haven't got to the really scary bit yet. My dream then changes, I see the albino dwarf and he is talking to me but I can't hear what he says. Suddenly he attacks me and I disappear and find myself trapped in the blue ooze that we felt when we transported here. A new figure appears, it is man wearing a dark cloak. He has a skull-like head and blood red eyes." Rhys continued to describe the creature in detail, "It emanates evil and I feel terror when I look into it's eyes. It is muttering just one word over and over and over again, DEATH. That's when I wake up. The thing that frightens me most though is that I feel I know the evil figure and that it is real. I know it's stupid but I cannot shake off that feeling."

Rhys looked at Michael who had gone a deathly shade of white, "Bloody hell! You're not going to believe this but I've just had a dream about that creature too."

They were freaked, Michael continued, "At first everything is great, we're walking through grassy hills above a large town with a group of centaurs. There are dark mountains behind us. Suddenly one of the trees changes into the form of a dragon. It grabs me in its claws and flies towards the mountains. The next thing I remember is being in a large tower, the creature that you described is in front of me holding something in his hand. Light flies out from this object and strikes me in the head, it feels like my brain is burning and I hear myself screaming. Then I woke up."

The three fell silent, after a while Rhys looked at Michael, "Are you having us on?" he asked.

Michael shook his head, "No honest to god. My dream is as I just said. The same creature that you described."

Rhys frowned, "There is no way that this is just coincidence but Ashley may be right about the Runestone. Maybe it sends out some form of radiation that is screwing with our brains. I think the sooner we get out of here the better. Do either of you know how long it's been since Kyrie left."

"Stars have risen, now they fall! Soon waking time for one and all!" the three jumped, unaware that Lan was lurking in the shadows a little distance from the Runestone. They stared at each other in amazement, Rhys spoke first, "Is he answering my question and talking to us?" he turned in LAN's direction. "Lan, do you know what time it is."

There was no reply, "Lan, do you understand what we are saying. Are you telling us that it will soon be morning?"

Silence. Whatever had prompted Lan to communicate with them had now gone. The three fell silent once more and laid back down. None of them slept any further though, all were lost in thoughts of home and about their dreams. Michael in particular was filled with trepidation. He had liked the theory of the radiation of the Runestone effecting their brains but he, like Rhys, felt that the skull head creature was real. He worried that he had just foreseen his own death.

The teenagers lay there for what seemed hours before they heard the familiar noise of the secret doorway being opened. They jumped up as one and made their way to the far end of the chamber, even Lan followed. The doorway eventually scraped open and Kyrie entered the chamber, behind her followed a male centaur and another female centaur possessing similar facial features to Kyrie. The sheer size of the male centaur was daunting. He stood some nine feet tall, a good two feet taller than the two females, and possessed both a muscular human torso as well as strong powerful animal hindquarters. He wore a dark brown beard and unruly curly brown hair. He stared sternly at the group as he entered. The teenagers guessed that the two newcomers were Kyrie's parents.

All three centaurs carried food and drink and laid it down on the floor as they entered. The male centaur spoke first, "I am Fyros, this is my wife Karia, you have already met my daughter Kyrie. My daughter has told me how you came to be here. If we are to believe your story it would appear that you have been most unfortunate and had no control over your transportation to our world. However, I, like my people, believe that nothing happens by chance. I am convinced that your arrival has been decreed by the fates for some reason."

Rhys started to speak but Fyros raised his hand for him to remain silent. "Also you are not the first strangers to visit us of late. A few days before your arrival a human male rode into town. He carried a message from the south and delivered it to the house of Hesh, one of the Centaur Council members. I have questioned Hesh on this matter but he is adamant that this rider is merely a madman and has locked him away. I believe that there may be a link between these two events. Your arrival would seem to suggest that there is much happening in our world at this time which we do not understand. I will take you to the council and ask that they hear your story. I will also demand that Hesh releases the human and that the council give an audience to this alleged madman."

"But what if the Council decide that we are a threat to them and decide to shut us away too?" asked Michael.

Fyros looked him in the eye, "I cannot speak for how the council will react but, I promise you, I will not let them harm you in any way whilst you are under my protection. However, if they feel that you are a threat to us, and prove that to me beyond any doubt, then I shall willingly hand you to their custody."

The teenagers made faces at each other, clearly not overly impressed by this half hearted guarantee of protection.

However, they had little choice other than to comply. Fyros continued now avoiding eye contact as he continued, "I need to ask one thing of you however. I am going to tell the council that I myself found you here in the chamber whilst I was checking the workings of the secret entrance. I do not want the council to know that Kyrie was here without permission. I am sure that they would be lenient with regards her continuing to practise her pipe music, however, but I know they would punish her severely for trespassing on these grounds. My daughter is foolish but I know she meant no harm and she does not deserve to feel the wrath of the council over this matter. Will you agree to this?

Ashley stepped forward and to answer for the group, "Only if you promise to keep us in your protection no matter what the council may think. From what we've heard about them so far it sounds like that they sometimes make hasty decisions. I don't want any of us to be the victims of any injustice that they may chose to hand out.

If you cannot make this promise to us then I feel that we would have to be truthful to the council. We'd be stupid to lie to them." Ashley looked apologetically at Kyrie feeling that she had let her new found friend down a little. Kyrie just smiled back at her and winked her support.

Fyros looked furious and stamped the ground, Ashley began to fear that she had spoken out a little too much and had alienated Fyros but finally, the centaur calmed himself and nodded his agreement, glaring at his daughter as he did so. He continued, "I am sure that the council will act wisely and there will be no need for this negotiation. However, before we worry about that you should eat and refresh yourselves. We have brought food and drink as well as some soap and flannels to allow you to wash. Karia and myself will go to find Cambor from whom we will request an audience with the council. Kyrie will remain here with you until we return."

Fyros turned to Lan with a concerned look on his face. He addressed Ashley, "Do you think this dim witted one will comprehend what is happening?"

Ashley shrugged, "We have no idea. Sometimes he seems to understand things and others he seems completely loopy, uh, I mean, mad. He seems to trust Rhys though and I think he may follow us when we leave if Rhys encourages him to do so."

"Good, then we will leave now and return forthwith. Come Karia."

The two adult centaurs left, gathering up Kyrie's instruments and belongings as they left. Karia smiled at them as she followed Fyros through the secret entrance, "Don't worry children, all will be fine." It was the first time she had spoken and the teenagers were enthralled with the beauty of her voice. She seemed almost to sing the words rather than to have spoken them.

When her parents had left, Kyrie thanked her new found friends for their help and co-operation and then they sat to enjoy the food that had been brought to them. Even Lan deserted the protection of the shadows to eat and even stayed close to the group. As usual though, his table manners were not at best and Kyrie stared disapprovingly as he crammed the food in his mouth ravenously. By the time they had finished breakfast and washed, their spirits had raised and they felt completely refreshed, despite their night of broken sleep.

Rhys paced the chamber impatiently, waiting for the return of Fyros. He was eager to be out of this place and to find a way back home. He walked to the Runestone and felt the pattern of the knot embossed on the solid stone. "I've always wanted to see something truly magical," he whispered to the Runestone as if it could hear him, "but now I am here I wish that you had never existed. If it wasn't for you and the portals created by the wizards then I'd be playing on the beach back home in Wales now." He slapped the cold stone in frustration. Standing up he found himself in front of the pedestal again. He stared at it for few seconds, cursing the loss of the key which would have offered an easy journey back to Salty's Cave. He traced the line of the Celtic knot on the pedestal and looked at the octagonal hole where the runestone key had once be inserted. He wondered if the centaur council may have access to the key-stone despite Kyrie's earlier report that it had been lost long ago. This thought cheered him but, to avoid disappointment, he made a conscious effort to tell himself that this was unlikely and that getting back home would not be that easy. He moved his hand up the pedestal until his finger tips rested on the edge of the octagonal notch.

Immediately a wave of energy seemed to flow through him. Rhys saw in his minds eye pictures of different places, similar to those in his earlier dream. In his head he watched as portals opened and closed, revealing images of deserts, snow, green pastures, mountains, sea views, lakes, towns, villages, forts and castles. Various creatures appeared in many of the portals, some strange, others more familiar. Salty's Cave came into view, the dark of the inner chamber lit by the blue glow of the portal. The images continued to change at a frantic pace and seemed to be accelerating. Rhys tried desperately to slow the images down without success, the images were now flying past in a blur of colour. He was feeling dizzy, there was a growing feeling of pressure and his head hurt, it felt like his brain was going to explode.

Suddenly he was aware of hands being placed on his

shoulder and he felt a sharp tug. The images gave way to blue haze and then a dark shadow slipped over his vision and the world went black.

A few minutes passed, Rhys opened his eyes to stare up at concerned expressions on the faces of his colleagues. Ashley was saying something that wasn't making any sense, but gradually he heard her voice and was able to put meaning to her words.

"Rhys, are you alright, speak to us." Rhys was partially moved and partially amused when he saw that Ashley's eyes were welling up with tears. "Rhys, please talk to us."

Rhys groaned. A smile lit up the faces of Ashley and Michael. "Uhhh, I'm OK, I think. What happened?"

Kyrie replied, "We're not sure, one minute you were standing there normally and the next you were holding the pedestal and seemed to be lost in thought. Your eyes were staring into space and you didn't respond when we spoke to you. Suddenly you started to twitch and moan as if in great pain. We ran to help you but Lan was nearest and reacted quickest. He grabbed you and pulled you away from the pedestal. I'm not sure how he did it though as you were fighting like a mad dog to remain where you stood. You were gripping onto the stone as if your very life depended on it. I'm afraid you gave him quite a thump with your elbow when you were trying to fight him off and his nose is bleeding quite badly."

Rhys shook his head, and took Kyrie's hand as she offered to help him to his feet. He had a blinding headache but otherwise felt fine. Rhys picked up one of the damp flannels and walked over to Lan. He gently placed his hand on the old man's shoulder, "I am sorry Lan. Thank you for helping me." Lan looked back at him with a blank expression as Rhys wiped clean his bloodied nose.

Rhys turned back to the others and noticed that Fyros had

returned accompanied by Karia and an older male. This centaur stood as tall as Fyros but his beard and hair had greyed. His body still exhibited a frame that had once been as muscular as Fyros' but now age had taken it's toll and his muscles had started to waste a little. The older centaur smiled at him and spoke, " I hope that you are not hurting too much young man. My name is Cambor, I am a member of the Centaur Council and I would like to welcome you to our city. "

Rhys acknowledged Cambor and commented that he was fine but for the headache.

"In that case let us leave here and we will find some feyberry powder to remedy that. I am sure that all of us would like to know what just happened here but, for now, I will lead you to the council chambers. The members are eager to meet you and your friends and to hear your story. Rather than making you have to re-tell the account of what happened to you a few moments ago, I would suggest that we wait until we are before the whole council." Cambor turned to address all three of the teenagers, "I understand that you are quite frightened, after all you are but children, however I would like to assure you that you will not be harmed. Fyros has sworn his protection and I have joined with his voice to offer mine too, if you will have it?"

Ashley resumed her role as spokeswoman, "I think we'll need all the friends that we can if we want to get back home. We'll most definitely accept your protection too. Thanks Cambor."

Karia who had been listening intently now spoke. "I have some Feyberry powder with me." She reached into a small bag that she held. She removed a small packet of white powder and poured it into one of the breakfast cups. She then mixed this with water from the cat's head and handed it to Rhys. "Here, drink this. It will cure your headache quickly." Rhys looked at the liquid suspiciously. "It won't harm you, it is used by all creatures throughout Portalia, including humans." Karia spoke softly and Rhys was reassured at the sound of her voice. He swallowed the mixture. It tasted bitter but not overly unpleasant. "Thank you," said Rhys as he drank the last of the liquid.

Within seconds the pain that had throbbed in his brain was washed away and was filled with a light-headedness. Rhys looked at the empty container in amazement.

"Whoaw! That is what I call a pain killer, my head feels better already." He tried to stand but had to be caught as he almost fell over. The light-headed feeling was making him dizzy and affecting his balance.

Karia raised her eyebrows, "It seems that the mixture may react with you a little differently than to those humans on Portalia. I have never known Feyberry to react so quickly. Do not worry though, the light headed feeling will leave shortly. It is often a symptom of those that have not taken Feyberry before."

Rhys stood there trying to regain his balance. True to her word, his head started to clear and he began to feel like himself once more.

Mike poked Rhys in the ribs playfully, "You know what, if we do find a way back home we have to take some of that stuff with us. We could sell it to one of the big medicine companies and make a fortune! Think of it, Michael and Rhys' Cure All, the worlds greatest headache and hangover remedy."

Rhys smiled too but sobered a little as he saw Cambor watching them impatiently, "If you two have finished and Rhys is feeling a little better I'd like us to get going."

Rhys and Mike both nodded and the band set off through

the secret exit of the chamber. Lan however did not make a move, he watched them until they paused at the doorway and he was urged to follow by Rhys. Encouraged by his new friend, he finally set out, falling in step a few feet behind Rhys but as far from the others as he could manage.

When they had all passed through the exit, Fyros sealed the doorway behind them. It was far more complex than they expected. Belts, cogs and a number of hidden switches had to be pulled, pushed, twisted or flicked. They realised that without the help of a centaur, they would never have been able to operate this exit, either from the inside or the outside. After the tenth door had slid into place behind them they exited into daylight.

The sun seemed incredibly bright after the dark of the chamber. They blinked to clear their vision and saw that they were in a city. Single storey buildings were all around them, built from white stone with thatched roofs. There were centaurs milling all around, going about their daily business. All paused and stared inquisitively as they saw the group leave the forbidden chamber and head in the direction of the council chambers. Some started to approach but stopped their advance when they saw Cambor and Fyros leading the group. Many bowed their heads in respect to Cambor.

Ashley turned to Karia, "Why do they bow?"

Karia looked towards Cambor and smiled, "Cambor told only part of the truth when he introduced himself. He is the most respected of the elders and in fact he now heads the council. The fact that he offers you protection is a great honour and most unusual. Now that you have his support none will harm you."

After a short walk they approached a building that, although still single storey, was much grander than the others.

It possessed a large arched central doorway that rose twenty feet from the ground. The doors were propped open to allow the summer air to flow through the building. The group entered and were immediately stopped by four centaur guards. The leader of the guards acknowledged Cambor and stepped aside to allow the group to continue.

Inside the building Rhys was reminded of old Roman buildings where an arched alcove ran around the four sides on the outer edge of a central rectangular room, the floor was decorated with fine mosaics. The thatched roof, thirty feet above their heads was multilayered. The centaurs had cleverly rigged up sections of the roof that could be raised or lowered to allow the central area to lay open to the skies. This provided lighting in the room and allowed fresh air to flow around the interior. In times of inclement weather, the thatches could be lifted back into place, keeping out the wind, rain, hail, sleet or snow.

At the centre of the room stood a large low rectangular table made of a deep red wood. Around three sides of the table ten centaurs sat on large magenta cushions made from a silk-like material. Most of the centaurs were old and greyed, but some appeared younger, a similar age to Fyros. There was no mistaking that this was the Eumor Centaur Council. All fell silent as the group entered the room turning to look at the teenagers who suddenly felt a great deal of trepidation.

Cambor sensed their discomfort and made an effort to reassure them, "Do not be afraid. No-one here means you harm. Some look very grave as we face serious times and they wonder if the peace that we have enjoyed is at an end." Cambor led the teenagers to the side of the table where no centaurs sat and signalled for them to sit on cushions that had been placed there. A young human male was already sitting at the table.

Ashley examined the boy and guessed that this must be the messenger to which Fyros had referred. He was about eighteen years old and looked just like any eighteen year old would back in her hometown. The youth stood about six feet tall with bright blues eyes and a shock of blonde hair. She thought that he would not look out of place carrying a surf board on a Californian beach. His clothes told of his alien roots though as he was dressed in animal leathers and furs. He smiled at her when he caught her looking at him. She blushed and turned away hastily.

Fyros, Karia and Kyrie sat on cushions a little distance away from the table. Cambor made his way to the empty seat at the centre of the council members and called the meeting to order. He started by introducing each of the council members before moving on to the visitors. He introduced the young man as Meld, of Fortown. He then turned to Rhys, Michael and Ashley and asked them to convey to the council the story of how they came to be in Portalia, and indeed in Eumor City itself. Rhys stood and began to tell their tale.

He was interrupted a number of times by a centaur to his right who Cambor had introduced as Hesh. Hesh was similar in stature and age to Fyros. His skin tone was darker than that of the others and he possessed a large black beard, long curly black hair and dark grey eyes. He sat with a scowl on his face all through Rhys' rendition, "You expect us to believe that you had no idea about the powers of the Runestones and that you came here by accident. You say you found the pendant one day and just 'happened' across the ring the very same day. Considering that these items have been lost for generations, how could this be. I suspect that you are part of a greater plot and are here to spy on us."

At these words Rhys, Ashley and Michael began to panic,

very much afraid that the others would agree. All three started to shout their innocence. Many of the council members joined in with the youths but a few sided with Hesh, the meeting was in chaos. Cambor hammered on the table and let out a roar, "SILENCE!".

The whole room fell silent, no-one dared to argue with Cambor who made no effort to hide his anger. "I will not have these chambers turned into a market place." He turned to face the teenagers, "Children, I would ask that you do not all speak at once no matter what is said here. Let Rhys be your spokesman for now." He then turned to the centaur that had provoked the outburst, "Hesh, too often of late have you spoken out of turn. You will desist with these incessant interruptions."

Hesh stared back at Cambor and spoke sarcastically, "So are we not allowed to express our opinion? Is the great Cambor no longer interested in the freedom for all centaurs to voice their concerns?"

Cambor paused and met Hesh's gaze, "You know the law Hesh. All are entitled to speak their opinions and you will get your chance. However, your timing on when you express that opinion needs to improve significantly." Cambor turned back to Rhys, "Please continue."

Rhys described how they had all arrived in the chamber and found themselves trapped. He swallowed and then went on to embellish the truth a little, "We had been there for hours and we were trying to work out how to get out, or better still back home, when we heard the secret entrance open and we were found by Fyros."

Hesh could not resist interrupting once more, he turned to Fyros with a sly look and said, "And what business had you in the Runestone Chamber? Perhaps the noise of the pipe music in your house became too grotesque and you sought out solitude."

Ashley held her breath, and wondered whether Hesh knew of Kyrie's secret habit. Fyros did not show any signs of surprise or anger and calmly replied, "As the council is aware, my family are charged with the maintenance of the Runestone Chamber even though it is no longer in use. I regularly check the mechanisms for the secret passage and check the foundations for any cracks or damage." He looked directly at Hesh, "As a council member yourself Hesh, I am surprised that you were unaware of this fact." Some of the other centaurs snickered and Kyrie beamed in pride. Hesh did not look happy at having his knowledge of council matters questioned and he glared at Fyros.

Cambor prompted Rhys to explain what had occurred earlier that day when he had touched the Runestone pedestal. Rhys paused to collect his thoughts, unsure as to how to explain what had happened. He continued hesitantly, trying his best to describe the incident. However, he had decided not to mention his earlier dreams and told the details of what had happened at the pedestal as if they had been in isolation.

An old centaur sat at Cambor's left spoke, "My name is Horos. I have spent many years studying the arts and legends of magic, documented in old books and scrolls. During this time I have read that in the days of the wizards, some of their kind could visualize the portal gateways by being in the proximity of a Runestone. All such cases referenced the fact that this ability was only held by High Wizards with a natural skill for the magic of the Runestones. I have never read of anyone possessing this portal-vision skill without such knowledge."

Rhys looked towards Horos, "So is that what you think I saw, the portal gateways?"

"It is possible but highly unlikely. It may be that your mind was creating a vision of what you thought each portal would look like at the other end."

Rhys thought about this, "But one of the locations that I saw was Salty's Cave and we know that is a portal point."

"Unfortunately that fact does not mean anything. We know that the cave location is real but that does not mean the others that you saw were also real."

Cambor raised a question, "Horos, although it seems unlikely, could it be that this young man possess some of the skills of the old ones. It could be that those skills lay dormant within him and that the proximity of the Runestone and the ancient magic triggered the skill in some way?"

Horos rubbed his chin, "I suppose it is possible. We know that during the times of the wizards trade routes existed between our worlds. It is possible that young Rhys is a descendant of a wizard line. The area known as Wales is mentioned often in the old scripts and was visited by wizards, centaurs, dwarves and sea elves." Horos looked at Rhys, "Is it not true that you have many tales of legend and myth in your world?"

Rhys nodded, "That's true, we have lots of tales of strange creatures in Wales and other places. We've always thought these to be just stories but maybe some were based on visitors from Portalia."

Hesh interjected, "Be that as it may, it is clear that even if this human is a descendant of the wizards, he possesses no knowledge of the old skills and clearly would not be of any use to us." Hesh raised his hand, palm upwards, "Is this not true boy? Tell us, do you know anything of the old magics?"

Rhys shook his head, "I'm sorry but no, I have no idea what you're talking about."

The centaurs were forced to agree with Hesh. Cambor

looked around at the faces of the council members. "My friends," he said, "Earlier we have already heard from Meld that Black Eagles fly the skies over Dargoth," Hesh let out a guffaw at this point but was silenced by the look given to him by Cambor "Now we find these Earth children transported to our world by ancient magic. The wheels are turning, Portalia changes. We have been at peace for many generations free from evil. Something now stirs and the fate decrees that we are involved. We must decide on a course of action. I therefore call a vote. Majority will rule."

Cambor now stood, towering above the table, "First of all, do we send aid with Meld to investigate events at Fortown? All in favour of offering assistance raise your hands."

Cambor counted the hands, there was a strong show for this first point, eight voted to assist Fortown with only Hesh and the two centaurs sat either side of him voting against. Cambor turned to Meld, "We will respond to your request for assistance. I will send a group of centaurs with you to Fortown to investigate and assist. I hope that the other messengers that you mentioned reached their destinations and that they have received better treatment than you did at Eumor City when you first arrived. I apologise for the lack of belief that we exhibited earlier." Cambor looked towards Hesh who merely grinned at his words.

Meld stood and bowed, "Thank you sir, I accept your apology and am heartened that you will come to our aid."

Cambor turned back to the council. "I would now ask for a show of hands regarding the Earth children. We have heard that they came here by accident and wish merely to return to their home. Some amongst us have expressed that they believe them to be spies. So, who amongst us believes them to be friends, thrown here through misfortune?" This time the vote was closer. Not only did Hesh and his cohorts voted against, but two other centaurs expressed doubt. Cambor scanned the vote, "Then we are honour bound to assist these inadvertent visitors and to help them find a way to return to their home land. Does anyone amongst us have any ideas on how we can aid them with this?"

Horos stood and picked up a scroll that had been sat on the table. He unrolled it and showed it to everyone present. "This is a Runestone diagram. As you can see it depicts the twenty points of the Runestone. As we all know the Runestone key is needed to activate the portals for each of these twenty locations. I believe that colours represent three separate worlds. The first is our own, Portalia, where all positions are shaded green, this includes the three Runestones hubs themselves." Horos turned the diagram towards the teenagers and ran a finger around the rim of the octagon, "These five positions shaded in purple are locations on your home world, Earth. One of these will be your cave in Wales. The final five positions relate to a world known as Roccore. I have little information on this last world other than it is mainly of water and possesses only a single land mass. Winters there are extremely cold and summers blazing hot. As such it is a very inhospitable place to live." Horos turned to the council, "We know that no Runestones exist on their home world so, the only way of getting our new friends back home is to get them to a working Runestone on Portalia. Until now, we believed that none of the Runestones were operable, but if we consider the stories that we have heard today, both from Meld and from the Rhys, then I would suggest that someone, or something, has discovered a way to utilise the Runestone power once more." There were murmurs of disapproval.

Horos continued, "There are only three Runestones. One lies in the Old Forest and is in the care of the Dark Elves.

Stories tell that the elves destroyed their Runestone and the Runestone artefacts long ago and chose a life of isolation and solitude, cut off from others. We have no reason to doubt this given our knowledge of the Dark Elves. The Runestone artefacts for Eumor City and Dargoth were lost long ago, during the Warlock Wars and, once again, many believed that they had been destroyed. We have evidence in front of our eyes that this is not true. We see three pendants and the ring of the Celtic knot, but alas, no keystone. We know that our Runestone has not been used, yet the children saw a dwarf and a portal opened on their home world. Further, Meld reports to us that the Black Eagles fly over Dargoth once more. I therefore believe that someone now possess a Runestone key and that the Runestone at Shangorth Towers has been re-activated."

Although most of the council had suspected this themselves, there was much mumbling and muttering as Horos voiced these words. Cambor gestured for silence, "I believe your logic is sound Horos. This means that Portalia faces grave danger. It is highly unlikely that those using black eagles intend the use of the portal for good. But how does this help our friends here?"

Horos looked at the council leader and grinned, "I suggest that we escort the children into the Dargoth mountains, locate the active Runestone and use it's power to return them to their home."

The meeting broke into a cacophony of noise. Hesh stood and hammered his hand on the table top, "This is ludicrous, such a mission is doomed. If we are to believe that evil rules again in Dargoth then the journey would be futile, we would lose both centaurs and humans. If Horos is wrong and the news from Fortown is nothing but an exaggerated sighting of large black birds, then the journey is nothing but a waste of time."

Cambor once again signalled for order, "We have heard the logic, let us vote on this matter too. All those in favour of Horos' suggestion show their hands." Cambor looked around the room, five hands had been raised supporting the proposal, five remained down, his final vote would decide. He raised his hand in support of Horos. Hesh let out a snort of derision, "Madness! Utter madness!"

Cambor glared at Hesh, "Do you question the vote of the council" he bellowed.

Hesh was ambitious and eager to wrestle power from Cambor but he was not so foolish as to question a democratic council vote. He shook his head.

Cambor continued, "Then it is decided. Rhys, Ashley, and Michael will accompany Meld and one hundred centaurs to Fortown. Once there, we will decide how best to pursue our plan to return the children to their homes."

Rhys raised his hand, Cambor nodded for him to speak, "What about Lan? We know he is human but we have no idea where he came from."

"He will accompany you to Fortown. In the meantime if we discover anymore of his home then we will endeavour to return him to it. If not then he can remain with the other humans in Fortown. I also feel that fate played a part in his involvement and that he is with you for a purpose. Time will tell."

"That seems like a good plan. Thank you Cambor." Another thought came to Rhys, "What about the spiders that we saw with the dwarf, what do you think he was doing?"

Cambor looked around the council members but no-one spoke, "It seems that we do not have any knowledge of this. I believe that the purpose was for no good though. I dare say time may tell us more."

Horos leaned close to Cambor and whispered something to him. The leader of the council nodded, "Before you make your journey south we have one more task for you to undertake, a task that must be undertaken by the bearer of the Runestone ring." Cambor paused and turned his attention to Michael, who reddened when he realised he was suddenly the centre of attention, "To the north of Eumor, where the plains meet the Pinnacle Mountains, there is a small temple built into the hillside. This temple was raised many years ago, shortly after the Warlock Wars. Here can be summoned forth a dramkaan, an ethereal creature made of pure energy. The dramkaan is the warden of Cormion's Crystals, a set of small magical orbs that allow communication over long distances with the Servants of the Runestone, those wearing the Eumor pendants."

Horos picked up the story, "Cormion was a centaur who had studied with the wizards. He created the crystal set to allow communication with the centaurs that wore the pendants of the Celtic knot. During times of peace they proved invaluable when our travellers were negotiating trade treaties. They allowed immediate discussion and authorisation to take place with the council no matter of the location of those wearing the pendants. Of course, when the Warlock Wars broke out the Cormion Crystals proved their worth once more. When the Runestones fell into disuse after the wars, Weldrock the Wizard took the crystals and gave them into the care of the dramkaan. I often wondered why the crystals were not destroyed, maybe Weldrock knew that there may come a time when they would once again be needed."

Cambor continued, "Michael, we need you to travel to the temple immediately and retrieve the Cormion Crystals. You will be accompanied by Kyrie for she knows the way. The temple is a few hours ride from the city, do you know how to ride a horse?"

Michael who had ridden often back home in Wales replied, "I do sir, but I'd be happy to give the ring to another so that they could summon the warden." Michael did not like the sound of being face to face with a spirit at all.

Cambor shook his head, "I am afraid that this cannot be. I have a strong feeling that there is a reason why the artefacts of the Runestone have found there way into your hands. Whilst our law prevents the artefacts being taken from you, it does allow for you to give possession to another. I would ask though that each of you carry the burden of the objects that you carry. I believe that there are greater forces at work here than we know."

Hesh objected loudly once more, "But Cambor, he is but a child and clearly has no spine for this venture. Boy, give the ring to me, I will take it to the temple."

Michael looked at Hesh, he was fed up with the rude centaur's persistent interruptions and now angry that he was calling him a coward. He wished that the centaur would leave and allow the others to sort things out.

Michael looked down at the ring on his finger, he toyed with it, lost in thought, he really did not want this responsibility but now felt trapped as he did not want to appear cowardly. He looked at Rhys for advice, "Mike, I think you should keep the ring. Although it sounds like we won't need it to get home I feel that it is important too."

Hesh interjected yet again, "DO NOT BE SO FOOLISH! THIS BOY IS GUTLESS AND CANNOT SHOULDER THAT RESPONSIBILITY!"

Michael glared at Hesh before turning back to Cambor, "OK," he said reluctantly, "I'll carry the ring and will get the crystals for you." Hesh let out a snort of derision.

Cambor smiled, "Thank you Michael. Well, unless there are any other questions from the council I would suggest that this is a good point to adjourn." He paused but no-one spoke further. "Kyrie and Michael, you will leave within the hour. I want you back as soon as possible so that you can get some rest before leaving on the morrow."

Kyrie looked surprised, "I am to accompany them to Fortown too?"

Cambor nodded, "Yes Kyrie, I believe that you have a greater part in this than has been made obvious to the council. I want you to be with them during this journey. Fyros, I hope you have no objections to this?"

Fyros shook his head, "No Cambor, Kyrie is now full grown. It is time she explored the world a little. I would sooner she do that accompanied by a hundred centaur soldiers than on her own."

"Then it is decided. Kyrie, you will find a suitable mount for Michael and then head straight for the temple. Come and find me immediately when you return. I will remain here within my chambers. Everyone else should help prepare for tomorrow's journey. We will all meet up again outside the council chambers at sunset."

Kyrie prompted Michael for him to follow her. Rhys, Ashley and Meld were accompanied by Fyros. As usual Lan followed closely behind Rhys, muttering to himself nonsensically. The council members left to prepare the soldiers and to arrange the provision of supplies for the journey.

Meld approached Ashley and Rhys as they walked to the home of Fyros and Karia, he raised his right fist in greeting and said, "We have not been properly introduced. I am Meld, messenger of Fortown, it is good to meet you."

Rhys and Ashley responded in like, Ashley looked at Meld

and replied, "It is good to meet you too , a rather curious way to meet each other though." Ashley smiled at him and her face flushed as Meld looked back with steel blue eyes. "So, you said you were from Fortown, how far away is that and tell us more about these black eagles?"

Meld replied that it would take three days to reach his hometown and preceded to tell them the story of how Ramsey the shepherd had discovered the Black Eagles, he also gave them an account of the eagles and the Warlock Wars, similar to the one they had heard from Kyrie earlier. He spoke fondly of his brother Molt. He hoped that he had travelled well and had found the Pinns a little more accommodating than the centaurs had been when he had first arrived. He told the pair of his frustrations, he had not been treated badly, in fact he had been well looked after, but fuelled by the sceptical Hesh the council had initially refused him an audience and branded him a liar and scaremonger.

The arrival of Ashley and Rhys had changed all that and he thanked them for their inadvertent good timing. Ashley listened intently to Meld as he spoke, a feeling like butterflies in her stomach. Rhys took an immediate liking to the Fortownian youth. He treated Rhys as if he was an equal, despite the five years that separated them. They continued chatting to each other as they followed Fyros into his home.

***

Michael held the reigns of his horse as he trotted alongside Kyrie. His mount was a beautiful chestnut colt called Firmstar. Kyrie had chosen the colt for him because Firmstar possessed a good temperament. It was not the fastest of the horses but would get them to the temple safely and relatively swiftly. When they left the council chambers, Michael was surprised to find that the horses had not been stabled but were left free to roam on the Eumor Plains. They had made their way to the outskirts of the city and climbed up a small hill from where Kyrie had called out the name of his mount. Firmstar had galloped to them. Kyrie had introduced the pair and asked Firmstar to carry Michael on their journey. Michael felt a buzz of excitement as Firmstar allowed him to attach saddle and reigns.

As they made there way north, Kyrie surprised Michael, "Long before the portals were built there were no horses in Portalia. It is told that horses were brought here through trade, so they may have originated from Earth. There have been many theories about the relationships between centaurs and horses. It's never been explained how we possess this close bond whilst we come from different worlds. Our equine features are so similar that there must be a link somewhere. But how could this be if our worlds were separated before the time of the portals. It is certainly a mystery. One legend tells that centaurs are not in fact of Portalia but came here after being outcast as abominations on their home world. If that is true then how did our race arrive here? Centaurs have walked on Portalia long before the creation of the wizards portal web. It truly is a mystery, although I believe that there is an element of truth in this tale and that horse and centaurs once originated from the same world."

Michael thought on this, "Then it is possible that centaurs actually originated on Earth?"

Kyrie smiled, "Who knows, it could well be," she replied.

A few hours passed and they continued to canter over green and yellow grassy plains under a blue sky and the warm summer sun. It felt good to be out on the plains, especially after the dark of the cave and the Runestone chamber. They were fast approaching the mountains and eventually Michael could make the shape of a small temple like building.

"Is that it?" he asked. Kyrie nodded and they broke into a gallop. As they approached, Michael could see that the temple had been formed of the hill rock itself. It was single storey and only just big enough to allow entry to a full grown centaur. The walls themselves had been chiselled out of the hillside and the entrance lay open to the plains with no outer doorway to prevent entry. He dismounted and rubbed Firmstar's nose. "Thanks Firmstar, you wait here we won't be long." The colt whinnied in reply.

Kyrie and Michael entered the temple. It was dimly lit inside with only two small windows offering light. Like the walls, the floor was made of solid rock, hewn from the hill. The temple possessed an inner chamber that housed a wooden door. Michael opened the door and walked into a shrine. As they stepped inside torches burst into life on the wall and the door slammed shut behind them.

The inner shrine was almost completely bare but housed a plinth on the wall that held the imprint of a hand. In the centre of the palm was a triangular slot, the same size and shape as the slots on the pendants. Michael looked at Kyrie. "I presume I place my ring in the triangular slot to summon the dramkaan?"

Kyrie shrugged, "It would seem so."

Michael approached the plinth with some trepidation. He raised his finger and, with eyes closed, pushed the ring into the recess. He waited a few seconds and then dared to peek. Nothing. He looked at Kyrie questioningly but she just shrugged and looked equally puzzled. He turned his back on the plinth and made to step away.

Suddenly a sharp blast of air burst from the centre of the hand imprint and he was almost knocked off his feet. The small shrine was filled with the noise of the wind as the air rushed around the room like a hurricane. Michael struggled towards Kyrie and she grabbed his arms to pull him towards her.

They became aware of a new sound at the same time. At first distant, but growing by the second. It was the sound of a tormented scream and was being carried on the wind. The scream grew louder and louder until their ears hurt with it's intensity. An explosion of energy was emitted from the triangular recess and whipped around the room a dozen or so times before slowing. The wind dropped and the screaming subsided. Michael and Kyrie had raised their arms over the faces to protect their eyes but now lowered them as things became calmer. In front of them they saw the energy that had spewed from the hole beginning to form into a man-like shape. It hovered a few feet above the floor and reached the roof a few feet above their heads. Slowly, features began to form on the shape, a long thin face, hairless but with vast goat like horns sweeping back across it's head. A human torso with a lower half that faded from substantiality to a blur of energy, giving the perception of a large glowing tail. The creature opened its eyes and it's sockets exposed depths of sheer energy, glowing with a pure white light.

The dramkaan spoke and Michael shivered at it's voice which sounded like that of a number of people speaking at once. There were so many pitches and tones that Michael had to check that there was indeed only one creature present in the shrine. "Who dares to disturb me and call me forth?"

Kyrie nudged Michael to respond as he was transfixed. "Step forward, raise your ring high and ask for the Crystals," she whispered.

Michael was not happy but he had little choice. He stepped forward to face the dramkaan. He could not hide a quivering in his voice as he responded, "I am sorry but it was me. I wear the Runestone ring and I have been sent here by the Centaur Council to ask for the Cormion Crystals."

The dramkaan turned his eyes to look directly at Michael. The young boy had felt fear over the past few days but the dread that struck him now was far worse than anything he had experienced previously. The eyes of the dramkaan seemed to look into his very soul. He was reminded of his dream and the pain that he had imagined as he faced Shangorth. He shut his eyes almost expecting the same pain to strike him down but relaxed after a few seconds when no pain surfaced. He was aware however of a curious feeling in his mind. As if something was moving in his head. The dramkaan continued to stare at him with those terrifying eyes. Michael started to feel sick and wanted this to stop. Then, as suddenly as it had begun, the feeling stopped and the dramkaan withdrew it's stare.

"Why should I release the crystals to your care?" thundered the dramkaan.

Kyrie responded first, "Because he wears the ring and has the right to demand them."

The dramkaan turned to Kyrie, the myriad voices ushered forth once more, "This is true but I was also charged to protect the Crystals and prevent them falling into the possession of evil. In this boy I sense conflict, a heart of pure good tinged with something which I struggle to understand. I cannot be sure of his intentions."

Kyrie hesitated but continued his support, "Perhaps you sense something alien to our world, he is of Earth not Portalia."

The dramkaan shook his head, "Perhaps that is so, but I

think there may be something else. It leaves me undecided as to whether I should hand over the ring or destroy this human."

Michael gulped at these words and realised that he was bathed in sweat. He looked pleadingly at Kyrie. She raised her hands to signal for him to calm himself and spoke again.

"Michael was sent here by the Council of Eumor, they have decided to trust him, will you not also."

The dramkaan closed his eyes as if in thought, Michael dared not move as the creature floated above him. "Very well, I will trust the council's view on this boy. I will give him the Crystals."

There was a blinding flash of light and the dramkaan broke apart into rays of energy once more. Michael ducked and covered his head again, afraid that the dramkaan had changed it's mind and had chosen to strike him down. The wind they had felt earlier returned but this time blew in towards the plinth. The dramkaan in it's pure energy form disappeared through the triangle, four white crystals were now sat on the floor beneath where it had floated in thin air. Kyrie rushed forward and picked them up. The crystals were the size of plums and sat comfortably in the hand. They were strung onto a metal chain to allow them to be worn about the neck. Kyrie slipped two around her neck and the other two around Michael's. She let out a sigh of relief, "That was a close call. For one minute there I thought the dramkaan was going to refuse to give them to you. I think your strangeness spooked him a little, I doubt he has ever come across one of your kind before." She smiled at Michael who finally relaxed and smiled back, "C'mon" he said, "Let's get out of here. I don't like this place, and for one minute there I thought it may be the last thing that I'd ever see."

He ushered Kyrie outside and the pair set off back towards Eumor City with the satisfaction of having completed their quest for Cormion's Crystals.

CHAPTER ELEVEN
Questions

Fyros cantered along at the front of the platoon of centaurs. He ran with Griff, the Captain of the Centaur Soldiery, Kyrie proudly by his side. Overnight the centaurs had tailored common clothing for the teenagers and they now wore light sleeved shirts, jerkins, brown leather trousers and soft comfortable socks. The centaur had even found pairs of boots for each of them, hidden away in the back of a merchant's store. There was not a great deal of trade in Eumor for human clothing but occasionally they entertained a visitor and the shops kept a small stock to cater to these travellers.

The teenagers rode in the middle of the centaur platoon, flanked on either side by fifty centaur soldiers. They noticed that the centaurs, who by large walked naked whilst at home in Eumor, were now clad in protective combat leathers which covered their upper human torsos as well as across their horse-like backs. The upper parts of their legs were also protected by long black leather battle stockings. All of the armour was decorated with a shining metal that looked like a cross between copper and bronze but was much more lightweight, it glowed as it caught the sunlight. The metal, which Kyrie had called wroughtore, had also been used to form light helmets, each exhibiting a representation of the centaur's family. Kyrie had explained that wrought ore was mined and reworked by the dwarves in the White Peaks. It was ideal for use as armour as, not only was it light weight, but it's density was such that it resisted blows from other metal weapons.

Rhys laughed and Kyrie stared at him a little confused, "What is funny Rhys?" she asked.

"Oh not much really," he replied, "It's just that when on Earth our stories always depict the dwarves as miners. This has always bugged me as I couldn't understand why such tough creatures would want to do such a horrible job. Now I find out that it is true. They really do exist and they really are miners. It's just too weird!"

Kyrie still looked confused so Rhys changed the subject, "These horses are superb Kyrie. They're so tame too."

The teenagers were all mounted on colts from the Eumor Plains with the exception of Meld who rode his Fortownian army horse. The previous afternoon, whilst Michael and Kyrie were on the quest for the Cormion Crystals, Fyros had taken Ashley, Rhys and Lan to the hills to find for them a suitable mount. Ashley had ridden previously so, for her, Fyros chose Quickhoof. Quickhoof was a great sprinter and could match even the fastest of the centaurs. Rhys had never ridden before, so, for him Fyros called Farseeker, a steady mount who was used to carrying novice riders but who was also capable of travelling great distances with little rest.

Whilst the colts were being chosen Lan watched intently. Fyros had earlier tried to communicate with Lan to enable him to find a suitable horse but the old man cowered from him each time he was approached. Rhys tried too but was unable to get any sensible answer from him. Having found the two colts for the children Fyros now frowned at Lan wondering what mount to select for the fragile old man. As he did so Lan touched Rhys shoulder and whispered in his ear, "DiamCret," Lan struggle with his words and shook his head. "DiamondCrell, cres, crest! DiamondCrest!".

Rhys looked blankly at Lan and shrugged, "I don't understand Lan."

Lan looked frustrated and said louder, "DiamondCrest!"

Fyros looked startled, "Did he just say DiamondCrest?"

Rhys nodded, again he was amazed at how Lan seemed to follow the conversation and understand events despite his apparent madness. Lan turned to look at Fyros, a glimmer of expectation in his eyes. Fyros spoke to Rhys, "DiamondCrest is one of the Eumor Cloud Horses, native to these plains for many generations. The Cloud Horses are magnificent regal creatures and possess enormous power and strength. I have never known anyone ride a Cloud Horse, although it is written that they once carried the wizards of Portalia." Fyros turned back to Lan, "How do you know of DiamondCrest old man?"

Lan just stared back, panic was beginning to set in and he was looking agitated, his eyes darting from Rhys to Fyros and back again, "DiamondCrest!"

Fyros shook his head, "No! You are not strong enough to handle a Cloud Horse even if it did agree to take you as a rider. You will ride Fallon, she is a strong mount with a good heart." Fyros turned his back on them.

Lan went wild, he jumped up and down waving his arms wildly, "DiamondCrest! DiamondCrest! DiamondCrest! DiamondCrest! DiamondCrest! DiamondCrest! DiamondCrest! DiamondCrest!" he shouted again and again.

Rhys raised his hands to calm Lan, "Fyros, can't we try to call DiamondCrest. If we show Lan that DiamondCrest won't let anyone ride him then he may settle down and accept Fallon."

Fyros let out a resigned sigh, "Very well, but the Cloud

Horses owe allegiance to no other, including the centaurs, he may not come when I call." He turned to the hills and called out for the Cloud Horse. Fyros told them to sit, the colts that had been selected for the teenagers lived near to the city and were always close at hand when called, the Cloud Horses however roamed throughout the plains and were not always within calling range. Time seemed to drag as they sat and waited. Fyros called out once more.

They had been waiting for an hour when Lan suddenly sprang up, "DiamondCrest comes!" he said, jumping up and down in excitement, a large and manic smile on his face. Fyros and the teenagers stood but could see or hear nothing, just as they had been about to sit down again they heard hoofs thundering towards them and a few seconds later a horse appeared, galloping across the hills to the south.

Ashley and Rhys both stared, they had never seen such a magnificent horse. DiamondCrest was a white stallion shimmering in the sunlight as he galloped towards them, muscles rippling. His mane flowed in the breeze he exuberated freedom and power. Rhys was reminded of the idealised pictures that he had seen of foam formed white horses galloping amongst the breaking waves. On the nose of the Cloud Horse there was dark black diamond shaped patch, making it obvious how the stallion had earned it's name. Even Fyros looked on with awe in his eyes and the children understood why the Cloud Horses were considered regal. DiamondCrest continued towards them, slowing as he neared their location. He went straight to Lan, nuzzling his face and neighing a greeting. Lan returned the affection, rubbing the horses nose and mane and placing his face against the horse allowing DiamondCrest to feel his breath in it's nostrils.

Before Fyros could carry out the ritual of requesting that

Lan be allowed to ride, the old man had leapt with unexpected agility onto the back of the Cloud Horse and they galloped around in circles, both emanating the type of pleasure that one feels after meeting a long lost friend or relative.

Fyros' mouth hung open in disbelief, "I cannot believe what I am seeing. I wonder how it is that Lan is known and accepted so trustingly by the Cloud Horse. In the past I have stood and observed council centaurs come here with important visitors and be refused by the Cloud Horses. I wonder who Lan is to hold such a friendship. It has been so long since any human has been seen riding a Cloud Horse."

The four had then returned to Eumor. Looks of wonder greeted them when the centaur townsfolk saw Lan riding through the streets on DiamondCrest. Lan looked proud as he sat there, his madness temporarily receded as he rode his mount through the streets. Even Diamond Crest seemed to hold his head up proudly as others looked on. Lan's rediscovered sanity proved but an illusion though. Some of the centaurs tried to approach him and were met by barrages of verbal meanderings and screams, causing them to back off rather swiftly.

Fyros led them back to his home and left them there whilst he went to talk with Cambor. He felt it important that he report the fact that a Cloud Horse has responded to Lan's need. Once informed, Cambor had thought a while on this. Eventually he smiled and merely stated that this reinforced his theory that the fates had thrown the four together for a reason.

Whilst Fyros was at the council chamber making his report, his daughter and Michael returned with the Crystals. Fyros watched as Cambor removed them from Kyrie and placed them in his pocket. He then took one from Michael and hung it around his own neck, leaving Michael wearing the other. He then showed Michael how to use the crystal. He told him to hold the crystal in his hand and, as he did so, to make physical contact with the Runestone Ring. Fyros watched and saw the outline of the bones in Michael's hand as the ring and the crystal glowed brightly in his clenched fist. A fraction of a second later Cambor's crystal echoed the glow and a ray of light emerged from both to form images in mid-air.

The image in front of Michael showed what was being viewed through the eyes of Cambor, whilst the image in front of Cambor reciprocated by showing the surroundings as being viewed by Michael. The council leader had then explained that it was believed that the crystals would work anywhere, even on the other worlds of Earth and Roccore. It was believed that the crystals tapped into the magic of the portal web to transfer the images.

Once these matters were settled Fyros, Kyrie and Michael returned to the others to take rest before the long journey to Fortown.

***

As planned they had set out at sunset. It had been decided that they would travel as lightly as possible, carrying weapons and enough supplies to provide for two days. They would then pick up additional supplies in the town of Ralle.

Ralle sat on the Snake River at the foot of the White Peaks and was one of the few multi-race cities still existing in Portalia. It was home to twenty thousand inhabitants counting amongst it's citizens dwarves, humans, centaurs and wood elves. This route also offered the quickest path across the river, utilising the Ralle bridge, and would mean that they did not have to use the slower ferry crossings that dotted the great river. The previous day Cambor had sent scouts ahead to the town to prepare additional supplies to restock the travellers on their journey as they passed through. However, it would take them a day and a half to reach Ralle, so they would camp that evening on the Plains before pushing on to the bridge and the town.

They continued their steady progress throughout the day, pausing occasionally to take on food and water and to allow the colts to rest a little. The smaller colts were using up more energy in keeping up with the steady canter of the centaurs and the larger horses. Surprisingly Lan did not stay close to Rhys during the journey but chose to ride on his own, trotting up and down the line of centaurs, occasionally breaking into a gallop, before circling the group. Lan wore a huge smile and DiamondCrest whinnied in pleasure. The sight of the two, so wrapped in the joy of being together heartened those that looked on and the looks of the centaurs soon changed from those of awe and disbelief to expressions of pleasure and amusement.

Rhys had been nervous about riding but had found it much easier than he had expected. When he had first mounted Farseeker, the colt had sensed his uncertainty and had been careful whilst moving so that Rhys would not fall from his back. As his confidence grew the colt increased his speed of travel. Rhys still felt a little unsteady but could now keep up with their current pace. Another few hours practice and he felt that he would also be able to master a full gallop. He knew that this success was more to do with the way Farseeker carried him than his own skills and he patted his neck gratefully, whispering his gratitude in his ear.

Griff and Fyros led the troop on through the day and into late afternoon. Eventually Griff ordered the troops to stop and break camp for the night. Ashley eagerly grabbed the opportunity to spend some time with Meld. She asked him more questions about Fortown and Portalia and he replied, in like, with questions about Earth.

Meld spoke of a land of beauty and peace, broken only by the occasional disreputable act of a theft or murder. True he had told her stories about coastal pirates and about thief mobs hiding within the woods, but more often he spoke of those that travelled across Portalia and found hospitality and friendship and expressed his desire to travel as much as he could. At first she was shocked by his accounts of robbers and pirates but, on describing her Earth to Meld, realised that her world was generally more violent than the world into which they had been thrust. By the time they broke for camp she had not only developed a good knowledge of the lay of the lands but also formed the basis of a strong bond with Meld.

After hearing Ashley describe life on Earth, Meld for his part, felt that he was happy living in Portalia and had no desire to live in her world, although he also conceded that he may change his mind on this if war broke out once again across Portalia. Later, when she talked to Rhys and Michael about her discussions with the Fortownian, Rhys commented that she was really more interested in Meld than Portalia and that she wasn't fooling them, and probably not fooling Meld either. She reddened in embarrassment and threw verbal abuse at Rhys before storming off. She found herself heading off to find Meld once more, realising that by doing so, she was proving Rhys right. She paused arguing quietly with herself about her attraction to Meld, eventually deciding that he would have no interest in her as she was too young for him so, by that logic alone, decided she was only searching him out to find out more about his world in order to help her, and those infuriating Brits, find a way back home. Armed with the logic of this she proceeded to search him out, brushing her hair back and tidying herself up as she did so.

As she left, Rhys gathered some food and took it over to Lan. The old man would not approach the campfire where the meat roasted on a spittle. Rhys was pleasantly surprised when Lan took the offering from him gently, almost politely and with a slight look of thanks in his eyes. Unfortunately this improvement did not quite stretch to Lan's eating habits. He immediately started to tear at the food and cram it in his mouth, mumbling and drooling as he did so. Rhys looked at him and shook his head. He walked back to sit with Michael and the boys sat quietly enjoying the hot food. It was still early evening and not yet twilight. Stomach finally full, Michael laid back on the grass and let out an enormous fart. The two boys roared with laughter.

"Good one Mike!" commented Rhys.

They continued to act like animals for a while, trying to conjure up farts and burps, each trying to out do the other. Eventually, their stomachs aching with laughter, they settled down.

Michael suddenly felt a little melancholy. "Did you dream again last night Rhys?" he asked.

Rhys looked at him and nodded, "Yes, the same dream as before. It must mean something. Now that we know a little more of Portalia I believe that it may be linked to our journey to Dargoth. How about you, did you dream again?"

Michael shook his head, "No, I slept like a baby. I think I must've got stressed out by my little encounter with the dramkaan," Michael paused as he thought again about the spirit creature which led him back to thoughts of his earlier dream, "You know that bloke that was in our dreams?" he asked.

"Yea, what about him?" replied Rhys.

"Do you think he's real? It just seems too much of a coincidence for both of us to dream up the same person, especially one that is not exactly what you'd call normal."

Rhys shuffled uneasily, "Yes, unfortunately I believe he is very real. I also have a feeling that he is somehow related to everything that's happening. Even when I wake up I can't help shaking the feeling that he still watches me. It gives me the willies!"

The boys fell quiet for a short time until Michael broke the silence again, "You know what Rhys?"

"What?"

"I'm bloody terrified! How about you?"

"Yep, almost scared enough to need new pants." replied Rhys with a grin.

Their conversation was interrupted as Fyros and Griff joined them. Fyros apologised for disturbing them. He asked Michael to contact the council through the crystal. It was time to give them his report.

Michael held the crystal as Cambor had shown him and the artefacts glowed in his hands. Rhys watched in fascination as this was the first time he had seen the Cormion Crystal in use. Fyros and Griff spoke briefly with the council assuring them that all was well. Cambor reminded them of the planned route and they could hear Hesh moaning in the background as usual. The council thanked him and wished them luck and Fyros indicated to Michael that he could close the link. Their report made, Fyros and Griff thanked the boys and left.

"What does that feel like Mike?" asked Rhys.

"Nothing really, just a very faint tingling in my hand. I'm not sure I'd even notice it if I wasn't looking at it. It doesn't hurt or anything and the glow is just energy, it doesn't feel hot or cold, it's just there."

Rhys looked at the gem hanging around Michael's neck, "Could I look at the crystal?"

Michael removed the crystal from around his neck and handed it to Rhys.

As the gem made contact with Rhys' fingers it stared to glow. Michael looked at Rhys in amazement but this quickly changed to concern as he watched energy move quickly up Rhys arms to enter his body through whatever hole it could find. Rhys' eyes rolled back in their sockets and his whole body started to twitch violently. Michael tried to pull the crystal back from him but Rhys had shut his fist tight around the stone, he could not get his fingers to open. Michael screamed for help and was soon surrounded by a number of centaurs including Fyros and Griff.

Rhys was oblivious to all of this. In his mind the portal exits had returned once more, appearing and disappearing faster than ever. His brain was spinning and he could not slow it down. The cycling portal gates were making him dizzy and he felt his mind slipping away. Instinctively he knew that he had to focus his thoughts, to slow down the images and reach towards the portal gates. He was trying desperately to gain some control but he felt giddy and seemed unable to master his thoughts. With extreme effort he gradually managed to increase his sense of the portal gates and they slowed momentarily. This was only a brief success though and soon they started to speed up once more. No matter how hard he tried, his mind could not slow them down and he felt his hold on them slipping again.

Fyros and Griff were trying desperately to prise open Rhys fingers. His fist had been shut unnaturally tight. With a loud crack a bolt of light streamed from Rhys and formed an arc of blue light a few feet away from where they stood. The arc shimmered and, for a moment, appeared to form a portal gateway. It had only been there for a fraction of a second but all had seen it and wondered at what they observed. Regaining their composure they refocused their efforts of removing the crystal from his grasp.

Rhys tried once more to touch the portal exits with his mind but he was tiring. He refused to give in and tried hard to force the wild images into some level of stability, to regain the hold that he had touched earlier. His efforts now started to cause him pain and thankfully he felt blackness sweep over him and, as he fell, the contact was lost.

Michael was holding his friend in his arms, tears in his eyes. The centaurs were still trying to open his fist when all of a sudden Rhys went quiet and fell back unconscious. Michael panicked, wondering if Rhys had died, but relaxed a little when he saw him breathing steadily. Rhys' fist opened and the crystal fell to the floor where it was picked up by Fyros who, in turn, placed it back over Michaels head.

Ashley came over and placed her hand on Rhys forehead, "He's very hot. Rhys, can you hear me?"

Rhys groaned and opened his eyes to see Ashley leaning over him. He groaned, "Oh no, not again and why is it that every time I pass out I have to wake up to your ugly mug looking down at me." Rhys smiled up at her.

"Up yours Brit!" she said with a wide grin on her face and then she hugged him. "Don't tell me, you've got another one of those blinding headaches and you need more feyberry tea. Am I right or am I right?"

"Right again Ash, I must be getting addicted to the stuff or something."

Ashley smiled at him and then her face changed to concern, "Seriously though, are you OK? You had us worried there. That was even worse than when you had that fit in the Runestone chamber."

Rhys nodded but then wished he hadn't, "Yea, I'm fine except for another of those blooming headaches."

A centaur that Rhys did not know stepped forward and passed Rhys a hot mug of feyberry tea. Ashley helped him sit up and Rhys slurped the tea down, eager for its healing properties to ease the pain in his head.

Fyros whispered to Griff who, in turn, ordered his centaur soldiers to go back to their business. The soldiers obeyed without question. Fyros looked concerned, "When you feel recovered a little more we'd like to hear what happened."

Rhys nodded, "OK, just give me a few minutes and I'm sure I'll be OK."

Rhys sat quietly as the feyberry tea worked its magic. He felt the familiar light headed feeling again although less so than previously. Karia had been right the after effects of the tea were lessening..

Michael leaned close and whispered to him, "There was a portal gate open right here. Only for a fraction of a second, but it was here. It was created when a surge of energy leapt from you into the air, it looked like you created it."

Rhys tried to concentrate on what Michael was telling him but his head still swam and ached. *A portal gate, Mike said I created a portal gate!*

Eventually the pain subsided as the feyberry worked it's magic. He waited for the light headed feeling to pass and then recounted to all what he had sensed when he had taken the crystal from Michael. Fyros frowned, "Rhys, you must think. It appeared to us that when you were linked to the crystal you opened a portal gate. Do you remember how this happened? Were you aware that you were opening a portal?"

Rhys thought hard. He could not link the confusion that took place in his mind to the events that occurred in the real world. If he had opened a portal then he had no idea how he had done so. He shook his head, "I'm sorry Fyros, I have no idea what happened. If a portal was opened then I had no control over it and had no idea that I was doing it. At the end there, before I passed out, I felt that my brain was going to get fried so I don't think I'll be touching the crystal again in a hurry either."

Fyros had Michael open a communication portal to Cambor. He had left the council chambers and was at his home, he walked to a mirror so that Fyros could see him eye to eye as they talked. Fyros recapped what had happened. Rhys filled in some of the detail.

Cambor thought a while but could offer no explanation, "I will speak with the council again in the morning. It maybe that Horos has some idea of what is happening to our young friend. In the meantime I would urge that you keep away from any magical artefacts, especially the Cormion Crystal."

Rhys' hand went instinctively to his pendant, "What about my Runestone pendant, can I keep that?"

Cambor nodded, "Has contact with the pendant triggered any such reaction in the past?"

Rhys hesitated before answering, his thoughts went to his strange dreams. Were these being caused by his close proximity to the pendant?

He quickly weighed up the risk of telling of these dreams and feared that Cambor would ask him to give up the Runestone pendant, something that he was not willing to do. He looked at Cambor's reflection and replied that the pendant had not caused him any problems as yet. The old centaur looked back at Rhys. He had a look in his eye that suggested that he knew that there was more to tell. He did not press this however and bade Rhys be careful and to get some rest.

The rest of the evening was largely uneventful. Later in the evening a hyrax, a large pig like creature the size of a small horse with a coarse hairy hide and vicious tusks, wandered close to the camp late, but it was more curious than threatening. The camp fires kept it at bay and the creature soon got bored and moved on, letting out a derisory grunt as it left. Michael watched it and smile, it had sounded just like Hesh.

The camp then settled for the night, sleeping under the watchful eyes of the centaur sentries.

CHAPTER TWELVE
Ohrhim

Gorlan sat himself down on his blankets, it had been a frustrating day. They had risen that morning and he had accompanied Molt to his family home. As he suspected the house was empty and there were no signs of where the family had gone. It was obvious that things had happened too quickly to allow the luxury of writing messages for absent friends and relatives. Molt's mood darkened as he searched the house from top to bottom. Finally, after Gorlan called a halt to the search, Molt reluctantly agreed that the house held no clues.

They had also searched a number of buildings around the town and found the same signs of a hurried exit. Wherever they found corpses they took the time to bury them, some in a second mass grave in the cemetery and others in smaller graves on the property where they had been found. They continued to leave the skeletons strewn about the town but took time to move them into communal piles whenever they passed.

Whilst they did not find this work physically difficult, it was a harrowing task that left them stressed and drained. They detected more corpses from survey from the air. By the middle of the afternoon they had removed all of the decaying bodies from the town and had filled in the second grave.

This grisly task complete, Gorlan turned his attention to the tunnels. After Molt had returned from his fruitless search of his home, Gorlan had ordered him to the library once more to look for more information about the maze beneath their feet. He felt that there was probably not a lot to be gained by this but he saw that the boy was hurting and did not want him to be involved in the task of burying his townsfolk. His belief had proved accurate, apart from a few more pieces of map that added no new information to the scroll they had discovered earlier, Molt's efforts failed to turn up anything that would be of use.

The Pinns had then ate refreshments before entering the tunnels.

Gorlan ordered Stern to remain behind and tend to his brother. The WarLord had decided to keep his men together in case they met any resistance but, other than the footprints of many people that had recently travelled through the tunnels, they did not come across anyone, friend or foe. It was heartening to discover no corpses or skeletons though, as this suggested that those making their escape had not been pursued. This raised their spirits and lightened the darkness that had dogged Molt all day. He even joined in a well known folk song with Kraven and the others as they picked their way back through the tunnels. The sounds of the eight men reverberated along the rock walls and filled the gloom with song. By the time they returned to the sanctuary of the hall Molt was smiling again.

As Gorlan laid back to grab some sleep he hoped that Lloyd and Pinnel were making all haste back to Pinnhome and that reinforcements would soon arrive.

***

The centaur platoon awoke to grey skies and a threat of rain in the air. Ashley observed that Rhys seemed brighter than usual and he went about preparing for the journey with a spring in his step. She asked him if he was alright and he told her he'd never felt better, in fact he had slept all night without being disturbed by his dreams.

They set off in their usual formation, heading due south to the Snake River bridge and the town of Ralle. There was a heavy, stormy look to the clouds above the White Peaks and Rhys watched them with some trepidation. The clouds above the group were thickening the further they travelled south. By mid morning the wind had blown up into a gale and the skies began to empty their load of water. The rain was falling almost parallel to the ground. Carried along by the southerly wind it was being blown directly towards them, stinging their faces as it hammered against exposed skin. All general talk had stopped as it was difficult to be heard, their voices being carried away by the storm. Fortunately the southerly winds always blew warm, heated by their passage across the Blistering Desert. Rhys stuck out his tongue to let the rain fall in his mouth. In surprise he realised that the rain was warm and tasted sweet. He likened it to drinking a very weak cup of black tea. Even so, the light hearted mood that Rhys had enjoyed earlier was now fading as he struggled to push Farseeker on through the driving torrent. One of the centaur soldiers had noticed Rhys dilemma and shouted to him to let Farseeker go at his own pace and not to try to drive him on. He relaxed his grip and found that the centaur was right, Farseeker progressed much more effectively by Rhys simply doing nothing other than just sitting there. Feeling better he raised his head to taste the rain once more.

Michael looked across at him and looked quizzically at Rhys who was now sitting on his horse with his head back and mouth wide open. Rhys glanced back and smiled. He made a gesture for Michael to try it. This in turn piqued Ashley's interest and soon all three were sat with heads back, gargling the tea-rain and laughing at how ridiculous they must look.

They continued through the storm, trudging southwards until, at last, they came to the Snake River. Here they turned eastward towards the bridge crossing. They followed the banks of the river and after a few miles they reached an elevation, the land rising up a slow incline. As they climbed the hill the landscape became rockier. Michael estimated that they had climbed to around one thousand feet above the plains when they eventually arrived at the bridge.

The crossing itself was nothing more than a very large rope suspension bridge. Rhys, who had expected the crossing to be made of stone and was used to the solid bridges of Britain, looked at the rope and wood bridge with some concern. Fortunately the direction of the wind was directly over the bridge, rather than against it, but even so it was swinging from side to side, moving a yard or so in each direction. If the wind had been blowing from the east or west then he was sure that it would have been impossible to cross.

From their earlier discussion with the centaurs, Rhys knew that the town of Ralle lay on the other side of the bridge. He peered across the river ravine but could not make out the other side, his vision obscured by the heavy rainfall.

Fyros approached the teenagers, "Griff is going to split his men into groups of ten to twelve for the crossing. The bridge will hold our weight easily but he wisely wants us to cross in groups due to the storm. When you are on the bridge the movement feels a lot worse than it looks from here. It will be easy to lose your balance so proceed cautiously. You will need to dismount and lead your horses. You'll cross with me and six of Griff's platoon. We'll be the third group to cross, that way we'll have assistance on either side should we require it."

They dismounted and waited for their turn to cross. The first band of centaurs started over the bridge. They watched as the band slowly picked their way across. As the group approached the centre, the swing of the bridge seemed to amplify and the whole group had to pause their progress to keep their balance. Rhys noticed that to the sides of the bridge span, rope had been threaded to form a net. This would easily catch a human if they fell, preventing them slipping off the bridge, but he felt that a centaur could easily fall over the top of this safety netting. This observation offered more reassurance for the crossing for himself and the other humans but increased his anxiety for the centaurs.

The first group had to pause their progress for some time at the centre of the bridge, waiting for the oscillation to subside so that they could continue. Eventually they started to make progress once more. A few meters beyond the halfway mark the spectators lost sight of the group as they disappeared into a haze of rain water.

Griff watched the vibration of the ropes on the bridges as an indication of the first group's progress. When the movement reduced he ordered the second group to make their way across and called the teenagers forward to the bridge entrance.

The passage of the second group was similar to that of the first. It would appear that the movement seemed at it's worst towards the centre, this group also had to pause at this point to keep their balance before continuing. Kyrie accompanied this second group and Fyros sighed in relief as the tell tale signs of the bridge movement suggested that they had made it safely across to the other side.

Rhys looked at Ashley and she had gone white. He remembered that she suffered from acrophobia, a fear of heights, "Don't worry Ash," he shouted through the storm, "You'll be fine. You go between Michael and myself, we'll keep you in the middle. Don't look down, just keep looking ahead directly across the bridge."

Ashley tried to smile but it looked false and she had not regained any of her colour as she replied, "Thanks guys. Take it slowly out there though will yer?"

Meld had overheard what was being said and shouted that he would take both his horse and Quickhoof for Ashley. "That way you will have both hands free to hold on," suggested Meld.

Their turn came, three centaurs led, followed by Rhys and Michael, leading their horses, Ashley sandwiched between the two boys. They were followed by Lan and DiamondCrest who walked side by side. Behind Lan came Fyros and Meld leading the two horses and finally three more centaur soldiers brought up the rear.

The bridge seemed fairly steady when they first set out but, as they made advanced, the movement began to increase. Ashley kept her gaze straight ahead as she had been told and she linked arms with both Rhys and Michael. They were making steady progress and were approaching the middle of the bridge.

Suddenly the wind seemed to shift direction and started to blow more towards the north east. The increased force that was brought on the bridge caused the walkway to swing even more severely. The group felt their balance give way and were pushed violently to the left side. With their combined weight on this side of the bridge, coupled with the force of the wind, the bridge began to tilt dangerously.

One of the front three centaurs lost his balance and fell. His feet slid towards the edge and caught in the net, but the safety device was not high enough for the centaur and he toppled over the edge, his expression contorted with fear as he looked death in the face. His comrades both moved quickly and, as he began to fall, he felt four hands grab his arms and he was held, his hoofs dangling in mid air.

Ashley had been thrown heavily against Rhys and they both fell to the floor. The netting held their weight easily but even so Ashley was screaming in terror and shaking.

Thankfully, just as suddenly as it had turned to the north east, the wind returned to it's original direction and the rest of the group were able to regain their balance.

The leading centaurs pulled their comrade to safety and he thanked them, a look of relief clear for all to see.

Ashley had stopped screaming but she cowered on the floor, Rhys tried to get her to stand but she refused. The whole group remained at the centre of the bridge whilst both Rhys and Michael tried to calm Ashley and get her back to her feet.

Griff was shouting something to them from the bank but they could not hear above the howling wind. Fyros urged them to continue, fearing that the wind would change direction again, but no matter how hard they tried, they could not persuade Ashley to continue.

Meld stepped forward towards them and looked at Ashley, her head and gaze was directly at her feet so she did not return his look. He winked at Rhys and shouted, "Ashley, for goodness sake get up. If you don't then I'm going to start to swing this bridge even more." The others stared in disbelief as Meld started to jump up and down. In reality his weight was making very little difference but Ashley still looked up at him with utter terror on her face. Meld continued, "Come on little girl, get up, you're not a baby anymore you know. No one is going to carry you over," he sneered.

The centaurs looked dismayed at Meld and Fyros was about to interject, however Rhys, who understood what Meld was doing, stopped him. Ashley glared at Meld and her temper began to rise, she got herself to her feet and shouted insults at him. Having completely lost her self control completely she even told him that she no longer fancied him and wondered what she had seen in him in the first place. Meld hastily retreated, his job done, he was pleased that she had found him attractive but now he privately wondered if she would ever forgive him. He liked Ashley a great deal but could think of no other way to get her to continue, he hoped that this had not damaged their friendship.

The group continued their way over the bridge, Ashley once again linking arms with the boys but this time she also clung tightly along their forearms, She was still terrified but she was not going to show that to Meld.

Eventually they made it across and saw that they were on a rocky bank of the Snake River. A short distance to the south they could see Ralle and beyond the mountains. They could not see the legendary White Peaks though as they were lost in the cloud. This side of the bridge also offered more protection from the wind and rain, a fact that pleased them all.

Ralle itself was surrounded on three sides by wooden battlements, much like the forts of the old west in the United States. No such protection was needed to the rear of the town as it backed up against the solid rock of the mountains. From this direction there was only one way into the town. A rocky road twisted out of Ralle and up through the mountains. A large wooden gateway served as the entrance to the town from both the north and south. Rhys thought it strange that the buildings inside the town were built from stone but the protective walls manufactured from wood. Later he discovered that Ralle was a relatively new town by Portalia standards and that many of the mixed race citizens did not even feel it necessary to have a protective wall. The wooden barrier only existed as a suggestion of fortification. This served it's purpose as it appeased both those that wanted some form of defence and also those who felt it unnecessary. It also allowed quick, easy and cheap modification to accommodate growth of the town which had been extensive in recent generations.

The remaining centaurs crossed the bridge without any further problems. Rhys admired the camaraderie that was exhibited as many of the centaurs stopped to hug their comrade who had been saved from death. Griff led them to a natural alcove in the rock where they were completely protected from the wind. He ordered that they all remain here whilst he went to Ralle to collect the supplies that should await them there. Rhys and Ashley expressed their disappointment and begged to go with the centaurs as both had wanted to see the town, but Fyros had refused. Their frustration became even greater when they found out that Meld was to accompany Griff. Fyros calmed this frustration though when he pointed out that later they would have to travel through the town to reach the road through the hills. He explained that at this point they wanted to minimise contact with the townsfolk as a precaution. The tongues would already be wagging at the sight of a small centaur army camped outside it's gates. They did not want to fuel rumour further by having the citizens of Ralle discover that there were those amongst them that were not of Portalia. The teenagers recognised the wisdom of this and settled themselves down to await the return of Griff and Meld.

The rain had eased a little and the sun was trying to break through the cloud. Every few minutes though the storm would revive and throw down torrents of rainfall in short sharp bursts.

The centaurs lashed together some canvas to form a quick and temporary shelter and took the opportunity to prepare a warm meal. Griff and Meld set out for the town. Much to the surprise of all, Lan galloped after them on DiamondCrest. When Griff saw the old man following he pulled up and commanded that he return to the camp. Lan just stared at him and refused to move, every time the pair made towards the town he would continue to follow. Three times Griff stopped and repeated his order, eventually Meld placed a hand on Griff's arm and said, "I don't think he will do any harm, let him follow. This is the first time that he has left Rhys since he arrived at Eumor. The way the fates have been working lately there may even be a reason for him to accompany us. If not, then at least it will give Rhys a break from always having Lan around." Griff agreed reluctantly and the three set off again..

As they approached the main gate of Ralle, two young male centaurs galloped out to meet them. They raised their arms in salute and confirmed to Griff that they had purchased the additional supplies. The goods were now being stored at a local inn, The Traveller's Tavern. This was a friendly inn and was renowned for providing excellent facilities to cater to the whims of the various species visiting the town. They had slept here the previous night and had been undisturbed, the locals used to strangers. A few had started to ask questions when they had purchased the large quantities of supplies. These were quickly appeased though when the young centaurs had explained that the supplies were for a centaur platoon that would be passing through the town on a training mission. Griff told them they had done well and added that they should tell the townsfolk that they were headed for the Blistering Desert for this mission. He also told the two young centaurs to remain behind for a couple of days to ensure that this story spread. If anyone asked about the humans amongst their ranks then they should be told that the platoon were accompanying a trade envoy back to Fortown.

This story agreed they made their way to the inn.

***

Calem Ford was a stout jovial man, ideally suited for his role as landlord of the Travellers Tavern. He heartily welcomed the centaurs and Meld although he looked suspiciously at Lan who failed to respond when addressed and had taken to humming a tune to himself. They shared some ale and some general chit chat with the landlord. Eventually Calem led them through to a store room at the rear of the inn. This room faced onto a delivery yard, where traders delivered their wares to the establishment. The young centaurs had arranged to hire transportation for the day and they immediately began to load the supplies onto a flat top cart that had been parked in the centre of the yard. Griff thanked the landlord for his hospitality and asked how much was owed for the additional storage. Calem laughed and slapped Griff on the shoulder, "No charge my friend, I'm happy to help out. Your colleagues have been more than generous with their tips during their visit and have been quick to settle their debts. All I ask is that you come and enjoy the hospitality of my tavern each time you visit our town."

"That I shall do. Thank you again," replied Griff.

Calem returned to his customers leaving the centaurs and Meld to complete the loading of the supplies. The sun had now broken through the cloud and even the wind had dropped off a little, the storm being carried north towards Eumor City and beyond to the Pinnacle Mountains.

Lan stood by and watched the group load the wagon. He

was still humming to himself and every so often burst into song as he remembered words, more often than not startling the others each time he did so. Occasionally Lan would stop singing and glance back towards the shadows at the rear of the delivery yard as if distracted by something. Meld eventually noticed this, "What is he doing?" he asked Griff gesturing towards Lan. Griff turned to look and followed the gaze of the old man. He looked into the shadows where Lan stared but saw nothing.

"Who knows," he replied. "He's probably just trying to remember more words to that infernal song he's been humming all day." Meld nodded in agreement and went back to loading the wagon.

***

In the shadows Ohrhim decided to chance a move closer so that it could hear their talk more clearly. It was nervous to do so at first as the old one that accompanied the centaurs seemed to sense it's presence. However, when it realised that no alarm was sounded by the old man, it's confidence grew and it took a few steps closer. As it did so it's flattened body began to change. It examined the contours and lines of the stonework and mimicked them precisely, effectively disappearing into the background. Some of the supplies that were destined for the centaur platoon stood only a few feet from it, but the young centaurs did not sense it's presence as they collected these and returned them to the wagon.

It listened to the group for sometime before it decided that it could learn nothing more. It now knew that the centaur platoon was camped outside the town and felt it would learn more there. Clearly this Griff was the leader but was not going to share any of their mission with the young centaurs. Ohrhim crept slowly back out of the yard and into the alley, all the time hugging the wall, it's perfect camouflage preventing detection. When it was out of sight, it checked that the alley was clear and allowed it's body to melt as it changed it's shape and colour once more.

As usual Ohrhim returned to it's natural form, a smooth blob like creature of translucent grey with no visible features. A Runestone pendant was visible, loosely suspended in it's flesh, before it disappeared into the shapechanger as it allowed it's flesh to flow into the form of a large crow. It's molecules, perfectly replicating the feathers of the real bird, now provided it with the power of flight. It knew that to the eye it would be indiscernible from any other crow. Only to the touch would one be able to tell that it was a Shapechanger, for despite the perfect replication of any creature or object, ShapeChangers never lost the tacky feel to their exterior epidermis. The crow leapt into the air and climbed high above the town, it's keen eye soon found the location of the centaur platoon camped out in the protection of the rocky alcove. With a flap of it's wings and a change of direction, Ohrhim soon covered the short distance to the platoon. It landed on top of the canvas shelter. As it did so four crows, that had already perched themselves there waiting for scraps, leapt up in panic and took to the air screeching in fright.

Rhys turned towards the fleeing crows and watched them disappear as they flew towards the town. It was a common site though, both here and on Earth, so he thought nothing more of the incident. He turned his attention back to Ashley who was still chatting to him about her love of football and recapping some of the games that she had recently played. Rhys loved football too but he was only an average player and was a little jealous of the stories that Ashley told. She was still calling it soccer too which irritated him immensely. He had tried to get her to refer to the sport as football and, for a while, she had managed this, but now she was back to using the soccer word again. Eventually it seemed that Ashley had finished. Rhys ran his finger absentmindedly along the ground making a trail in the dirt as he did so. The sun was now out again and the dirt was swiftly drying in it's rays of heat. Rhys drew an octagon in the dirt, "Ash, " he said, "I'm really sorry that we got you into this. If we hadn't used the ring and the pendant then you'd never have been brought here."

Ashley looked back at the younger boy, "It's not your fault silly. You weren't to know. If it had been me that found the stuff then I'd have probably done the same thing."

Rhys was grateful that she felt that way, "Do you think we'll really get back home?" he asked her.

"Yea, I'm sure of it. We'll get to Fortown and then we'll find out where this dwarf dude is. If he won't help us then we'll get the centaurs to sort him out and Fyros will get us back home. You watch, I bet I won't even have to miss a soccer game."

Rhys laughed, "You mean football!"

"Yea, that's right, football! Geez you Brits are so fussy!" Ashley retorted, smiling at him as she did so.

The crow watched the pair as they teased each other. It's beady eye glinted.

Rhys continued his conversation with Ashley, "From what we have heard from Meld about these black eagles it may be a little tough to force this dwarf to give us access to the Runestone, even with the help of the centaurs. I don't even pretend to be as clever as Cambor, or Horos, but even I can see that there must be some connection to all this."

Michael joined them clutching a tray. On the tray were

three large plates of boiled stew, each with a hunk of bread. "Here you go, fresh from the Olde Centaur Kitchen." He passed them both a plate and spoon, smiling as he did so. He looked at Rhys, "You're right about those eagles, they sound scary. Mind you, Meld also told us that there had been other messengers sent out so we may find that there are more than just centaurs heading towards Fortown. And anyway, we're the good guys so we're bound to win. Haven't you seen the movies?"

The crow continued to stare at the teenagers. Ashley saw it and threw it a piece of bread. The crow watched the bread fall on the ground but ignored it. Ashley shrugged and figured that the bird was too scared to come any nearer.

"Well we'll be there in a few days and then Mike can contact the council with his crystal and they'll tell us what we need to do next. I for one think that Cambor knows what he is doing. He'll not only get us home but I'm sure he'll be able to stop this evil that they believe is rising up in Dargoth," she spoke with a look of certainty on her face.

The crow squawked in delight, it had heard what it needed to know for now. It leapt into the air and headed towards Dargoth. When it was safely over the mountains it landed and transformed into a grey dragon, it's massive wings beating the sky. In this form it would be back with the warlock within hours.

***

It was late afternoon when Griff, Meld and Lan returned with the supplies. They approached the camp to a curious sight. Four large poles had been stuck in the ground, two at either end of a large rectangle which had been drawn in the dirt. Between these two poles stood Ashley at one end and Rhys at the other. A ball had been made from some leaves and leather wrapping and twelve centaurs were chasing it, kicking around the rectangle. Six centaurs wore shirts, whilst the other six were bare-chested. One of the centaurs broke away from the others and bore down on Rhys, at the last moment he flicked the ball from his rear hoofs to his front and kicked the ball. Rhys made a dive for it but was unable to reach the ball as it sped between the two poles. Ashley and the six bare-chested centaurs raised their arms in celebration. "Goal!" shouted Ashley, "That's three to two to us."

When the centaurs saw their leader approaching they called the game to a halt, some reddened a little at being caught playing the game. Griff pulled up by the side of the rectangle, "What is going on?" he bellowed.

"It's soccer," replied Ashley.

"Football actually," corrected Rhys.

"Either will do," said Michael who was sitting with another six centaurs, two of whom were Fyros and Kyrie. All were still sweating a little and had clearly been playing the game too.

Ashley explained, "It's a game that we all play back home. It's very popular."

Griff frowned, "So let me get this straight. Whilst we were working hard in the town, all you could do was play games and teach my men how to play this football, soccer thing? Do you know what makes me so angry about that?"

Ashley looked a little coy, "No, what?" she replied quietly.

"Simply that I wasn't here to join in the fun." He smiled at Ashley and the other centaurs laughed. "If we had a little more time I'd insist you teach me the rules immediately but I think it would be wiser for us to start to head out once more. When we have more time I insist that you teach me too though, it looks fun."

"You've got it!" replied Ashley beaming.

The make shift camp was soon packed away and the platoon formed once more. The wind and rain had now blown away, far to the north and the day had returned to one of summer's heat, although a little fresher than the previous day, the air cleared by the passing of the storm. The townsfolk of Ralle must have set up watchers on the town walls for, as they entered the town, the centaurs were met by throngs of townsfolk lining the streets. All were cheering and waving the platoon on their journey south.

Ashley, Michael and Rhys were astonished and stared as they rode through the town. They were now used to the sight of centaurs mixing with the humans but this was the first time they had seen dwarves and elves. The creatures were just as they imagined. The dwarves were short and stocky little people with solid build. The males wore large beards and moustaches and were dressed in heavy leathers. The females exhibited the same tough features as the males and were far from pretty, their faces were a picture of health though and most possessed chubby pink cheeks. Some even had the suggestion of small moustaches of which they were very proud and which the male dwarves found particularly attractive.

By contrast the elves were a handsome race. They had long thin faces, ears pointed at the ends. The males were all clean shaven and had similar blonde hair cropped at shoulder length. They only saw four elven females but all were exceptionally beautiful, with long flowing blonde hair, high cheek bones and soft fair skin. All of the elves, male and female, wore soft cloth dyed in various shades of green and red. The teenagers noticed that only a few of the watching crowd carried weapons. Some of these wore a brown uniform and were clearly a town guard or police force of some kind. Others carrying weapons were few and were intermingled with the crowd. They guessed these to be out-of-town travellers passing through Ralle like themselves.

One of the centaurs moved closer to the teenagers and wisely suggested that they try not to look as if this was all new to them and to stare a little less. They recognised the sense in this council and hid their astonishment by smiling and waving at the crowd. Ashley whispered to Rhys and Michael, "It's like a Disneyworld procession in reverse. The dwarves and elves are stood watching the procession instead of taking part in it."

It only took a few minutes to move through the town and they were soon exiting by the southern gateway, riding up into the White Peak mountains. Almost immediately they arrived at a junction on the trail. A signpost marked the way, right to Drenda, mountain city of the dwarves, backwards to Ralle and left to the Portalia Meadows and Fortown. The group veered to the left and Griff ordered them to pick up speed, eager to make it out of the mountains and onto the open meadows before evening.

They continued along the trail continuing to climb for a few miles before coming out onto a flat hilltop. To the southeast they could now see that the mountains gave way to a few hills and then to the rolling Portalia Meadows. Griff slowed the pace a little to allow the platoon to conserve energy. They would make it to the meadows well before sunset and would have ample time to form a camp for the night. He smiled at Fyros and Kyrie. So far everything was going to plan.

***

Pinnel and Lloyd looked across at one hundred fire eagles brought to combat readiness by Toran, Overlord of Pinnhome. When called upon, the fire eagles, clearly sensing the needs of their bonded riders, offered themselves willingly. None rejected the call, even when the Overlord made the unusual order that each rider would carry a fellow Pinn soldier to Fortown. This would slow the squadron of birds down a little but would deliver over two hundred troops to reinforce the town within two days.

One thousand mounted cavalry had already set out for Fortown and should reach there within four days. A further five thousand troops were being readied and would follow by foot. They would be dispatched within the day and would follow, this time skirting around the Halfman Forest to avoid the halfman horde.

Pinnel had been given the honour of leading the fire eagle riders back to Fortown.

The Overlord gave the order and the eagles took to the air. They soared upward, a truly awesome sight, as they made towards Fortown, eager to reinforce their comrades at the town.

***

High in the mountains overlooking Pinnhome a hooded figure tied a message to the leg of a pigeon. The figure released the bird and it immediately flew south west, straight towards it's breeding home at Shangorth Towers. It was as the warlock had foretold. The massed armies of Portalia would now awaken and be defeated at Fortown. The warlocks would rule the world again and he would be given the city as reward for his loyalty.

The dark figure grinned. He would have his revenge over OverLord Toran, the one who had banished him, Nexus, from the lands of Pinn for all time. That banishment was his punishment for merely studying the writings of the dark arts. With it he had lost the ability to access the scrolls and volumes that he had needed to learn the skills of a warlock. Soon there would be plenty of time to revisit those publications once the warlocks ruled once more. He would then be able to take his place alongside them as an equal, part of a new ruling Council of Warlocks that would oversee Portalia for the rest of time.

He played with the pendant that hung around his neck, a token given to him by Shangorth himself. His finger followed the line of the mountains embossed on the surface of the pendant. *Soon*, he thought, *soon I will have what I desire and Toran will be made to grovel at my feet.*

CHAPTER THIRTEEN
ReUnion

Gorlan stood on the roof of the office buildings that adjoined the town hall. The rain had all but stopped and the sun caused him to squint, it's rays brightening the green hillside for the first time that day. He was looking in a northerly direction , across the hills and towards the White Peaks. His attention had been drawn there by Tor who, during his watch had reported that he had seen some movement in the hills.

"Maybe it was a group of animals, a family of hyrax or a group of deer," suggested Gorlan as he failed to see anything of interest.

"That's possible I suppose, although it looked like these animals were bipedal," replied Tor. "Mind you, that said, I did see the movement through the rain so it could have been the light and the rain drops playing tricks on me. Anyway, all seems quiet up there now. I am sorry Warlord."

"No need to apologise Tor, it is good that you are alert. Return to your vigil and let me know immediately if you see anything unusual."

"Shall I stand down the others?" asked Tor, looking over at the other Pinn warriors who now lined the roofs about the town square.

"No, I'll do that, but I am going to double the watch for a short while. I think it may be wise to check out the hills from the air too. I'll ask Kraven and Flare to go on a little sortie to investigate. You say that the movement was close to the hill with the humped peak?"

"That's correct Warlord, it looked like something was moving through the hills along the ridge line."

"Very well," the WarLord made his way down from the building calling to Tosh, Kraven and Flare as he did so. The three warriors rushed to his side, "Tosh, can you talk to the others and double up the watch for the next four hours. Put one man on the roof and have him pay particular attention to the north and northwest. Carl should now be fit enough to take a short shift or two also. He has not yet regained his full strength though so be cautious and check on him regularly." Tosh raised his hand in salute and rushed off to carry out the order. Gorlan now addressed Kraven and Flare, two fire eagles swooped down as he did so. "I want you to check out the hills to the north for any signs of life. Be very careful, we know the enemy walks in these hills. Use altitude to your advantage and report back here what you see."

Kraven and Flare jumped to their mounts and took to the air. The more experienced Kraven shouted instructions to his comrade and, as one, their war birds climbed steeply and they headed northward. The wind was at their backs and had increased as they climbed. Hurried along by the air flow they were fast approaching the hills where the movement had been seen.

Kraven stared down into the valleys and gulleys. The grass below was a vivid healthy green, refreshed by the morning rains. They flew in blue skies, the sun beating down on their backs and onto the hills, causing tiny flashes as it reflected off the rain drops clinging to the blades of grass. Grey rocks and boulders, already dried by the sun, lay exposed amongst the greenery. Occasionally a wild animal could be seen, scampering away from the shadows of the warbirds as the warriors surveyed them from above.

They were now directly over the unusual shaped hill top. Kraven scanned the area, he signalled for Flare to remain at altitude and then dropped his own bird to a lower flight path to get a closer look. At the base of the peak the land looked to have been folded by nature. Approaching from the southeast all that could be seen was the usual green face of the hills, however, passing over this fold and looking back, the landscape looked entirely different. A narrow deep gulley, overhung by grass covered rock ran to the southwest for a good ten miles or so. The gulley would make a superb natural cover for anyone trying to hide. Kraven signalled for Flare to join him. "We need to check out this gully as best we can. I think we should risk going a little lower or we'll never see in there. I'll drop down as low as I dare, you stay above and keep watch for any movement."

Flare nodded his understanding and the two riders turned their great birds towards the earth. They continued to follow the gulley, eyes actively searching for any signs of life. They flew the entire length before turning and heading back for another pass.

Kraven's nerves were on edge. His eyes told him that the gulley was empty but his senses screamed at him that they were being watched. They made a third pass down the length of the gulley before Kraven increased his altitude to rejoin Flare. The younger warrior spoke, "It looks like it's empty. Shall we head back?"

Kraven shook his head, "Not yet. I have a nagging feeling that this gulley hides something. I want you to stay up here and keep circling me, I'm going to land and take a closer look."

Flare raised his eyebrows in surprise, "Is that wise Kraven, remember what the Warlord said."

Kraven nodded, "Yes, I remember but I also remember him asking us to check for any signs of life. Don't worry I'll be careful. If anything happens to me, do not follow. Fly back to the town and get help."

Flare reluctantly agreed as Kraven directed his bird towards the gulley. The fire eagle fell like a stone before adjusting it's flight to glide into a smooth and silent landing. Kraven dismounted and walked to the edge of the gulley. From this northerly aspect, it dropped away sharply and offered a difficult route to the gulley bottom, forty feet below.

Kraven gazed across the gulley where the overhang formed a dark shadow. Every so often he could make out even darker patches in the shade of the overhang. He assumed that these were damp moss patches caused by the lack of sunlight in this shaded aspect. He walked the rim of the gulley for a short distance, checking that Flare was still watching him from overhead. Eventually he decided that the only way down was via the steep descent in front of him. He signalled to Flare and eased himself over the edge, half scrabbling, half falling down the steep slope. He made it to the bottom with less trouble than he had imagined but his spirits were dampened a little when he looked back up the slope and saw how difficult the climb back out would be.

Kraven wondered whether his warbird could be called to lift him out. He assessed the width of the gulley and felt that it would be a close call. The wingspan of the bird would fill the entire width, from bank to slope. He was not sure that it would have sufficient space to stretch it's wings for take off. He therefore decided that when it became time to climb out, he would first try the steep bank and then, if unsuccessful, would call for Flare's assistance.

On the thought of his colleague, he looked up to check that the warrior was still watching from above. Kraven waved that all was well and signalled that he was going to investigate further as he disappeared from view under the overhang.

Here Kraven found that a crude path had been formed. It ran the length of the gulley, hidden from view by the natural protection above. He walked along the path. He had only gone a short distance when he came to one of the dark mossy patches that he had seen from the other side. He looked at the dark green patch, he had indeed presumed correctly that it was moss, however, as he stared at it something struck him as unusual. The moss seemed very symmetrical. It was straight at the edges and curved into semi circles at the top and bottom. He ran his finger through it and realised that the moss grew on wood of some form. He smiled, his brain registering that he was looking at a door. He placed his hands on the moss and gave it a push. The panel swung inwards on hidden hinges, revealing a small tunnel leading into the hillside.

Kraven stepped forward through the door. Almost immediately it slammed shut behind him as he came face to face with a circle of swords and axe-heads preventing his advance or retreat. Twelve pairs of eyes looked at him through the gloom and he was forced to the ground by the waving of the weapons.

Outside, on the hillside, Kraven's fire eagle became very agitated and began pacing about and beating the air with it's wings. Flare saw the reaction of the war bird and shouted to his colleague. He dared to drop lower but could see no sign of him. He checked Kraven's fire eagle and was relieved to find that it remained where it had landed, indicating that his colleague was still alive. He continued to wait, circling overhead, but eventually deciding that something must have befallen Kraven. Following his earlier order, he turned his own fire eagle back towards Fortown.

***

Gorlan was fuming, "I told you both to be especially cautious! Did I not?"

The young Pinn warrior nodded, "You did Warlord, but Kraven was adamant that something was hiding in the gulley. He felt it important that he find out what. I believe he felt that it could be a threat to us."

"THEN HE SHOULD HAVE RETURNED HERE FOR MORE HELP!" bawled the Warlord, "He should not have taken the risk on his own. At least he had the sense to leave you out of it though!"

Flare looked down, "I realise I should have stopped him sir, but you know how adamant he is. I wish now I had accompanied him into the gulley."

Gorlan saw that Flare was struggling with guilt at having left Kraven. He softened a little, "Do not blame yourself for that. If you had done so things would be even worse. We may have lost both of you. Also, I know Kraven well and he is renowned for his stubbornness. Though this time he has added foolishness to it."

Flare looked at down at his feet, "So do we go after him?"

Gorlan glared at him, "Of course we do, I will not leave him alone. However, this time we will go prepared and as a group. It means we will have to leave the town unprotected but that is just the way it is. Carl and Molt will remain here, the rest of us will fly to where Kraven disappeared. If his warbird remains waiting for him then we will know that he is still alive and in need of our aid." The Warlord frowned, "If however the bird has flown......" Gorlan did not need to finish this sentence.

The Warlord turned to leave, shouting orders as he did so, "Gather some ropes, we'll need them to get into the gulley. I will fly with Tosh again, stay close to us and let us lead the way."

Eight Pinn warriors stormed out of the town hall and mounted their fire eagles. As they climbed away from the town Tosh pointed to the northwest. "Look!"

All eight looked in the direction that was indicated. A lone fire eagle and rider were heading towards them.

"It seems that he does not need our help after all," quipped Flare.

The riders adjusted their flight path to intercept. "It seems also that he has some company. Look on the hillside."

Gorlan turned his attention to the hills and saw that Kraven was being followed on foot by a mass of creatures. They were too far away to make out any detail but the masses were following Kraven straight towards the town.

Tosh spoke quietly to his Warlord, "By all that's sacred, he's leading them back here. What does he think he's doing? He must know that we cannot hope to protect the city against so many."

Gorlan frowned, something did not make sense.

In front of him, Tosh asked for orders. Gorlan responded, "Let's fly with all speed to join him. Kraven has an old head on his shoulders and may have a plan."

The eight fire eagles swiftly closed the distance to their comrade and detail became clearer to discern. As the scene unfolded before them, Gorlan's jaw hung loose and he stared in disbelief. "Well would you believe it!" he exclaimed.

Kraven was flying towards them, a huge grin on his face. "I've brought you a present Gorlan!" he shouted.

The Warlord smiled, "So I see! You do seem to have a knack for finding things in unusual places."

Gorlan looked down from the back of Tosh's eagle. Dwarf and human faces looked up at him, their arms waving as they cheered and shouted greetings.

Kraven's fire eagle beat it's wings against the air as it reached the others and began to hover. "They were hiding in the hills and making their way back to the town. It seems the Fortownians travelled through the tunnels and on to Drenda. The dwarves, who had heard the words of the messenger a few days previous, were already preparing to march. When the survivors arrived, King Swiftaxe increased the commitment to five thousand of his army. These were tasked with escorting the humans back to their home and to purge it of the enemy. Tor must have caught sight of some of them as they made their way from the White Peaks down into the gulleys."

Gorlan smiled and waved at the throng below, "This is great news. How many humans survived the assault on the town?"

"Better than we expected. About three thousand in total. They have quite a tale to tell and I have only heard a short summary. When they captured me in the gulley they could hardly believe it themselves, especially when they saw my fire eagle. I informed them that the town had been deserted by the enemy, so they decided to come out of hiding and move more swiftly back to Fortown. King Swiftaxe himself is leading the return. He's quite a character."

Gorlan looked to the crowd below and, sure enough,

there was King Swiftaxe. He led from the front, striding along and flanked on either side by solid looking dwarves, carrying heavy war axes and wearing practical wroughtore armour and leathers. Gorlan watched the king as he led the humans and his own dwarf soldiers across the hills towards Fortown. "I guess I had better go and pay my respects," he sighed, secretly not relishing the prospect. Swiftaxe had a fierce reputation for being forthright and outspoken and somewhat brash.

Gorlan spoke to Tor and he guided his fire eagle down to the ground. The WarLord dismounted and approached the King. The advance of the crowd paused as Gorlan bowed low to introduce himself.

"I cannot tell you how pleased I am to see you King Swiftaxe. We had feared for the survival of the towns folk and it gladdens my heart to see so many marching back to their homes with your soldiers. My name is Gorlan, Warlord of Pinn."

The Dwarf King gestured for Gorlan to stand. "I know who you are Gorlan and I do not expect you to bow to me. Neither do you need to use the term King when you speak to me, just plain Swiftaxe will do fine." Gorlan hid his astonishment, this was not what he had expected at all, "I too am glad that so many escaped through the tunnels. It is also good to see your fire eagles, although my heart aches that so many were lost to the halfmen. Kraven also told me that you have sent for reinforcements. You acted swiftly and wisely, you are clearly well fitted to the rank that you have achieved. However, I feel that you have made an error of judgement."

Gorlan raised an eyebrow, "I have? And what would that be?"

"Kraven tells me that there are but ten of you in total and yet you storm in to save one warrior from an unknown

fate. You could have been flying straight into an enemy trap!.."
Swiftaxe paused for a reaction but Gorlan merely stared back
at him, exhibiting no sign of offence or emotion. He measured
his response before speaking, "Swiftaxe, your exploits are
renowned across Portalia. It is known that you love to hunt and
have taken your dwarves on various adventures throughout our
lands. I have heard many stories of when you yourself have
risked the lives of many to save that of the few. Would you ask
differently of me? Would you chastise me for rushing to the
aid of a comrade who we thought captured by the enemy?"

Swiftaxe looked into the eyes of the Pinn Warlord before
throwing his head back and letting out a might guttural
laugh, "Well said my friend, well said indeed. We shall talk
more when we reach the town, I think you and I will get along
splendidly, but for now take your eagle riders and return to the
town. We will continue our advance and join you there."

Gorlan nodded and bowed as he turned to leave. Swiftaxe
waved his hands at Gorlan in frustration, "And I've told you to
stop doing that. That's an order!"

***

Gorlan almost had to tie Molt down. As soon as the Pinn
warriors had returned and told him that his people approached
he was ready to mount up and ride to meet them. "Molt, calm
down a little, I know what this means to you but you would
do better to wait here at your family home. There are eight
thousand men and dwarves out there, by the time you found
your kin they'd be back here anyway." Gorlan then excused
him and Molt ran all the way to his father's house, flush with
excitement.

He would never forget that wait, sat on the grass in the
front garden, Molt stood and paced and even thought about

ignoring the Warlords advice. Common sense told him that Gorlan had been right though and this would be the quickest way to meet up with his kin folk once more. Time dragged. He went inside and began to tidy the home which had been deserted so quickly when the attack came. He re-filed his fathers books and dusted the furniture. He wanted it to look just as his mother had left it.

He smiled when he thought about how house proud she was. He could see her now, rushing around the rooms, tidying up after her husband and offspring, nagging then affectionately when they didn't leave things as they had been found. He let his mind imagine the smell of the home, scented by bouquets of flowers that she would cut from the garden. He suddenly realised that even though he had tidied, the bouquets were missing. He immediately returned to the garden to cut some summer flowers. Returning inside he placed them in a number of vases and spread them throughout the house, closing his eyes as he breathed in their perfume. Yes, that was better.

Finally, he heard the approach of the crowd. He stood at the gate of their family home and waited. He saw the dwarves enter first, marching their way to the town hall. Then the people of Fortown arrived. He felt his excitement rising and saw the happy smiles on the faces of the townsfolk. He also noticed how these expressions turned to grim frowns as the returning citizens came across the stacks of skeletons and noticed the large mass graves that had been dug by the Pinns. Molt had become so accustomed to these sights over the past few days that he had not considered how shocking they would be for the returning townsfolk. Even so, the Fortownians were made of strong stock and Molt watched as their looks of horror turned to anger and determination. He could feel their desire for revenge.

Molt waited and watched as the people streamed back into town and made their way back to their homes. He was heartened to see that so many had made it out of the city, but, as the crowds started to thin, his trepidation began to rise. The crowd that passed was gradually turning from human to mainly dwarf as the rear guard of the throng arrived at the town.

Molt stood their at the gate waiting, even as the last of the dwarves entered the town. He stood and stared back towards the empty hills in utter disbelief. *Surely they cannot all be lost!* He felt panic begin to rise within him and his eyes filled with tears. He did not know what to do, he fell to the floor and dropped his face into his hands. His mind took him back through his memories of his mother and father, of Jade and Amber his beautiful sisters. His thoughts then turned to Brianna and he leapt to his feet and raced to her family home. He stormed up the garden path and through the open door. Brianna's mother looked up in surprise, she stepped towards him and hugged him, "Oh Molt, it is so good to see you." She pulled a little away from him and as she looked into his eyes, her own eyes filled with tears. "They took her Molt. The beasts took her and we couldn't stop them. Her father tried but they sent the spiders after him. He died as we watched. I would have died there too but my sons pulled me away and we ran to the tunnels."

Molt brushed his own tears away, "Who took her?"

"The Graav." Molt's heart raced when he heard this name. *So Kraven's theory had been right.*

Brianna's mother continued, "They attacked us, killing our men but sparing many of the women. Then they sent the spiders into the town. There must have been thousands of them although they worked together as if they possessed one mind. They were easy to kill individually but for every one that you could squash under your heel, hundreds would climb up your legs and begin to weave their victim's death." Her face went deathly white and Molt held her close as she began to cry violently.

Molt waited for her sobs to die down a little, "What of the women they spared, what happened to them?"

There was no reply, Molt held her at arms length and saw utter despair in her face.

"Please tell me, what happened to the women!"

A door opened to his right and Brianna's older brother, Ben, walked into the room. "We're not sure Molt. Some say that they saw the rock creatures heading into the hills with the women they captured. They must have taken over two hundred. After that neither the rock creatures nor the spiders cared who or what they killed." Ben stepped forward and took hold of his mother, "Here let me have her, I'll see to her. I am surprised she even spoke to you, she has been like this ever since she watched my father die."

Molt bowed his head, "I'm sorry Ben, I should have been here to help fight."

Ben shook his head, "Don't be stupid Molt, you're presence would not have made any difference. You were sent for help and you brought back Pinn Fire Eagle riders, that is more than most were able to achieve."

Molt sighed, not comforted by Ben's kind words, "Ben, do you know what happened to my parents? Have you seen them since the attack?"

Ben shook his head, "I'm sorry Molt I have not. There was much confusion during the journey through the tunnels and things didn't improve much once we got to Drenda. TownMaster Cortrain led us into the tunnels but then returned to the town hall to stand with his guard. They fought the enemy whilst everyone fled. It seems that he and his guard all lost there lives there. I presume that your parents did not return to their home?"

Molt shook his head, "No, I waited but they did not come."

Ben's shoulders sagged, "I am afraid that is not a good sign my friend. I am so sorry. If there is anything that......" but Molt had already turned and fled from the house.

Molt kept running, leaving the main town behind he headed for the hills and to a small meadow which he had often visited with Brianna. The meadow sat on an incline that provided a vista across Fortown. Molt sat on the grass and looked across the roofs, lost in thoughts of those that were lost. He watched the activity in the streets below as the townsfolk, assisted by the dwarves, buried the remaining skeletons. Despite what had occurred the town seemed even more alive than usual, it's numbers swelled by the Dwarven army.

A few yards away from him two small cooburrows skipped out of the cover of some bushes. He sat still watching them play in the grass, taking it in turns to chase each other and wrestle the other to the ground. The small grey furry creatures had small front legs and large powerful rear legs allowing which allowed them to hop swiftly over the grass. Molt moved and the two cooburrows froze, listening intently with their small pointed ears, their large black eyes open wide in fright. Molt stayed still and eventually the cooburrows returned to their play before finally running back into the one of the burrow entrances under the bushes.

Molt's thoughts returned to the TownMaster who he knew had kept cooburrows as pets. He found it hard to think that the friendly portly old man was now dead. At the same time he also felt proud in the way the TownMaster had given up his life, fighting side by side with his men as the citizens of the town escape through the tunnels. When all of this was over the town would need to recognise that act and honour him in some way. The realisation of the bravery that had been shown by TownMaster Cortrain and his guards made Molt feel ashamed of how he had left town. He resolved to strengthen his thoughts and with this in mind he rose to his feet to return. He would make a short stop to see Tom and apologise for his earlier behaviour. Then he would return to Gorlan and plan how to gain revenge for those who had fallen. Deep inside he sensed that Brianna still lived and felt that she was out there somewhere, probably facing untold horrors. He would find her and bring her back. Those that had taken her and killed his parents would regret ever setting foot in Fortown.

***

Gorlan sat in the town square and listened as Fleck gave his account of what had happened. He told them of the initial attack by the Graav and of how many of their women had been captured and carried off. He gave an account of the enemy tactics. Of how they would use the spiders to sweep away the bulk of resistance before sending in the Graav.

Gorlan listened intently. Molt entered the chamber and took a seat next to the two men. Fleck was a tall and striking figure in his late forties. He had short cropped dark brown hair and grey eyes. He wore an emerald green gown and carried the seal of office pinned to each arm. He was the official Town Counsellor, He also happened to be Brianna's uncle so was well known to Molt. Fleck was second in command of the town, behind TownMaster Cortrain, and had been ordered by the TownMaster to lead the fleeing people through the tunnels to

Drenda. Fleck had not liked the idea of leaving his TownMaster behind but he knew the sense of this order and obeyed the command. He nodded to Molt as the youth took his seat and then continued, "At first we could not find any way of stopping the Graav. Then, through sheer chance, someone happened to strike a creature at the neck. When the heads of these rock creatures are removed a spout of lava erupts from their neck and they literally crumble into a pile of smouldering rock. You need to be quick to retreat too. Once the head is removed there is a risk of burns from the spouting lava. Although it tends to cool fairly quickly."

Gorlan pointed to the pile of rocks that they had stacked outside the town hall, "We found the rubble and stored it over there. Kraven, one of my men, told us of an old story-song that identified these creatures. We doubted that this could be true but it seems we were wrong. Tell me, how were you able to identify the creatures? Is the song known in Fortown?"

Fleck pointed in the direction of the farmhouses, "No, but we have a number of farmers who previously lived in the cities of the Gates. When they saw how the creatures could be killed by removing their heads they remembered the old song and guessed what these creatures were."

"I'd be interested in speaking with those farmers. Kraven could not recall the words from that story-song and it may offer more clues as to the origin of these creatures and what there purpose is here in Portalia."

Fleck called to a young man to his right, "Boy, run to the farm of the Stillwaters and ask for Gareth to attend us." The boy nodded and ran off to do as he was bid. Fleck continued his account, "The spiders are not difficult to kill. They range in size. From those as big as a pin-head to larger species, the size of a human head. Even the bigger ones can be crushed with weapon or foot, but it is the mass of the beasts that makes them effective. They swarm over a body and spin their webs. It takes just seconds to cover a man from head to foot. The spiders then secrete their acid, liquidising the flesh and they literally drink the poor soul to death, clothes and all. Only the bones remain.

It is not a good way to die. You can see the panic of the web wrapped forms as they struggle to break free. Some of the spiders appear to carry a venom too. Those that are attacked by these poisonous creatures are the lucky ones, they die much quicker than those eaten alive. The spiders also seem to act intelligently. They attack as one, as if the are obeying commands. Those that are crushed under heel are devoured by the others. This is why you see no trace of dead spiders around the town.

The Graav fight amongst them, but the spiders give them a wide berth. They attack side by side, but show no signs of communicating or of any kinship. The best fighting tactic is to get close to the Graav and to fight the stone creatures face to face. The spiders give the rock men a wide berth. So, if you are fighting the Graav, it is rare that you have to concern yourselves with the spiders too."

"Did they show any signs of why they attacked?" asked Gorlan

"Well we assumed they wanted the town but that appears not to be the case. Some of the Graav also focussed on the library and were more interested in securing that location than chasing anyone down the tunnels."

"Yes, we noticed the interest in the library too. Many of the volumes were taken. All related to magic," added Molt.

"I guess that should be of no surprise," said Fleck. "These Graav must be honed via magic. Clearly the behaviour of the spiders is due to a magic spell or binding of some kind too. Whoever controls these monstrosities is using the black arts and is probably hungry for more knowledge and power."

"What of the black eagles?" asked Gorlan.

"They covered the sky, there must have been hundreds of them but they did not attack. They circled above and observed. Not once did I see any swoop to join the affray."

King Swiftaxe spoke to Gorlan, "My guess is that the eagles were being held in reserve, just in case the attack of the Graav and the arachnids failed to secure the town."

Gorlan nodded, "That would seem most likely." He turned to the Town Counsellor once more, "What more can you tell us Fleck?"

Fleck looked embarrassed, "Well there is one more thing. Some of the townsfolk from the edge of our boundaries saw two figures on the hillside. One was a short dwarf-like creature dressed in white, with pale hair and skin. The other was tall with long flowing grey hair and a skull like face. He watched the battle with light blazing from his eyes and carried a glowing red staff."

Gorlan looked at Fleck, "Why do you redden as you tell me this, Fleck?"

Fleck cleared his throat, "Warlord, I believe that my people saw something but I think the tale is prone to exaggeration. Some are even saying that the grey cloaked figure was Shangorth the Warlock himself! Resurrected to wreak revenge on those that defeated him all those years ago."

The Pinns looked up in surprise, Gorlan shivered, "Shangorth is long dead. More likely that another has learned his secrets and revives the dark magic. I cannot believe that the dark one himself has returned to plague the land."

Fleck agreed with Gorlan but even so, both men lacked conviction.

Molt broke the silence, "But what of the women that were taken? How shall we find them?"

King Swiftaxe stood, "There are many actions that we need to take. Rescuing the captured women is just one. However, until we find out more about our foe, we cannot send out troops on a wild goose chase. We need to understand more and plan accordingly. Gorlan, Fleck and myself will talk further and will formulate a plan."

Eager to chase after Brianna, Molt started to object but was silenced by a look from Fleck. The King turned to him, "Counsellor, could I ask that your townsfolk provide food and shelter for my army whilst we are here."

Fleck nodded, "But of course, what is ours should be considered your own. I will nominate a handful of my people to act as wardens to find accommodation for your men. Alas, events have provided for many empty houses and no-one will object if you utilise them for your soldiers whilst you help protect our homes." Fleck ordered that preparations be made to house the dwarves and the three leaders made their way into the chambers of the TownMaster to discuss the situation in private.

The three were deep in conversation when a knock on the door announced the arrival of Gareth Stillwaters. They gestured to Gareth to join them and asked him what he knew of the Graav.

Gareth voice was a little shaky, nervous at suddenly being the centre of attention of these great leaders. "Not much I'm afraid. What little knowledge I have is from the verses of an ancient song-story. It tells the tale of the trader sailor named Llewellyn. It is long and has many verses but part of the story tells of a strange race of stone like beings called the Graav. The description seems to match that of the creatures that attacked Fortown."

"Can you recite these verses?" asked Swiftaxe

Gareth nodded, "Do you want to hear the whole story-song or just the section regarding the Graav."

Gorlan spoke, "Just the verses relating to the Graav will do for now. You can share the whole song with Kraven later and decide with him if there is anything else of interest in the tale."

Gareth cleared his throat, "Very well, I will pick up the story-song just after the crew had fled from the second island having just escaped from the man eating cannibals that lived there. I am no bard though, so I will recite the words rather than sing them. If you heard my singing voice then you would thank me for this." Gareth relaxed a little as the three leaders smiled at his witticism. He began the recitation,

> Llewellyn's crew flew to the west,
> Relieved at last to take some rest.
> We sailed a day and through a night,
> Sails a-billowing as we made our flight.
> And then a cry from overhead,
> "More land Ahoy!" The watchman said.
> The crew looked out to volcanic heights,
> Grey ash, lava flows, power and might.
> But the western shore, looked green and clear,
> Towards it we soared without fear.
> We anchored there and made to shore,
> Llewellyn with twenty men at oar.
> We searched the woods, discovering there,
> Exotic fruit, apple, plum and pear.
> No beasts were seen, of feather or fur,
> Not a movement in the trees did stir.
> We then pushed east, to the lava flows,
> To sulphur smells where nothing grows.

In the flow, where naught could live,
The red surface bubbled and started to give.
And in that fire, with horror we saw,
Creatures form, from hells own core.
Grey lava rock they had for skin,
A fiery heart gave life within.
They marched toward the men in hordes,
Stone weapons, edged as sharp as swords.
Their faces were as lifeless stone,
As they slashed and stabbed through human bone.
We tried to fight but many died,
Our weapons bouncing off their hide.
Then Llewellyn struck in fear and dread,
His vicious blow removed a head.
A spurt of flame, a lava bubble,
And the creature fell to a pile of rubble.
We rallied then and killed some more,
As we retreated to the shore.
Six took a boat and fled to sea,
Four of the crew, Llewellyn and me.
We reached our ship and climbed aboard,
And stared back at the frightful horde.
Some chased us still, maintaining their pace,
They sunk in the sea without a trace.
From the old elvish word, for stone making ways,
We named them, the Graav, for the rest of their days.
That night in my log, this ode I did pen,
So that others are warned of these lava made men.

Their was a slight pause as Gareth completed the verse. "The story-song then goes on to tell of the rest of their journey and does not mention the Graav again."

"Is their any reference to the spider army in the story?" asked Swiftaxe.

Gareth shook his head, "No, I'm afraid not. I have been over the words a hundred times in my head, and recited them for other folk, but there appears to be nothing else of relevance. Until the arrival of the Graav here in Portalia we all thought the whole story-song was just a fantasy and not based on any fact. Now I wonder what truths lay in those words. The tale tells of other strange creatures and races and of islands packed with treasures. I wonder where the truth ends and the myth begins."

"Understandably so," replied Gorlan. "I trust your judgement that there is nothing else of relevance to our current plight, but I would ask that you review the rest of the tale with Kraven. He knows many other story-songs and tales and is well placed to know if there is anything that may increase our knowledge of these creatures."

"Then, if you have heard all you need from me, I will go and find him immediately," replied Gareth.

Gorlan nodded and directed Gareth to the courtyard.

When he had left Swiftaxe resumed their conversation, "Well it seems to me that these rock creatures are undoubtedly the Graav but how they come to be here in Portalia remains a mystery. The creatures seem to operate on instinct. I cannot imagine these beings building ships and sailing here."

"I agree," added Fleck. "Having fought against these creatures they appear single minded in their desire to kill but show no other signs of intelligence. There were a number of times when the Graav wandered into a mass of spiders. They squashed their allies without acknowledgement of their existence."

"No wonder the spiders give the Graav a wide birth," commented Gorlan.

Swiftaxe walked to the window and looked over the hills

to the west. "What about these reports that Shangorth has arisen. Do we give them any credence?"

"I think we have to," replied Gorlan. "Just review what we already know; black eagles fly in the skies, the portal pathways are in use again, an evil army of spiders, the appearance of the Graav and the mythical halfmen. All of this smells of Shangorth's work although common sense tells me otherwise."

"Maybe so, but what do we know about how he was killed?" offered Fleck.

"In truth, fairly little," answered Swiftaxe. "The stories tell of how the allied armies, bolstered by the Pinn fire eagle riders, defeated the warlock army and that the warlock was slain at Shangorth Towers by the wizards. We don't know how that was done or, indeed, if it truly happened. Only two wizards survived that battle, Weldrock and Farspell, and they have not been seen in generations. In short, unlikely as it would seem, Shangorth may well have returned. I do not think we should discount this.

For now though, I suggest that we await the arrival of the reinforcements from Pinnhome and then dispatch a force to the east to Shangorth Towers. In the meantime I will send a pair of dwarf scouts into the mountains to see what additional information can be gathered." Swiftaxe then addressed Gorlan, "How long before we can expect the reinforcements?"

"We could receive fire eagle reinforcements as early as tomorrow. I presume that the Overlord will also send both cavalry and infantry. These will take a further three to seven days depending on how they travel, by what route and if they travel together. They may choose to detour around the Halfman Forest at this stage rather than fight the Halfmen on their own territory."

Swiftaxe stood deep in thought, "Then I reinforce my

earlier suggestion. I will send forth the scouts and we will await the bulk of the Pinn army here at Fortown. I know that our people yearn for revenge, but I feel that this path is the wisest. Our scouts may gain additional information and, should the enemy decide to attack once more, we will be entrenched here in Fortown and much better placed to defend the town.

Once the reinforcements arrive we will decide the next course of action. My thoughts at this stage would be to dispatch a portion of our forces east to Shangorth Towers but we can ponder these issues over the next few days. Agreed?"

"I think that we may have a few problems keeping my people here in the town but, yes, I agree that this is the best course of action."

Fleck and Swiftaxe looked at Gorlan, "I agree but with one addition. The scouts should take one of my fire eagle flyers to accompany them to provide protection and a faster means of communication. Agreed?"

"Agreed!" they replied.

As the others left the chamber, Swiftaxe sat again, wearied to the bone. He looked through the window towards the mountains, "So is it you Shangorth? Have you returned from hell to strike down those that defeated you so long ago?"

CHAPTER FOURTEEN
Shangorth Towers

Zarn, the White Dwarf, stepped through the portal gateway of the mountain Runestone.

"I have delivered the women to Stycich as you commanded Shangorth."

"Very good. Did the worm grovel as usual?" sneered the warlock.

"Of course. I'd like to see their faces when they realise that the women that you deliver to them are barren and will be unable to bear them babies. Stycich dreams of leading a new breed of halfmen, born from the wombs of the human women that you give to him."

The warlock smiled, "I merely promised to deliver to them women captives in return for their loyalty. I did not make any guarantees about their state of health, body or mind! Anyway, once the halfmen have served their purpose and we have subjugated the peoples of Portalia, I will eradicate them from existence. They are ignorant and repulsive creatures."

The White Dwarf grinned, he despised the Halfmen and would relish their destruction.

He stepped off the Runestone and looked into the face of his master. There was very little of humanity left in that cold skull-like face. The warlock looked at Zarn through blood red eyes. His thin grey lips gave the impression of a permanent sneer. His face had grown increasingly sunken and pallid. He wore a long black flowing cloak and around his neck hung two items. The first was a Runestone pendant bearing the mark of the mountain. On his finger he wore the matching Runestone ring. Zarn possessed the second mountain pendant and knew that the third hung around the neck of the human, Nexus. These gave Shangorth the power to call them back to Shangorth anytime that he desired.

Zarn looked at the second item hanging around Shangorth's neck. It was a small amber orb held by a silver chain. The orb glistened and danced with light almost as if it were alive. Zarn did not know for what purpose the warlock wore this trinket, or indeed, what magical power it possessed. This was not unusual though. Shangorth held many secrets and rarely shared information with the dwarf. One that burned Zarn's curiosity more than most was the locked doorway in the Runestone chamber. His master used magical incantations to prevent access to the space behind the door. Zarn knew that whatever lay there could not be large. Behind it was a closet which he estimated to be no more than four feet deep. It was built across to the side of the round room and intersected a section of the Runestone, covering one corner of the triangle completely. This was also curious. The closet could just as easily been placed elsewhere in the room, well away from the Runestone. Why did it need to occupy that precise floor space?

A few weeks earlier he been on the stairs when he heard the warlock chanting the incantations to open the door. He had sneaked into the room and tried to peek into the closet. The door had been open for a fraction of a second allowing him to catch sight of a blue glowing interior. At that point Shangorth had sensed his presence and slammed the door shut.

He had been severely punished for his curiosity and his head still throbbed when he recalled the pain that had been invoked on him by the angry Shangorth. Since that day, the warlock would frequently secure the main doors to the Runestone chamber whenever he needed to use the magic of the closet.

Another secret that his master refused to share was the story of his resurrection and how he came to be in possession of the Mountain Runestone artefacts. Magical items that had been destroyed by the wizards many years ago.

Zarn recalled how his master had first found him and taken him under his wing.

Zarn was desperate for money to pay off gambling debts. He had broken into a house in Drenda. The dwarf that owned the house, a local merchant, had returned early, interrupting the theft. The two dwarves fought and Zarn killed the merchant. He had escaped from the city in shame and fled to Shangorth Towers where he found shelter.

He had been sleeping in this very room when a glowing blue archway appeared and Shangorth emerged. The dwarf immediately thought that he had been hunted down for punishment and recoiled from the warlock. Shangorth had taken pity on him and, after hearing his story, asked the dwarf to join his cause. Zarn had pledged his allegiance that day, his eyes glowing with the promise of riches and power.

A shout from Shangorth brought Zarn back to the present. "Take your eyes off my orb minion! You are NEVER to go near this. I don't even want you looking at it. Do you understand!"

Zarn realised that he had been staring at the wizards amber orb as he reminisced. Fearing more punishment, Zarn cowered and placed his hands over his head, "I am sorry master, I was lost in thought about the day that you first arrived here. What a great day it was for Zarn." The White Dwarf relaxed a little as he realised that no punishment was forthcoming. A little gentler Shangorth spoke again, "The orb is very delicate Zarn, no-one must ever touch it. Not ever."

Zarn nodded. The warlock turned away from him and wandered to the easterly window. He looked across the peaks and saw the approaching dragon, "Ohrhim returns. I am going to the roof to meet it and hear what news it has brought. You will go to my spiders and see that they are settled. Take the Spider Gem. Some may have aroused."

Zarn rushed to obey, a blur of white as he moved across the room. He grinned as he picked up the Spider Gem staff, relishing the chance of once again holding the orb that would control the arachnid army. Scuttling to the northern stairway he descended to the rear of the tower. On reaching ground level he made his way into a newly forged tunnel to the new chamber beneath the main tower structure. Here Shangorth had used fire magic to clear an enormous cellar that was now filled with millions of spiders.

Zarn looked proudly over the mass of spiders. All of the creatures were comatose, held in suspension by the power of the gem. He looked around to check that the warlock was nowhere to be seen and then raised the staff above his head. He grinned in manic delight as the creatures awoke and looked at him, his head felt dizzy with the power that he wielded. He ordered the creatures to rise and they stood as one. The air was filled with the ticking of the arachnids. The noise seemed to remind the dwarf as to who and where he was. He quickly returned the creatures to their sleep, once more frantically looking around to ensure that his master had not seen him use the gem without his bidding. The warlock only allowed Zarn to use the staff on his command, such as when he was asked to return waking arachnids to sleep if they broke out of the spell of the gem. This rarely happened. Zarn double checked that all of the creatures had returned to their comatose state and made his way back to the surface above. He crossed the open courtyard behind the main tower and walked through a large gate that was set in the rectangular walls that protected the tower complex. Black eagles were perched on all the surrounding walls and the battlements of the four towers that gave the complex it's name. Others circled overhead and some flew towards their eyries, high up in the mountains to the northeast.

On the plateau that stretched before him were over five thousand Graav. Most stood in long straight ranks as if frozen in time, however a few, those last used for battle and for guard duty, bathed in a large pool of molten lava.

The pool was formed by a small channel of lava that flowed from the ground at the west end of the plateau. It ran to the centre, where it formed a small lava lake, before returning to ground to the east via another channel. Zarn watched as the Graav walked through the pool of fire, replenishing their energy before returning to their positions within the silent ranks. There they would rest until summoned by Shangorth. Here was another mystery to Zarn. Where had the Graav come from and why did they follow Shangorth's bidding? His presumption was that they did so because they had been created by Shangorth himself. In this he was wrong.

As Zarn inspected the twin armies of Graav and spiders, the warlock climbed the south stairway to the roof of the tower. Ohrhim had landed and had transformed into the shape of a man. This form was it's favourite and it utilised it whenever it could. It liked the sensation of walking on two legs as well as eating and sleeping like a human, although in reality Ohrhim did not truly sleep. It had two human forms, male and female and enjoyed spending time as both. It ensured that both forms appeared physically attractive to the opposite sex and was amused when the humans started to flirt with it. A number of times it had, for fun, pretended to be interested in a human partner but would change it's body into it's normal non-descript form on the first kiss, just to see the horror in their eyes as the human's lips touched the sticky gelatinous skin of the shapechanger. When the frightened human ran away it would calmly change back to human form. It would then depart, leaving no evidence of it's presence to those returning with the frantic individual, who was subsequently labelled as crazy.

Ohrhim approached the warlock and spoke in a clear voice, "Shangorth, I bring you news."

The shapechanger then imparted all that it witnessed at Ralle. The warlock smiled, "You have done well Ohrhim. Things progress as I expected. Soon the combined armies of Portalia will meet at Fortown and we will eradicate the main resistance in one devastating strike."

Ohrhim examined it's fingers, "Why do you not strike now and destroy the centaurs on the road to Fortown?" "It would not suit my purpose," replied the warlock, "To strike early gives warning of my strength. Also, to control the entire spider army will take immense concentration. I therefore follow a careful plan that will lead me to complete victory and ultimate power.

From the first, when I allowed the shepherd to witness the black eagles, I have driven events to a large confrontation at Fortown. This is where I will gain my first major victory. My spider army sleeps until needed, the Black Eagles now number some nine hundred and I have portal access to many more Graav should we need them. In addition, with the promise of gold and riches, Nexus has formed a force of five hundred dwarves and men from the pirate town of Dargoth Sands. Even as I speak they camp a few miles to the west, awaiting my order to advance on Fortown.

So you see my shape shifting friend, everything goes to plan. I will therefore bide my time and strike a blow at the combined forces at Fortown that will rock Portalia. The fear and confusion that will follow will forge the path for complete domination."

Ohrhim looked at the warlock, "You have waited a long time for your revenge Shangorth. I want to be there to enjoy the moment with you. I pray my gods allow me that before they call for me to transform."

"I'm sure they will Ohrhim. I believe that your gods are already pleased with the way you serve my purpose." Shangorth smiled inwardly as he played this card yet again. "However, I now have a new mission for you to undertake. I want you to return to watch over the humans that accompany the centaurs. From your account it would seem that these humans have runestone artefacts in their possession. I had not envisaged this and I would know more. Stay close and learn all you can. Take action as you see fit and report progress back to me."

Ohrhim bowed it's compliance. Shangorth looked at the shape-changer and watched in admiration as it began to transform.. He even managed to feel a small amount of pity for the beast. He knew Ohrhim was the last of it's kind.

Once there had been many of it's race, but a great disaster had struck their world as a multitude of fireballs began to fall from their skies. The ShapeChangers believed that this was their fate, brought upon them by their gods. A fate that would take them to the next stage of their evolution, a transformation to pure energy and a place at the side of their creators. Ohrhim had gone with the others to the temples, to ready itself for the passing from solid being to that of pure energy. It had seen the first of the fireballs strike and watched as buildings burned. It had heard the roof of it's own temple give way and had felt the intense heat. As it's kinfolk erupted in flames, screaming in terror and pain, doubts about the afterlife entered Ohrhim's mind.

It was no longer sure of what happened next. It remembered that the doubts plagued it in those last moments and it felt itself starting to melt in the heat. As it lost consciousness it imagined transforming itself into pure energy. It returned to consciousness on a cold flat stone and had been found laying there by Shangorth. It was grateful for the sign of life and mimicked the shape of the warlock and decided it liked this form.

Ohrhim knew instinctively that it was the only survivor of it's race. It believed that reawakening on this strange world was it's punishment for that final loss of faith. It therefore chose to work for the warlock who had befriended him, under the belief that this was a test from it's gods. It was determined that it would pass that test allowing it to pass into the state of pure energy and to join with it's creators. It felt no remorse for it's actions, or those of the warlord. It saw the creatures of this world, Portalia, as primitive and expendable for it's greater cause.

Shangorth watched Ohrhim disappear in the distance. Surprisingly he actually felt a small liking for the creature. He had pondered long for an explanation of how the shapechanger had appeared on Portalia. After much thought, he had finally reached a plausible conclusion. Shangorth believed that in those dying moments, as Ohrhim had melted, the ShapeChanger had somehow transformed itself into the same form of energy that formed the portals, and, as such, had transported itself via the portal web, to the Runestone. This had proven so very fortunate for the warlock, especially when he discovered Ohrhim's belief that this new life was a test from his gods. Not only could this be used by the warlock as a weapon to persuade Ohrhim to carry out his will, but also meant that the creature would stay loyal to him and could be trusted not to betray him.

Unlike the human agent Nexus. He knew that his agent desired to be considered an equal. He was too eager to search for power of his own. For now though, Nexus served a purpose and could always be eliminated later.

Zarn was another matter. Shangorth trusted the dwarf to do his bidding as he believed him to be too stupid to grasp power for himself. The dwarf was also terrified of pain and could easily be brought into line with a few simple spells. This was tedious but necessary.

Turning his back on the mountains, Shangorth made his way back down the spiral staircase. He descended to the floor above the Runestone chamber and entered a small room. A large pile of volumes and scrolls were stacked on the floor near an oak desk. These were mostly the writings that had been removed from the library at Fortown, although there were a few other manuscripts scattered around.

It had been easy to remove these volumes once the town hall had been secured by the Graav. The old portal gateway, once used to give access to the central Portalia Meadows, opened onto the hills above Fortown. With the town won, Shangorth had opened this portal, transported himself to Fortown and walked to the library. He had then used his Graav to transport the more interesting volumes back to the Towers via the open portal.

Shangorth looked at the large stack of writings and sighed. During the ransacking of the library he had noticed nothing of particular note. Informative documents were becoming increasingly hard to find. He was not relishing the prospect of picking through all of this information. He estimated that probably ninety-nine percent of it would be knowledge he already possessed, or merely speculation and rumour. However, he resigned himself to search these tomes for that one percent of information that would further his knowledge of magic and the dark arts. Knowledge was power and therefore he craved it.

On the desktop were four volumes, their covers marked with a red 'W'. He had reviewed these books earlier and all four offered up knowledge of the old dark arts. He picked up the books and made his way down the stairs to the Runestone chamber. He checked that the room was vacant and noticed that the dwarf had returned the Spider Gem staff. He then shut both of the doorways to the stairs and barred each shut.

He walked across the room to the closet that he kept magically secured and mumbled an incantation to unlock it. The door popped ajar, a blue glow seeped out of the door cracks. Shangorth entered a small space filled by an arch of blue light. It was another portal gateway. The closet door automatically closed behind him, reforming the magic seal as it did so. Without hesitation, Shangorth stepped forward into the blue power of the portal gateway.

He reappeared on a flat, featureless triangular Runestone. This stone was made in a similar fashion to those at Eumor and Shangorth but the stone was much brighter in colour tone, it had not yet weathered and was clearly much newer than the ancient Runestones. No decoration adorned the centre of this Runestone though. A control pedestal was evident in the centre of the triangle. Like the Runestone in Shangorth, this pedestal possessed an octagonal key.

As Shangorth appeared bearing the books a young man

stepped forward. He bowed his head and welcomed his mentor, accepting into his possession the volumes that were offered to him. "Bring them to my library," commanded the warlock as he stepped from the Runestone and exited the chamber.

Over an hour passed before Shangorth returned to the Runestone chamber at Shangorth Towers. He exited the closet, and, as before, it sealed itself behind him. Even so, Shangorth double checked the door to ensure that it was safely secured. He knew that it was essential that the existence of another set of portal pathways remain a secret. He would not trust this knowledge to anyone, not even the ShapeChanger and certainly not the dwarf or Nexus.

He smiled as he unbarred the entrances doors to the Runestone chamber. During the past hour he added the new volumes to his main library. He had also met with his twelve young apprentices and had heard a report on their progress. He was pleasantly surprised, it seemed that he had chosen correctly. These twelve would indeed make a fine coven. Disciples that would follow his every wish and command.

Initially he had taken one hundred youths, mostly from the gutters and sewers of the larger towns, but occasionally torn from more influential backgrounds, those that had fallen out with their wealthier families. Most showed no talent for the magic and he had killed these immediately. Of the twenty that he had spared only twelve had survived, eight had failed the numerous tests that he had placed before them. He was not concerned however. Thirteen was enough. In fact his studies showed him that many of the ancient warlocks had worked with a coven of this size, believing the number thirteen itself to be darkly magical. He was therefore happy to emulate this. Together, he and his coven would preside over all of Portalia and the islands of the Seas of Mist.

CHAPTER FIFTEEN
Crow's Watch

The centaur camp was nestled on the edge of the Meadows. Rhys, Michael and Ashley shared a tent in the centre, whilst Lan chose to sleep in the open air at the entrance. Very little stirred in the camp. Only the movement of the sentries as the guard changed and the hopping and fluttering of wings of a black crow that had perched itself on the tent of the teenagers. All three inside were asleep. Or at least they were trying to sleep, for Rhys was fitful once more. His dreams were trying to take hold of him again and he kept waking with a start, his mind trying to avoid this night journey. Eventually exhaustion won and he fell into a deep sleep.

Almost immediately his portal dream returned. Rhys felt himself spinning, as the visions cycled over and over in his head. He tried hard to focus, once again feeling the need to control cycling of the portals images, but the harder he tried to fight the images, the faster they seemed to spin. He continued the struggle, hopelessly clutching for some kind of order. Then he recalled the words of the centaur that had offered riding advice earlier that day. "Do not force her, let her find her own rein." The words swept over Rhys and he suddenly knew what to do. He turned his focus away from the portal images and forced himself to relax, watching as the images continued to change. At first nothing seemed to change but then, as Rhys became calmer, so did the images, slowing by the second until they eventually came to a full stop.

In his dream Rhys looked through the portal gateway onto a snowy evening scene. He could see houses in the distance and could hear the sound of children playing in the snow. It sounded welcoming and he moved closer to the blue glow to get a better look. As he watched, a woman approached the portal from the other side. As she neared the portal. the features of the woman became much easier to discern. Her face was lit by the blue glow of the gateway and Rhys could now make out every feature. He continued to stare at the woman, her face seemed curiously familiar. Then it struck him. This unknown woman greatly resembled his family line, with features very similar to his Auntie and his mother. She frowned as she stared at the portal. At first her vision seemed distant, as though focussed on the horizon, but, after a few minutes, she seemed to focus directly on Rhys and her face changed from a look of inquisition to that of astonishment. Then rather surprisingly she smiled at him. Rhys smiled back. She raised her hand in welcome and beckoned for him to step through to her. Rhys looked at her, at first uncertain but then, reassured by her smiling face, he began to walk into the blue light.

All of a sudden the wind was knocked from him as something crashed against him and threw him to the floor. Pain racked his body as his back came down hard on a rock and he felt his head slide down canvas of the tent wall. He opened his eyes with a start and saw the blue portal disappear with a pop. Ashley was on top of him, pinning him to the ground. He pushed her off angrily. "What the hell are you doing!" he shouted.

Ashley climbed off him and stood up.

"You were going to step through Rhys. There was a portal here in our tent. The blue glow woke me and I saw you standing there. I watched for a while wondering what was happening, but then I saw you step toward the gateway. You were going to step through. I had to stop you."

Rhys stared at her as if she had lost her mind, "What are you talking about Ash. It was just a dream. It wasn't real, there was no portal here. You were imagining it. It must have been like when Michael shared a piece of my dream about the skull head bloke."

Michael was sat up in his bed, staring at them both in amazement, he shook his head, "No, it wasn't the same. The portal was here in this tent. A REAL portal. I saw it too."

Rhys looked scared but thoughtful. The tent was suddenly very silent. Eventually Rhys looked at Ashley apologetically. "Thanks Ash, sorry for shouting at you. In my dream the portal led to a woman that resembled my Mother and my Auntie, it seemed safe and homely, but who knows where it led in reality."

Ashley shrugged, "That's OK Rhys, you would have done the same for me. What I'd like to know though is where the hell the portal came from. We are, more or less, in the middle of nowhere and it seems more than coincidental that the portal happened to appear inside our tent. Who do you think opened it?"

A voice mumbled something from behind them. They turned to look and saw Lan's head poking through the canvas door. They smiled, he looked quite silly, almost as if all that he had was a decapitated head with no body. The old man was making faces at them. He stuck his tongue out and rolled his eyes. He made his cheeks puff out and forced himself to go red. They could not help but laugh. "That's funny Lan" said Rhys between giggles.

"Lan make smiles!" replied the old man.

They all looked at each other in surprise. Yet again Lan had said something that made sense.

Rhys did not comment on this but spoke again to the old man, "Why thank you Lan. We appreciate it."

"Most welcome, most welcome. Rhys fear! Bad! Bad! Rhys must not sleep! Make webholes!"

Rhys looked at the others, "What do you mean Lan?"

Lan looked into Rhys' eyes and the young boy could see the change take over him as this brief moment of sanity passed away. Lan mumbled and bubbled spittle and removed his head from between the tent flaps.

"What the heck was that all about?" Rhys asked himself as much as anyone else.

Ashley was staring at Rhys, "Well, this may sound crazy but I think Lan thinks that YOU created the portal in your sleep."

Rhys told her she was talking rubbish but he went white. Mike spoke, "No Rhys, I think Ashley is right, Lan believes that you created the portal."

"Aw, not you too Mike. Give me a break will you."

Michael ignored the dig from his friend, "Were you dreaming again, Rhys?" he asked.

Rhys nodded. "Tell us what happened," prompted Ashley.

Rhys gave an account of his dream. Afterwards both Michael and Ashley were sure that Rhys had created the portal. "The fact that you were able to stop the chaotic cycling of the images must have been the key!" exclaimed Michael.

Rhys felt differently. He offered that the images in his mind only slowed down because someone had opened a portal in close proximity to him. It was a weak argument and he knew it. Eventually though they agreed to disagree over the matter for the sake of some peace. "So what do we do now?" asked Ashley, "Should we go and tell Fyros what happened?"

Rhys looked worried, "I'm not sure. I'm worried that they'll think me some kind of threat. Remember what happened back at the council with Hesh, he wanted to lock us up as spies. I think I'd like to ask that we keep this a secret for now."

Ashley started to object, "But it could be dangerous. What if it happens again and non-one is here to help you?"

Rhys looked down dejectedly but Michael jumped to his defence, "We'll help him Ash. One of us needs to stay with him all the time, even at night. If it happens again then we'll be watching and can stop him before he steps through the portal. Remember it did disappear as soon as Rhys woke up."

Ashley frowned but the look of pleading in Rhys' eyes made her reluctantly agree. Michael winked at Rhys and he smiled back.

"Two conditions though," added Ashley. The two boys groaned.

"OK, what are they?" asked Rhys.

"The first is that if this does happen again we go straight to Fyros."

Rhys and Michael looked at each other, they both agreed. "So what's the second?" asked Michael.

Ashley smiled, "That you stop bugging me about calling soccer, soccer."

The two boys laughed, "OK, we'll try, "replied Rhys, "but no promises!"

On the roof of the tent above, a crow sat listening. If it's beak would have allowed, then it too would have smiled. It would now wait for the teenagers to settle down to sleep once more.

***

In the dark of the early hours a black snake slithered passed the feet of Lan and made it's way into the tent. Once inside Ohrhim raised it's snake head to look around. The girl and the boy nearest the door slept soundly. The third youth thrashed back and fore in his sleep disturbed by his dreams. *This must be the youth that can dream portals* thought Ohrhim, and it glided across the floor until it was a few inches from the face of the sleeping youth. The shapechanger watched as the boy tossed and turned in his sleep. *The warlock will be very interested in you young man*, thought Ohrhim. The shapechanger sat and waited until it heard the steady rhythm of breathing from all three youths. Once satisfied that all slept soundly it began it's latest transformation, morphing into a bipedal form with two arm like protrusions. The first terminated in a large open pocket, similar in shape to an empty pillow case. Instead of a hand, the second arm ended in a short sharp blade. Ohrhim concentrated and used his ability to harden it's structure around the blade, without this the blade would have been far too soft to cut anything. The shapechanger frowned as the skin hardened, causing it discomfort as it did so. Ohrhim looked at the youth again. Observing that the he was still deep in sleep, it gently placed it's pillow like flesh over the face of the human and contracted it's skin. It felt the boy start as the skin tightened cutting of the youth's supply of air. Ohrhim had now perfected this technique having used it to good effect to capture other humans. It watched and listened to the boy and released the pressure around his face as he sunk into unconsciousness. The shapechanger then used it's body knife to cut the canvas of the tent wall. Transforming itself into human form with normal hands, Ohrhim dragged the comatose boy out of the tent. One last check to ensure that no-one had been alerted to his presence and then another swift transformation into the form of a black dragon. Clutching the boy between soft claws, it took to the air, invisible against the night sky as it beat it's wings and headed back towards Dargoth.

***

The sun had not yet risen when Ashley awoke. She crawled from her sleeping bag and out of the tent. Lan snored noisily at the entrance and she had to step carefully to avoid stepping on him. As she passed, her nose caught the odour of sweat and dirt from the old man, she really wished Lan would take a bath. Ashley made her way to the campfire where Kyrie sat drinking from a mug. She looked up as Ashley approached, "Good morning Ashley, would you like some?" Kyrie pointed to a large pot sat on the embers of the fire.

"What is it?" she asked.

"Sweetgrass tea. It is brewed from the tall red grasses that you see growing on the Meadows. It can be used fresh or dried and brews up into a sweet refreshing drink. Here try it." Kyrie took a large ladle and filled a mug, she handed it to Ashley who took a large swig allowing the liquid to slip down her throat.

"Mmm, this is good," she said, "It tastes like the tea-rain that fell yesterday."

"The what?" asked Kyrie.

"The tea-rain," replied Ashley with a smile, "Your rain here in Portalia tastes sweet and a little like the tea that we drink back home."

Kyrie looked confused, "Do you not get rain where you come from?"

Ashley nodded, "Yes, of course but it just tastes of water. Not like the rain you get here."

"How strange. You are right about the sweetgrass taste though. The plant absorbs the rain water without any filtering

259

and carries the fluid directly to it's leaves. The grass then picks up the taste as the rain water is absorbed into the leaves, feeding the plant."

Ashley finished her drink and Kyrie refilled her cup. The centaur looked thoughtful as she stared into the embers of the campfire. "Ashley, what do you think would happen if the portals between Earth and Portalia are opened once more and your people become aware of our existence?"

Ashley pondered this for a moment and lines formed across her brow. "I'd like to say that it would be a great thing, but I can't. So many people on our world feel they need to control the lives of others. There are things here on Portalia that would bring out the greed of the men of my world. I don't think opening the portals between our worlds would result in good. Our ways are very different. Whilst we have progressed technically, our world is driven on materialism and the need for ownership is great, especially amongst the stronger nations of Earth. I think Portalia would change beyond all recognition and that would be a sad day for us all."

Kyrie looked shocked, "You talk as if your world would be as much a threat to our way of life as the evil that grows within our own world. Surely your world is not controlled by evil."

Ashley shook her head, "No, it is not controlled by evil, it is just very different." She knitted her brow, wondering how best to explain, "In our world good and evil exist side by side, even within individuals. There is no magic and the only truly intelligent species that reside on Earth is human. The way we communicate and interact is entirely different. We have invented devices that can allow us to converse over great distances without the aid of magic. Weapons have been developed that are so powerful that they could destroy our own planet if used in anger. We have built space ships that can fly to the stars, aircraft that fly in the skies faster than the speed of sound and yet we cannot live in harmony and peace. We choose to fight and bicker and argue amongst ourselves. Here on Portalia you have lived as you do for generation after generation, hardly changing your ways. Some on my world may say that the inhabitants of Portalia are backward and uncivilised. They'd be wrong though, I have only been here a few days and I feel that it is us that has it wrong, not you."

"But we are far from perfect Ashley," replied Kyrie, "There have been wars on Portalia too and there are many who have turned to a life of crime, especially around the coastal regions to the West. As you know, we now have the threat of evil rising once more in the mountains, once again threatening our peace.

Maybe your world has found a way of diluting this evil, breaking it up into small pieces that exist in all and that can be fought more easily. Here on Portalia that evil would exist as a pure force, completely absorbing those touched by it and, as a result, all the more potent and more capable of destroying our world. You say that evil exists everywhere in Earth and because of it you have developed the power to destroy your world. In truth you have not yet done so. Maybe your world's fight against evil is more successful than you realise."

Ashley had not considered this viewpoint and thought about it for a while, "Maybe, but I still believe that our worlds would do better kept apart. Our ways and beliefs are far too different from those of your own."

Kyrie nodded, "I must agree Ashley, and yet my heart yearns to visit Earth, especially given the theories that we may once have originated there." Ashley looked confused so Kyrie explained to her the theories of how horses and centaurs came to Portalia.

"So centaurs are not naturally of Portalia!" exclaimed Ashley, "How curious. It would certainly be weird if you had come from Earth." Ashley continued to ponder this and then spoke excitedly. "Kyrie, what if the theories were wrong? Maybe your race was not driven from Earth but chose to leave when they witnessed what man was doing to the world. From what I have seen of your race, they seem to be content with living their way of life and don't strive for technical advances. Perhaps they saw how men were demanding more and more power for themselves and decided to use the portals to move to a world where they could be who they wanted to be."

Kyrie shrugged, "Perhaps, but I guess we'll never know."

The sun had risen as they talked and offered the promise of another warm summer's day. Ashley and Kyrie turned as they heard stirring from within the teenager's tent. They could make out a figure rising within and heard a cough and a clearing of the throat as Rhys stepped from the tent. Still stretching and eyes squinting against the light, he stepped straight onto Lan's head and the old man awoke with a shout, causing Rhys to jump comically into the air. "Oh bugger, sorry Lan." Rhys apologised but then felt a touch of annoyance, "You know, you really need to stop getting under everyone's feet." Rhys furrowed his brow as he spoke, "And, you need a bath big time, you are starting to smell worse than ever!"

Rhys stumbled over to join Kyrie and Ashley, "Good morning Rhys" said Kyrie.

"Morning Rhys," added Ashley, "I think I can guess which side of the bed you got out of this morning!"

Rhys yawned, "Oh, morning Kyrie. Morning Ash. Sorry about that, it just gets a bit annoying having Lan hanging around all the time."

"Did you not sleep well Rhys?" asked the centaur.

"Not too bad thanks. I just woke up a few times dreaming about my family and of my home. I'm afraid it's made me a little irritable this morning. Nothing that a full belly won't fix though," he winked at Ashley.

Ashley poured Rhys some sweetgrass tea, "Try this Rhys, you'll love it. It tastes like the tea-rain but thicker and sweeter." Rhys drank the warm liquid and licked his lips as he finished it, he felt better already. He helped himself to a refill.

The camp was stirring around him and the three sniffed the air as the smell of cooking eggs met their noses. They made their way over to where half a dozen centaurs busied themselves preparing breakfasts for all.

All the food was fresh having been brought from Ralle the previous day. Rhys and Ashley ate hungrily as they tucked into fried eggs, bread and a meat which tasted very much like a spiced ham. Kyrie remained with them and others were milling around so they did not speak of the events of the previous night.

They finished their breakfasts and returned their plates. "Looks like Mike is sleeping in this morning. I suppose we'd better wake him or he'll miss breakfast. It looks like they are just about ready to stop cooking," observed Rhys.

"I'll go and get him," replied Ashley. "I'll roll up the beds whilst I'm there."

Rhys sat down and helped himself to third cup of sweetgrass tea as Ashley made her way to the tent. A sudden shout of distress from her caused him to choke on a mouthful of tea and he rushed to the tent to find out why she sounded so alarmed. On entering he saw Ashley looking out through the hole that had been cut in the canvas. She turned to him as he entered, "Mike's gone! Something or someone must have taken him in the night. Look at this," she pointed to the cut in the canvas. Rhys stared in disbelief but recomposed himself. The cries from Ashley had drawn the centaurs to the tent and Griff entered.

The centaur immediately assessed the situation and realised that Michael had been abducted. "Ashley, stand still! Do not disturb the ground." Ashley froze as Griff pushed passed her to study the dirt floor around the bedroll. Fyros thundered into the tent, "What has happened!" he shouted.

Griff looked at the older centaur, "Michael has been taken."

"How?" replied Fyros.

"I'm not sure. The tracks here and outside the tent are confusing. Look here," Griff pointed to a line in the dirt. "this looks like the tracks of a snake. They lead from the doorway straight to Michael's bedroll.," Griff pointed to scuffled footprints, "These are clearly the mark of a man, but there are no man-made tracks leading here, either from outside or inside the tent." Griff pulled open the torn canvas and stepped through, as he did so he examined the patch of ground outside the tent. "Here we can see the man's footprints again and this," he traced the line of a pair of long lines in the dust, "must have been caused by Michael's heels as he was dragged from the tent. You can also see the indentation in the dirt where his body was laid out. He was unconscious when pulled out or he would have struggled."

"Or dead," added Ashley tears welling up in her eyes.

Fyros put his arm around her, "I don't think so Ashley. This looks more like an abduction than a killing. If someone had wanted him dead then they could easily have killed him whilst he slept. There would have been no reason to remove the body."

Griff was still busy examining the prints, "There are a

number of footprints here. Most are human but these are new." He indicated a series of imprints, "I believe that these were made by a large four footed reptile of some kind. They walk a few steps and then weight is placed on the hind legs before they disappear. It seems the abductor then took to the air. My guess is that the beast carried both the man and the boy."

Fyros looked up in alarm, "You are suggesting that a dragon swept the lad away! But how did it pass in and out without being seen, and, why abduct Michael and not the others?"

Griff shrugged, "I'm not sure. Maybe they came across us by chance and only had the means to take one of the youths. I suggest that we provide a closer guard for our Earth friends for the rest of our journey to prevent a reoccurrence. I wonder why they abducted him? Surely with such easy access to the tent they could easily have killed all three whilst they slept. It's curious that none of the guards saw anyone entering or leaving the camp though."

Rhys caught Ashley's eyes looking for approval before his next comment, "Maybe they used a portal gateway," he offered. Fyros raised his eyebrows questioningly and listened intently as Rhys explained all that had occurred that night. He looked especially thoughtful when told that Lan had suggested that Rhys himself had created the portal. When Rhys had finished Fyros scratched his head, "Well young man, it seems that you may well possess unique ability. We need to discuss this with the council once more. I feel we need to seek advice."

"But how will we do that, the crystal was lost with Michael, "asked Rhys.

Fyros reached into his vest and pulled out a long chain.

"The Cormion Crystal!" exclaimed Ashley, "but how?"

Fyros smiled, "Michael retrieved all four crystals from the

dramkaan. Cambor kept two for use by the council and gave me a spare just in case something of this sort occurred and the original crystal was lost." He placed the crystal around Ashley's neck. It's chain was shorter than the Runestone pendant and hung much closer to her throat. She was about to find out that there was a reason for this. Fyros continued, "Ashley, you will wear the crystal and provide our link to the council."

"Me?" replied Ashley, "But I can't use it, I don't have the ring. Why don't you take care of it until Mike is found?"

Fyros smiled at her, "You also possess the ability to use the crystal. The pendant that you wear around your neck is the catalyst. The crystals were created for communication with all Servants of the Runestone, so four were forged, one for each of the pendant wearers and the other for the ring bearer. We know that Rhys cannot touch the crystal, therefore the task must fall to yourself. Use it in the same manner as Michael, but touch the crystal to the pendant instead of the ring."

Ashley nodded, "Well OK, but only until we get Mike back." She did not look happy about it.

Rhys had been listening to this and spoke out, "Fyros, if I understand how the pendants work, isn't it right that images will be created for all of those who have a crystal?"

"That is correct," replied Fyros.

"Well Mike probably still has his crystal around his neck. If we use this one then whoever has Mike will be able to see and hear us."

Fyros nodded, "That is true Rhys and likewise we will see through the eyes of Michael. Therefore we must be cautious when we use the crystal. If Michael is awake and wearing the crystal then we cannot avoid him being part of the communication, however, if he sleeps, or if he has removed his crystal from around his neck, then he will not be a part of that communication."

"Then should we not try this immediately Fyros," commented Griff. "Michael may still be unconscious and it will give us an opportunity to talk openly with Cambor and the council. If he is conscious, then it will give us some indication of where his abductors may be taking him."

"That is true Griff," replied Fyros turning to Ashley. "Ashley, can you please make contact with Cambor. Take the Runestone pendant in your hand and hold it against the crystal. You need not do anything else other than hold the two together so they make contact during our communication. Initially though we will need to check what links are opened before we impart any information to the council however."

Ashley did as she was bade. She held the pendant in her right hand and lifted it to make contact with the crystal. Almost immediately the pair began to glow and the familiar projection emanated from within. Only one image appeared to them, that was the world as it appeared through the eyes of Cambor, the centaur council sat conversing with their leader. They all stopped as the images of Fyros and Griff appeared to them, projected as seen through the eyes of Ashley.

Cambor sensed that something was different but he did not know what, he looked at the image of Fyros and saw that he was troubled. "Good morning Fyros, what ails you?" he asked.

Fyros nodded a greeting and told Cambor and the council of all that had occurred, of Rhys' dream, the creation of the portal and the abduction of Michael and the loss of the first crystal."

Cambor shook his head and the image before Fyros swayed from side to side as he did so. This is not good news, it means that we will have to take great care when using the magic of the crystals. At present we can assume that either Michael is asleep or unconscious or that he, or another, has removed the crystal from around his neck. The latter would be both a blessing and a curse, for it would mean our discussions are safe from prying eyes but also that we lose a way of knowing of Michael's whereabouts. Although, from your description of events, I think we can make an educated guess that he has been taken into Dargoth by the enemy."

Fyros nodded, "It would seem that way. Let us hope that he has had the wits about him to hide the ring and the crystal. Given all that has occurred I am fairly sure that our foe would quickly recognise the items and use them for his own purposes."

"True," the image changed to the figure of Horos as Cambor looked directly at him, Horos continued, "But at least the ring is of no use to him without a Celtic knot pendant to initiate it's power. Also there is not much that our enemy can gain from the use of the Cormion Crystal. We will know when he uses this magic and we will be prepared. He cannot use it to spy on us without us seeing what he sees too, so the problem works two ways. All that he will be able to glean from it's use is the location of Cambor, who will be here in the city and, of course, the location of Ashley. Of these two only the latter would be of any import."

The vision in front of Fyros and Griff moved again as Cambor nodded and they heard him speak. "Despite what has occurred we must continue with our original plan. The council will need time to discuss and better understand the abilities that Rhys possesses. No-one has ever been able to create portals through thought alone and we will need to theorise how this could be. Also we must review the consequences and decide whether it is of use to us or a threat to our mission."

Cambor was rudely interrupted by the voice of Hesh.

The image quickly changed to that of the scornful centaur, "Well that at least I can answer for the council. This ability is nothing but a threat. Rhys obviously has no control over it and the portals have only appeared when he has been asleep or effected by the touch of powerful magic. I believe that this is not a latent ability within the boy but our enemy tapping his mind to create a portal opening. He desires this so that he can attack us from within. For all we know this is exactly what happened to Michael. The tracks left behind may have been a deliberate ploy to throw us off ." The image in front of Fyros and Griff became narrower and they realised that Cambor scowled at the ranting centaur. "Hesh, be silent, this is but personal supposition. You will have your chance to voice your opinion during our discussions." Cambor's voice softened as he addressed Fyros once more, "Fyros, continue as planned." There was a short pause before he continued, "Ashley," she jumped as Cambor addressed her, "Yes Cambor."

"I want to thank you for taking the role of communicator. Look after the crystal as best you can. Wear it so that it does not make contact with the Runestone pendant. We do not want accidental communication opened. This is even more important now that the enemy has possession of a crystal of his own."

"I will Cambor," she replied, suddenly feeling important.

Cambor now addressed them all, "Travel well! We shall talk again in a few hours after we have discussed the question of Rhys' portal creations."

Ashley released the pendant and the link was broken. Even though the chains differed in length, to avoid inadvertent contact, she tucked the crystal inside her shirt but wore the pendant outside.

Fyros spoke quietly to Griff, "Give the orders to break

camp and continue. I will stay by Rhys' side for the rest of our journey. I want to be around if another portal gateway is created."

Griff nodded and within a few minutes the platoon was once more winding it's way through the hills towards Fortown.

***

The boy had remained still as Ohrhim swept across the mountain tops. Now as it approached the plateau that housed Shangorth Towers it felt the youth beginning to stir.

Michael awoke and stared down at the jagged peaks of the Dargoth Mountains. Glancing upwards he saw that he was being carried by a black dragon. He began to scream and writhed in terror. Thrashing out with his arms and legs.

"Be still you fool or you'll fall!"

Michael fell silent on hearing the voice, he was not expecting the dragon to talk. The words brought him to his senses though and he glanced down at the rocky peaks below and realised that escape was not an option. He reluctantly calmed himself and sat still in it's grasp.

Maybe things are not as bad as they appear, after all the dragon could easily have killed me by now. He then began to feel panic rising once more as his thoughts. *But what if the dragon was keeping him alive to feed its young. He could be bound for it's home right now. He imagined the young dragons starting to tear at him with teeth and claws, fighting to pull him apart as they satisfied their hunger!* He screamed once more and began to struggle again.

Ohrhim lost patience with the youth and released his hold. Michael felt himself falling and screamed even louder. As the rocks below roared up to greet him he passed out. Ohrhim followed and skilfully gathered up the unconscious youth long before he struck the mountain peaks below.

They soon reached the plateau and Ohrhim looked down on the army of Graav. As they swooped overhead, Michael regained consciousness once more. Shaking with fear and petrified, he stared down at the citadel of Shangorth Towers and at the Graav army. At first he had thought them nothing but statues, similar to those stone armies buried with the ancient Chinese rulers, but then he saw the movement around the lava pools as the creatures bathed in the furnace. He felt dizzy and light headed as the dragon swept across the walls, adjusting it's flight to land at the top of the tall central tower.

Once landed, Ohrhim released his hold on Michael and the youth rolled away from the dragon. Michael turned to look at his captor, his eyes wide with terror. He realised that he was whimpering and tried to force himself to stop. With hands to his face, he watched in fascination as the shapechanger transformed from dragon to human form. Ohrhim smiled, "What's up kid, haven't you ever seen a man changing before?" Ohrhim threw back his head and laughed at his own quip. Michael continued to stare and gradually some of his composure returned. With a very shaky voice he asked, "Who are you and why have you brought me here?"

Ohrhim grinned, "To meet my good friend Shangorth, why else."

At hearing the warlocks name Michael's fear amplified. His head began to spin.. *Hadn't Kyrie told them that Shangorth was dead?*

Ohrhim pointed towards the tower stairs. "This way."

Michael stayed where he was. "No! If he wants to see me then he'll have to come up here," he responded defiantly. His voice still trembling.

Ohrhim stared at him, "I wouldn't advise that. Despite his lust for power, Shangorth is usually fairly controlled and calm. I fear that if you refuse to move, his temper would be raised. That would not be good for any of us. He can get very nasty when he is mad. I would suggest compliance as the best route to avoid needless pain."

Michael thought on this and realised the hopelessness of the situation. Dejectedly he rose to his feet and, with head bowed, shuffled after the shapechanger.

They descended two floors into the Runestone chamber. Michael and the warlock stared at each other at first sight. The youth felt fear totally overwhelm him as he faced the creature of his earlier nightmares. He looked into those evil red eyes and remembered the searing pain that had seeped through his brain during his dream. Shangorth sneered at him, the thin grey lips revealing yellowed teeth and fangs. "Welcome to Shangorth Towers, I trust you enjoyed your flight?"

Michael felt the blood drain from his head as blackness once again swept across his vision and he fainted, falling heavily to the stone floor.

Shangorth looked down at Michael, "What have you brought me here then my friend?"

Ohrhim imparted the events of the night before, unaware that he had captured the wrong youth. He told Shangorth that Michael seemed to possess the ability to open portals in his dreams.

Shangorth threw back his head and let out a roar of laughter, "Impossible! I fear that you have been misled Ohrhim. It is not possible for an individual to control the power of the portal web without the use of a Runestone. I know that for a fact. However, it is clear that something unusual happened. You did the right thing by bringing him to me. We will bend him to my will and we'll find out what he knows. It may be that this one possesses blood of the old line. Through that he may have the ability to create illusions, but he will not possess the ability to create a true portal. I suspect it is nothing more than that, a cheap illusion. Even so, as a friend of the others, he may prove useful."

As the warlock spoke Zarn entered the chamber. The White Dwarf looked down at Michael, "I know this one. I've seen him before somewhere." Zarn stood in thought, it didn't take long for him to remember, "It was in the cave. This boy is from Earth, I saw him and another when I was gathering spiders for our army."

Shangorth struck Zarn, "You mean you let him through the portal! You fool!"

Zarn cowered, "No master, I returned here and closed the portal behind me immediately. No-one followed."

The warlock paused, he walked over to Michael and rolled him over. He saw the ring almost immediately and tore it from Michael's finger. "The Eumor Runestone ring! How did this boy get hold of this? It was lost long ago." Shangorth searched Michael and found the crystal. He took it from Michael and examined it. "I think I have a good idea what this is too." He touched the crystal to the ring and they began to glow, he quickly pulled them apart. "A Cormion Crystal! Now that is interesting. I think this may prove to be of some use." The warlock slid the crystal into a pocket inside his cloak and pushed the ring over the middle finger of his right hand, it pulsed once and adjusted itself to fit perfectly. He looked at his hand, now adorned with two Runestone rings, the Ring of the Mountain and the Ring of the Celtic Knot.

"Arouse the boy Ohrhim, I have a few questions for him. Maybe there is more to this story of portal creation than I at first gave credit."

Ohrhim filled a cup with water and threw it over Michael's

face. He came too and scampered across the floor cowering away from them. When he eventually gathered the courage to face them, he saw Shangorth staring at him again. The warlock glared, "Who are you boy and how did you arrive in Portalia?"

Michael did not say a word, he sat staring at the warlock as if transfixed. "I command you to speak. What is your name?" bellowed the warlock. He was not used to being ignored and his temper was beginning to rise. Ohrhim walked to Michael and whispered in his ear, "You'd do better to answer."

Michael looked at the shapechanger and nodded, he breathed in deeply and found a determination to face his fear, "My name is Michael."

Ohrhim cursed silently, it's mistake suddenly apparent, he had taken the wrong boy. It was the youth Rhys who had dreamed the portals. Ohrhim looked at the irate warlock and chose not to inform him of this mistake.

"And how did you get here?" prompted the warlock.

Michael found the courage to sit up and look at his tormentor, he remained silent.

"ANSWER ME BOY! How did you come here and tell me what you know of creating portals through your dreams." screamed the warlock.

Michael was feeling braver by the second, he looked Shangorth in the eyes and said, "I don't think I like you and I'm definitely not going to answer your questions!"

Michael was taken by surprise by what happened next. He expected the warlock to lose his temper, instead he started to laugh, "Oh, how amusing, you have chosen to defy me. I guess that I may as well let you go then, what do you think?"

Michael was confused, he hadn't expected this, "I guess that's the best idea," he stuttered.

Shangorth suddenly stopped laughing. For Michael the pain was about to begin.

The orb around the warlock's neck began to glow and two red beams of light streamed from his eyes towards Michael. The youth had enough time to register this image with his earlier dream. He began to scream even before the agony started and his brain began to throb against his skull. Michael felt that his very being, his memories and thoughts were being pulled from him and sucked into the warlock. As he felt the final piece of himself disappear into darkness, the last thing he saw was the manic sneering face of the warlock and the grey evil lips uttering, "Come to my Soul Orb—now all that you are and all that you know will be mine!".

CHAPTER SIXTEEN
Reinforcements

The dwarves on watch had been the first to see the black eagle. It flew alone, hovering high above the town, a mere dot in the sky. Gorlan and Swiftaxe watched the bird circle overhead.

"It seems our enemy is feeling more bold and openly chooses to use his black eagles to spy on us," said Gorlan.

King Swiftaxe nodded, "Aye! I feel that too! Although I am not sure how as the eagles carry no riders, they possess no voice and, as far as I am aware, they do not have any mind bond with any other. Even so, they appear to spy on us and our foe must have a way of communicating with them." The pair watched as the eagle continued it's vigil. "Shall we send up the fire eagles to kill them?"

Gorlan shook his head, "We already tried that earlier. As soon as any of our birds take to the air the black eagle flees. Even though our birds are faster, the distance is too great to catch up with their prey before they are well over Dargoth. I do not want to send our forces away in chase until we have received reinforcements. Our enemy may have forces spread all over the mountains and we cannot afford to lose anymore of our fire eagles."

King Swiftaxe was troubled but did not disagree with the WarLord. "Then I suppose that we will have to put up with being watched for the present. Our scouts should be well into the mountains by now. Hopefully they will provide some information about our enemy when they return. It annoys me that our enemy spies on us whilst we remain blind to him!" As they watched a second black eagle joined the first.

Above the heads of the watchers the eagles floated on the air currents. Clinging to the feathers of the birds were a handful of small spiders, their tiny webs blowing in the breeze.

Far to the south-west, in his stone tower, Shangorth stood deep in concentration, his eyes closed. In his hand he held the Staff of the Spider Gem. It was throbbing with energy. Waves streamed from the gem, dancing and writhing over the warlock's body, as the current carried the flow towards the head of the sorcerer where it seemed to seep inside through his exposed ears. In Shangorth's mind images were formed, allowing him to observe all of Fortown through the eyes of the spiders riding on their winged hosts.

***

Meanwhile, as Shangorth spied on the town, two dwarf scouts picked their way through the mountains heading directly towards the citadel of the Towers. Folken flew overhead, urging his warbird to stay low against the mountainside to avoid detection. The group had stopped to hide themselves on a number of occasions, warned of the approaching presence of black eagles by the superior eye-sight of the fire eagles and their telepathic ability to detect danger.

When they set off they had chosen a route that would run adjacent to where Carl and Stern had discovered the Graav a few days before. Whilst this proved much more rugged than the well trodden path, the dwarves, experienced mountain travellers, progressed through terrain that would have been impossible for many.

The dwarves rarely spoke to each, other than to discuss their progress and notify each other of danger. They knew that they were better served to conserve their energy and move swiftly towards what they believed to be the base of their enemy. Each dwarf carried an assortment of weapons and tools, some sheathed to a belt around their waist and others stored in a grey rucksack that they carried across their backs. Both possessed a vicious looking battleaxe, a telescope, an ice-pick, numerous ropes and grappling irons for climbing, a compass, basic maps, cold rations for five days and implements for recording what they observed. When they had been introduced to Folken and advised that he would accompany them, they had greeted him politely and had then turned to each other to discuss the best use of this new resource. Folken, who was not involved in this discussion, could not help but smile when they finally informed him of his part in the mission. Their decision was precisely as that ordered by Gorlan when he had sent him to find the dwarves. On the journey to Shangorth, Folken would provide cover and scouting from the air. Once there, the group would gather as much data as possible and would send the fire eagle rider back with this information as speedily as possible, leaving the dwarves to return alone. At first Folken had been concerned about this plan as he did not want to leave the dwarves to fend for themselves. However, after a few hours of watching them traverse the rugged landscape, he realised how tough these mountain breed were and his worries were forgotten.

Folken watched the pair as they arrived at a small ravine. Observing that they had halted their progress, Folken directed his mount to land to the side of the pair. "Is there something wrong?" he asked.

Borst, the first dwarf looked at Folken but did not speak.

Yam, the second dwarf, replied for him, "Borst is worried that this ravine may provide an opportunity for our enemy to ambush us."

When Folken had first met them earlier that day, he had presumed the two to be brothers, or at least related in some way, but they had both assured him that they were not. Both possessed a thick mane of red hair which hid their ears and joined a full growth of beard that stretched to their chests. Both were stocky and solidly built, even by the standards of dwarves. They possessed short stubby arms and legs that were rippling with sinew, ideal for the journey they now faced. They shared similar facial features that included a short flattened nose, two dark brown eyes and a pair of very full pink lips. Folken had also soon discovered that Yam was the more vocal of the two. Borst was very serious and wore an almost permanent scowl. He hardly spoke other than to request information or to discuss their plan.

Folken watched as Borst signalled to them to remain where they were and then ducked cautiously into the ravine. A few minutes later he returned, "I believe that the ravine offers a safe path, there are no signs of any enemy." He addressed Folken, "Your warbird may find it easier if you walked through the ravine and allow him to fly freely until we reach the end. The channel is narrow and in places would offer difficulty for it to fly whilst carrying a rider. The way is dotted with twists and turns."

Folken thanked the dwarf for this insight and agreed to accompany them on foot. With this agreed, they continued, Folken welcoming the opportunity to chat with Yam as they progressed.

***

The black eagles and their passenger spiders continued to watch over Fortown, oblivious to the danger that approached. The first alarm came when they heard the rush of air as the fire eagles approached and they turned to face vicious claws bearing down on them. The black eagles had no time to react as talons tore into the skin around their necks. Their final sense of feeling was the burning of their flesh as the fire eagles took hold and flames erupted from within. Their lives were sparked out. Black eagle and spiders fell to the ground as charred flesh.

Below in Fortown the entire population was on the streets, waving and cheering as a hundred fire eagles carrying Pinn warriors descended from the skies. Gorlan had seen them coming and watched as they swiftly dispatched the black spies from the sky.

Pinnel led the reinforcements and brought the riders in to land as the crowd in the town square parted to provide space for them. He brought his eagle to halt in front of the three leaders and dismounted, bowing deeply when he realised that he was facing King Swiftaxe.

Gorlan ushered him to his feet and stepped forward. He hugged his warrior in welcome, "It is good to see you old friend," Lloyd joined them as they spoke, "You too Lloyd. You made good speed. What word do you bring from the OverLord?"

"OverLord Toran sends greetings and wishes all that protect our lands a safe return to their homes. He places you in command of the forces that he has dispatched to utilise as needs demand." Pinnel cast his eyes over the crowd and noted the presence of the dwarves. "The OverLord also expressed hope that other allies would respond. It is good to see that we have already been joined by the dwarves." Pinnel turned to King Swiftaxe, "Thank you for your swift assistance sire." The King bowed his head in acknowledgement.

"What size of force has been dispatched from Pinnhome?" asked Gorlan.

"As well as the riders you see before you, one thousand cavalry and five thousand infantry have left our capital. The OverLord demanded that they avoid the path through the Halfman Forest so, their journey will take a little longer but it will prevent any losses to the Halfman Horde."

"An unfortunate delay but a wise decision none the less," commented Gorlan

"The cavalry should arrive here within two days, the infantry a further three days. If the weather continues to hold, and we avoid summer storms, then they may even improve on that."

"Let us hope that they can. The sooner we receive additional forces the better I will feel." Gorlan turned to Tosh, "The town is fast becoming over crowded. Take our forces and make camp at the outskirts. A semi-permanent camp can be made there. Ensure all are comfortable, we may have rough times ahead of us."

Fleck stepped forward, "If I may, we have already considered the housing of your troops Gorlan. There is a large stable to the north of the town. Sadly, with the exception of the mother and eldest son, all of the family that ran this stable perished at the hands of the Graav. They have already cleared the stables for use by your cavalry when they arrive. There is also plenty of open land there to accommodate the warbirds and their riders, as well as to camp the five thousand infantry that make their way here."

Gorlan bowed his head, "Thank you Fleck, that is kind of your people."

"The honour is ours Gorlan," replied the Fortownian counsellor.

***

True to his word Fyros trotted alongside Rhys and Ashley. Much to Ashley's dismay they were joined by Meld who had taken to avoiding her since the incident on the bridge. Even Lan, mounted on DiamondCrest, had taken to riding calmly alongside Rhys rather than galloping madly to and fro around the party.

Ashley was too embarrassed to speak to Meld. She had long forgiven him for the way he had treated her on the bridge and through discussion with Rhys, now realised that he had intentionally angered her so that she would forget her fears. She was still angry with him though as he was clearly avoiding her. She had even started to believe that he truly did look upon her as an immature little girl. Eventually, unable to bear the silence between them any longer, Ashley spoke, "Meld, How far is it to your home?".

Meld looked at her, surprise clearly shown on his face. He knew that she was fully aware of how long the journey would take and wondered why she had chosen to talk to him now and ask such an inane question. He responded politely but was very suspicious about her intent. "We should be there within a day. If we did not camp this evening then we could reach there by first light. However, Griff is most insistent that we rest tonight. Although I myself am eager to be back home with my kin."

"Then why don't you ride ahead of us?" Ashley had not meant this to be a suggestion that Meld part company with them but, given his suspicious demeanour, this was how he interpreted her comment. He glared at her, now feeling his own anger rising, "Perhaps I shall!" he exclaimed and turned his mount. Ashley watched in astonishment as the Fortownian galloped away towards the front of the platoon.

Rhys looked at Ashley and raised his eyebrows, "Phew, what's eating him?" he asked.

Ashley shrugged, "Who knows. And who cares!" she said, her face set grimly. Inside she felt differently. She really had not intended to hurt Meld and she realised he had misinterpreted her comment. For a moment she pondered whether she should ride after him to apologise. She decided against this though. If he wanted to act like a spoiled brat then let him stew a little. Her thoughts turned to his words on the bridge and she decided that there may have been more truth in his comments than Rhys realised. Perhaps he truly did prefer the company of others rather than herself. Despite not wanting to, she could not help but feel sad at that thought.

They had been riding through the hills for a number of hours when Griff brought the party to a halt. He ordered the platoon to rest for a while and to take on food and water. After checking that all had heard his orders he joined Fyros, Rhys and Ashley and together they opened communication with the council once more. All felt relief when they saw that no third link had been created by Michael's crystal.

The image that they saw before them took them by surprise. Instead of the council chambers, they looked out of Cambor's eyes upon a large rectangular room. It was sparsely furnished. A couple of very old chairs and a few small occasional tables were set around the room. In the centre, on the stone cast floor, pillows and cushions had been placed for the comfort of centaurs. The room was lit by the suns rays that shone through four large stained glass windows.

These windows depicted various scenes. Two showed the various races of Portalia, busying themselves about their daily tasks. One focussed on centaurs, elves and dwarves, the other, on humans. Another showed the Celtic knot Runestone, surrounded by the depiction of the twenty portal web points picked out in tiny pieces of coloured glass. It was on the final window that Cambor let his gaze rest. Depicted in the relief was a group of wizards, all with hands linked forming a circle. Their faces were well defined and showed that their eyes were closed. All appeared to be in deep concentration.

Around the wizards, in the background, were representations of all the races of Portalia. Dwarves, centaurs, man and elves watched the wizard circle. The wizards themselves were shown standing on a blank Runestone. At the centre of the triangular stone the glazier had formed the image of an open portal gateway. The blue stone that had been used for this depiction was extremely beautiful. Tiny facets had been cut in it's surface and caused the sunlight to refract. It seemed that the portal itself seemed to glow on the glass and appeared to reach out of the flat surface.

Cambor turned his head slightly and Horos appeared in the crystal image. "We've come here to the reading room. This building adjoins the library at Eumor and is now used as a place to sit quietly, a place to read and to reflect. It is very old. We believe that it was once used for consultations with the wizards when they visited the city. We came here to show you this." Horos pointed to the window that depicted the wizard circle. Cambor approached it so that they could make out the details even more clearly.

"This window has been discussed by many over the years. No-one truly knows what this shows, but it is clearly related to the creation of the portal web. We also believe it may have some bearing on what Rhys is experiencing. Look closely at the Runestone in the glass. You'll notice that it does not bear any emblem. No Celtic knot, no mountain or oak tree. Neither does the stone possess a pedestal. Some argue that this was just 'artistic license' but, it has been theorised, that this was how the portal gateways were opened before the wizards created the control devices and keys.

If this is true then it would suggest that the wizards possessed an ability to naturally control the portal web. This may well be what Rhys is experiencing. It could be that he possesses the genealogy of the great wizards from his ancestors. We know that some of them travelled to Earth. It is not unfeasible to suppose that some may have taken human partners whilst there."

Even Fyros raised his eyebrows at this suggestion. Before anyone could speak though, Horos continued, "However, look again at the window. Count the wizards and observe their level of concentration. If our supposition is correct then the control of the single portal that we see depicted here requires the linking of at least eight wizards. How then could it be that Rhys, alone and with no knowledge of the magics, is able to create the opening of a portal unaided? Maybe it was always so. Perhaps the wizards of old possessed the ability to create a random portal but, could only control the destination of that portal through their combined minds? It is clearly a puzzle."

Horos was suddenly interrupted by loud decipherable mutterings from Lan. He had approached the projection and was staring at the window, clearly fascinated by the image. Cambor, observing Lan through the eyes of Ashley, immediately moved his gaze away from the window. Lan's concentration waived and he fell silent once more. They heard the council leaders voice. "It seems this picture troubles Lan. Here is another mystery. Who is this old man and what does he know about these ancient magics? The council and myself are agreed that his presence is not coincidental. He is somehow linked to all of this."

Rhys could not contain himself any longer, "So let me repeat what I think you are telling me. Basically you are suggesting that I am the descendant of the old wizards and that I possess the ability to open portals through a natural talent. However, without the assistance of other wizards I will never be able to control these portals and their creation could come upon me at anytime while I'm asleep. Is this correct?"

"More or less," replied Horos, "We also believe that the ability could be honed to allow you to create portals whilst you are awake. Of course, we are guessing and have little to go on other than this stained glass window and a few scribbles on ancient texts, but we now deem it possible that all wizards possessed the ability to *create* portals but not to control them, much like yourself."

"But if this is true why haven't I always been able to do it?" asked Rhys.

"We're not sure but it is possibly one of three things, or even a combination of all three. The first, that you are closer to the heart of the portal by being present here in Portalia. The second, that you have used the portal web to get here and have 'touched' the magic. The third, being that you wear the Runestone pendant. All could explain the awakening of this power."

Rhys looked thoughtful, "I think I understand, but what good does it do. If I can't create them at will or control them then they are unusable, aren't they?"

Horos looked sympathetic, "I'm afraid that's true. In fact, the portals may prove more of a threat than a blessing. You may inadvertently open a gateway that would allow others to travel here. Because of this, we insist that you are accompanied at all times, especially whilst you sleep. At least until we understand more about what is happening. We want someone to be close-by should you open a portal during your dreams."

Rhys did not like the thought of being watched twenty-four hours a day. It was bad enough having Lan under his feet from morning until night. However, he realised that this was the only real option that they had. "OK Horos, I get it, and I understand why you'll need to watch me. One thing though. Deep down inside I feel that this is a good thing. After all, if I can learn to control this I may be able to open a portal back home to Wales."

Horos nodded, "I hope you are right Rhys. I fear though that without the assistance of others with wizard blood, you will be unable to control the portals. Therefore I ask that you do not get your hopes high about creating your own route back home. To travel through a randomly generated portal could prove extremely dangerous."

Rhys nodded, "I know Horos, but it makes me feel good that there is possibility of another way for us to get back home."

The communication continued with Fyros providing a report of their progress to the council. Griff explained that he intended to camp one more night before moving on to Fortown and the council nodded their approval of this. The rest of the conversation was spent with the passing of messages for and from loved ones back in Eumor.

Whilst Ashley had to remain to keep the link open, Rhys left the gathering. He saw Lan sitting on the grass away from the others. The old man was doing something, Rhys walked nearer to take a closer look. As he approached Lan took no notice of him but continued his activity, deep in concentration. He sat with his eyes closed and his legs crossed. His only movement was his arms, which he moved from outspread on either side, to folded across his chest and them upwards to touch his lips. He constantly mumbled words to himself under his breath. Rhys spoke his name but Lan ignored him and continued with these strange arm movements. All of sudden Lan leapt into the air, looked at Rhys and started to jump up and down on the spot. With a great big grin on his face he shouted, "Lan knows, Lan knows!" Then, just as suddenly, he paused, looked at Rhys, stuck out his tongue and fell silent. He turned his back on the youth and walked to where DiamondCrest was grazing. He wrapped his arms around the horses and rested his head on the horses neck. "Lan knows, Lan knows! Far he was! Far he was!" he whispered to the horse, his face now crestfallen, the earlier smile lost as a silent tear ran down each cheek.

**

Shangorth was disappointed in Ohrhim. Despite the shapechanger's assurance that he had not realised that he had abducted the wrong boy, the warlock felt that he lied. Still, the boy had proven extremely useful so he had decided to forgive his minion on this occasion. The power of the Soul Orb had sucked the life essence from the boy, transferring all his memories, and mental abilities for conscious thought, to the warlock. Shangorth grinned as he contemplated the power of the Soul Orb. He had now used it over a hundred times, yet he still felt a buzz of excitement and elation each time he called upon it's power. He raised his hand to hold the Orb and contemplated what he had learned from Michael. Even though Shangorth basked in his own brilliance and felt no fear, he now knew that there were other factors at play within Portalia. Factors of which, until now, he had been completely unaware. If this boy, Rhys, truly possessed the ability to create portals from thought alone, then he could prove a threat. Although, if the youth could be turned to join with him, then conversely he could become a powerful ally.

Shangorth dismissed Ohrhim and Zarn to consider these events. He kept Michael with him but had insisted that Zarn secure the youth to the wall, leaving him only a few yards of chain to allow minimal movement. Michael was now rolled into a ball on the cold stone floor. He mumbled and murmured nonsense, occasionally humming out an unfamiliar tune. His mind was in turmoil. Changing from blank to confused thoughts. Each time his brain latched onto a coherent idea or memory, searing hot pain tore through his head causing him to writhe in pain and groan out loud. Better then to let his mind wander insanely. No focus, no pain.

Shangorth's concentration was disturbed as a pigeon flew into the chamber. It landed at his feet and he bent over to pick it up. He removed Nexus' message from it's foot and threw the bird back out of the open window. "Aha, so the Pinns march, just as I predicted. Perfect timing," he said out loud, reading the report from his agent. He called out for the dwarf, "Zarn! Find Ohrhim and bring him here. We need to ready ourselves for the next stage of my plan."

Only a few minutes had passed when both Zarn and Ohrhim stood before him. The warlock was seated on a large ornate chair of carved black wood. The seat and chair back were covered with a cloth of dark, blood red velvet.

He gestured for the dwarf to approach him, standing as he did so. He removed the Celtic knot runestone ring and the Cormion Crystal and handed them to the dwarf. "Wear these! I have an important task for you."

Zarn could hardly believe what was happening. He grabbed at the items hungrily and quickly placed the crystal around his neck. He felt a brief moment of panic when he placed the ring on his finger as he felt it tighten, re-adjusting itself to fit snugly.

Shangorth continued, "When I give the signal, I want you to stand in front of me and hold the ring against the crystal. Do not be startled with what occurs. Images will appear projected in front of you. They will flow through you but will not harm you. When I give another signal you are to break the contact between the objects. Do you understand?"

The White Dwarf nodded.

Shangorth waited for the dwarf to take up position, "Good now focus your eyes on my face, come closer so that little else can be seen." Zarn hated being close to Shangorth as it usually resulted in pain but he did as he was bid. "Good," commented the warlock, "Now hold the ring to the crystal."

Zarn held the objects together, they began to glow and he immediately let go, worried that he would be burned.

"Fool! Hold them together, they will not harm you!" raged Shangorth.

Zarn swallowed hard and brought them back together again, he relaxed as he realised that the glow possessed no heat. Only fear of the warlock prevented him releasing the items again as two projections emanated from the crystal to either side of him. He kept his gaze on the warlock as ordered. He could also make out other images at the corner of his vision.

Simultaneously images appeared to Ashley and Cambor.

"Look! Centaurs! How cute!" scoffed Shangorth. "You will bend to me you know. Shangorth will rule over Portalia. Humans, centaurs, dwarves and elves! All will be my servants."

Lan looked at the image of Shangorth and screamed in fury, he jumped from DiamondCrest at the projection, snarling and bearing his teeth. He passed through the image and hit the ground hard. Shangorth watched in amusement as Fyros moved forward with haste and pulled the crystal over Ashley's head. This image disappeared. However, he had not been swift enough to prevent the warlock learning that the travelling band were only a day away from their destination.

The other image remained and the figures of the centaur council appeared. The warlock smiled as he saw the surprise and fear in the faces of the centaur's.

Horos spoke, "So you have returned evil one. You know that you will be defeated once more, do you not?"

The warlock laughed loudly, "Cute AND funny, what a wonderful species, such a pity that you have such limited time left in your existence." Shangorth let the smile disappear from his face and sneered at the centaurs, "It is you that will feel defeat this time fools. There are no wizards to help you this time and I have an army that is capable of defeating anything that you could put in my way, even those accursed fire eagles." He paused to let his words sink in before continuing, "Now I am bored, I think I may take a few thousand souls to amuse myself in the next few days. Bye for now." He smiled at them and signalled for Zarn to break the connection. The images disappeared. Shangorth spat on the floor, the spittle landed on Michael who was crawling under his feet pulling at his tight chain. "I hate centaurs, so self righteous."

Shangorth turned his attention back to Zarn and Ohrhim, "Ohrhim, I think your carrion form would be useful again. Fly to Fortown and spy on our foe. I have recalled the Black Eagles to prepare for battle. Tomorrow we will send the Graav, the eagles and the dwarf and human army to march to Fortown. We will join them with our spider army via the portal. Go now and watch for anything unusual."

The shapechanger left as ordered, glad to be heading away from the Towers and back in the freedom of the skies once more. For a few seconds he considered whether he could have been mistaken about the task that his gods had set before him. He quickly shook this off though and reassured himself that this was his destiny, beating his wings hard as he headed for Fortown.

As Ohrhim climbed into the sky, far below two dwarves, a dismounted Pinn rider and a fire eagle hugged the hillside. They continued their progress up to a high peak that overlooked the Shangorth Tower plateau. Moving cautiously to avoid being spotted by the black eagles, they found a suitable overhang that would allow them to spy on the forces below. They pulled their cloaks around them, protection for the snow that covered the peaks at this height. Removing telescope devices from their packs they began a closer inspection of their foe. They remained here for a number of hours, counting eagles, Graav and men and searching the terrain fruitlessly for the army of spiders. Finally they documented their findings and handed two sheets of parchment to Folken. The Pinn and his fire eagle made their way back from the plateau and down the mountainside. Once they reached a suitable point, he mounted his warbird out of sight of the black eagles and took to the air. Turning his bird towards Fortown, Folken stayed low and hugged the hillside.

Back in the sanctity of his tower, Shangorth had retreated to his study and was pouring over parchments. He paused at a particular passage relating to the manipulation of beings with simple minds. He read it with interest and then looked up and grinned, "Oh yes, now this could be very useful". He rolled up the parchment and tucked it under his arm. Rising to his feet, he descended to the chamber below. Michael was alone in the room, chasing a small bug around the stone floor but simply not quick enough to catch it. The warlock looked at him and nodded. "Yes, I am sure this will work." He held out a biscuit and the boy looked at it hungrily, "Michael, come to me, I have a little experiment that I'd like to try."

Michael stared at the food. At first he did not move, but the temptation of the biscuit finally overcame his fear and he lunged forward to snatch at the offering. As he did so, Shangorth grabbed both of the boy's wrists. Bending them upwards he forced the boy painfully to his knees. The warlock released Michael's right hand and placed his palm flat on top of the boy's head. Mutterings the enchantment that he discovered in his library, Shangorth cast his spell.

Almost immediately Michael began to twitch violently and his eyes rolled back. The warlock increased the pressure, bringing his thumbs to the boy's temples. Michael's twitching became excessively violent. Bruises were already beginning to form where the warlock pressed against his skin. Suddenly, with one last quiver, Michael stopped moving. Shangorth released his hold and Michael stood in front of him. He stood silent, as if waiting for something, or someone. The madness and erratic ramblings were gone.

Shangorth looked at his new creation. "Who is your master?"

Michael looked into the warlock's eyes. "You are sir!" he replied.

Shangorth decided to test the depth of the enchantment. He walked to a table in the corner of the room and picked up a small knife and a napkin, left there from his earlier meal.

"Here, prove yourself. Drive this knife into your arm."

He threw the knife to Michael. It landed with a clatter at his feet. The youth picked up the utensil in his right hand and, without hesitation, drove the blade into his left forearm. Shangorth winced as he saw the tip of the knife blade enter the boy's arm. Michael did not even acknowledge any pain. His face remained passive as he awaited the next command.

This was even better than Shangorth had hoped. It seemed that the effects of the new spell had combined with the powers of the Soul Orb. Not only would Michael follow his every command but the youth would be oblivious to any pain or feeling of emotion. Shangorth smiled broadly, pleased with this new found power.

He approached Michael and removed the knife from the wound. He then used the cloth napkin to tightly bandage the wound to quell the bleeding. Searching the eyes of the youth and finding no hint of individualism, Shangorth gave him a new order. "You will stand at my side and will protect me from anyone that means me harm. Even if this means the loss of your own life. "

Shangorth removed the chains from the youth and returned to rest in his chair. Michael followed obediently and took up a standing position at the warlock's side. His mind was focused on that last order. If he had to he would kill to save his new master.

CHAPTER SEVENTEEN
Portals from the Mind

Griff had brought the platoon to a halt four hours to the northwest of Fortown. Camp had been struck and Ashley had taken the opportunity to make good on her promise to Griff by setting up another football game. Rhys was reluctant to join in given the loss of Michael , but Ashley had persuaded him that the game would help him relax and take his mind off things. She had been right once again.

Given that the centaurs were over four feet taller than the teenagers and possessed an additional two legs they decided to take up position in goal for their teams. Michael's place on the third team was taken by Meld. Rhys had asked him to get involved as Ashley had point blankly refused to approach the Fortownian. It did not take long for Meld to adjust to the game and he was soon playing like a natural, diving to his left and right with amazing agility to push the ball away from the goal.

Ashley's team were sitting the current game out, having beaten Rhys' team in the previous game by one goal to nil. Ashley herself was refereeing the game. She watched in admiration as Meld bravely dived at the feet of an attacking centaur to scoop the ball up and roll it away to safety once more. Ashley smiled as she thought of the goalkeepers that she knew back in the USA, not many would have been brave enough to dive amongst the flashing hooves of a full grown centaur!"

Griff was playing on Rhys' team and seemed to be enjoying the game even though he was struggling to get to grips with some of the skills required to project the ball in the direction he desired. A few of the other centaurs, who had played a few days before, took advantage of this and seemed to enjoy getting the better of their leader. Teasing him in a light hearted way. Griff took this well though and responded in like.

Ashley checked her watch and blew her whistle for full time. Meld's team had won by one goal to nil and would now play against her team. A win would secure the mini tournament for Meld's team and Ashley was determined that this wouldn't happen. After all, this was an Earth sport and, as such, should be won by either her team or Rhys'.

The two teams lined up against each other, Rhys blew his whistle to start the game.

Despite having only just learned the intricacies of the game, the centaurs were totally immersed in the competition. They had already caught the fever and desire to win and played with a passion that rivalled that of the parks and fields around Earth. The ball was taking a hammering as it was kicked back and forth. The centaurs had learned to pass the ball accurately as well as how to use their strength to fire it at the goal with some force. Ashley had played in goal many times and she was determine to match the agility that Meld showed. Time and time again it looked like one of the teams had taken the initiative only for Meld or Ashley to fly across their goal and punch the ball away.

Eventually, with the two teams still tied with no goals for either, Rhys blew his whistle to end the game.

"So what happens now?" asked Fyros sweat dripping from his brow.

"Well we can either call it a tied game, or, we can have a

penalty shoot out," replied Rhys. "I think a penalty shoot out would be fun."

Rhys explained how this worked. Each team would get five penalties each, one on one with the goalkeeper. He checked that they all understood. Meld and Ashley chose five players to take the penalties for their teams before taking up position in goal. Both wore expressions of grim determination.

The first three penalties for each team flew into the goal with neither Ashley or Meld anywhere close to making a save. Ashley was first to make a breakthrough, diving to her left to push a poorly hit shot around the post.

She grinned at Meld in triumph as he took up his position to face his fourth penalty, "Top that then!" she said as he passed her.

Meld frowned and set his stance for the penalty. He adjusted his balance across both legs and bent his knees, ready to jump either way. He need not have bothered, the shot he faced was far too high and sailed over the cross bar of the goal. He took no notice of Ashley as she passed him to take up her position to face her fifth penalty.

Ashley looked at her opponent. She noticed that this penalty was being taken by a centaur who had shown particular talent for the game and had a shot like a cannonball. The centaur sprinted to the ball and let fly. The ball was screaming to Ashley's left and she dived at the last minute and got her hands to it. Unfortunately the ball was hit with so much power that she failed to hold the ball. She watched in horror as the ball squirmed out of her hands to bounce once and then trickle over the line.

She bowed her head and walked to the side of the goal to watch Meld face the final penalty. Unlike the previous shot that he faced, the ball was kicked firmly and accurately, heading for the top left hand corner of the goal. Meld made a desperate lunge to towards it and threw his hand up towards the ball as it flew over his head. His finger tips caught the very edge of ball and it was enough to re-direct it's path and tip it just over the top of the cross bar. Ashley stared in disbelief, it truly was an awesome save. She felt that she should be disappointed but the save had been so spectacular she could not help but clap and cheer, even though the save had cost her team the tournament.

She ran over and hugged him, "Great save Meld, I think I'm going to take you home with me to Earth. I know a few teams that could use a goalkeeper like you."

Meld beamed back at her, "Thanks Ash. You were unlucky though, you nearly made a great save yourself."

She smiled at him and was about to respond but Meld's team-mates had now engulfed them and had raised him up onto a willing back in celebration. He was swept away from her.

Griff walked off the field alongside Rhys, "This is a great game Rhys, I think that it will grow in popularity even after you are gone. Who knows, maybe we'll even have a regular tournament in your honour."

Rhys smiled, "Now that would be something, centaurs versus dwarves in the final of the Ashley-Rhys Football Challenge Cup. I bet the BBC would pay a small fortune to televise that game!" and Rhys laughed out loud. Not wishing to offend, Griff smiled back, but truthfully had no idea who the BBC were or indeed what televise meant.

Later that evening Rhys was laid down in his tent deep in thought. Ashley and Meld, now back on good terms, had recently left Rhys alone with his thoughts whilst they took a walk in the hills close to the camp. Fyros had ousted Lan from his place at the entrance to the tent and had taken up residence there himself. He wanted to be close to Rhys in case he created another portal. However, he was also conscious that the youth needed some privacy, hence his reason for remaining outside the tent.

Rhys was lost in thoughts of home. He recalled his bedroom and the games he played with his parents. A sudden flapping and breath of a breeze broke Rhys' concentration and he sat up as Lan entered the tent. This was the first Rhys had seen of the old man since he had seen him so distraught earlier that day. Unusually Lan had kept well away from him and rode a little behind the platoon mumbling and muttering to DiamondCrest almost incessantly. Rhys looked up, "Oh, Hi Lan, it's you." he said, not expecting any answer.

Lan looked at the boy quizzically and Rhys could see that something still troubled him. He sat himself down next to Rhys and started to gesture with his hands. Rhys frowned, unsure of Lan's intentions. Lan pointed to his neck and made an arc movement before raising his hands to his head and groaning as if in pain.

"Steady Lan. Take it easy and calm down."

Lan drew in a deep breath and closed his eyes. Rhys waited for a couple of minutes but Lan did not stir or open them again. Just as Rhys suspected that Lan had fallen asleep, the old man's eyes suddenly flew open and he started to make darting movements with his hands. Lan grabbed Rhys left hand and forced it upwards to clutch the Runestone pendant. Rhys tried to pull back but the old man held him tight. Rhys began to panic. In his mind, he saw the spinning images of the portal gateway, just as before. He groaned out loud, he did not want to go here again. He pulled hard with his hand and tried to tear his thoughts away from the images. As he did so he heard a strong voice in his head telling him to remain calm and to focus his mind on watching the portal. The sound of another's voice stopped him from withdrawing. He listened to that voice and felt a recognition there that immediately calmed him. As his panic subsided, the images in the portal began to slow and the voice urged him to calm himself and to look for a stable, single image within the portal gateway. He did as he was bid and his concentration became focussed on that one activity.

In the tent Lan watched Rhys closely but still held on tightly to Rhys hands. The pain in Lan's own head was getting intense and he started to groan. Fyros was alerted by the sound and stepped inside just as Rhys succeeded in finding a solid, single portal image in his mind. Fyros stared in fascination as a portal gateway burst into being before his very eyes. He saw Lan and Rhys locked together and it was evident that Lan was in severe pain. He was however, reluctant to pull the two apart, unsure of what effect that may have on either of them.

The voice in his mind spoke to Rhys once more, "Leave your thoughts here on this portal and open your eyes. See what you have created."

Rhys opened his eyes and looked into the portal. In his mind Rhys could see that the gateway led to a place where rain lashed against a rocky shore, it was night-time. Through his eyes Rhys could not see through to the other side of the portal. All his eyes could discern was the blue glow of an open gateway, just as they had first seen in Salty's Cave.

Rhys stared in fascination. Realisation hit him with a shock. This portal was under his control, he had created it and he could control it. Staring at his creation and wondering how he had achieved it, he did not, at first, notice the pain that Lan was experiencing. A comment from Fyros made him more aware of his surroundings and he then saw the suffering in Lan's face. Rhys immediately lost concentration on the portal, terrified at what this link was doing to his friend. The portal immediately disappeared and Lan fell to the ground, thoroughly exhausted.

Both Fyros and Rhys rushed to the aid of the old man. They helped him to sit up and Fyros called for some feyberry tea. Ashley and Meld entered the tent, drawn by the commotion of Fyros shouting. They were both relieved to see that Rhys was fine but their faces showed concern when they looked at Lan. The old man looked drawn and exhausted. "Like death warmed up!" muttered Ashley under her breath.

A centaur brought in the tea but Lan refused to drink the brew. His eyes held fear and confusion and Rhys noticed that although he did not like to be touched by the centaur, he did not have the strength to back away.

Fyros spoke quietly to the old man but he did not reply. Turning to the youths he said, "I think he is going to be fine, but he needs to rest." He then left the tent and returned a few seconds later with two centaurs companions.

Fyros watched as the centaurs picked up Lan and carried him away, "I've arranged for him to sleep in a bed in a tent next to your own. I think if we moved him further away he'd probably crawl back here anyway. At least this way there is some chance of him getting the rest that he needs."

When Rhys had snapped out of his trance state, he had been entirely focussed on helping Lan, now, with his friend safe, his mind returned to the extraordinary events that had just occurred. He spoke to Fyros with an excited look in his eyes, "Did you see it Fyros?" he asked.

Fyros nodded, "I did indeed Rhys. Can you explain what happened?"

"Yes, I think so, it seems quite clear now, not like when I created the portals in my dreams, everything seemed so cloudy and distant then." He went on to explain how Lan had entered his tent and had linked himself and Rhys with the pendant. "Almost immediately I could feel the, the...." He paused, unable to explain what it was he had felt.

"The magic?" offered Fyros.

Rhys thought on this and nodded, "Yes, the magic! It flowed through my mind and I could sense the portal being created and then the images started. I almost panicked and backed away but a voice helped me relax and concentrate so that I could focus on the portal. I could feel the magic even stronger then. I knew instinctively how to mould it so that the portal became solid and real." Meld and Ashley looked at each other and raised their eyebrows in surprise.

"Did you know who's voice it was? Was it Lan's?" asked Fyros.

"Yes, I think so, but not the Lan that we know. The voice sounded much younger, strong and powerful and yet kind, not harsh. He requested, firmly and politely, that I concentrate on the portal, rather than order that I did so. I think that's why I listened. I trusted the voice and knew he wanted to help me."

"Perhaps that is how Lan sounded in his youth, before this madness took him. Go on," prompted Fyros.

"Well, everything seemed easy from then on. I forged the portal with the magic and was able to slow the images until they stopped. I had no control over where it stopped though, all I did was slow the chaos until a single image formed." Rhys turned to Ashley, "It's a bit like a one armed bandit fruit machine at a fairground where you have a button to stop the wheels turning. You pull the handle and the pictures spin. You can stop the wheel anytime but the images are turning so fast that you have no idea of what will show." Ashley nodded her understanding.

Fyros prompted Rhys with another question, "So where did this portal lead? Do you know?"

Rhys thought on this, "I guess the answer to that is yes and no. I know *what* was on the other side but not *where* it was. The gateway opened onto a rocky coastline. It was raining heavily. Strange white birds hovered in the skies, similar to seagulls that we have on Earth, but much whiter.

Once the portal was locked I heard the voice tell me to keep concentrating on the portal but to open my eyes. That was weird. In my mind I could still see the images on the other side of the portal but my eyes could only make out the blue glow. What did you see Fyros?"

"Just the normal iridescent glow of a portal, I could discern no detail. That ability must only be open to you. The ancient magic must flow through you Rhys. I believe that this confirms that you are of wizard blood, a descendant of the old ones."

Rhys frowned at this comment, "Do you really think that Fyros? If I am it seems strange that I don't know it."

Fyros placed his hand on Rhys shoulder, "Yes I believe it young man. I do not know how or when, but I suspect it was a very long time ago, when journey's from our world to yours were more common. At that time your line was crossed with the wizard line."

"Then that would mean that either my father's or mother's ancestors also possessed wizard blood. I wonder if they know." Rhys' mind wandered to his parents and grand-parents. Instinctively he felt that any connection to the magics of Portalia were from his mother's side of the family. He had always felt closer to her and they shared an almost uncanny ability to know what the other was thinking. As did his Auntie Glenys, his mother's sister.

Rhys continued, "When I opened my eyes I only saw the portal at first and I was able to keep it open fairly easily. As soon as I saw Lan and the pain that he was in, I lost concentration and the portal closed."

"Yes, I was by your side then and I was witness to that. You opened your eyes and they held a strange distant look as you gazed on the portal. As soon as you saw Lan's pain, your vision cleared and the portal disappeared." Fyros considered what Rhys had told him before speaking once more. "It would seem that Lan possesses some knowledge as to how you use the magic to create portals. He really is a mystery. I suspect that a memory was triggered by the images of the wizards that he saw in the stained glass windows of the Eumor reading room. When he recovers we should try to ask him some questions and see if we can glean anymore information from him."

Rhys shrugged, "You can try but I think you'll find it useless. Lan goes crazy if you ask him questions. It's better to just talk to him so he doesn't have to think too hard about what you are asking. That way you get more sense out of him."

"That is a good point. Thank you Rhys we'll try that. In the meantime I must ask, do you think that you could create a portal again in the same way?"

Rhys thought on this and considered lying. Eventually he decided against this and spoke truthfully, "I'm fairly sure that I could, with help from Lan again. However, you saw the pain that it caused him. I would not want to put him through that once more."

Fyros agreed, it was clear the incident had caused the old man a great deal of discomfort. "Did you feel any pain yourself Rhys?"

"No, none at all, in fact I felt better than I have for days. Weird really, when I had my visions before I ended up with a blinding headache. This time it was as if Lan took all that pain away. Maybe that is what he did. Maybe he was feeling the pain for both of us."

Fyros frowned, "Possibly. Perhaps Horos and Cambor may have some ideas."

Fyros turned to Ashley and noticed that she had been joined by Griff who was listening intently. "Oh Griff, I am glad you are here. Ashley, can you open a communication with the council for me please, they must know of this."

Ashley smiled, "No problem Fyros." She touched the pendant to the crystal and the two began to glow. Almost immediately two sets of images appeared in front of them. The first was the home of Cambor in Eumor. The second showed a large chamber, filled to bursting with spiders of various shapes and size. Fyros immediately signalled for Ashley to break off the link.

"Hells hounds, it is as I feared," cursed Fyros, "The enemy now wears the crystal. The information that we must discuss with the council is far too sensitive for the ears of our foe. We will have to wait and try again later." Fyros looked at Rhys, "For now I suggest that you rest. We arrive at Fortown tomorrow and do not know what we will find there. We may need all our strength as well as your newly found ability."

***

Zarn ran to the tower, eager to tell Shangorth about the attempt by Fyros to contact the council once more. His short legs pumped as he scuttled up the spiral staircase. He reached the chamber and crashed through the door. He paused as he entered. Something was different. He scanned the room and realised that it was Michael who had changed. The youth was no longer chained to the wall and grovelling on all fours, he stood erect to the right of Shangorth, free of his bonds. Zarn stared at him suspiciously but Michael's gaze was focussed in mid air and he did not look back at the dwarf.

Shangorth grinned as Zarn entered. "Ah, Zarn. Look what I have." He gestured to Michael. Zarn looked at the boy and a look of puzzlement came over his face.

"Oh, I see you don't understand," teased the warlock, "Here, let me show you."

Shangorth pointed to Zarn and said, "Michael, strangle the dwarf."

Michael ran forwards arms outstretched. Zarn screamed as Michael's fingers found his neck and the youth's fingers began to squeeze. The dwarf reached for his axe but Shangorth emitted a bolt of magic that burned the albino's fingers. Zarn looked terrified and gagged out pleadings for mercy. Shangorth laughed, "Enough Michael. Return to my side."

Michael immediately let go of the dwarf and returned to his position.

Zarn rubbed his neck and cursed, "Why did he do that master? I have not hurt him in any way."

"Because I told him to do so you idiot," replied Shangorth. "The boy is nothing but a shell, he has no thoughts of his own. His true self is captured in the Soul Orb and I have used the dark arts to tie his mind and body to myself. He will do whatever I ask of him. A wonderful man servant, don't you think?"

Zarn did not reply. He stared at Michael and felt a wave of jealousy as the boy stood so close to his master. He did not like this turn of events at all. Eager to find additional favour from his master Zarn hurriedly informed him of the failed attempt to contact the council.

"Excellent. We have cut off a significant line of communication. The centaurs will have to act without the combined wisdom of their council during their time at Fortown. I want you to keep the crystal around your neck at all times and come to me immediately if they try to open a link again."

"Yes master, I will." Zarn stood smiling at the warlock, waiting for instructions.

The warlock watched him with amusement in his eyes, aware of the dwarf's discomfort. "Well Zarn, do you have anything else to report?" The dwarf shook his head. "Then why do you hang around here. Be gone!"

Zarn turned and left, disappointed. His heart fell even further as he left the room and overheard his master order Michael to lock the doors to the chamber. In frustration he realised that the boy was going to be allowed to share the secret behind the locked door.

CHAPTER EIGHTTEEN
A Call to Arms

Nexus had run out of patience. He had expected Shangorth to have recalled him by now, ready to start the offensive that would allow him to take his revenge on the OverLord Toran. He removed the black leather gloves that he wore and looked at his right hand. Now no longer of solid flesh but shaped like a ball, a sphere of energy that shimmered and moved like liquid. His thoughts returned to the time when he had lost his hand. Toran had been responsible for that loss and now revenge burned deep within Nexus.

Once he had been a trusted advisor to Toran. Advising him on decisions associated with the general running of the kingdom. He considered Toran a friend and indeed, thought of him almost as a brother. All he had wanted was to bring Toran more power and greater wealth. To achieve this Nexus had turned to the multitude of books on the dark arts that were locked away in Pinnhome. Tomes that were considered forbidden to touch, let alone to open and study.

He could remember clearly the scorn that Toran heaped upon him when he had approached the Overlord with his plans to use the dark arts. Toran had lectured him severely and removed his access to the vaults where the books were secured.

Nexus was not to be diverted so easily however and he had already secured copies of the keys to the vaults. For days he would sneak down there at night, pouring over books and scrolls that held the secrets of the warlocks. Slowly but surely, the power of the books changed him as he learned more and exposed himself to the writings of the dark arts. The text showed how he could gain great power and how wealth and fame would be open to him. After a time he eventually mastered a simple spell that turned water into an undetectable poison, a venom that once drunk would burn from within. With this success came the realisation that he did no longer needed the co-operation of Toran to achieve greatness and power. He would master these powers and grab control of the kingdom for himself.

However, his plans were thwarted. Someone was spying on him and had reported his activities. The day after he had cast that single spell the guards were waiting for him. They arrested him immediately and dragged him before Toran.

The OverLord looked at him with tears in his eyes as he decreed that the man should be branded an outcast and banished from the lands of Pinn, never to return.

He remembered how his anger had boiled over. The Overlord had no right to do this. He had served him well for many years. Even his work with the dark arts had only started so that he may better serve the OverLord. As he argued his case he had reached for a dagger hidden in his cloak, but, as he drew the weapon and raised it to strike the OverLord down, the guards had leapt to protect their leader. One had swung his sword in a swift arc striking the hand that held the dagger. The weapon fell harmlessly to the floor. Next to it Nexus' severed hand landed with a soggy thump. He could still feel the pain when he thought about that moment.

Another guard stepped forward to run him through with his sword but a shout from the OverLord had prevented the next strike. Toran had ordered his guard to bandage the arm and to escort Nexus to the borders of Pinn for banishment.

Nexus had wandered Portalia for the next two years, unsuccessfully trying to find alternative sources of information on the dark arts. He had been run out of many a town for questioning the existence of such documents but, eventually, at Urtwatch, he had enjoyed some success and had discovered an old volume referencing alchemy, describing how to manipulate everyday objects into gold. Here too, from an old tinker who traded in the town market, he had purchased the cloak that he now wore. The tinker had assured Nexus that the cloak would provide invisibility during times of danger. Nexus had paid him well in gold dust for the cloak. For months he wore the garment but, no matter what he tried, there was no sign of it's power, even when he had purposefully placed himself in danger. At first he felt angry at the tinker who he knew must be laughing behind his back at having fooled Nexus into purchasing the cloak. He had had the last laugh however. The gold with which he had paid had been magically forged using the alchemy spell but it would return to sand after a few days as the power of that spell diminished.

Nexus had continued to wander the lands for months. Despite his ability to use basic alchemy spells, none of the gold he created would remain in a permanent state. This prevented him from using such gold as payment in any town where he hoped to spend any amount of time. As a result he wandered the lands through all seasons, usually staying at places for only a few nights so that he could utilise his temporary wealth.

It was winter when Shangorth had found him. Wet and cold and with his stump throbbing with pain in the cold, the warlock had befriended him. He still did not know how he had found him, but his suspicions were that the warlock had spies in place throughout Portalia. One of these must have reported his interest in the dark arts back to Shangorth.

The warlock had shown him compassion and had taken him under his wing. He showed him how to cast some basic spells and how to invoke the power of the cloak of invisibility that he wore. Nexus found much amusement in this, the tinker had indeed been right about the cloak and had not even known it. Now the fool would be without the cloak and the false gold.

Eventually Shangorth had shared his plans of conquest with Nexus. He had then given him the mountain Runestone pendant to wear as a sign of trust and loyalty. The warlock had even taken pity on Nexus and formed for him a replacement hand, made from pure energy. The hand held no special power but did respond to Nexus will and worked as well as a normal hand, allowing him to carry out tasks and activities. In return for his pledge of loyalty, Shangorth had also promised that he would help him gain revenge on Toran and that he would be given the rule of Pinnhome once the humans were defeated.

At that time Nexus had been content with this. He knew he needed the warlock to help him develop his power. However, as time passed and he learned more of the dark arts, his desire for more knowledge grew. With this came a burning ambition not only to conquer Portalia with the warlock but also to sit at Shangorth's side and to rule with him. Not as an advisor as he had been to Toran, but as an equal.

The warlock had also shared with him that he was training a coven. Nexus was now determined that the warlock put him in charge of that coven. With the aid of others his knowledge would grow even more, even to a point where his skills may allow him to challenge the warlock for overall control.

It was this ambition that formed the basis of his new

name, Nexus. A name that expressed his desire to be the focus, the centre of the coven.

Shaking himself back to present, Nexus approached the gates at Pinnhome. As he stepped from the cover of the bushes he pulled the cloak around him and forged the magic that would rend him invisible. The gates, normally left open to the outside world, were now closed and secured from within. Clearly the threat from the west had made the citizens of the town more cautious.

Nexus waited until a large wagon approached carrying produce from the local farms. He heard the guards shout a welcome as they recognised the driver and the gates were opened. Nexus slipped in easily, completely undetected under his cloak. He moved slowly through the streets, ensuring that he made no noise and taking large detours to prevent physical contact with anyone. Eventually he reached the building where the OverLord lived and presided over his realm. Access into the building itself was easy. The main doors were propped open, the large hall at the front of the building also served as a city administration area.

Nexus moved stealthily through the hall and made his way up two floors into the area reserved for the private use of the OverLord. He watched the movement of the sentries that guarded this area of the palace and timed his movement to avoid detection. He made faster progress than he expected and within minutes reached the corridor that led to the rooms where the OverLord worked and slept. At the end of an exceptionally long corridor stood two guards, one either side of a pair of panelled wooden doors. The doors were closed.

Nexus sat and waited for over two hours until the guards were relieved. He knew that he now had four hours until the next changing of the guard. Plenty of time for him to finish his task.

This area of the building was rarely visited by others, the OverLord choosing to entertain visitors in the official chambers on the floor below. There was always a small chance that someone may approach the private rooms before the next guard change but this was a risk that he would have to take.

Moving closer to the guards he removed a needle like knife from within his cloak. The knife was tipped with a quick acting poison that would bring death to it's victim within seconds. Nexus stepped close to the first guard. The man frowned as his killer neared, almost as if he sensed his presence. Nexus noticed the movement in the man's face and quickly thrust the knife into the front of the his throat. The guard grunted, twitched once, and fell forwards, the wound hidden from the view of the second guard. The wound caused by the weapon hidden, the other guard stepped forward to see what ailed his companion. A second swift lunge with the knife into the throat of this guard ended his life too.

Nexus waited a few seconds to ensure that both were dead and moved to prop them as best he could against the wall. The needle point of the weapon and the congealing ability of the poison ensured that very little blood was spilled, a perfect combination for an assassin's weapon. He arranged the dead guards as best he could and balanced their weight against the walls to each side of the door. Fortunately, both wore heavy leg armour which enabled Nexus to prop them upright. The position of the guards would not fool anyone up close but, from the end of the long corridor, a mere glance would not alert anyone that something was wrong. Taking one last look at the guards Nexus placed his hand on the door handle and pushed it downwards.

It popped open with very little sound. Nexus peered through the crack in the door at a large office. Toran was not in the office but he could hear the OverLord in one of the rooms to the rear. Nexus slipped into the office and closed the door behind him. He walked across the room and through the doorway that led to a sitting room which was situated behind the office. The door to the bed chambers led off this room and Nexus could see Toran within. The OverLord was sifting through some papers on a desk and Nexus watched as he selected a thick document and returned to the sitting room to lounge in a chair.

Nexus closed the door to the sitting room and Toran looked up in surprise. Seeing no-one the OverLord stood to investigate. Nexus stepped towards him and pushed him violently back into the chair, removing the invisibility spell as he did so.

To his credit, the OverLord did not show any fear as he cast eyes on his old advisor but, he was unable to hide his surprise.

"So," the OverLord said, "It has finally come to this. I presume that you have now succumbed totally to the dark arts and have come here to kill me?"

Nexus stared at the OverLord, "But of course Toran. What did you expect? Surely you did not think I was here to read you poetry!"

Toran looked saddened, "I see that the darkness has also destroyed your sense of humour my old friend, I had hoped that your exile would bring you to your senses and that you would throw off the desire to pursue the darker arts and return to your former ways. I should have known that this was not to be. They had already poisoned your mind."

Nexus laughed, "Why would I want to turn my back on the dark arts. You are a fool Toran. I came to you with the knowledge that would have led to great power and wealth for both of us. We could have ruled all of Portalia together if you had but shown me the loyalty that I once gave to you."

"Rule! After using the power of the dark arts to bend folk to our will! What sort of rule is that! It is you that is the fool" exclaimed the OverLord. He looked at his would be assassin and softened his voice, "But how could you understand, I do not believe that you stood a chance at resisting the call of the dark arts once you had opened the books. You are not even of this world so could not hope to understand the power that they held within. Exposure to the dark arts can corrupt even the gentlest of minds."

Nexus frowned, "You are mistaken Toran. The power does not corrupt. It enlightens!"

"No! It corrupts to the core," Toran exclaimed, raising his voice once again and rising to his feet. "Step away from it my old friend. Come back to me and help me beat the evil that once again threatens our peace!"

Nexus, concerned that the noise would alert others, raised his hand and struck the OverLord. Toran fell back heavily into the chair.

"Silence you fool. The time has come. You tried to take away my chance for power but I have survived and I will now succeed and realise my destiny. Shangorth walks the world again and I will be by his side as he leads me to greatness. Unfortunately Toran, you will not be here to witness my victory."

Nexus drew out the needle dagger once more. The OverLord was sprawled across the chair, head still spinning from the blow. Nexus stood over him. He raised his hand to strike the final blow.

Suddenly his expression changed as he felt the familiar pull of power. Nexus watched in horror as the room disappear into a sea of blue He felt as though he was floating. As he recognised the feeling he screamed in frustration, "No! Not now!". The portal quickly dissolved around him to leave him stood before Shangorth. He was stood on the Mountain Runestone in Shangorth Towers. The warlock stood with his Runestone ring firmly inserted into his pendant. Nexus snarled in frustration, "Why now?" he shouted at the warlock, "I was busy!"

Shangorth glared at Nexus, the bewilderment on his face turning to anger. "You dare to question me!" he shouted, raising his hand towards his agent. Energy shot forth from his outstretched palm and Nexus was thrown across the room; to lay in a heap at the far end of the chamber. He groggily rose to his feet and muttered his apologies. His whole body ached from the force of the blow.

Ohrhim, waited on the Runestone. It had still been in the guise of a crow when it was recalled, but had now transformed back to the appearance of a human. In this form it let the Runestone pendant hang around it's neck and played with it between false fingers as it watched Shangorth punish Nexus for his outburst.

Head bowed in submission, Nexus returned to the Runestone, to join Ohrhim and Zarn. Michael still stood at Shangorth's side. As usual Ohrhim merely watched and took all in it's stride, it did not raise any questions. Nexus however, who had not at first noticed the youth, was now burning with curiosity but dare not risk questioning Shangorth once more. He decided to wait to see if the warlock offered any explanation as to the presence of this human child.

Shangorth now addressed them. "The time has come to strike. Today I have dispatched the main force of our troops. Black eagles, Graav and the army from Dargoth Sands advance to Fortown. This is why I have recalled you. Tomorrow we will open the portal and will commence the transportation of my spider army to the battlefield. When all are safely through, we will use the gateway to follow and we will join our forces in the hills above Fortown, ready to lead them to victory."

Nexus and Zarn smiled. At last it had begun. Ohrhim looked on with fixed, impassive expression.

The warlock continued, "Zarn and Ohrhim will accompany me to the Fortown battlefield," both acknowledged this order. "Nexus, I have a different task for you."

"Master?" queried the agent with an inquisitive glance.

"The boy you see before you is called Michael. He has travelled here with another called Rhys. These boys are from another world, a world called Earth."

Nexus' jaw dropped open in astonishment. *How could this be?*

"It would also seem that this other boy, Rhys, has an ability to create portals. This is not something that I had foreseen but I do not believe that it poses us a problem. However, I am going to adjust my original plan as a result." Shangorth placed his hand on Michael's shoulder and continued to talk directly to Nexus. "Michael is now converted to my cause and will serve me no matter what I ask. He will accompany me to Fortown to the battle there. Because of the information that Michael has shared with me about his friends, I want you to take a Graav force to meet the advancing Pinn infantry on the Meadows. That force must not reach Fortown. To complete this task I have held back five hundred Graav, more than enough to wipe out the five thousand human infantry that approaches. Under the cover of darkness you will use the hill portal gateway and travel south. This will prevent detection by those in the town. Once clear of that risk, you should head east to meet the Pinn forces head on. You will find the Graav more than adept in combat. They are not fast but they are immune to any strikes to their body and they have learned to protect their heads well, a single Graav can easily slay thirty or so soldiers before he is killed."

Nexus nodded, "Very well, but what of your original plan to destroy the main forces of Portalia in one strike?"

Shangorth scowled at Nexus. He was not happy about changing his plan and he did not need to be reminded of this by his agent. He fought hard to stop himself striking out at him again. He knew he needed Nexus in good physical shape for the task ahead. "As I said, the existence of this youth changes things. I want to isolate the one they call Rhys quickly. If I can bend him to my will, as I have done with Michael, then he may offer additional power useful to our cause."

At the sound of Rhys' name, Michael twitched, a small electrical impulse flashed in his brain and he struggled to awaken the memory that resided there. Pain racked his brain as an image of another youth entered his mind.

Nexus saw the logic in Shangorth's words but was disappointed as he wanted to find out a little more about these Earthlings himself. "Once we have destroyed the Pinn infantry should we then turn west and return to Fortown?" asked Nexus.

"Actually no!" replied Shangorth with a grin, "Take the remaining Graav and march to the Halfman Forest. I will send Zarn to Stycich to notify him that you will be arriving with your Graav and to offer every assistance. You will take up camp and befriend Stycich. At night, when they sleep you will kill all of the Halfmen and their captive human women. The Halfman horde has more than served it's purpose and I no longer need them to fulfil my plans. They are frightful creatures and I have no desire to allow them to remain on a world where I rule." On hearing this the White Dwarf grinned from ear to ear. "Once you have finished your mission remain at the Halfman Camp and I will open a portal for you when I am ready for you to return."

Nexus pondered the plan for a few seconds, "How will I control the Graav without your presence?" he asked.

"Both the Graav and the Black Eagles know my will. They follow me instinctively, they were born to do my will. I believe that they recognise my greatness and my destiny to rule all. They will follow you merely because I wish it."

Nexus nodded his acknowledgement and left the room accompanied by Zarn. They descended the stairs to inspect the Graav and make ready for the journey.

When the two had left, Shangorth requested that Ohrhim report on his spying mission.

"There is not much to tell," said the shapechanger, "as you know the centaurs approach and will arrive at Fortown within a few hours. The dwarves have sent scouts into the mountains to spy upon Shangorth Towers. They suspect that you are behind recent events. At present they await the arrival of further forces to decide upon a course of action."

Shangorth seemed pleased with this news and even thanked his spy before dismissing him. "Let them spy on me, it matters not," he spoke out loud as if to Michael who's face held no acknowledgement that he was being addressed, "They will be dead in a few days anyway."

At his side Michael sweated and grimaced, still struggling through the pain in an attempt to grasp the memory of the name Rhys and the face that smiled at him in his head. As it eventually came to the surface, he made a last effort to clutch it.

Immediately the pain intensified and became unbearable. The memory plunged back into the darkness of his subconscious.

***

Looking out from their plateau high in the Dargoth Mountains, Borst and Yam watched as Shangorth's army was dispatched. There was no doubt in their minds as to the destination. The mass of humans, dwarves, Graav and black eagles were heading straight to the north-east, bound for Fortown. The two dwarves reacted immediately, gathering up their belongings they beat a retreat to Fortown as fast as they could travel, eager to provide prior warning of the coming force to their comrades. Over their heads nine hundred black eagles blackened the skies.

***

Meld was the first to draw their attention to the town. They had crested one of the higher hills and the town had appeared to the south. Rhys and Ashley squinted in the sunlight, they could just make out the outline of the buildings. Both smiled in relief. Lan, now recovered from the events of the previous evening, rode silently at Rhys' side. He had not uttered a sound all day. As they stared in the direction of the town, they saw two large birds approaching their location. Ashley and Rhys felt panic rising, believing the birds to be the black eagles of which they had heard so much. "Do not fret," advised Meld, "They are fire eagles, ridden by warriors from Pinnhome in the northeast. It seems aid has already arrived at Fortown and also means that my brother, at least, was able to reach his destination and return with help."

The teenagers watched in astonishment as the fire eagles, and their riders, glided down to the head of the platoon to meet Fyros and Griff. They moved forward through the ranks to take a closer look at these giant birds. Ashley in particular was enthralled. She leaned close to her friend and whispered, "Rhys, they are the birds of my dream. Remember, I told you about them when we were back in Eumor?"

"Of course I do," replied Rhys. "That worries me though, remember the dream that Mike had? If his has come true too then he may be being tortured as we speak."

Ashley looked down despondently, "That's true I hadn't thought of that. Mind you, my dream wasn't exactly fun either. I was actually riding one of those things and was attacked by another bird. Hopefully not all of the things that happened in those dreams will come true!" Their mood, earlier buoyant, was suddenly pulled down by these more sobering thoughts.

It took another hour before they reached the outskirts of Fortown. They were greeted warmly by the townsfolk and led to the town hall. As they walked along the streets Ashley and Rhys were fascinated by the dwarves. They had seen a few in Ralle but not up close like this. Ashley had to nudge Rhys a number of times to stop him staring.

As they approached the main square, Molt ran out to greet his brother. They threw their arms around each other in delight and relief. Ashley watched from a distance and her heart sank as she saw Meld's glee turn to dismay and grief as he talked quietly to his brother. She guessed that the news was not good.

Griff and Fyros left the others and they entered the town hall to meet with Swiftaxe, Gorlan and Fleck. A few minutes later Fleck returned and ushered the Earth teenagers and Kyrie into the hall. The five leaders and the teenagers talked for over an hour, sharing their stories and experiences. An attempt was made to contact the council using the crystals, but, once more the link had to be cut as Zarn still wore his crystal.

Swiftaxe stared at Rhys in amazement when they shared the news about his ability to create portals.

"So, even the portal magic finds new life. These are indeed interesting times," muttered the dwarf leader. "this news worries me though for there is a portal gateway in Drenda. If our enemy controls the gates once more then he also has the ability to attack our city from within."

Fleck waited for the King to finish before speaking, "There is also supposedly a portal point in the hills not far from Fortown. It was created long ago when the town was nothing more than a few farmsteads scattered along the hills. It was used to transport produce to the major cities of Portalia. If the enemy does have control of the portal web, it may also explain the rumours that a warlock and a dwarf had been seen in the hills to the south west."

As they spoke a Pinn warrior interrupted them apologetically and whispered to Gorlan.

The Warlord stood up, "Excellent, show him in immediately."

The others turned to the door as Folken entered. He looked exhausted, having just arrived back from the scouting trip in the mountains. Acknowledging all he made his report.

Fleck reacted first, "So, our supposition about Shangorth Towers was correct! However, we did not perceive that he possessed Graav in so many numbers. He must have only used part of his force when he attacked us."

"I wonder where the spider army is housed?" added Gorlan.

Rhys had been wondering this too and offered a suggestion, "Maybe the warlock uses the portals to transport them. After all, we did see the dwarf taking spiders from our own world."

Fyros shook his head, "It may be so Rhys but I believe

that the transportation of so many would take too long. I believe that they are housed here somewhere. I just wish I knew where."

"Well one thing is clear," said Swiftaxe, "it would be folly to try to attack our foe on his own territory with the forces that we currently have. We will remain here until we are joined by the main Pinn forces. We can then plan a strike on our enemy at Shangorth Towers." Swiftaxe turned to address Rhys and Ashley, " I realise that you are anxious to find your friend Michael and to return to your own home but we cannot help you with this yet. When we have a force that is large enough to mount an attack on the Towers, then we will take you with us and endeavour to free your friend and to aid your return. If the power is rekindled, we may be able to use the Mountain Runestone to send you back. Be aware though that there is much risk in this. The enemy may destroy the Runestone before we have a chance to utilise it. Also, your friend may already be dead. I say this not to make you downhearted, but so you know the reality."

Both teenagers saw the sense in the King's words but could not help but feel a little despondent.

"In the meantime," continued Swiftaxe, "Work has already begun to dig in and prepare the town against any attack."

Gorlan added, "This is true, both Pinn and dwarves prepare the town for assault and we are heartened by the joining with us of the centaurs If our enemy attacks we will be prepared. Although I must admit that I wish we knew the size of the spider force. It would help to know precisely what we are facing."

"Aye, that is true, but if our enemy does choose to attack us here, I have a plan to help us with those accursed spiders," replied Swiftaxe with a wink. He did not expand on this and suddenly changed focus to address Rhys, "I would like to talk to you more on this ability of yours and even see if we can recreate events. Get some food and come back here with Lan in a few hours."

Rhys looked at Lan with some concern, "Sir," he replied, "the last time we did this Lan suffered incredibly."

Swiftaxe looked sympathetic, "I realise that Rhys and if things were different I would not ask this of you or the old man. However, we must know whether you do indeed possess the ability to create portals, it could be a significant factor."

Rhys reluctantly accepted but his face gave away his true feelings, he looked across at Lan. To his surprise Lan smiled at him and nodded, the old man seemed to understand the request and Rhys felt a little more confident as he agreed to return with Lan later that day.

The leaders continued to talk and decided to set up a constant vigil. The fire eagles would begin around the clock scouting of the hills to the west. Fleck then arranged for the accommodation of the centaurs within the outer perimeter of the town and led Ashley, Rhys and Lan to an inn, close to the central courtyard. Here they were given a large room to share. Lan had still not spoken but he did at last decide to follow Ashley's prompting and actually stepped into the bath. He was about to jump out again though when Rhys intervened. Quickly pushing him back into the water he ensured that the old man received a thorough soak and scrub. When he had finished Rhys stared in disbelief at the state of the scummy water that remained. Lan spat, mumbled and cursed at him as he grabbed a towel to dry. It was worth it though. If Lan was to share their room at least they would no longer have to smell him.

Rhys scrubbed the bath clean and decided that he'd like

a soak himself. Fleck had arranged for clean clothes to be supplied for all. Rhys selected some he liked and laid these out on his bed. As he did so Ashley skipped by him and nipped into the bathroom. He shouted and cursed her but she just giggled and told him it was a ladies prerogative to bathe first "Ladies first, Rhys. You must know that even in England!"

"Yea, yea, yea. But remember that I am Welsh, not English and actually we Welsh are more gentlemanly than the English so take your bath first. You'd better clean the tub afterwards though." he teased, "You smell almost as bad as Lan!" This comment was met with a stony silence.

An hour or so later Rhys was laid back in a hot bubbly tub. As he sat back he realised how tough the long walk from Eumor had been. He relaxed as the aches and pains were soothed by the warm water. He put his head back and closed his eyes. His thoughts wandered but, inevitably, they soon returned to his ability of creating portals. He reached for his pendant which he had laid the side of the bathtub and held it in his hand. No longer afraid of the magic, he concentrated on the events of the previous day and tried to recall exactly what had occurred in his tent.

Soon a glowing arch image appeared in his mind. In his thoughts he recalled the memory of the stained glass wizard circle and imagined himself amongst them, sharing their strength. He remembered how confident he had felt with Lan's voice speaking to him in his mind. Gradually he felt the familiar pull of the magic inside him. This time he felt no panic. He did not need the strength of his friend Lan. The portal in his mind now began to show images of other places. He tried to count them but there were far too many, there seemed to be hundreds upon hundreds, definitely more than could be opened from a Runestone gateway. He realised that, once again, he was struggling too hard to forge the magic and tried to focus his mind to go with the flow of the portal web. Time and time again he felt that he was almost there, only to have his concentration broken by a doubt or an abstract thought.

What if this magic harms me when used alone? I wonder what Ashley's dream meant? What is happening to Mike? What will him Mum and Dad do when they get back and find me missing?

Eventually, after five or six attempts he gave up. He felt that the ability to create the portal was almost there but he realised that he was unable to conjure up the single mindedness required to complete the task.

With a start, he suddenly realised that Lan was watching him from the doorway. "Hey, get outta here will you! Can't I get a moments privacy in this place!" He splashed water at Lan who screamed and dived out of the door. Rhys jumped out of the bath and shut the door. He climbed back into the tub and smiled. Submerging himself in the warm waters once again he laid back amongst the bubbles and began to snooze.

He awoke to a loud thumping on the door. The water was cold and the bubbles long gone. "Rhys! Are you awake?" It was Ashley. "We need to get back to the town hall. Are you coming or what?"

Rhys mumbled an apology in reply and quickly dried himself off. Pulling on his clean clothing he combed his hair and rushed out of the inn with Ashley and Lan at his side.

The three arrived at the town square, acknowledging the polite welcome of the human and dwarf guards as they entered the main hall. "Ah, you have returned. I hope that you are refreshed?" It was Swiftaxe who spoke.

"Yes, thank you," replied Ashley.

Swiftaxe turned to Rhys, "Rhys, we discussed your ability

whilst you were gone and I feel that I must insist that we ask you to try to create a portal gateway once more. I realise that this caused Lan great discomfort previously but the need is great, we do not ask this of you lightly. We must know if you do indeed possess the ability."

Rhys looked at the faces around him. All of the figures were looking at him hopefully, even Ashley. He turned to Lan. The old man had been quiet since they entered the hall. He sighed to himself and, taking care not to pose any question in his words and tone, he said to the old man, "Lan, we need to try the portal magic again. I'll need you to help me. Here, give me your hand." Rhys held the pendant in his hand and reached to grasp Lan's free hand. The old man looked straight into Rhys' eyes and he could see fear there. However, he did not withdraw as Rhys held him and joined with his hand holding the pendant.

The speed with which the portal was created in his thoughts took him by surprise. Perhaps it was due to the attempts that Rhys had made during his bathing, a latent magic already formed within his mind, but essentially, as soon as Rhys had touched Lan's hand to the pendant he felt the magic rise within him.

The voice was back, he was now certain that this was Lan. "Now steady Rhys. Go with the flow of the web, concentrate entirely on it's ebb and flow, nothing else matters. I will take away your other thoughts."

For a fleeting moment, Rhys felt the pain that this concentration cost his friend, but this too was swept away and he became totally focussed on the portal. He climbed into the images, riding them with a feeling like elation as he received momentary glances of world after world. Gradually he built a resistance to the flow of the magic. Later he described this resistance as being like a brake on a bike. You squeeze gently to slow the motion down, knowing a quick jerk could result in disaster. The portal images began to slow down. Rhys' excitement grew as he took in more of the images before him. Men running here, a violent electrical storm there, a red planet, barren and desolate, a world where dinosaurs still roamed, all flashed through his mind. He saw a world where he stood on a hillside overlooking a city that spread below him. He could make out movement along the streets and realised they were cars. Earth! Could this be his home-world? He tried to latch onto this image and follow it and nearly lost the magic. Lan saved him at the last, pulling his thoughts away from home and back to the task at hand. The pause in concentration had caused the portal images to speed up again and Rhys, once more, had to hitch a ride and build his resistance, causing the deceleration needed to form a stable portal. A few minutes later Rhys looked through the portal at a scene, not dissimilar to that of the Portalia Meadows. Gold and green grass stretched before him for miles. Amongst the growth Rhys saw young centaurs and horses, galloping and playing under a pale green sky. Wherever this was, it was clearly not Portalia or Earth. He watched them as they continued their play and realised that they were clearly communicating with each other. Not verbally but through thought. Watching from a short distance were adult horses and centaurs. They too stood and looked at each other as if in conversation.

Rhys suddenly heard Lan's voice, "Rhys, I am still with you. Swiftaxe wants to speak with you but it will be difficult. I will help you, though. In a moment open your eyes and you will see the real world. Do not let go of the portal however, keep it in your thoughts. I will do all I can to stabilise it whilst you converse with Swiftaxe and the others. My strength will not last long though so be quick. Now! Open your eyes!"

Rhys did as he was bid and immediately felt his hold on the portal slip as the real world exploded into view. He felt the voice of Lan, more distant now, helping him to keep the link open. Before him he saw the portal that he had created, blue haze to the eye but with a clear image of it's destination in his head. He marvelled at how he was able to hold the image whilst still being aware of the world in which he existed.

Suddenly he saw that Swiftaxe had approached the portal and had picked up a chunk of stone. The dwarf king threw the stone at the portal and Rhys watched as it appeared on the other side and fell to the ground on the golden grass. To the others it appeared that the stone had just disappeared into the portal.

"Rhys, where does this portal lead?" asked Swiftaxe. As Rhys tried to concentrate on the King's question the portal began to flicker. Once more Rhys felt Lan in his mind and he instinctively turned towards the old man. Lan was stood as if in a trance. His eyes were open wide but they focussed on nothing. Sweat dripped from his brow and his face was held in a grimace. Rhys quickly turned away, knowing that to think on this would break the link to the portal.

With extreme effort he answered the question and explained precisely what he could see through the portal. All of the centaurs in the hall looked up with a keen interest, particularly Kyrie.

Swiftaxe continued, "Rhys, can you hold the portal solid long enough for someone to pass through to the other side and back again?"

Rhys felt his mind racing and Lan groaned in pain as he helped to keep the link active. Even so Rhys had to close his eyes to shut out the scene before him to enable the portal to be maintained. He stuttered a reply, "I, I, I think so, but I don't know for sure."

"Well that will have to be good enough," replied the dwarf, "We need someone to try the portal to see if it can be used by living beings and that the force remains solid. This is not a task that can be taken lightly as we have no way of knowing whether a return is possible. Therefore, I will undertake this myself."

Kyrie stepped forward, "No!" Fyros tried to stop her but it was too late. "The council said that they felt I was linked to this mission by destiny. I have a strong feeling that this task is mine. Through the portal Rhys can see an image of centaurs and horses. It is therefore less likely that I will raise suspicion by my presence there. Also, King Swiftaxe is far too important to risk on this venture." She approached the King, "Sir, your leadership and experience are required here."

Swiftaxe nodded, acknowledging the truth in her words. Fyros looked upon his daughter with mixed emotions, proud of her bravery but angry at her foolishness to risk her life so. He was about to speak when Rhys raised his voice in alarm, "We need to hurry! Lan and myself cannot hold this portal open for much longer."

Swiftaxe looked at Kyrie and bowed to her, "You are brave and honour your family. Travel back swiftly."

Kyrie returned the bow and without hesitation stepped into the portal.

Rhys watched as she entered. He felt a ripple in the flow as she travelled along the portal web. He saw how she seemed to float in mid air for a few minutes before making the transition to the world. He closed his eyes and shut himself away from the town hall to concentrate on maintaining the link. Almost immediately he heard Lan let out a tired sigh and some level of consciousness told him that the old man had lost consciousness, exhausted from the effort. Rhys was now alone with no support to hold the portal open.

Almost immediately he felt the panic rise and heard Fyros shout in alarm as the portal began to flicker to a close. Rhys recovered himself in time, remembering the need to stay entirely focussed on the portal to prevent the image deteriorating, he set his concentration and restored the portal to solidity.

Rhys watched as Kyrie stepped onto the grass under the green sky of the alien world. The young centaurs and horses stopped playing as they saw her appear as if out of thin air. The adults galloped over to stand between her and their offspring, alarmed by her sudden appearance. He continued to watch the scene as Kyrie approached the group with arms outstretched. He saw the stern defensive posture of the adults relax as they appeared to communicate with Kyrie. The conversation that took place was silent and it took but a few seconds but, to Rhys it seemed like hours. Eventually, with great relief he observed that Kyrie had turned back to the portal. Waving and smiling at the group of horses and centaurs she stepped back through to her own world. *So much for going unnoticed* thought Rhys momentarily but he let this observation fade as he returned his focus to the gateway.

As Kyrie stepped back into the town hall she was hugged lovingly by her father, a tear of relief splashed down his cheek. Rhys allowed himself to let go of the portal image. Although he felt no pain this time, on the release of the magic, the blood rushed from his head and, exhausted, he fainted. Ashley was ready though and she caught him before he hit the ground.

Rhys came around to the smell of feyberry tea and drank the offered cup eagerly. He looked up from his bed in the inn into the concerned faces of Ashley, Meld and Kyrie. Kyrie, smiled as he came around, kneeled down and kissed his forehead, "Thank you Rhys. You have given me a wonderful gift. I learned much from my journey even though it was but a short time" With this, she turned and left the room.

"What on earth was that about?" asked Rhys.

"You showed her a world where centaurs and horses lived as one race. She believes that it is the source of all centaurs. The centaurs are thrilled with this information as they have always felt that they were not truly of Portalia, and most did not believe the theories that they originated from Earth. You've provided them with proof of that. Fyros has agreed that Kyrie should return to Eumor immediately. The council must be told of this great discovery. Of course, you have now confused the heck out of the others. They do not understand how you could have opened a portal to a completely alien world. Anyway, never mind that now. How are you feeling?" asked Ashley

"Fine thanks," replied Rhys, "Not even the sign of a headache like other times." He sat up and looked across at Lan's bed. The old man was tucked up there, fast asleep. "How is he?" asked Rhys.

"He's doing OK," replied Ashley. "Swiftaxe had his physicians check him out and he's going to be fine. They are worried about him though. He is old and the effort obviously takes a lot out of him. He seems to be in terrible pain too. When you closed your eyes and went 'back in' to control the portal, the pain on Lan's face was horrible. He screamed in agony and collapsed. For a minute there I was sure he was dead!"

Rhys frowned, "Well hopefully we won't have to ask him to do this again." Rhys looked at Ashley as he spoke and saw the contradiction in her face. "Do you think?" asked Ashley rhetorically, "I think we both know differently, if we're honest."

He sighed, knowing that she was right. Even Rhys himself felt instinctively that his presence here was part of a greater picture. He also suspected that his ability would be called upon again in the near future. He vowed to himself that he would have to find a way to do so without the assistance of Lan. The old man had clearly suffered a lot and should not be asked to endure even more hardship.

"Rhys, if you are feeling OK I need to go back to find Fyros. He wants to try to contact the Eumor Council once more. Will you be OK?" asked Ashley.

Rhys nodded, "Yea, I'm fine. I'm going to try to get a little sleep myself though. I'm still feeling pretty tired."

So saying he turned over and pulled the blankets over his head. Ashley looked at him affectionately and smiled when she heard his steady breathing as he fell asleep almost immediately. Picking up the Cormion Crystal and placing it back around her neck, she left the room and close the door quietly behind her.

CHAPTER NINETEEN
A Treasure Found

Shangorth stood at the centre of his twelve disciples, Michael stood silently by his side. The coven members sat in a circle surrounding their mentor and listened intently as he spoke to them about the progress of his plan.

"Soon, you will follow me back to Portalia. We will complete your education of the dark arts and you will take your places as my barons. Rulers over all the lands of Portalia."

The twelve clapped in appreciation, their devotion to Shangorth unquestionable. Their ambition fuelled by a common lust for power and wealth. Their desires became a catalyst for the energy forces of the dark magics which grew within them, consuming what was left of their humanity.

Shangorth approached Stack his most prized student. He leaned close and quietly whispered in his ear. The warlock had found the young man thieving for a living in the streets of the river town of the Gates. He had taken the boy in, and nurtured him to become the first member of the warlock's coven. Stack had worked hard and made every effort to please the warlock. He had shown great ability in the mastering of the dark magic and even Shangorth had to express surprise at his rapid progress.

"Stack, I want you to prepare more Graav in case they are needed. Go to the lava cavern and use the dark arts to call forth more of the creatures. You will discover that they will bond with you on their creation. as they did with myself. They will then follow your command without question. As each stone man is created, picture my image in your mind and command the Graav to follow both of our wills without question. They can then be allowed to join with others in the lava pools. I want another two thousand ready to go to war, ready to reinforce my army after we have taken Fortown."

Stack nodded, proud to be asked to carry out this great task "I will not fail you." The young apprentice grinned as he thought about the control that he would have over the Graav that he would create in his master's name.

Shangorth returned to the centre of the student circle and commanded all to return to their studies. The coven dispersed swiftly, leaving the warlock alone with Michael. Shangorth watched them leave and then turned to depart himself, looking back over his shoulder to ensure Michael still followed him. The pair made their way to the Runestone chamber and stepped back through the open portal to Shangorth Towers.

***

Fyros had sensed their approach even before the horses were spotted by the fire eagle sentries. One thousand mounted Pinn cavalry had joined the allies. A most welcome addition to bolster the defending force. The cavalry were warmly welcomed and within a few hours, as Fleck had promised, were stabled on the outskirts of the city.

Fyros and Gorlan had assisted with this task but had now returned to the town hall where they found Swiftaxe and Fleck deep in discussion with a pair of bedraggled looking humans. As they entered the dwarf king raised his gaze to meet them, "Ah Fyros and Gorlan, this is Niles of Fortown and Yanto Flow a Gatesman. Niles was the messenger sent from Fortown to the Gates to request assistance. They bring us good news in response to this request."

Swiftaxe signalled for Yanto to speak. Gorlan looked at him. The man was clearly exhausted from his journey but he possessed a proud and confident stance, typical of the riverfolk of the Gates. Yanto stood a little under six feet tall and his brown hair was long and swept back into a pony tail. He wore light leather riding clothes and spoke quickly in a lilting accent with each sentence ending on a high pitch. It was peculiar to the city-men of the Gates.

"Aye, it is good news I bring, although I would rather that times were different and that the need was not so great. Like many of my colleagues I do not relish the thought of war and fear for the safety of my kin and my friends," said Yanto.

"Indeed," replied Gorlan, "But times are grave and undesirable actions are called for. What news do you bring?"

Yanto pointed to the north-west, "When Niles arrived at the Gates there was much debate. Some felt that the problem was not one that should involve us, but these were soon swayed by the politicians of the city who spoke of the olden times when evil ruled. More discussion followed, as is the way of men. It was finally decided that if evil was once again brewing in the Dargoth Mountains, then the source would most likely be Shangorth Towers. Although some suggested the source to be the despicable city of thieves and pirates at Dargoth Sands. Our leaders therefore dispatched a force of fifteen hundred men and commanded they sail south down the coast to Dargoth Sands. If they were unopposed there, then he ordered that they march east, towards Shangorth and the Dargoth Mountains. Their mission was to destroy any signs of evil or servants to the dark arts that they encountered.

At the time this seemed a brave and wise decision. However,

after discussing the Fortown events with Fleck and Swiftaxe, I fear that the mission is doomed to failure. If they meet the combined force of the spiders, the Graav and the eagles then they will be hopelessly slaughtered. I therefore request that I be allowed to leave as soon as I have taken refreshment. I would travel to Dargoth Sands as earnestly as possible in an attempt to warn my kinfolk of the impending danger."

Gorlan shook his head, "I understand your need Yanto but this is not the best way. For a start you are exhausted and need your rest. How long before the ships arrive at Dargoth Sands?

In response to the Warlord's words, the Gateman looked even more tired and crestfallen, "Winds allowing, they should arrive at Dargoth Sands tomorrow."

Gorlan flinched, "So soon! Even if I did allow you to leave, by the time you reached the main force the Gatesmen would already be at Shangorth Towers. There is only one option. We will dispatch a fire eagle to head west to meet the oncoming army. If he can intercept them in time they can hold their position to the west, between Dargoth Sands and Shangorth Towers. We can then send word when we are ready for them to strike.

Yanto immediately perked up at this suggestion and smiled broadly as he nodded his agreement. "Yes! Yes! That way we could have them avoid battle until we could co-ordinate our forces to attack from two sides. We must take action immediately and dispatch a flyer."

Gorlan agreed and excused himself to assign the task. He had already decided to send Folken once again. He knew this was a lot to ask as Folken had only recently returned from his scouting trip, but, he was aware that his Pinn warrior possessed knowledge of the enemy and the mountains, obtained during his first scouting mission. This would be invaluable intelligence for this task. To reach the advancing human army, Folken would need to get past the enemy unseen and speed his way west. Gorlan was glad that he had instructed Folken to rest when he had returned and therefore he should be refreshed and capable of undertaking this new assignment.

As Gorlan made his way through the streets he watched the hustle and bustle going on all around as the citizens and the soldiers prepared the town against any further attack. Glancing up he saw the small groups of fire eagles scouting overhead, looking for any sign of the enemy. He watched the birds for a while and frowned quizzically as he observed a number of fire eagles swooping westwards towards the fringes, where the hills met the mountains. They hovered over a particular area and then swept down. Gorlan continued to observe their flight path for a while before quickening his step to find and brief Folken.

***

Carl and Stern called to each other as they scouted the hillside. Carl was glad to be back in the air once more, now fully recovered from his wounds and even more delighted to see that Tosh had assigned the brothers to sentry duty together. The pair soared the heights, watching the ground and the mountains ahead for any sign of the enemy. The sky over Fortown was now ruled by the fire eagles, the black eagles no longer spied on them as they had long fled the area when the Pinns had decided to use their warbirds to guard the skies.

Carl and Stern were assigned an area of hillside directly to the west of the town. They flew a zigzagging line from the outskirts of the town, over the hills and into the mountain fringes. The brothers were heading west, approaching the point where the hills began to rise sharply as they met the Dargoth Mountains. Carl encouraged his warbird to drop to a lower attitude, skimming a few feet above the ground. He felt the elation as his mount raced along the hills. The close proximity of the grassy surface amplified the feeling of speed and he could not help but let out a cry of delight as he instructed his eagle to bank to the left to follow the contour of the steep hillside. Stern stayed well above his brother, watching the hillside for any sign of a threat. He didn't object to his brother's antics as he knew he needed to blow away the frustration and lethargy of the last few days of convalescence.

Carl had passed over the grass below and moved into an area of rocky terrain that formed the rugged mountain landscape. He spotted a thin ravine and signalled to his brother that he was going to drop into it. Carl had a penchant for flying his fire eagle low and fast, using his riding skills to avoid obstacles at high speed. He loved the thrill and the pump of adrenaline and he could sense that his warbird felt similar elation.

As the warbird dropped down into the rocky crevasse Carl increased his vigil, inspecting the flight path ahead for unexpected outcrops of rock and stone. As the pair flew, swerving to the left and right to follow the contours of the ravine, Carl grinned and his eagle screeched in delight. They picked up speed, bare rock flashed by just inches from the mighty birds wingtips. Ahead Carl saw that the ravine turned sharply to the left and he tightened his grip on the bird as he willed his mount to make the turn at break neck speed. The giant eagle responded, lunging sharply to the right, dropping a few more feet as it did so before it soared to the left to make the curve with little room for error. As they levelled out the colour drained from Carl's face as man and bird faced a solid wall of jagged rock face as the ravine abruptly ended. The giant bird realising the danger immediately veered upwards. Carl clung onto the bird for all his worth as they climbed an almost vertical path, narrowly missing the top of the ravine as they did so.

As they reached open sky again Carl yelled out loud in a mixture of relief and elation. The shout echoed back and forth the steep walls, reverberating around the ravine. Suddenly, from the corner of his eye Carl caught sight of the movement. He turned his head just in time to see someone, or something, dive for the cover below.

With one eye trained on this area, he began the climb back up to his brother. Stern saw his approach and shouted, "So do you feel better now? You know that if Gorlan or Tosh saw you doing that you'd be reprimanded don't you?"

Carl smiled, "Ah, maybe so brother of mine, but then if I had not been following my instincts to scout the ravine, then I would have not detected movement in the hillside at the lip of that ravine." he grinned even wider as he made this statement and winked at his kin.

Stern's expression changed to one of alarm, "Movement? Did you see who or what it was?"

"No. Whoever it was was watching me in the ravine though. Our steep climb out of there must have taken them by surprise and caught them in the open. As soon as they realised their predicament they ducked for cover. In fact, it was the movement that gave them away. If they had remained stationary then I probably wouldn't have seen them. I was far too busy trying to ensure I stayed mounted as my eagle climbed out of there."

Stern removed a small round mirror from his inside his garments. "Time to investigate then. Let's get some help." So saying he used the mirror to signal other fire eagles that scouted the adjacent areas. Within a few minutes four others had joined them.

"What is it Stern?" asked the first to arrive. Stern raised a hand for patience and then when all four were hovering alongside explained what Carl had seen.

Stern organised the six into a staggered line and on his signal the six birds descended to the top of the ravine. Starting at the rim they began a systematic search of the ground below.

At first all appeared quiet but as they reached the end of the ravine Carl signalled towards a slight disturbance in the grasses below. Stern signalled for the group to hover over this location. It was clear from their aerial vantage point that there were multiple beings hidden amongst the tall fronds that fringed the edge of the ravine. The creatures seemed oblivious to the fact that their progress was visible through the swaying of the grass blades. The group below was travelling slowly, heading in the general direction of the town. Stern estimated that there must have been around a dozen or so of the creatures. Unlikely then that this was a strike force of any kind. He surmised that it was probably a group of enemy scouts.

Signalling to the others to spread their line wider, he arranged the group to cover an area where they could easily drop on his command to intercept their quarry. The sky warriors obeyed, drawing their swords as they readied for combat. Stern watched and waited, using hand signals to adjust the positions of riders to ensure that the entire group remained in line with the progress of their prey. On the ground, the hidden creatures continued their slow progress through the grass, still seemingly unaware of the war birds watching from above. Stern looked ahead and saw that they were now only a hundred or so yards away from where the grassy cover gave way to a clearing. Stern knew that if those below were truly oblivious to their presence, then a great advantage could be gained by using the element of surprise. If their quarry reached the edge of the grass cover then they would probably scout the way ahead, as well as the skies, before leaving their position of cover. It was this that made his mind up for him.

Stern signalled for the group to dive, judging the interception of the hidden quarry to perfection. The war birds swept down as one, talons outstretched and with warriors brandishing their steel ready for the kill. The Pinns let out a loud yell as their birds met the grasses. The long slim fronds parted as the majestic beasts beat their way through. They looked ahead and saw that the noise they made had caused their prey to come to a complete stop. Shapes were now visible amongst the grass and, as they bore down for the kill, forms began to scatter in all directions, thrown into disarray by the advancing riders.

Stern was first to his target by a fraction, his jaw dropped in surprise and he was bearly able to manoeuvre his mount upwards and away from their prey as the eagle stretched with it's talons of fire. He looked anxiously from left to right. To his relief he saw that all of his companions had avoided any contact and were climbing out of the grasses. The group below were now breaking from the cover and Stern was able to count them. Sixteen in total. All were human, all were female and every one of them was screaming in terror. Suddenly, one of the women turned and let out a shrill whistle to the others as she sprinted towards the lip of the ravine. The fleeing women looked and changed their direction to follow her.

Stern watched as Carl and his fire eagle swooped down and plucked the lead woman into the air with ease.

The others immediately froze at this sight. Carl shouted

to the woman to be calm and then lowered her to the ground. The other five fire eagles swooped down to join them as Carl dismounted. The woman stood before them and called for calm amongst the others.

Carl looked at the group of women. All wore clothes that were worn and dirty, no more than rags. The ages varied, from teens to middle age. They all seemed tired and wore the grime of hardship. Each held a similar grave expression of defeat. Two of the women fell to their knees to plead for mercy.

The leader of these women was looking at him defiantly. She held her head proudly and Carl was struck by her good looks even through the dirt that blackened and smudged her features. She was not as old as he had first thought, perhaps only in her late teens. Momentarily he marvelled that one so young could rise to lead this group of women, many of whom were much older.

She continued to look him directly in the eye, still with that stubborn look of defiance. After a few moments she broke her stare and allowed herself to peruse her surroundings. She let her gaze wander over his companions and their fire eagles. He could see she was processing her situation, formulating a way to escape. Suddenly her expression changed. He watched her demeanour soften and saw hope light up in her eyes. "Are you Pinn riders?" she asked excitedly.

Carl nodded. In response the woman threw her arms around him and squeezed him. Tears flooded from her as she kissed his cheeks. She turned to her companions and shouted, "We are safe, these men are Pinn warriors. Look at their eagles. They are fire eagles, not the dark creatures of our enemy."

The other women looked around in disbelief, but then, as realisation dawned, they mimicked the reactions of the first woman. They cheered, hugged and kissed the warriors in relief and all of the men reddened in embarrassment.

Stern raised his hand to his mouth and cleared his throat to draw their attention, "Steady now. All is well. Who are you and where did you come from?"

The young woman answered for the group, "We are from Fortown. We were attacked by an evil army of spiders and stone-men. They killed our kin but captured and enslaved many of the women of the town. We were lucky, all of us," she swept her arm in an arc to indicate the others, "We were able to escape. I do not want to think about what may have happened to the others."

Stern nodded, "We are aware of what happened in Fortown. We arrived here to help. The town is now full of dwarves, centaurs and Pinns ready to fight the evil. Many of your kinfolk escaped using the tunnels but have now returned to defend their homes. Tell me, how were you able to escape?"

"As I indicated, just luck. We were placed in a circle of the stone-men and hustled along into the hills. All of the women were secured and ordered to march through a glowing blue archway. I believe that this may have been a portal gateway."

Stern nodded, "In this you are probably correct. It seems our enemy has use of the old magics."

The woman continued, "We were at the back of the line and roped together. Suddenly it was as if the stone-men lost interest, they wandered off and ignored us, believing that we would just follow the rest of the women. The spiders had already gone, taken through the portal before the women were forced through. We took our chance and crept away. We realised that we were unable to return towards Fortown, there were still many stone-men in that direction and the black eagles still flew above the town. This left only one option. We fled further west, into the mountains beyond the hills. Once we felt we were at a safe distance we removed our bonds and started to work our way back towards the town. We had to travel slowly though as we observed black eagles throughout the hills. We took turns to watch the skies and went into hiding each time we detected any of the birds." She paused and pointed to the ravine, "We found our way here and saw one of you flying in the ravine. Looking down into the shadows from above you looked like a man on a black eagle. We hid in the grasses to let you pass. Lucky for us we obviously did not do a very good job!"

The Pinn warriors looked upon these women with renewed respect. "What a remarkable escape," commented Stern, "Your story will hearten those in the town and you will all return as heroes." Stern struck his head with the palm of his hand, "Sorry, I mean heroines."

"Well I don't think any of us feel like heroines," replied the woman, "But I do know that we all want to be back with our loved ones. The news that you bring about their escape through the tunnels and subsequent return to the town is a joy for us all."

"Then let us make haste and carry you back there without delay," replied Stern. He gestured for the woman to join him on his mount. "I will carry you back to Fortown and send more eagles to pick up the others. The warriors will remain here with the others whilst we get assistance."

The woman hesitated, "I do not want to leave the other women," she said, "We have been through a lot together."

One of the women stepped forward, she was a little older than the rest, "Go with him! You kept us together and alive in the mountains but we are safe now, your work is done. We will wait here with the other riders." She smiled and turned to the men, "I'm sure they have many stories to tell us whilst we await your return." The leader turned to her colleagues who added their encouragement, all speaking at once and excitedly urging her to fly with Stern.

She looked at them and smiled, "Thank you," she responded. She turned to Stern, "It seems that I will be riding with you after all. I trust you will hold me tightly. I did not escape the clutches of monsters and vile insects for you to drop me over my own town!"

Stern laughed, "Do not fear my lady, you shall be safe. Anyway, I have you marked as a survivor so even if I did drop you, I reckon that you would probably land on something soft," he replied, smiling and bowing to her as he did so.

They both mounted the fire eagle. Stern held her tightly and spoke quietly in her ear, "I'm sorry, but when all your colleagues were speaking I did not catch your name."

The woman shook her hair out of her eyes, "My name is Brianna," she said and she gave a little start as the giant bird leapt into the air and sped her back towards her home, her kin and, hopefully, back into the safe arms of Molt.

***

Meld and Molt were working side by side filling cloth bags with dirt to form defensive blockades. It was hot work and the pair had stopped to quench their thirst. They chatted idly, glad to be back together again. A sound caught their attention and they looked up as a pair of fire eagles flew towards the town from the mountains. Meld pointed out to Molt that one of the birds was carrying two riders. Molt squinted up at the war bird, watching in awe as it beat its wings against the air. Suddenly he leapt into the air, "Meld! Look! It's Brianna! The firebird is carrying Brianna!"

Molt's brother tried to calm him down, "Are you sure? They are a long way up and you may be mistaken. You know that grief can play the cruellest of tricks on your mind."

Molt shook his head vigorously, "No Meld, it's her, I'd recognise her anywhere," and with this Molt dropped his tools and raced to follow the bird. He ran through the town, bumping into people as he kept his line of sight on the great bird as it made it's way to alight at the central square. He reached the edge of the square and stopped, doubt crept into his mind for a moment. He hardly dare look but, breathing deeply, he finally turned to face the eagle and watched the two riders dismount. His heart began to raise, it was unmistakably Brianna. Molt beamed and sprinted towards them screaming her name as he did so. Onlookers watched in amazement but then cheered loudly as they realised what was occurring.

Brianna looked towards him, "Molt! Oh Molt!" she returned his shout and raced towards him. They met and hugged each other, kissing away the tears that flooded down both of their faces.

Molt held her at arms length and looked into her eyes. "Brianna, I thought you were dead! Hold me close, I never want to let you go again."

Brianna squeezed Molt so hard that his ribs hurt. They clung to each other there in the square, neither speaking, just both glad to be in the safety of each others arms. The crowd continued to cheer and after a few minutes, closed in on the couple to welcome Brianna home.

***

Borst and Yam left the mountains behind and clambered over the hills towards Fortown. They quickened their pace as they spied the town and were soon at the main hall reporting of the advance of the dark army to Swiftaxe.

The Dwarven king immediately called a council of war and shortly the dwarves were joined by Gorlan, Tosh, Fleck and Fyros.

"The enemy will be on us much sooner than we hoped. This will mean that we will not have the support of the Pinn infantry when they first attack," observed Gorlan.

"Then we must ready the town to fight with the troops that we do have," replied Swiftaxe frowning in defiance. The stocky dwarf king turned to the others. "Gorlan and I have already discussed a battle plan for this eventuality. Our troops have been building trenches around the town and filling them with tons of wood and coal covered in oil. We believe that by lighting this inferno we can halt the advance of the spiders. As luck would have it the ring of fire will also prevent the advance of the human and dwarf forces that opposes us.

The Graav are a different proposition however. Borst and Yam have confirmed our fear in what they witnessed at Shangorth Towers. The damned creatures are born of flame, the fire pits will not stop them. They are formed from the burning heart of Portalia and re-energise themselves by bathing in pools of molten lava. I fear that the fire pits will not only be ineffective against the Graav but may also replenish any strength that they lost in the march from Shangorth Towers."

Gorlan continued, "There is little that can be done about this but we have a way of fighting the Graav utilising our centaurs and the Pinn cavalry. The additional height of both can be used to good advantage. We plan to line the rim of the fire pits with the centaurs and cavalry. As the Graav climb from the pit they will be extremely vulnerable to attack from above and it will give our troops opportunity to strike at the heads of the stone creatures. As Fleck has informed us, the Graav are not swift in combat, but they protect their heads well and their advance is relentless. Blows to their bodies fall away leaving them chipped but otherwise unharmed, but their heads are the weak point and as they climb from the fire pit they will be exposed. The wind blows in our favour on the hillside of the town where we expect the main thrust from the dark army. Here the wind will blow the smoke into the faces of our foe blinding them as they move forward."

Fyros frowned, "But what of our forces on the other side of the town? The smoke here will blow into our own troops eyes."

Gorlan nodded, "This is true but we also have an advantage here as we do not need to advance on our foe. Our troops can hold their position and wait for them to come to us. We also expect our enemy to be over confident and we expect them to strike from the south and west, directly from the hills."

The two centaurs nodded approval. Fyros rubbed his chin and spoke, "If we can make the fire pit walls steep, especially at the rim, then it will slow the Graav down to such an extent that we should be able to pick them off with ease." He grinned and slapped the Warlord on the shoulder, " I like this plan Gorlan!"

Gorlan continued, "What we do not know is how intelligent the creatures are in combat. Will they realise the danger and retreat? Our hope would be that they do not. If this plan is effective we may be able to destroy the bulk of the Graav using this tactic!"

Fleck looked thoughtful, "But what of the enemy force that do not enter the fire pits? We cannot keep the fire burning forever?"

"This is true," responded Gorlan, "But Swiftaxe has prepared for this event too."

The king took up the plan, "This is where my dwarf army will come into the plan. My forces have been manufacturing a number of large catapults. These will be aimed on the area on the far side of the ring of fire. My dwarves have already built over forty of these devices and have gathered a large amount of armament that we will use to strike across the pits at our foe. There are two types of missile. Fireballs, formed from thickly compressed vegetation soaked in oil. These will do little harm to the Graav but will hit the humans, dwarves and spiders hard. Secondly, large rock projectiles that will kill and maim those of flesh and blood but also, with luck, may strike off the heads of any Graav that stand in the way."

Gorlan took up the briefing once more, "My Pinn riders on their fire eagles will protect our force from above, battling any threat from the black eagles. We had hoped that the ratio of fire eagles to black eagles would have been more even, but they will be out numbered nine to one in the skies. The numbers will make it difficult for my riders to do anything other than keep back the enemy eagles. I do not think they will be able to offer much assistance to the battle on the ground."

Tosh offered up an idea to assist with this, "Warlord, we also have one hundred Pinn warriors and almost a thousand Fortown men. We could station these around the catapults. They could protect our artillery force from ground attack or from any black eagles that break through our fire eagle defence."

Gorlan smiled, "You are ahead of me Tosh, this is precisely what I had in mind too. I myself will command that force. We should also send a rider to meet the Pinn infantry. They will need to know of our plan as they may well arrive during the battle and find themselves cut off on the wrong side of the fire ring. The rider can also carry the intelligence to the infantry about the type of foe that we face."

Tosh pointed to Gorlan's chest, "And what of the Horn of Summoning sir, do you intend to use it?"

Gorlan raised his hand to the horn, "If the needs demands it then I will use the horn."

"A red dragon in our ranks would be formidable sir," suggested Tosh.

"Undoubtedly Tosh, but it has been many years since the horn was last blown. We do not even know if the call will be answered. Even if the promise is still true, there have been no red dragon sightings for generations so there may indeed be none to answer the call. For this reason we have not included the horn in our plans. *If* the need arises I will sound the horn and *if* a response is made then it will be treated as an added bonus to our defence plans. A huge bonus I grant you, but a bonus none the less."

"This is a wise decision," commented Fyros, "To form our plans around the summoning of a red dragon would be foolish. In the past centaurs have always been friends to the dragons and sometimes, although rare, they visited our city at Eumor. Communication with the red dragons stopped many generations ago, so I too fear that they may no longer exist to answer the call of the Horn of Summoning."

The group fell silent. King Swiftaxe looked around their faces before speaking, "So we have now laid out our plan. Raise your hands if you approve." The king scanned the gathering and the vote was unanimous, all had their hands raised in approval.

"Then it is decided. We must hasten to complete our preparations. Our focus should be on completing the fire pits and gathering additional munitions for our catapult artillery. Gorlan, I would ask that you brief the Pinn and Fortown troops. Griff, you take control of the centaurs soldiers and the cavalry. I will brief my own dwarves on our strategy. Fleck, I want you to speak to your townsfolk. Keep two hundred fighting men with yourself and assign the rest to Gorlan's command. The women, children and older folk, should be ordered back into the tunnels for their protection. I would also ask that you accompany them with your small force into those tunnels to....."

"But Swiftaxe, I cannot leave...!" Fleck's interruption was cut short by the raised hand of Swiftaxe.

"I am sorry Fleck, but we need you to lead those women and children into the tunnels. They must be protected and led to safety if the battle does not go our way."

Fleck saw the sense to this and was forced to agree, albeit rather reluctantly.

King Swiftaxe looked around the throng once again, "Then all is settled, go to your people and prepare. Tomorrow we likely go to war."

Anyone watching the town that day would have seen the sudden increase in activity. Urged on by the reports from the scouts, the whole town prepared for the upcoming battle. Fleck made arrangements for his people to retreat to the tunnels but many of the women, particularly those that had already lost family members, chose to stay and support the men. Fleck drew the line at children however, ordering that no-one under the age of fifteen could chose to stay with the army to fight. In fact, it was only this order, which raised the need for adults to nurse the children, that allowed him to gain the support of many of the women. The old men were just as reluctant, almost all wanted to stay and fight. Fleck was forced to make a decree that anyone over sixty five must retreat to the tunnels. Some argued, but rescinded when Fleck explained that those not fighting fit would hamper the soldiers if they remained behind as the defending army would feel honour bound to protect them during the conflict.

With these decisions made, Fleck ordered the able bodied men to report to Gorlan, the women were split into two groups. Those with weapon skills and bearing a physique for battle were ordered to report to Gorlan. The others were divided into groups and would be used to fetch, carry and nurse for the fighters.

Griff approached the stables where the Pinn cavalry was housed and could not help but feel apprehensive. He was greeted by Kul, captain of the Pinn cavalry. Kul listened to his orders and welcomed Griff warmly before introducing the centaur to his soldiers. Whilst, in general, the men appeared to understand and support the order to follow Griff's command, he saw some whose expressions showed clearly that they did not approve. Griff knew that some of his force would be uneasy at following the orders of a centaur. There was ancient bad feeling between the centaurs and the Pinns from the Valley. Feelings that went back generations to when the races of Portalia were split apart to live in different regions. Men and centaurs once shared the Eumor Plains, but during the time of the split, humans were forced to vacate Eumor and move either into the Valley of Heroes or to the Coastal Range, handing over their lands to the centaurs as they did so. Most of the people obeyed this decree, but a few small pockets of defiance had to be removed by force. For some human families, feelings of hostility towards the centaurs still existed to this day. Aware of this, Griff quietly discussed this concern with Kul but the captain was quick to reassure him that his warriors would follow orders, regardless of their personal feelings. Some may do so unwillingly but they were all honourable men who obeyed orders.

Meanwhile, Gorlan met with and briefed the fighting men of Pinn and Fortown. The women and older men assigned to his command by Fleck joined his force as he spoke and he welcomed them openly thanking them warmly. Finally content that his orders were understood, he split the force into five, and placed each section under the leadership of a veteran Pinn warrior. Finally, he spoke with his section leaders and gave them instructions to work with the new recruits to ascertain their abilities and to assist with the collection of munitions and in the building of the fire pits. His force organised, Gorlan searched out Griff and a cavalryman was assigned and dispatched with orders to ride east to meet and brief the approaching Pinn infantry.

King Swiftaxe watched the activity buzzing around him. He smiled and encouraged those he met and talked confidently of victory and revenge. Inside he secretly feared that even these preparations would not be enough to hold back the might of the forces that they would face.

***

Folken and his fire eagle were racing through the mountains. He had just finished a meal when the Warlord found him and dispatched him to meet the oncoming human force from the west. Despite Gorlan's insistence on explaining his choice of messenger, the thought to question his superior had not even entered his head. He knew that he was a logical choice and that this was his duty.

As earlier, when he had travelled with Borst and Yam, he kept close to the rock face, looking for enemy silhouettes in the sky. He used his own instincts for direction, aided by the position of the sun, to pick his way south-westwards. He had been briefed that the approaching human army would be located either somewhere between Dargoth Sands and the Tower or, more likely, just off the coast approaching Dargoth Bay. Gorlan had given him a brief to ask the advancing army to hold their position to the west of the Towers until they received additional word from the main force at Fortown.

Folken knew that speed was of the essence. If the force

had already landed at Dargoth Sands, then they would be less than half a day's march from Shangorth Towers. If they reached the Towers unsupported then the might of their enemy would simply annihilate those forces. His mind wandered a little as he imagined the horrors of this potential slaughter.

This momentary lapse lack of concentration was all it took. As Folken followed a ravine and his eagle made a sharp left the sky was suddenly filled with hundreds of Black Eagles, part of the main strike force heading for Fortown. A moment of panic set in but, with relief, he realised that they had not seen him and he veered downwards to hug the lower rock-face. Too late did he realise his mistake. As he made his descent to avoid the flock, he flew straight into a barrage of arrows, shot from the bows of human archers that filled the ravine below.

In desperation Folken swerved his mount left and right, avoiding the shafts as they swept towards him. The activity below had now drawn the attention of the black eagles from above and, as Folken veered upwards to climb out of the range of the archers, he flew straight into the heart of the flock and was surrounded by the dark birds.

Folken and his fire eagle fought bravely. Folken himself slayed two of the black creatures whilst his fire eagle incinerated another five. The odds were too great however and eventually, one of the black eagles was able to strike Folken from his mount.

Folken looked up in fear and loathing as he fell and watched as a mass of black eagles chased his fall. His body never reached the ground in one piece. The black mass siezed him and tore him to shreds. Folken's fire eagle looked down and with a dejected posture watched it's companion die. The black eagles ignored the golden bird as it passed by them, aware that it no longer offered any threat. The fire eagle took one last look at the scene of Folken's death and began it's journey west, into oblivion.

CHAPTER TWENTY
Blood and Rubble

There was no moon to illuminate the night, a fact that worked to the advantage of Nexus and his Graav as they exited the portal and swept south and east to avoid contact with Fortown. Nexus was mounted on a large black stallion, his dark cloak billowed out behind him as he rode near the front of his force. He had been ordered to make haste on this mission so, once they were sure they were clear of the ears of the town sentries, he ordered the Graav to break into a run. If Shangorth's spies were correct, they should meet the Pinn infantry to the south of the Halfman Forest by sunrise.

As he rode Nexus stared through the gloom at his army of Graav. They jogged with a steady rhythm, seemingly untiring. They were formidable creatures and Nexus was eager to see them in battle. He had heard of their effectiveness in combat but had never witnessed it himself. He looked at the faces of those closest to him. They were human like in form but it was clear that no oxygen passed through those solid rock noses. Their grey mouths were capable of movement but he had not heard a single sound from the Graav and he suspected that they did not possess any vocal mechanism. The eyes fascinated him though. Clearly they were functional, but they appeared as mere slits in their faces, their eye balls formed from two small orbs of orange and red fire. In the darkness the Graav appeared as just two glowing eyes, floating in mid air above the ground. Nexus marvelled at the creation of such beings and felt jealousy that the Graav had chosen to follow Shangorth. *Oh, what he would give to lead these creatures and have them follow him as if he was a god.* He wondered what it was that drove the creatures' loyalty to the warlock. He vowed to himself that he would one day discover that secret and then the Graav would be his, together with the power that their possession would allow him to seize.

Nexus shivered and felt a moments panic as he remembered the current loyalties of the Graav. Could they even now sense his own thoughts?. Doubts began to gnaw at his mind. Had Shangorth spoken truly when he had commanded this quest? Would these creatures follow Nexus' commands simply because Shangorth willed it? Or was the warlock sending him to his doom against the superior forces of the Pinn infantry?

Nexus was becoming frantic. To reassure himself he commanded the Graav to halt. Even before he had uttered the words the creatures came to abrupt stop. Nexus knew then that the Graav were indeed reading his thoughts. Even so, they were clearly not disturbed by his own desires for control and it seemed that the warlock had spoken truly, the creatures would obey his command.

He smiled and decided to play with them a little. He ordered them to raise their arms in the air and wave at the skies. He laughed as the creatures followed his will. His earlier thought returned to him, could they make any sound? He sat up straight on his horse and ordered the Graav to scream as loud as they could. As one the Graav opened their mouths wide and Nexus suddenly regretted this command as he stared into their rock faces, all contorted as they delivered a silent scream. There was something incredibly unnerving about them. Goose pimples erupted on his arms and legs.

Shaking off the feeling and now content that the creatures would follow his lead, he continued the quick march eastward.

***

Shangorth sat with his lead apprentice, Stack. The young student was eager to hear why his mentor had summoned him. "It has come to my attention that a force of humans are advancing on Shangorth from the West. I had not foreseen this as I had expected the Gates people to push south and to join their comrades in Fortown. However, it poses little problems to my plan and merely calls for a slight modification and some assistance from yourself."

Stack beamed, "Anything sir, just tell me what you need. It would be an honour to serve."

Shangorth smiled at the willingness of his student, "Ah, the enthusiasm of youth!" he commented. Stack hesitated before smiling back, unsure if the warlock was pleased with his response or whether he mocked him.

"I want you to take two hundred and fifty Graav to meet the human army headlong. The force you will face is around fifteen hundred strong and should be no match for the Graav. How many do I now have in reserve?"

"Over a thousand sir. I have been busy creating additional Graav since your last visit. I have hardly slept," replied the apprentice searching eagerly for approval.

"Excellent work Stack. However, I'd suggest that you go and rest for a few hours now. I want you to return with me to Portalia within a few hours. I will instruct the rest of the coven and have them prepare the Graav. Go now and rest."

Stack made no move to leave, "Sir, will I be allowed to use magic in the up and coming battle? I have been practising a spell which generates a fireball and I think I now have it mastered. My directional control is not perfected yet but as I will be fighting with the Graav, they will be impervious to the flames so this matters little. Providing I can direct the energy in the general direction of the enemy then it will prove effective."

Shangorth considered this and then laughed, "You know, that is quite a good idea. I had planned to transport the coven to Shangorth Towers after our victory at Fortown. Now you suggest it though, I think it is time to let the world know that the return of the warlocks is imminent. Yes, whilst I fight the forces of Fortown you should be seen commanding the Graav against the humans in the west. In fact I now insist that you use that spell and be seen to wield the power of the dark arts during the battle. The news that two warlocks are seen fighting the battles, added to that of Nexus' activities in the east, will show that we are fast growing in strength. This will strike fear across all of Portalia. Also, I suspect that Nexus will utilise the power of his cloak during combat as I cannot imagine the weasel fighting hand to hand. This too will add to our propaganda as it will appear to all that there are already three warlocks with enough power to lead. Once the rest of the coven reach your level of skill and with the bulk of Portalia's resistance annihilated at Fortown, no-one will dare to oppose us."

Stack grinned feeling pleased with himself, he even dared address the warlock by name, "Also Shangorth, I have something to show you. Something that will be of use in the battles ahead."

The warlock looked on quizzically as his apprentice led him down a corridor to a store room that led off a vestibule. "The coven thought much about your reports of the Graav's first battle at Fortown. Although they fought impressively it was clear that they were vulnerable to blows to the neck. We have therefore produced these." Stack opened the door to the storeroom. Inside were boxes on boxes all neatly arranged. Stack opened the nearest box and Shangorth peered at the contents. It took a moment for him to realise what he was looking at but then he started to laugh. He took out one of the items and examined it. "Brilliant." He commented, "My coven does me proud. Simple but brilliant!"

Smiling and full of self congratulation, the pair left the room together.

***

A few hours later Stack accompanied Shangorth through the portal and was soon heading west to intercept the oncoming human army. Unlike Nexus, Stack held no doubts that the Graav would follow his command and as he rode with his force, he practised the creation of fireballs, using groups of the Graav as targets. He had not exaggerated earlier. His aim was indeed poor and he more often than not completely missed the group for which he aimed.

Back in his tower, the warlock made the final preparations for the transportation of his arachnid army to Fortown. He had left the White Dwarf in charge of the spiders and was pleased to see that for once his minion had followed his instructions to the letter. All the spiders were dormant and secured in the control of the spider gem. The warlock took the staff from the dwarf and immediately the red glow intensified. The arachnids awakened and the room was filled once again by their eerie ticking. "Zarn! Go! Prepare the Graav escort for my spiders. It is time to send my creatures through the portal in readiness for the assault on Fortown."

As the dwarf rushed away, the warlock cast his eyes over the millions that looked at him in obedience. "Tomorrow you eat fresh meat again my creatures." The ticking intensified at the sound of his voice and the thought of liquified flesh.

***

The sky was just beginning to lose the dark shades of night as a still unseen sun began to paint it orange and red. Gorlan was awoken by the sound of alarm. He quickly donned his battle dress and made his way to the roof of the town hall.

On the hillside, a little distant from the town, the Graav had begun to take their positions. Over the hills the sky was dotted with dark silhouettes, as eagles soared and hovered above the rock men. Gorlan saw that the dark arts army of dwarves and men were intermingled amongst the Graav. He noted that they appeared to be leaderless, nothing more than an angry mob, undisciplined and no match for an organised fighting force, but still extremely dangerous through the support of the magical creatures and their superior numbers.

More terrifying than any of this though were the spiders. They had arrived in their millions, covering the hills beyond the Graav. Even as he watched he realised that their numbers were still growing and he traced their source to a particular hill. The peak in question was surrounded by a force of Graav and between the rock-men, spewed forth myriads of spiders, scuttling over the grasses to join their kind.

Swiftaxe stepped to the Warlord's side as he stepped out onto the roof level, "They are using a portal to transport the spiders from Shangorth. If you look carefully you can see the blue glow beyond the Graav."

Gorlan stared at the area indicated by Swiftaxe and was able to pick out the blue tinge, a sign that a portal gateway occupied this hill. "Well that explains how they were able to move their forces in and out so quickly for the last attack." Gorlan cast his vision across the lines of the enemy. "So many of them!" he whispered to himself but overheard by Swiftaxe.

"Aye!" replied the dwarf king, "The very sight of it will put fear into the hearts of our forces. We cannot show that fear though Gorlan. We must portray confidence at all times, no matter what we may fear inside."

"I know Swiftaxe. It is just the shock at seeing so many. Our rings of fire will hold them back for a while but I fear the very mass of the spider carcasses may put out the flames."

The two continued to watch the scene before them, Below in the city, their captains continued to work their soldiers in preparation for the defence of the town. Sentries stood by, ready to ignite the fire pit at the orders of Gorlan.

Fleck joined the two leaders on the roof and they greeted him warmly. "All of the citizens that are not part of the defensive force have now retreated to the tunnels. I will join them shortly. I wish you well and, Portalia willing, we will meet again soon to celebrate our victory." With this he took one last look across his home town, embraced the man and the dwarf and retired to the tunnels.

Tosh called up to the Warlord from the square below, "Shall we ignite the fire pits?" he asked.

Gorlan shook his head, "Not yet. Our foe will not attack until they are all in place, including their leaders. Once ignited the flames will engulf the pit quickly so time is on our side. As soon as we see the enemy begin their advance I will give the order."

"Aye sir!" barked Tosh in response.

Swiftaxe and Gorlan turned their attention back to the hills where the spider army continued to amass. The Warlord swallowed hard and took a deep breath. It would take all his self control to hide the fear he felt for the safety of his men and those that defended the town.

**

Far to the east of the town, two armies saw the dust rising from the advance of their enemies long before they saw each other. On the sight of the dust cloud, Nexus urged his Graav to greater speed whereas the Pinn infantry, warned on what tactics to expect by the messenger sent forth from Fortown, spread their line and dug in, ready to repel the advancing Graav.

"Remember, strike for their heads," shouted the commanders of the infantry. A cry began to rise up in the ranks, "Cut off their heads! Victory for Pinn! Cut off their heads!" Five thousand men chanted the battle cry.

As the sun rose in the east, Nexus, and his Graav crested a hilltop a few hundred yards from the Pinn lines and he ordered his army to halt their advance. The Pinn war cry could now be clearly heard and whilst the sound caused trepidation to rise in Nexus, the Graav remained impassive. Nexus cast his eyes over the two lines, his confidence began to wane. The Graav were outnumbered ten to one and the enemy had dug in. Could it be that he faced defeat here on the Portalia Meadows? The forces stood facing each other, each poised ready for the battle. The Graav remained perfectly still, unmoving, not a twitch or a cough to break the silence in their ranks. Nexus looked at his force and the very sight of these unmoving warriors renewed his confidence. With a shout to advance he ordered his Graav into battle.

As the first weapons met in anger and metal fell upon metal, biting into stone and flesh, Nexus pulled his cloak around him and dismounted from his steed to watch from the safety of invisibility.

The early exchanges saw the Graav cut deep into the Pinn line. The creatures fought with a steady ferocity. Although not fast, they were very adept at protecting their neck regions. Line after line of Pinn infantry fell as the Graav sliced and diced their way forward.

Cries of frustration and despair rose from some of the Pinn fighters as blow after blow rained down, only to be deflected away or to strike unyielding stone. The Graav were pushing forward protecting their heads before striking out their own death blows. The Pinns found it extremely difficult to strike blows to the vulnerable neck area of the stone-men.

Looking on, the infantry leaders realised that the battle was being lost. Over half of their force lay dead or dying and the Graav had lost less just a handful from their original numbers.

Almost in desperation, the Pinns changed their tactics. Instead of confronting the foe as two lines, the rear of the Pinn infantry was ordered to spread out, forming a longer and thinner line. This weakened the middle however, and the Graav were cutting their way through the dwindling ranks of the men. Nexus roared in triumph as he saw how close the Pinn line was to breaking.

Suddenly the Pinn leaders ordered the outskirts of their thin live to wrap around in a pincer movement and attack from the rear, sandwiching the Graav between the Pinn infantry.

Nexus watched closely and realised the danger. He used the cover of his cloak to move away from the battle centre and to ensure that he too was not ensnared.

This new tactic worked well for the Pinns and the balance of conflict swiftly changed. The soldiers were now able to strike at the Graav from front and rear, making it far more difficult for the creatures to protect their heads. Over the next few minutes increasing numbers of Graav lost their heads to Pinn swords.

However, even in death, the Graav proved a dangerous foe as the close proximity of the fighting from all sides, did not allow for retreat after the death blow and many Pinns suffered severe burns as the Graav dead exploded in a cloud of hot ash and lava rock. Still the Pinns battled on ferociously and the Graav numbers were now dwindling almost as fast as those of the Pinns.

The centre of the battle became a quagmire of mud, dust and rock as Pinns and Graav met their ends. For the men in particular, footing became difficult as they slipped in the blood on the warm lava rock that littered the battlefield. The Graav rallied for a while due to this, the weight of their own bodies, crushing stone and bone under them, allowing them a surer footing. It was only a momentary rally though and soon the superior numbers of the Pinns overwhelmed their foe. The Graav were reduced to a handful of fighters and Nexus watched in horror as his force was defeated. He wondered how Shangorth would react when he discovered that his Graav were not unbeatable. Feeling it was time to beat a retreat, Nexus looked for his horse but could not see it anywhere. Turning away from the battle, he started to head back westwards on foot, back towards Fortown. He did not relish having to face the warlock

The Graav were now down to six but they showed no sign of surrendering. The odds were hopeless for them but they fought to the last, taking down another twelve Pinn infantry before they lost their own heads and erupted in a pile of smoking rubble.

The battle was over. It had lasted less than thirty minutes but the Meadows were littered with the dead of both armies. The Pinn infantry had however, been severely hit, thousands lay dead and several hundred more were wounded or suffering from lava rock burns. The Pinns searched the rubble and the bodies for any sign of Nexus, who many had seen disappear into thin air. They eventually gave up the search having combed the battlefield and the surrounding area.

The Pinn commanders ordered their troops to bury their dead. This task complete, they marched their force west until the battlefield was lost from site. Although they were all eager to push on with what remained of their force to help at Fortown, they recognised that they would not make it to there in time to enter the city before the enemy lay siege. Also, the commanders were aware that their own men were suffering the weariness of a hard fought battle and desperately needed the rest. They were in no fit state to dive headlong into an enemy army of superior numbers. To ascertain the status of what lay ahead at the outpost, the Fortown messenger, who had survived the battle, was asked to scout ahead and to return with news on how the town fared. The Pinn infantry would rest for a few hours before continuing their way. Once they had met up with the scout again, they would decide the next course of action.

With camp set, they took stock of their forces. Of the five thousand that had set out from Pinnhome only fifteen hundred remained alive and seven hundred of those were wounded in some way, bearing the scars of battle, through weapon cuts or burns. The commanders looked at their ranks and wondered whether this had indeed been a victory.

CHAPTER TWENTY-ONE
Face to Face

Rhys and Ashley, accompanied by Fyros, had joined the Warlord and the King of the dwarves on the rooftops above Fortown. They watched the enemy lines growing by the minute and shared the small telescope that belonged to Swiftaxe. A few hours after sunrise, the flood of spiders from the portal began to lessen and finally, came to a stop. The enemy force covered the hillside, patiently awaiting their orders. As the allies watched, a movement amongst the Graav caught their attention and a large defensive circle formed around the portal as a figure emerged from the blue aura.

The White Dwarf was the first to arrive, as he made the transition, he glanced around at the town and the lines of the dark arts army. Swiftaxe cursed when he saw the dwarf through the lens of the telescope, "Foul Traitor! " he exclaimed. Zarn was closely followed by Ohrhim who was in human form.

Swiftaxe studied the figure, "I do not recognise this one. What about you Gorlan?" he asked passing the telescope to the Warlord. Gorlan shook his head, "Me neither." Two more figures stepped from the portal, side by side. Gorlan inhaled sharply as he looked upon the last two to emerge.

"What is it?" asked Fyros, concerned by the warlord's consternation. Gorlan looked at him with as serious expression and handed the telescope to the centaur.

Fyros brought the instrument to his eye and looked upon

Shangorth for the first time. The warlock was dressed in heavy thick black battle leathers. In his right hand he held the staff of the Spider Gem, it's orb glowing brightly in the close proximity of the spider army. Around his neck Fyros saw that the warlock wore a small pendant, which he recognised as a Runestone pendant, and another chain on which hung an amber orb.

Fyros muttered darkly, "Shangorth! So, it is true, the evil one has returned. I see the reason for your concern Warlord, it seems the Warlock wars did not eradicate our enemy after all."

"Grim indeed," replied Gorlan, "But look at the figure that accompanies him Fyros."

The centaur moved the telescope to focus on the fourth character. At first Fyros did not react but then recognition dawned and Fyros let out a shout of contempt, "This is a desecration. The lowest of the low! What evil magics have been used here." Handing the device to Rhys he continued, "You had better see this for yourselves."

Rhys looked through the lens, "It's Mike! He' s still alive." Rhys smiled broadly, relieved to see his friend again. However, his face soon turned from an expression of glee to one of puzzlement. As Rhys watched from the rooftops, it became obvious that Michael was not a prisoner. No bindings held him and no weapons were trained on him. He appeared to be stood at the warlocks side through free choice. "Mike, what the hell are you doing?" he asked out loud. Ashley reached for the telescope, "Here, let me see." Rhys handed the device to her, his expression now glum and severe. Ashley stared at the gathering on the hillside for sometime.

"This is weird," she said, "Why is Mike with them. He seems OK but he is acting a little strange. He has not said a word yet whilst the others are deep in conversation. He's just standing there at the warlock's side."

Swiftaxe took the telescope back and looked at the youth, after a while he said,. "I fear that Michael may have been enchanted by the warlock. He holds himself as if in a trance."

"Look, something else is moving through the portal," commented Gorlan.

The group continued to watch as a number of Graav carrying boxes appeared on the hillside. Shangorth shouted something and the boxes were opened revealing something metallic inside. The Graav removed them and began to distribute them along the lines of their ranks.

Swiftaxe, still watching through his telescope described the objects as hinged metals rings with a lower collar. As the first Graav fastened the ring around its neck, Gorlan realised the purpose of the rings. "Damn! They are devices to better protect the necks of the Graav. These collars are going to make it extremely difficult for our forces to behead the cursed stone-men. If they have been enchanted too, then our weapons may well prove ineffective."

Swiftaxe nodded, "This is true Gorlan but we must continue with our battle plan none the less. We had better warn Griff and Kul of this turn of events though. They will need to find an effective way of fighting the Graav." He called to a dwarf soldier and spoke to him. The dwarf ran off in the direction of the stables.

The enemy line remained passive for the next hour or so. Swiftaxe decided that he would remain on the roof, providing him with an excellent observation point for the battle. Gorlan left the rooftops to join his own forces who stood ready to protect the catapults of the dwarves.

Swiftaxe noted that the boxes were now empty, all had been distributed. The vast majority of the Graav now wore the device but there had clearly not been enough to protect all of the stone-men.

Since the completion of this task an eerie silence had fallen over the enemy ranks. Shangorth watched the skies and his army waited. As the sun reached it's zenith, the warlock let out a yell and raised his staff high in the air. The silence was broken by the sound of millions of spiders, clicking and shuffling as the spider army, passed through the ranks of the Graav, and began to sweep towards Fortown.

Swiftaxe continued to signal the allies to hold their positions. As the first wave of spiders entered the fire pits, he raised his arm ordering the ignition of their defensive ring. The pits exploded into a fiery furnace, completely surrounding the town. The spiders continued their advance regardless, marching into the furnace by their thousands. The air was filled with the smell of searing flesh as, driven by their craving for fresh meat and the desire of the mad warlock, wave after wave of the creatures met their deaths in the inferno.

Some of the insects actually managed to make it through the blaze, crawling along the backs of their incinerated brethren to avoid death. Those that did were in small numbers and easily dispatched under foot by Pinn or centaur.

On the hilltop Shangorth cursed. He had been overconfident and had not foreseen that the trench was filled with combustible material. He recovered his composure and brought his spider force to a halt but not before he had lost almost twenty percent of his arachnid army to the searing flames.

Furious at his own mistake and the loss of so many, Shangorth waved the rest of his force into battle. The black eagles soared through the skies towards the town and the Graav began to move forward at a steady pace. The dark army of men and dwarves, also unable to pass through the fire pits, turned to their bowmen who began to fire shafts across the pits at those protecting the town. Fortunately the smoke that rose from the pits fogged their vision and the vast majority of their arrows fell harmlessly to ground. By chance a few hit their targets, most bouncing off battle dress but a few piercing the flesh of the Pinn cavalry or burying their shafts into the sides of the centaurs who made up the defensive front line. The centaurs were strong and were not brought down by the effects of a single arrow, but it was clear that their wounds caused them discomfort. They held their ground, waiting for the advance of the Graav.

The stone warriors had now reached the fire pits and, as expected, the creatures continued their march through the flames and burning oil, completely unharmed. When they reached the other side, they found that the back wall of the pit was extremely steep and hindered their progress. The creatures began to claw at the earth to make footholds and handholds that would enable them to climb back to the surface.

Over head, black eagles met fire eagles and the air was filled with the screeches of the birds and the battle cries of the Pinn riders. The fire eagles were greatly outnumbered but their greater agility and their bond with their human riders more than made up for this. The air was filled with the smell of charred flesh as the fire eagles used their magical ability to incinerate their foe. As they did so they continued to fight with their beaks, ripping and tearing at any flesh that came close enough for a strike, their riders wielding their swords in ferocious arcs, cutting through black feathers and flesh. The superior numbers of the black eagles allowed them success too and Gorlan's heart sank as he saw the occasional rider-less fire eagle winging its way away from the battle towards the west.

Below, the dwarves had begun to use their catapults to good effect, firing projectiles into the stalled ranks of spiders, dwarves and men that faced them across the fire pits. Earlier the allied dwarves had spent significant efforts in aligning their target areas for the catapults, and the effect was to cover vast areas with huge piles of rock and fire. Whilst the spiders held their ground, seemingly oblivious to the dangers, the effect on the enemy dwarf and human forces was devastating. As bowmen and swordsmen met their deaths from catapult fire unable to advance on their foe due to the fire pits, the mercenary forces began to panic. As more of them fell they turned almost as one to flee the battle.

Shangorth, already fuming at the loss of the spiders, saw the retreat of his Dargoth Sands forces and, irate, he commanded his spiders to intercept. The spiders eagerly fell on the retreating meat and devoured men and dwarves to the bone. Shangorth, grinning manically, screamed out loud as he watched, "No-one turns away from my path! Feed my pets!".

Swiftaxe watched all of this from his vantage point on the roof and knitted his brow. At once sickened by the sight of the devastation of the Dargoth Sands forces but also elated at the early battle exchanges. The dwarf king nodded and turned his attention back to the fire pits.

Shangorth too had turned his attention back to the onslaught of the town. He frowned, this was not going to be as easy as he thought, the defenders had prepared well.. He was not too concerned however, he still held the mightier force and his Graav would soon be through the fire pits and then the tide of the battle would change. Conscious of the danger to his spiders however, he ordered them back from the area of the fire pits so that they waited outside the reach of the enemy catapults.

Noting this change, Swiftaxe responded and the dwarves ceased their use of fireballs and redoubled their effort to fire heavy rocks into the approaching Graav. Swiftaxe peered through the smoke as the heavy rocks slammed into many of the Graav. The creatures that were hit bodily were struck to the ground but, after a few seconds, stood and continued their advance as if nothing had occurred. However, some of the Graav were not so fortunate. The bombardment from the dwarf defenders struck their heads with so much force that they were removed from their shoulders, the metal collars offering no protection against this heavy aerial assault.

Even though the numbers that met their end this way were light, Shangorth observed this tactic and turned his attention to the air to redirect the efforts of some of the eagles. The black creatures screamed down towards the dwarves, intent on removing the threat of the catapults. As they closed on their quarry, Gorlan ordered his forces to intercept, surrounding the dwarves to protect them from beak and talon.

The black eagles held a great advantage from their aerial attack, and although Gorlan's forces were able to protect the dwarves, allowing them to continue their artillery barrage, the losses to those defenders proved great. The Warlord looked overhead, hoping that he could call on assistance from his fire eagles, but, to his disappointment, he saw that all still battled in the smoke laden skies above. Even worse, he realised that the black eagles were starting to make headway in their assault and had reached the first of the catapults. In amazement at their efficiency, Gorlan watched as the eagles quickly dispatched the dwarf crew and then used their powerful talons to tear the catapults to pieces. He shouted new commands to re-shape the defending line as another five of the forty catapults fell to the eagles. He paused and his hand moving to the horn around his neck. *Was it time? Should he now sound the Horn of Summoning?* As he stood to ponder this question he was suddenly brought back to the awareness of his surroundings as he felt an intense pain across his shoulders. In agony the Warlord fell forward, the talons of a black eagle dug deep into his flesh. The eagle thrashed its wings and began to lift the Warlord off the ground. As the creature began it's climb, Gorlan swiftly struck up instinctively with his sword and it stabbed deep into the chest of the animal, piercing it's heart. The eagle screeched loudly and black blood sprayed, covering the Warlord as he and the bird fell the few feet back to earth. Gorlan momentarily felt his feet make contact with the ground before the dead weight of the bird fell on him, pinning him underneath. As he tried to rise he suddenly realised that he could not move. His arms were trapped beneath him and the weight of the bird prevented him from pulling them free. He shouted for assistance but his cries were stifled beneath the bird and lost in the general noise of the battle. As he struggled in vain to free himself, he also realised with some trepidation that the Horn of Summoning was also trapped under his own body and he was incapable of reaching it with his hands or his lips. His frustration level was growing as, hopelessly pinned, he tried to kick and squirm his way free without success.

Meanwhile, back at the fire pits the Graav were making progress up the nearside bank to the crest. As they approached the rim, centaurs and Pinn cavalrymen charged forward and chopped at their heads. The swords of the town defenders struck the metal collars of the Graav and sparks flew in all directions, but unmarked, the metal of the armour protected the Graav. Time and time again allied swords swung back and forth but even the powerful swords of the centaurs hardly scratched the surface of the metal collars. Griff swore as he watched his troops and their lack of success, "Kul, the collars are preventing us taking out the Graav. We need heavier weapons to cut through."

Kul nodded, "We have some heavy axes in the armoury. I'll take some soldiers and will get them." The Pinn captain turned his mount and made for the armoury. Within a few minutes he had secured a bundle of large two handed axes. Kul rode forward and passed the axes out to the centaur soldiers.

The Graav had now crested the rim and the first of their line met headlong with the defenders. A centaur, now armed with an axe leapt into the fray. He was a huge warrior even by centaur standards. This centaur soldier stood ten feet high and his muscles rippled with power. Lifting the large axe he swung the weapon with all the force he could muster. A great cheer went up as the axe struck the Graav at the neck and lifted it off his feet. The Graav landed with a thud against it's colleagues and fell to the ground. It lay still for a few seconds before rising to its feet to return to the battle, the metal collar around his neck showing no more than a slight discoloration where it had been struck by the axe. The cheers quickly subsided as four Graav fell on the brute of a centaur. Even the bravest of the defenders felt fear as the huge warrior was dispatched, sliced into pieces by the stone men, whilst the centaur was unable to take down any of his tormentors with the weapons that he possessed.

Dejectedly Kul looked on and ceased handing out the heavier weapons, leaving them in a pile on the ground as he returned to face the advancing Graav. Raising his own sword he now rode into battle with his men and the centaurs. Realising that they could not destroy their foe, Kul shouted orders to his left and right, commanding the men to hold their line as long as possible to prevent the Graav advancing. He hoped that this way the catapults would be able to maximise their destruction of the creatures on the other side of the fire pit.

Kul's sword swept in giant arcs as he used the force of

his blows to deny the Graav any advance. Moving to block two Graav rising out of the pit to his left, Kul was attacked from his right by a third Graav. A blow struck his leathers with force, knocking the Pinn captain off his feet. As he fell his sword dropped from his grasp to land in the dirt. Kul turned at the sound of alarm from his men and watched as all three Graav raised their swords above their heads. As he looked at his death Kul thought of his homeland and the wife and children he would leave behind. He saw the blades of the Graav strike downwards and then miraculously stop short with a loud metallic crash as another sword blocked the blows. Griff stood over Kul and held the force of all three of the Graav. Too late, Kul realised that in doing so the centaur had left himself open to two Graav that he himself was battling. In horror Kul watched as the first Graav struck the tendons of both rear legs of the centaur. Blood spilling in the dirt, Griff fell to his knees as the Graav sliced into his front legs, removing the lower half of both. The second stone warrior, now presented with a large exposed target, thrust his own sword deep into the chest of the centaur and with a look of shock on his face Griff fell to the ground. Both Graav now fell upon him, slashing and slicing. Many Pinn cavalrymen saw Griff's ultimate sacrifice and in that fleeting moment, the centaur's actions successfully healed rifts that had existed for centuries between the families of these men and the centaur race.

Taking the chance that Griff had made for him, Kul leapt to his feet grabbing his sword as he did so. His vision was tainted with red as he felt an intense battle rage rise within him. Striking heavy blows all around, he started to drive back the Graav. Time and time again his blows struck the collars of the stone warriors but even in his battle rage, they were simply too strong to pierce and it soon became clear to Kul and the others that the collars were enchanted in some way. He continued to strike back at the foe though, slowly making his way to the Graav that had cut the tendons of the centaur. On reaching him, Kul's battle fury heightened and he struck with such power that the Graav was knocked off his feet. Using his sword like a dagger, Kul violently stabbed the blade of his sword at the midriff of the first Graav. The angle of the strike was such that the sword blade slid up the creatures chest and found it's way under the metal collar. With a final push, Kul forced the sword deep into the neck of Griff's killer. Kul immediately heard a loud hissing and observed steam erupting from the gash that his blade had left under the collar. Withdrawing his blade with some difficulty the noise became louder as steamed gushed from the stone wound. Realising the danger, Kul leapt backwards just as molten lava spewed from the Graav's collar, and with a dull thud, it's head exploded and the Graav fell into a pile of rubble, it's body spread around that of the fallen centaur.

On-looking centaurs and Pinns were heartened by this sight. It reinforced to them that it was still possible to kill the creatures but as they fought on they it extremely difficult to replicate what Kul had achieved. Even when they successfully forced a Graav to ground, it was rare that they were able to deliver a death blow under the collar, especially as another Graav swiftly replaced it's fallen comrade.

Even so, initially they were able to still hold their defensive lines, but, as they tired and more Graav clambered over the edge of the fire pits, the defenders started to fall back, losing increasing numbers under the incessant blows of the Graav.

In the skies above this battle, Tosh and his warbird continued to fight with the other fire eagles. Observing the tiring of the cavalrymen and centaurs below, Tosh rallied four other fire eagles and dived to attack the Graav, leaving their colleagues to continue the battle with the black eagles above.

Tosh's eagle was first to reach a Graav and as it connected with the rock man, it's talons dug deep into the stone. Immediately the creature was engulfed in flame but, instead of ending it's life, the creature lapped up the flames, replenishing itself. Tosh realised the mistake immediately and only some deft riding and swerving allowed him to escape the clutches of the Graav. The other riders had observed what had occurred too and turned their tactics to knocking the Graav off their feet, hoping that the ground force could deliver a death blow. This had limited effect, a handful of Graav were lost to sword and knife, thrust underneath their protective armour, but, more often than not, they recovered their feet quickly and returned to the affray. A few of the eagles tried to use their talons to strike the heads from the creatures but found that the stone men were not only adept at avoiding these strikes but also, once again, they were well protected by the collars.

Swiftaxe, still accompanied by Fyros, Rhys and Ashley looked on from his vantage point and saw that his forces were fast losing this frontline battle. His catapult force had now been reduced to twenty whilst the foot soldiers continued to battle the black eagles to protect the others. In the skies overhead however, the fire eagles had vastly reduced the numbers of the black eagles and many were now able to turn their efforts to helping the protection of the catapults and in supporting the frontline. The spiders were also still effectively cut off from the battle by the still burning fire pits. Nonetheless, the dwarf king realised that this advantage was limited as the Graav had now pushed his forces away from the fire pits so they had no way of replenishing the fuel. This would allow the spiders to cross in a few hours, if the Graav had not already won the day by then.

Swiftaxe spoke to Fyros, "We need a new tactic. We need a way to defeat these accursed Graav."

Ashley replied before Fyros had a chance to respond, "If we can't beat the Graav, maybe we should strike at the guy over there who controls them." She pointed towards Shangorth who stood commanding all from the hillside.

Fyros nodded and added his support to this, "I was thinking along the same lines myself. If we could attack that hillside then we may be able to take out the warlock and his minions. The Graav would then be leaderless. This may not stop them continuing the fight but their actions would not be so focussed without the leadership of the warlock."

Rhys was watching the hillside too and added, "If we could take Shangorth out, then we may be able to use the portal and travel back to his Runestone. We could save Mike and get back home from there too."

Swiftaxe pondered these ideas, "The warlock is powerful and greatly protected but I feel that a direct assault on the hill may be our only hope." As he spoke he looked at the fire pits and saw that the Graav were now making significant advance. The line of centaurs and cavalrymen was fast dwindling and the Graav were now spewing forth from the fire pits by the hundred. Realisation dawned that any assault on the hillside would need to take place quickly if they were to have any hope of winning this battle. He called to one of his dwarf men to carry messages to his commanders below.

In the heat of the battle Kul continued to fight like a demon. He had now been joined by Stern and Carl in the air and the three were at the centre of the battle, striking back the Graav and inspiring the other troops to great things. However, even they realised that time would bring defeat and each had begun to feel the signs of weariness in their muscles as they struggled against the formidable Graav.

Stern was sweeping in to strike at another Graav when he suddenly heard the familiar swish of arrows as they swept through the air all around him. The shafts screamed into the necks of the Graav, cutting through their collars with ease. Wafts of steam ushered from the pierced collars and the hissing of the released gas could be heard all around. This sound was closely followed by the explosion of the targeted Graav as they fell into a pile of steaming rubble.

Stern and Carl shouted to Tosh and he immediately ordered the remaining fire eagles to take to the skies to avoid the arrows that surrounded them. As the brothers climbed to rejoin the battle with the black eagles they looked to the north of town. There on the hillside, clad in their traditional green and brown cloth and protected by a light mesh armour, they saw over a thousand elven archers silhouetted against the horizon. The riders watched in awe as each elf, long blonde hair flowing behind them, and with grim determined faces bearing sharp features, waited and watched for gaps in the smoke. When an opportunity arose to target the Graav, a single elf would let forth a volley of four or five arrows at the creatures within seconds. The accuracy of the elves was incredible. Even in the reduced vision the vast majority of their arrows struck through the metal collars of the Graav as if they were made of butter.

Urged on by the sight of the enemy losses, the cavalrymen and centaurs rallied. The Pinn riders that had dropped to support the ground force, now returned their attention to the battle in the sky, a battle which they were fast winning. The black eagles had suffered many casualties and there numbers were fast declining. In their reduced numbers the giant birds could no longer threaten the dwarves and their catapults. As a result, many of the foot soldiers, now released from their catapult protection duties, turned to supporting their colleagues at the front line. Only ten catapults remained intact, but these continued to pound the far side of the fire pits, wreaking whatever damage they could.

Slowly but surely the defenders, supported by the piercing accuracy of the elven arrows, began to push back the Graav. In astonishment Shangorth looked on as his forces were forced back towards the fire pits. Peering through the clouds of smoke, he watched as many of his Graav met their deaths. His line of sight to the elves was obscured by a combination of the hills and the smoke so he did not realise the source of this destruction. Almost in a blind panic he decided to recall the Graav and what was left of his black eagle force, fearful that they would not be victorious without the support of the spider army.

As the enemy began to withdraw, realisation swept through the town and the defenders began to cheer and hug each other. They knew the battle was far from over but they felt elation at this first victory.

Swiftaxe who had watched the interjection of the elves swing the battle, now saw that the elves had left their point of cover and were racing towards the town. He looked at the enemy lines in alarm, fearing that the elves would be cut off by the spiders, but his heart leapt as he saw no movement towards the elvish forces from the dark magics army. Acting swiftly, Swiftaxe called for water soaked wooden platforms to be lowered across the fire pit to allow safe access to the town for the elves. These had been built in case the defenders had needed to cross the fire pits themselves. Reacting to the Dwarven king's order, the forces ushered forward and dropped the platforms over the fire pits. The wood spat and sizzled as the furnace below began to heat the surface. The Pinn cavalry galloped across the makeshift bridge and formed a protective escort as the elves crossed into the sanctity of the town behind the ring of fire.

Zarn, the White Dwarf had been the first to become aware of the arrival of the elves. He screamed alarm and pointed towards them but it was too late. By this time the archers and the cavalry had reached the platforms and were already swarming across to reinforce the ranks defending the towns. As the cavalrymen followed the elves, the wooden platforms, now scorched and charred by the heat, were lifted and place back into their holding ponds. The luck of the defenders had held once more, they had completed this task at a breakneck speed and before the enemy was able to react to their presence. Shangorth cursed under his breath as he watched the platforms lifted and then sighed loudly. He formed a fist and struck the White Dwarf, "Why didn't you tell me they were there before now!"

Zarn started to reply but fell back screaming as the warlock projected intense pain on him. Behind them, Michael stood impassive as he watched the creature shrivel in fear and agony. Ohrhim looked on with a slight frown on his face before speaking, "What now Shangorth. Do we regroup and attack again?"

Shangorth broke off his contact with Zarn to answer, "Yes, but first we need to douse the flames that stop my spiders from feeding. I am going to return to my library to prepare a spell to dampen the fires and the spirits of our foe. Stay here and watch the town. Let me know if anything unusual transpires. I will return in a few hours."

With this, Shangorth stepped through the portal to return to Shangorth Towers. In the west, the sun met the horizon as evening fell over the battle field. This day belonged to the defenders of Fortown.

***

In the East things were very different. The army of the Gates were taken completely by surprise. With no understanding of the power of the enemy, Stack led his Graav to an overwhelming rout of the human forces. Fighting against a force that did not know their weakness and protected by the metal collars, the Graav sliced and hacked their way forward slaughtering all in their path.

Stack laughed insanely as he cast fireballs to left and right, the burning orbs passing around his Graav but burning the men to a cinder where they stood. The battle, which took place on open ground between Dargoth Sands and the Tower, lasted less than two hours and by the end, almost fifteen hundred humans lay dead, the rest having retreated towards the coast in terror. Not a single Graav lay dead.

The men had tried to fight with sword, axe, spear and arrow. But, unlike the arrowheads of the elves, their weapons were not magically enhanced and could not penetrate the Graav rock exteriors or their protective collars.

Pleased with himself, Stack turned his army back to Shangorth Towers. He would await Shangorth there as ordered. The apprentice smiled as he thought about how easy it had all been and felt particular satisfaction at how he had perfected his knowledge of the fireball spell as the battle had progressed. At first he had felt a slight sickening feeling as he watched the fireball consume a man before his very eyes. However, by the time he had watched this scene a dozen times he had become to enjoy it and was even keeping a score in his head of the most effective fireballs. The more he created the greater accuracy he achieved. By the end of the battle he was even able to adjust the size of the fireball. Small powerful globes that burned intensely, or larger orbs that burned but did not incinerate the flesh so rapidly.

The apprentice warlock let his thoughts wander to the battle to the east. He contemplated whether he should try to join his master there but decided against this as he was sure that the town had fallen easily and swiftly as the army of the Gates. After all, Shangorth not only had the power of the Graav but also the might of the spiders and the Black Eagles. He was simply invincible!

CHAPTER TWENTY-TWO
Loss of the Lifebreath

I can still feel consciousness although I crave the peace of the creeping stone. Too long have I laid here waiting for the sanctity of death. I try to will my end, to close down my thoughts, but each time they resurface, tormenting me with images of my kin, now long gone.

More vivid than most is the scene that constantly plays in my head of the last few days of our kind. I remember laying on the hillside watching and hoping with all of my body and soul as Cyretha and Drentor waved their intricate love flight. Arching their backs and intertwining their bodies, their scales rubbing together sensuously as time after time they tried to call forth the Lifebreath. For months they flew, desperate to spark the inferno that would engulf the pair and create new life for our kind. But the power of the Peak was now dull and the Lifebreath did not arise. Finally exhausted to the point of death, our last mating pair fell to the earth, their spirits broken. Cyretha had ridden the Flame just a few days later, mercifully she had been offered a swift return to sit alongside her ancestors. Drentor and I separated. The last two of our kind. Drentor was still young enough to call forth the Lifebreath, but with Cyretha gone, there was no partner to create new eggs.

I sometimes wonder about Drentor. Was he granted a swift journey or, like me, is he doomed to take the slow path? Other images come to my mind. Faces and words, familiar and yet now so, so distant. Perhaps I will meet with them again soon. I resolve my brain to silence and once more I return my thoughts to the rock, willing it to engulf me. It responds! *But so slowly, oh so slowly!*

Once my ancestors that had chosen the way of the rock would leave this existence within weeks, the Peak was strong then and it's power aided my brethren on their chosen path. Now the power of the Peak was all but spent and the magic force that called the rock came more from within myself than from the source of the Peak. I search my body with my thoughts and find that the rock has still only progressed to the top of my legs.

Oh, so slow! So slow!

I pray and hope that there is enough essence left in the Peak to complete the task.

CHAPTER TWENTY-THREE
Confrontations

It was hours before they found Gorlan. The Warlord was livid. He had been stuck under the dead eagle for hours. He was able to hear the battle raging around him but had been totally trapped beneath the bird and unable to join the fight. Many of the men could not help but tease him a little, raising the question as to whether he had hidden under the eagle. They soon stopped this type of jibe though as Gorlan spat blood and thunder at anyone who dared to tease him.

The ground on the town side of the fire pits had been cleared of their fallen comrades and of the Graav debris. Reluctantly, the fallen had been respectfully cast into the fire pits for instance cremation, the defenders did not have the time to dig graves as they needed to prepare for the next assault.

Swiftaxe personally supervised the refuelling of the fire pits and Gorlan busied himself in reforming the foot and cavalry brigades. It was approaching midnight before the town started to slow down it's activities and finally, exhausted, many took the chance to rest.

Even then Gorlan and Swiftaxe called a war council before they retired for the night. Fyros, Meld, Rhys and Ashley were all requested to attend. Lan, who had not been seen by any during the battle, had once again latched onto Rhys' trail and accompanied him to the meeting. The council was also joined by Gabriel who had led the Elven archers to Fortown in response to the messenger that had been dispatched a few weeks earlier. All expressed their gratitude to Gabriel who's archers had saved the day. The elf merely shrugged and responded that thanks were not needed, for all of Portalia had a duty to fight against this common foe.

Two hours later the eight left the chambers and returned to their accommodations to rest. Molt heard his brother creep into the family home and could not help but raise questions. Meld swore him to secrecy and then briefed him on the discussions that had taken place. When he had finished Molt stared at him as if he was mad, "That is a daring plan and so full of 'ifs and buts'. To attempt to attack the warlock and his minions whilst they hide behind the combined ranks of the spiders and Graav is a desperate act."

Meld frowned, "Well, in many ways it would indeed be that. Of course, this plan would only be called upon if the battle on the ground starts to turn against us. Remember, until the elves arrived with their bows, we came very close to disaster today. If Shangorth can execute a plan to bring his spiders into the combat, then not even the elven archers can prevent us losing heavily. Remember too that the ammunition that the elves carry is not limitless. Whilst we can replace their spent arrows, our own shafts do not carry the same magical abilities as that of the elves. The shafts of the arrows that they carry are made from the wood gathered from the Forest of Lorewood and, as such, they are imbued with an inherent magic. Gabriel, the head of the archers, believes that it is this that allows their arrows to pierce the enhanced metal of the Graav collars. We have retrieved as many as possible but the arrows that hit their targets do not survive, destroyed by the heat of the Graav as they are destroyed."

"But brother, surely the fire pit will continue to keep the

spiders at bay. With the elves behind us we can defeat the Graav. Even in the air, the black eagles have all been annihilated by the Pinn riders."

"Yes Molt, this is true but what if the warlock chooses to wait. We cannot keep the fire pits burning for ever. He could choose to sit this out and wait until the flames subside. This is why a backup plan was needed. Remember too that we have promised to try to return Ashley and Rhys to their homes. A portal gateway to a working Runestone is located on that hill and it offers a way for us to achieve this promise."

"What about Michael?" asked Molt.

"Rhys and Ashley still hold hope that we can save him from the warlock but I have used the spyglass to look at him and I fear he is already lost. I, for one, am ready to discount any hope for Michael but I will try to leave my mind open. If an opportunity arises to save him then I will grasp it with both hands. Now, enough questions, I need my rest."

The brothers took to their beds but neither were able to sleep. Too many questions and fears were being processed in their heads.

**

It was still dark when Gorlan was awoken by Tosh.

"Warlord, something is happening on the hillside," commented the Pinn sergeant.

Gorlan made his way to the roof tops once more, where he was joined by Swiftaxe, Gabriel and Fyros.

The four looked up at the hillside where Shangorth stood surrounded by his forces. His hands were held high in the air. In the dark of the night he appeared a fearsome sight indeed. In one hand he still held the glowing red Spider Gem staff. Around his neck, the small Capture Orb pulsed with a bright amber light that pierced the night. The warlock was chanting and purple arcs of light were leaping from his outstretched arms into the night sky. Overhead, dark clouds began to form and grew ever thicker as the warlock continued his magical incantation.

Swiftaxe expecting an advance from the enemy, immediately ordered a bugler to call the town to battle once more. The defenders poured out of their resting places to take up arms once again.

Hours went by and the warlock continued to cast his spell. Once more the two armies faced each other across the ring of fire. The clouds overhead were now an unnatural black and had formed into a large ring, mimicking the shape of the pits of fire. Then, as the first light of dawn began to paint the sky, the dark evil looking clouds spewed forth their contents in a thunderous clap. Arcs of lightening lit the sky all around the ring and enormous hail stones fell from the heights to strike the fires below with a loud hissing. Gorlan watched and shouted a warning as one of the Pinn fire eagles was caught directly under the clouds. The barrage of hail stones was too thick for the warrior to avoid and Gorlan closed is eyes as the warrior was struck from his mount to fall into the inferno that still raged below.

Shangorth continued to chant and fuel the cloud burst. Slowly the fires were beginning to ebb as the huge lumps of ice fell onto the flames, melted and cooled them. Steam filled the air all around the town. The leaders of the defenders realised that the hail would soon extinguish the fiery defence and both the Graav and the spiders would have access to attack the town.

Swiftaxe looked across at Gorlan, "Regrettably I believe it is time my friend."

Gorlan nodded, "Tosh, go and find Ashley and Rhys and direct them here. Then report back here yourself and bring Carl, Stern and Kraven with you. We will have need of their fire eagles."

As the Pinn sergeant leapt to obey, Gorlan lifted the Horn of Summoning. With shaking hands, partly through excitement and party in trepidation, he placed the instrument to his lips and blew. A single resonant note erupted from the Horn and the sound rang out through the town and across the hills, carried north, born on magical currents that were invisible to the eye and of which only the dragons had knowledge.

***

As I lay, lost in my solitude I feel a stirring in the magic of the skies.

Something comes!

It has been a long time since I have felt the air magics move. I thought that they too, like the Peak, had lost their power but I can sense them, rising and falling as something uses their channels of currents to move through the skies.

And then a sound, unmistakable in it's calling, arrives at the Peak, resounding throughout the mountains as each echo amplifies it's call.

"No, not now! I will not answer!" I shout at the skies, but I know that this ancient magic formed a bond that could not be disobeyed. When my kin had been alive, one would be chosen to answer such a calling. Now, only I remained. Tired, I allow my thoughts to plot. *If I am the only one left then no-one would know if I ignored the call. All I need do is close my eyes once more and return to forging my rock spirit.*

Hardly convinced by my own insincerity, I close my eyes once more and listen to the fading sound of the horn's call. Not for long though as a second blast calls me back to reality.

I look at my body, now solidified up to my torso. I can feel the tingling there already as I almost subconsciously will life back into the flesh.

A tear runs down my cheek as I watch years of meditation disappear in minutes, the rock giving way to warm red scaled flesh once more. I sigh, knowing that I must answer the call of the horn. Spreading my wings I leap skywards, wriggling my toes as I ascend and as I feel the life return to them once again.

The air invigorates me, it has been so long since I last used my wings. My feet, recovering their sensation by each second, are throbbing, not with pain but in a rebirth of feeling.

As I fly through the sky, following the currents on which the horn's call had been born, my mood changes. *After all what harm could one last flight do. I'll answer the need of the horn bearer and will then return to my mountain meditation.*

I look down at the world below but there is little to see. All passes in a blur as I fly like the wind through the magic currents, bound for the bearer of the Horn of Summoning.

***

Twice Gorlan had blown the horn and stood waiting with bated breath,. He hardly dared to hope that the call would be answered. Now their hopes had turned to reality as they looked into the distance and saw the approaching dragon. Only Lan seemed to show no sense of awe at the arrival of the beast.

All gasped as the dragon dived from the skies. It's huge wings, each the size of a building, made thumping sounds as they beat against the air. It's arched body was covered in dark red scales and it's mouth showed lines of large, fearsome fangs. It's four legs, powerful and each terminated in talons the size of a man's arm, were tucked up against it's belly to ease it's flight.

"It's just like the dragons described in old fairy tales," said Rhys to Ashley, "I wonder if it can breath fire too?"

Ashley continued to stare up at the creature as it approached. Her heart beat fast, hoping that the dragon was indeed as friendly as the others believed. "Don't you have a red dragon on the Welsh flag Rhys?" she asked.

Rhys nodded, Ashley continued, "Hmmm, seems like yet another example of a link between our world and Portalia. I wonder how many other mythical beasts are actually real creatures here?"

The dragon slowed it's descent as it reached the town. The courtyard was swiftly emptied to make space for the giant beast, as it landed, with hardly a sound. The creature looked up at the roof, it's head level with those that watched from there. Gorlan stepped forward and bowed.

"Thank you for answering the call great one. We were not sure if you would still respond after all these years. My name is Gorlan, Warlord of Pinn, I apologise for disturbing you but," at this point Gorlan waved towards the enemy lines, "As you can see, our need is great. Will you aid us?"

Fangtor turned his huge head towards the lines of troops. He cast his eyes about and saw the myriads of spiders and recognised the ancient magic that controlled them. He looked at the Graav and stared at them. "What manner of beasts are they?" thundered the dragon, it's voice echoing from the buildings around the town.

"They are called the Graav, Great One. They come from another land and are born from the fires of new mountains," answered Gorlan.

For a moment Fangtor's thoughts returned to his people. Once, his race had been born of fire. So long ago!

Gorlan spoke once more, "Will you aid us against this foe.

They seek to destroy our world and are led by Shangorth the Warlock himself."

The dragon looked at the Warlord, if it had possessed eyebrows then it would have raised them in surprise, "I think not human. Shangorth took his journey from this life many years ago."

"As we thought also Great One, but as you can see he sits on the hillside, once again commanding forces of evil."

Fangtor turned to look in the direction of the warlock and gave a single guffaw. Wisps of smoke rose from his nostrils as he did so.

Ashley looked at Rhys, "Well I guess that answers your earlier question about whether this is a real fire breathing variety of dragon."

Fangtor turned back towards the Warlord, "I wonder if all is not as it seems human. Perhaps time will tell us what is truth and what is fiction."

The dragon turned it's attention to the others on the rooftop. He perused them all, acknowledging King Swiftaxe with a nod of it's head. When he came to Lan he stopped, "This one knows the truth. Oh, he does not realise it himself, but it is there, buried within." Fangtor continued to inspect the group, "I see you also have two that are not of Portalia. Their world is known to me."

As they continued to talk, Gorlan continued to watch the hill. With a wave of his arms and an arc of light that spewed into the sky to strengthen the clouds, Shangorth ordered his army to begin their advance once more. The spiders came first, swarming across the cooled fire pits by the million. Amongst them marched the Graav, swords raised for battle.

"Great One?" urged Gorlan.

"Oh please, call me Fangtor," interrupted the dragon.

Gorlan hesitated, "Oh! Fangtor, I must ask for your decision with some urgency as our enemy is on the move. Will you aid us?"

"Of course," replied the dragon, almost nonchalantly as he moved himself into a position for Gorlan to mount, "Now where shall we attack first?"

Gorlan was grinning from ear to ear as he climbed onto the great back of dragon. "Thank you Fangtor, we have a plan which we need you to help us execute. We are going straight to the throat of the enemy. Our task is to lead the others to the hillside and keep the forces at bay whilst our friends here confront the warlock and his minions. We hope to wrestle away from him his tools of power and to slip Rhys and Ashley back through the portal gateway that Shangorth has open. They can then use the Runestone to return to their home world. If we can remove the threat of the spiders then I believe that we can defeat the Graav with the aid of the elves."

"Very well, " replied Fangtor, "Let us fly. The sooner this is finished the better as I want to return to my home too."

With enormous strength the dragon flexed sinew and leapt into the air. Below, the forces of the defenders cheered as their spirits were lifted by the sight of the Warlord on this mighty beast. As they watched, the front line of their force met head to head with the spiders and the Graav. The carnage began once again.

Combating the Graav had been tough enough, but now, trying to dislodge the rock men and behead them whilst stamping on spiders proved incredibly difficult. Elven arrows hummed all around though and, as before, a large proportion of the arrows were finding their targets. By now, a great mass of spiders had crossed the dampened pits and many began to satisfy their hunger for fresh meat. Gorlan watched from above and knew that not even the dragon could prevent the mass of spiders and Graav from winning the battle for the town. It looked as if the defenders may be swept away before they had chance to deliver the plan on which they had decided. Sweeping his eyes around the battlefield and town dejectedly, Gorlan's spirits were suddenly raised once more. To the south he saw over a thousand reinforcement Pinn infantry sprinting towards the battle. He knew that this was not enough to sway the odds to victory but it would give the group more time to carry out their actions as many of the attackers were drawn towards the advancing Pinns and away from the town.

Back on the rooftop Swiftaxe was busy organising the others and soon Meld, Ashley, Rhys and himself were flying through the air on the backs of the fire eagles ridden by Carl, Stern, Tosh and Kraven.

Ashley clung tight to Stern, her terror was beginning to rise as the Pinn commanded the fire eagle into the air. She opened her mouth to scream as the earth raced away below her. All of a sudden a calm came over her. An inner voice called to her that all would be well. Her confidence immediately soared and her fears subsided. "You are of us Ashley. Do not be afraid." In wonderment she realised that the fire eagle was talking to her.

Below, on the ground, Lan had been almost hysterical when Rhys had turned to leave with Carl and had to be man handled by the dwarf guards before Rhys was free to mount the fire eagle.

As they climbed to join Gorlan and the dragon, they were joined by twenty fire eagle riders who surrounded them, providing a protective ring. Gorlan then screamed the order and they set out towards the enemy's command post.

Almost immediately, the air became full of the remaining

black eagles, some fifty attacked the group and the fire eagles riders met them head on. A few of the black eagles made straight for the head of the dragon, but with one exhalation of fire, they were charred to a cinder by the great beast.

On the hill Shangorth watched as the group approached. Ohrhim leaned close to him and whispered, "Leave this to me. Let's pit the black against the red." So saying the shapechanger allowed his body to flow into the shape of a Black Dragon once again. As it took it's new form, Ohrhim concentrated and hardened the tips of it's talons and teeth. It then leapt into the air to intercept the oncoming red dragon.

The pair met each other with a mighty crash and Gorlan wobbled, almost falling from his perch. Ohrhim scratched and stabbed with it's talons at the red dragon. The fact that the black dragon was much smaller and swifter that the red, gave the shapechanger an advantage at this close range. Fangtor had begun to bleed from several wounds and was finding it difficult to strike back at the agile attacker. When his claws were successful at raking through the black flesh, the skin of the shapechanger merely parted and reformed itself as if nothing had happened.

The red dragon beat his wings to gain more height but his black tormenter swiftly followed. They thrashed, dived and climbed, swinging out with flailing talons as both battled to destroy the other. Soon, Fangtor was covered in deep gouges, whereas his opponent appeared unscathed. The fire eagles' riders watched with concern, unable to get close to the dragons to offer assistance.

Quietly a plan formed in Gorlan's mind and he shouted instructions into the dragons ear. Fangtor suddenly dropped towards the ground. Ohrhim was taken by surprise and let a gap open up between the two. Swiftly though, he dived after his quarry. As the pair approached the ground, Fangtor swerved at the last minute, striking down fifty or so Graav as he did so. Behind him the shapechanger smiled and muttered, "Stupid beast, thinks it can out manoeuvre me and drive me into the ground."

With a swift swivel of its body and beat of the wings, Ohrhim did a sharp u-turn.

Suddenly he realised the red dragons intent as Ohrhim turned to see his quarry hovering in mid air and facing him. Ohrhim only had time to start a scream as a huge fireball erupted from the mouth of Fangtor to engulf the shapechanger. Ohrhim immediately felt the intensity of the heat and it's skin started to harden and dry out. As the shapechanger tried to battle the crisping of his glutinous flesh, Ohrhim began to lose shape and the black dragon soon looked more like a giant ball with dark grey wings.

Fangtor, urged on by Gorlan, moved closer to the beast and let out another sheet of fire, this time more concentrated and burning with an intense white heat.

The fire passed straight into the body of the shapechanger and with a mighty explosion, jelly like flesh, crisped at the edges, was thrown all over the battlefield. The flesh fell on the defenders, spiders and Graav alike as the shapechanger disappeared into a rain of grey and black.

The shapechanger now destroyed, Gorlan turned Fangtor back towards the hillside and was once again joined by the others. Sweeping down to the hill top, Fangtor used flame and talon to keep the enemy defenders at bay as Swiftaxe led the others down to land on the hillside, close to Shangorth and his minions. The Graav fell back from the dragon, not even the magical collars could protect them from the power of this mighty beast.

Leaping from their eagles, Swiftaxe and Meld were joined by ten other Pinn warriors, brought to the battle by the other Pinns riders. They drew their swords and ushered for Rhys and Ashley to stay behind them.

Their passengers now dropped, the remaining fire eagles, joined the Warlord to keep the enemy forces busy as the others approached Shangorth.

Above them, close to the crest of the hill, the warlock turned his attention to the approaching force. He laughed as he looked down and bellowed, "Fools, you think that you are powerful enough to take me!" Raising his arms once more, electrical arcs spewed from the warlock to strike at the Pinn warriors. Almost impulsively the warriors closed ranks around the dwarf king and the teenagers as, one by one, they fell to the power of the warlock.

Next to Shangorth, Zarn stood with axe raised, ready to protect his master. In horror, Rhys watched as Michael too unsheathed a sword and stepped forward to block their path to the warlock. The group continued their approach. Rhys felt terror beginning to rise and looked towards Ashley who was retching at the smell of the charred flesh. Rhys closed his eyes momentarily, "This is a dream, I'm going to wake up now," but he was suddenly returned to the fight as a Pinn warrior, black and charred to the bone, fell against him.

In horror Rhys realised that all of the Pinn warriors lay dead. Swiftaxe, Meld, Ashley and himself were all that were left of their band, their plan was doomed to failure. Rhys fell to his knees, tears welling up in his eyes, as he realised that they faced death here on this alien hilltop.

Swiftaxe and Meld stepped towards Shangorth. The Dwarf King brandished his golden axe, Meld with a one handed fighting sword. The warlock looked at them and laughed, "So,

King Swiftaxe himself has graced us with his presence. I am going to enjoy this." Shangorth made large circling motions with his hands and muttered strange words that Rhys could not understand. A throbbing green glow formed between the hands of the warlock and, as Swiftaxe and Meld rushed forward, the green glow rushed from his hands, grew and engulfed them. They suddenly found themselves trapped within a cocoon of pure energy. They both hammered their weapons on the surface of their cage but they had no impact, both were trapped within, unable to escape. As Rhys looked on, Shangorth made a small gesture and the cocoon lifted a few feet into the air.

"Put them down you horrible man!" shouted Ashley throwing a large stone at the warlock. Shangorth deflected the missile with a wave of his hand but the White Dwarf was not so skilled and the stone struck him in the side of the head. Zarn, his attention drawn by the blow, looked at Ashley and snarled. He made towards her, axe lifted high in the air to strike. Rhys realised her danger and looked towards Swiftaxe for help but he was still hopelessly trapped. Neither Rhys nor Ashley carried a weapon, so Rhys reacted with the only skill that he possessed. Almost instinctively he let his mind search out the portal web. Whether it was his continued exposure to the magic, his terror, or the adrenalin that flowed through his body, he was not sure, but he found the portal web almost immediately and latched on to the portal images.

Fortunately Ashley had seen the dwarf's attack and as he swung his axe forward, she dived to the left, the blade missing her by a few centimetres. Ashley rolled back onto her feet. She kicked out at the dwarf's legs and the albino fell to the ground with a thud. Screaming with rage he rose once more and lunged at Ashley who dived to avoid the blow again. This time the dwarf was ready though, and as Ashley rolled to recover, the dwarf leapt to her side, axe swinging wildly.

Ashley looked up to see the dwarf bearing down on her and realising she was cornered she screamed and curled into a ball. The expected blows never reached her. As Zarn lunged forward, Rhys steadied a portal gateway and it was projected, where he desired, right between Ashley and Zarn.

As the White Dwarf swung his axe downward he shouted in surprise and his face contorted with fright as he tried to stop himself entering the portal gateway. Unfortunately for him, his momentum was too great and dwarf, together with his axe, the Celtic knot ring and the Cormion Crystal fell through the portal to disappear into another world. Rhys, shouted in delight and immediately broke his connection, closing the portal and trapping the White Dwarf on the other side. Rhys only had a fleeting memory of where the portal had led, the landscape on the other side had been a barren hot desert wasteland, with no signs of life. Rhys was sure that the dwarf could not survive there but he was now far from feeling any remorse for his enemies.

Shangorth had watched these events, but as his fascination turned to anger, he pointed towards Rhys and screamed a command at Michael, "Kill him!"

Michael stepped forward, a sword held loosely in his hands, clearly not an item he was used to yielding. Ashley shouted a warning as he approached and Rhys turned to look towards him. In Michael's eyes Rhys momentarily saw torment as his friend struggled against the command, but this look soon dissolved, the warlock's spell too strong to deny. Michael increased his pace and ran towards him, swinging his weapon wildly.

As Rhys swerved to avoid the first strike by Michael, he

heard a horse whinny to his right and through the fighting Rhys saw DiamondCrest, galloping through the masses to leap over their heads. Michael's attention was also momentarily drawn to the sound and both boys watched as Lan dived from the back of the huge steed onto the surprised figure of Shangorth. As he did so, unnoticed by the warlock, Lan reached for the Capture Orb and tore it from around the neck of the warlock. As Shangorth was knocked off balance, the Spider Gem staff fell from the Warlocks grasp and, his concentration momentarily lost, the spell binding Meld and Swiftaxe was broken and the two fell to the ground.

The next few seconds seemed to happen in slow motion to Rhys. He was suddenly aware that Michael had moved closer and Rhys watched in disbelief as the youth swung his blade towards Rhys. In horror, Rhys watched and shouted his objection as Swiftaxe jumped to his feet. Almost in the same movement, the dwarf swung his axe, striking Michael in the chest. Ashley and Rhys both screamed their revulsion and denial as their friend sunk to the ground, blood spurting from the wound. Incredibly, though, he was still trying to lift his sword to strike at Rhys, still blindly trying to follow the command of the warlock to the very end. The wild, but weak swings of the sword prevented an approach from either Ashley or Rhys who continued to stare in disbelief.

To their left Lan stood and picked up two large rocks. "No more! No more!" he screamed at the glowing Orb and he brought the two rocks down on the orb to shatter it into a million shards. There was a blast of power and all around were knocked to their feet, only the Red Dragon was able to withstand the force of the release.

Waves of magic, blues, greens, oranges and reds swam in the air. Most flew off in various directions but two snake like flows streaked towards Lan and to Michael, wriggling and squirming as the energy burrowed it's way into their bodies. Michael immediately dropped the weapon and Rhys looked on as a calmness fell over his friend. Ashley and Rhys, both sensing that Michael had returned to his former self, rushed to his side, both in tears.

Michael looked up at them both and spoke weakly, "Huh, guessed I messed up good this time Rhys, didn't I?"

"Hush Mike, take it easy, we'll get some help," replied Rhys, trying to control the sobbing as he spoke.

Michael smiled, "I think it's a bit late for that Rhys. Um, by the way, I'm sorry I tried to kill you. I just couldn't stop myself."

Rhys shook his head, "Shh, don't be dumb, that wasn't you. Now you need to stay calm 'cos you'll need your strength later to get back to Salty's Cave. Of course, when we get home you know no-one will believe us, don't you? You're going to have to show them your scars."

Rhys tried to smile as he spoke to reassure his friend but, as he looked into Michaels face, he realised that there would be no answer. Michael lay silent in his arms, his eyes closed. Ashley and Rhys stared at each other in disbelief.

"No!" Shangorth screamed in frustration. He reached for the Spider Gem but Meld was way ahead of him and had already secured the item. On the battle field below, the spiders halted their advance as the staff changed hands. After a few seconds, when no new commands came from Meld, the control of the Spider Gem was broken, and the creatures began to scuttle off in all directions. The defenders in the town saw this and focussed their efforts solely on the Graav, crushing wayward spiders as they fought.

Meld turned to flee knowing that the warlock would

try to seize the staff from him. As he ran he was suddenly thrown off his feet as a blast of energy was let forth by the warlock. Fortunately for Meld, the arc of energy struck the staff and it's energy was dissipated, or he too would have been frazzled like the Pinn warriors. Shangorth summoned a second strike to finish the human. As the arc of light erupted from his outstretched hand, flying towards it's target, a shaft of blue intercepted it and the magical energies dissipated as they met.

"I think not Shangorth, or should I call you by your true name Weldrock!" boomed a voice from behind the warlock.

The warlock froze, his hand shot to his neck and searched fruitlessly for the touch of the Capture Orb. "Farspell!" replied Weldrock turning to face the challenge. "So you are free again, I presume that magical blast was you destroying my Capture Orb? I should have realised."

"Of course," replied Farspell. Rhys looked at the wizard and saw that all of the tiredness and despondency had now fallen away from the man he knew as Lan. Instead there stood an energetic man, still old, but with flowing white hair and beard and with a love of life clear in his blue eyes.

Farspell walked towards Weldrock and spoke, "Why did you choose this path Weldrock? After the defeat of Shangorth, when we retired to the mountains to live with the dragons, we spoke of the things we could do to help the world. Not to rule it by force. Why did you do this? Why turn to the dark arts?"

Weldrock grinned at his old colleague, "You'd never understand, Farspell, not in a million aeons! You are weak and would spend your life serving others. This is an abomination. We are born to power and all should worship us. It took me a long time to realise but the old warlocks were right. We should never have helped to destroy them. Come join me and I will show you how great we can truly be."

Farspell bowed his head, saddened by those words, "Never! I trusted you once before and you turned the power of the Capture Orb against me. You tore away my soul and free spirit! I became that poor creature Lan, half mad and tormented by disjointed memories. Some of my spirit remained with me though and when I saw the Orb once more I knew what I had to do. Weldrock I cannot allow you to continue this tyranny. You will not be allowed to resurrect the power of the dark arts!"

Weldrock threw back his head and laughed, "Oh really, and how will you stop me?"

Farspell indicated the battle all around. "Look before you. Your spider army is gone and soon your Graav will face defeat at the hands of the elves and the dragon. You cannot win here."

"And you think that I am stupid enough to place all my eggs in one basket. You are more foolish than I thought Farspell, I have planned for this eventuality," lied Weldrock. "You know, I don't know why I even bothered to capture your essence all those years ago. I feared you then but now, your time as the puppet-brained Lan has muddled your thoughts and I see you as you truly are, weak and insignificant. The next time we meet, you will die in agony Farspell, but you will scream for mercy before you do as you bow to the power of my coven."

With a flick of his wrist, Weldrock caused a blinding eruption of white light to fill the air, causing all around to avert their eyes. Taking his chance, Weldrock dived through the portal, only Swiftaxe was fast enough to follow him. The others moved towards the gateway but could only watch as the warlock's portal closed before their eyes.

Warlock and dwarf were gone!

CHAPTER TWENTY-FOUR
Return to Shangorth Towers

Weldrock stepped from the gateway into the Runestone Chamber. He reached for the control pedestal just as Swiftaxe began to appear. He removed the keystone from it's slot.

The portal closed. Swiftaxe, looked on helplessly as the chamber scene before him suddenly vanished, returning back to the shimmering blue of the portal web. With no means of escape, the Dwarf King shouted curses at Weldrock. Those words never reached the ears of the warlock as they were absorbed into the swirling blue energy. Even the brave and fearless Swiftaxe could not suppress a scream as he realised his plight.

Back in the chamber Stack looked on in confusion. "What is happening Shangorth?" he asked.

The warlock turned to his apprentice, "Things have not gone as planned. A Red Dragon was summoned and the magical ability of the elf wood turned the battle against the Graav. We must return to our island and to our coven. There we will discuss new plans. We will recover and strike back, but next time it will be with a coven that has grown in strength. Portalia *will* fall to our might."

Stack grinned, "The others will be pleased Shangorth, they grow stronger by the day and all yearn to use their new found powers." Stack looked at the Runestone. "What of Ohrhim, Zarn and our armies. Do they still fight our foe?"

"All were lost. Zarn, idiotic as usual, fell needlessly. Ohrhim battled bravely to protect us from the dragon but he was eventually destroyed by it's fire breath. The Spider Gem is in the hands of our enemy, but do not fear, they will not call upon it's power. It is honed from the dark magics and they are too weak minded to use such force. I fear though that they may destroy it. They now have the knowledge of the ancient wizard Farspell who knows many of the secrets of the magics."

Stack involuntarily raised his eyebrows in surprise. "Ah, do not fret yourself about Farspell my apprentice. His brain has become old and tired over the years. He does not pose the threat that he would have in his prime." Stack nodded obediently but was finding it difficult not to question the confidence expressed by his master. So much had gone wrong.

He was glad when the warlock gave him a new order. "Go now Stack and call forth the remaining Graav. Then return here. I have closed the portal to Fortown but the boy Rhys has a power which I do not understand. He may be able to re-open it. I am going to destroy the Mountain Runestone as a precaution. We have our own entry into the portal web so we do not need this one."

Stack nodded his assent and ran to obey the warlock's orders. As he left the room, Weldrock began an incantation of a spell that he had forged himself and which had earned him his name. Within minutes the Runestone began to melt into a featureless bed of stone. As it melted, streams of power were dissipated into the air in a fluorescent display of brilliant colours.

***

Back in Fortown the Graav continued their relentless advance. Fangtor continued the fight and was the single reason that the defenders were not over whelmed. Unlike Ohrhim, who had honed his talons to the hardness of a diamond, the Graav, armed with only normal blades, could not cut through the thick scaly hide of the dragon,. Very occasionally though, one would get lucky and find an already open wound with it's strike and Fangtor would roar out in pain as the blade tore the abrasion open even further.

In the town, the elves had long exhausted their supply of elfwood arrows and the foot soldier infantry had turned their attention from fighting the Graav to trying to retrieve ammunition for the elven archers. They sprinted into the fray to retrieve shafts where fallen arrows lay on the ground or sat embedded in trees or hillside.

Farspell, realising that Fangtor was needed to protect the town, called forth old magic and had conjured a shield around himself, Rhys, Ashley and Meld. Graav hammered on this shield in desperation, but their swords could not pierce the magical defence. Occasionally though, a wayward elven arrow would bounce off Graav stone skin and would be deflected towards the shield where it would pass through, requiring those inside to nimbly dodge them.

With the shield defence now fully formed, Farspell had turned his attention to a new spell. Rhys watched the old man as he created a series of small round pellets the size of marbles in mid air. The wizard continued to focus his attention on the pellets which began to spin and emit a green glow. Then, with a jerk of his arm, the wizard aimed the pellets towards the Graav. The missiles flew widely towards them, most of the pellets fell to the ground but, where the pellets met the stone skin of the Graav, the creatures fell into a pile of ashes and dust. There was no explosion or pyrotechnic display, the creatures merely crumbled to the earth.

Farspell continued to share his time between reinforcing the shield and creating these pellets. At one point Rhys watched in terror as one of the stone pellets deviated wildly and flew straight towards Ashley. Rhys screamed a warning as the pellet struck Ashley in the middle of her back. To Rhys' surprise the pellet passed clean through Ashley who was totally unaware of its presence. It then continued it's path before meeting a large boulder, forming a large hole at it's centre where it struck.

"No need to worry Rhys," shouted the wizard smiling as he created another set of pellets. "I created this spell a long time ago to help the dwarves in the White Mountains. It passes through everything other than rock. It's intended use was to help the dwarves mine and tunnel in the mountains, but as things have turned out, it is an ideal weapon against these Graav." So saying, Farspell returned to his task with an ever widening smile. Rhys found it increasingly hard to relate this confident wizard to the poor creature that he had befriended back in Eumor.

The battle continued to rage outside Fortown. The ground was now littered with bodies of the defenders and the rubble of the fallen Graav. In places footing was extremely precarious as loose rubble lay covered in human, centaur, Elven and spider blood. The Graav numbers were now dwindling and the defenders were beginning to sense victory as the dragon, the wizard and the elves continued to strike against their foe.

Above the town the sky was now clear of black eagles. The fire eagles, unable to make much impact on the Graav, returned to their tactic of swooping down to knock the attackers off their feet in an effort to aid the attackers gain access under the protective collars.

Unable to assist in any way, Ashley and Rhys sat next to Michael's body in the protection of Farspell's shield and watched. They did not speak, they watched events unfolding around them, occasionally looking down at Michael in disbelief. They had seen much and coped with things that most youths of their age could not even imagine, but with no activity to occupy their minds, shock was beginning to set in and both could do nothing more than merely stare at the carnage, willing it not to be real.

"Oh god, I want to go home!" commented Ashley.

Rhys looked at her, "Me too Ash!" he said, "Me too!"

***

Weldrock and Stack returned to their island hideway. Here the warlock had immediately closed his portal to Shangorth Towers. He had summoned his coven and was now sat before them at a large oval table in his quarters.

"My apprentices," he began, "I underestimated the strength of our foe but I will not do so again. You will now have my full attention in your development. I will remain here with you to hone your skills and together we will build a new army of Graav. We will bide our time and will strike when the coven is ready, the power of thirteen warlocks will be released over Portalia. Next time they will fall like flies."

Weldrock looked at their faces for any signs of fear or lack of respect but saw only excitement and adoration. "My coven. From this day you will call me by my true name and we shall be known through all time as the Coven of Weldrock!"

Stack began to thump the table in approval and chanted the wizards name, his actions were followed by the other elven apprentices.

"Weldrock! Weldrock! Weldrock!"

The wizard looked at them and smiled, his dark mood

from the earlier defeat already dwindling as new plans for conquest formed in his brain.

***

On the hills at the outskirts of the town, Fangtor lay, still bleeding profusely from his many cuts. The Graav were defeated and rubble lay scattered all around. Gorlan spoke to the dragon.

"We need to close those wounds. You have lost much blood," he said, climbing from the dragon's back.

"No! Gorlan, let them bleed," replied Fangtor with a sigh.

"I cannot do that Fangtor. Even a dragon would not survive such a loss of blood. It is your life essence."

"I know that Gorlan but listen to me," Fangtor snapped in response. The mighty dragon then turned it's huge head to look directly at the Warlord and softened his tone. "Gorlan, I am the last of my kind. For generations I have been alone, eager to join my ancestors. The power of the Peak is waning Warlord. I want to ride the Flame. I want to sit with my kin once more."

Gorlan looked at the dragon and felt sympathy for the great beast, deep inside him he sensed the enormous loneliness of the dragon. Even so, Gorlan struggled with the request.

"I understand Fangtor but I do not want you to lay down your life through protecting us. Let us heal your wounds. You could return with me to Pinn and live with my people in the Pinnacle mountains above the town. I know we are not dragons, but you would not be alone."

Fangtor shook his head, "No Gorlan. I thank you, but I crave my ancestors, I would not be happy in Pinn. However there is one thing that you can do for me and, in return, one thing I can do for you. Listen well as I ask a lot but I will give a lot in return."

Farspell, leading DiamondCrest, walked down the hillside towards Fangtor with Ashley and Rhys at his side. Meld had left them a few minutes earlier to return to the town to search out his brother. Farspell had laid Michael across the back of the Cloud Horse and covered him with a blanket so that the teenagers did not have to continually look at his lifeless body. As they approached they watched Gorlan back away from Fangtor. As he did, the dragon rolled onto it's side and the Warlord took out his sword. In horror they watches as the Warlord sliced down with the sword and drove it deep in to the soft vulnerable point at the top of the dragon's chest. Using all his force he pulled the blade downwards and opened the chest. Gorlan raised his blade once more to strike and the teenagers heard the dragon mumble something to the Warlord. Gorlan nodded and brought the mighty sword down with all his strength, cutting the still beating dragon heart from Fangtor's body, who fell to the earth with a sigh.

Rhys and Ashley turned their eyes away, unable to comprehend why Gorlan would do such a thing. Farspell placed his hand on their shoulders, "Wait, do not judge him yet. I believe he knows what he is doing and acts on instruction from the dragon himself."

At Farspell's words, Rhys and Ashley dared to turn back. They immediately wished they had not as they witnessed Gorlan hacking a slice from the dragon heart that still throbbed with life, pumping red blood from it's valves.

"Quickly Farspell, lay the boy on the ground!" shouted Gorlan.

Farspell did as he was bid and removed Michael from the back of the Cloud Horse. Gorlan sprinted to the body, clutching the slice of dragon's heart that he hacked from Fangtor's body. Removing a knife from his belt, Gorlan stabbed Michael in the chest and sliced his skin downwards.

Ashley retched in horror. Rhys felt nausea rising and let out a cry of derision, "No! Leave him be!" he shouted and he ran at the Warlord. Farspell quickly grabbed him from behind and easily held him still. Rhys was held in a firm arm lock. The strength of the old man took him by surprise.

Gorlan, ignoring Rhys' pleas, took the dragon heart slice and pushed it into Michael's body before standing and stepping back from the dead youth.

Farspell whispered into Rhys' ear, "Hush now Rhys. Watch and marvel at the gift that Fangtor gives to us."

Rhys calmed himself and looked at Farspell questioningly. The wizard pointed towards Michael and Rhys turned back to see that the dragon heart had started to pulsate. All around the slice, flesh began to join with the organ. As they looked on, the wounds on Michael's body began to seal themselves and they could see the heart, glowing with magical power, through the flesh and skin that was reforming around his chest. The new flesh was naturally coloured but Rhys noticed that the structure of it was faintly scale like.

"The mark of the Dragon Heart." commented Farspell.

Finally, the glowing and throbbing subsided and the damage to Michael's body was healed. Rhys' own heart was pounding and Ashley let out a surprised "Oh!" as Michael moved his head as if waking from a deep sleep.

"Uh, what the heck happened?" commented Michael, "'Cor, my head bloody well hurts!"

Rhys leapt to his friend and hugged him, "Mike! You're alive again!"

"Um, steady on there Rhys, you'll have the others talking about us," replied Michael pushing his friend away.

Ashley took her turn to hug Michael too, "Now this is not so bad," he joked winking at Rhys.

There camaraderie was broken up by Farspell, "We should get back to the town, there is still much to organise. Michael, do you feel well enough to walk?"

"Me? I feel better than I have for years. What did you do to me?" he asked.

"Don't you remember the battle?" asked Rhys.

Michael suddenly went pale. He put his hand to his chest and found the scaly skin that now sat there marking the dragon's gift. "What the heck?"

Farspell took Michael's hand and placed it flat on the scaly skin, "Concentrate on the beating, Feel the dragon's heart and you will understand."

Michael looked tense but with persuasion from Farspell he finally closed his eyes and let his concentration focus on the heart. A look of calm suddenly fell across his face and he smiled.

He was flying high above snow capped mountains. All around him young dragons played whilst their kin watched over them. The power of the Peak was strong and the dragons powerful. Life was good.

Then he was a boy, playing tag and hide and seek in the hills of South Wales. He waved to his parents watching over him from their home. Running through the long grass he came to the edge of the clifftop and breathed in the smell of the sea. Life was good.

The dragon dived towards the ground.

The boy leapt from the cliff top.

Dragon and boy met in mid air. Both stared at each other in wonderment. They met and merged as one. The boy felt the power of the dragon flow through him.

Michael opened his eyes again. "Bloody hell!" he cursed,

"I understand now, but…..well…bloody hell. I have the heart of a dragon!"

Farspell smiled at Michael. "This is a great and rare gift Michael. Very few have been so blessed. The gift of the Dragon heart means the death of the dragon. Over time you will find that the gift is more than life. You will discover that you know certain things, parts of the dragon's memories will come to you as if they are your own. Do not be afraid, learn from these events and use any knowledge you gain wisely young man."

"But why did Fangtor do it?" asked Ashley. She suddenly turned to Michael, "No offence Mike, it's great to have you back but why did Fangtor pay with his own life. He hardly knows us, we're just stranger's from a strange world."

Michael smiled at her, "That's ok Ash, I understand and I can answer your question. Fangtor was the last of his kind. He was incredibly lonely and yearned to ride the Flame and join his ancestors on the other side. For years he has been trying to call upon the mountain rock to take his body, but the power of the Peak, the source of the energy that created the red dragons, is all but exhausted and the process was taking too long. When he fought for us and he saw me die, he remembered another way for him to ride the Flame. A dragon had the right to lay down his life to save another. He chose this path, saving me and finding the final contentment he craved. Do not be sad for him."

Ashley rubbed a tear away from her eye, "That is so sad and yet so beautiful a story too. I'm still upset that Fangtor has gone, but it helps a little to know that this is what he wanted." She shook off her melancholy and paused before throwing a teasing jibe at Michael to lighten the mood. "Now that we do have you back in an 'improved' version, I hope you're not too clever with this new dragon wisdom of yours. You were bossy enough as it was!" Ashley winked at Rhys.

"Now why did I ever miss you?" responded Michael jovially.

***

In a gulley on the hill tops above Fortown, a fist sized lump of glutinous flesh flashed back into consciousness.

Is this it? It thought. *Have I passed into a being of pure energy? Have the gods called me at last.*

The glutinous blob sat in darkness waiting and listening. No-one called to it though, all it could hear was the sounds of it's own thoughts. Slowly the memory of the dragon battle returned to it and as it's life essence sensed other pieces of it's mass spread over the Fortownian hills, realisation dawned. It had not been called by it's gods. It had been blown apart.

Dejectedly the shape changer reached out with it's mind, calling it's body to rejoin the host. In utter dejection Ohrhim suddenly felt how far his parts had been spread and realised that the rejoining would take a very, very long time. It sat in a lonely dark world as it waited. It sensed nothing of the outside world. No sight, sound, taste, smell or touch. The rejoining would take thousands of years to achieve. Ohrhim screamed a silent scream as the realisation dawned and it began it's journey into insanity.

***

Back at a rejoicing Fortown, Farspell called a meeting of leaders.

The audience had changed since the first meeting that they held. Swiftaxe, lost on the hillside was absent so Farspell now took the lead. The wizard was now returned to his former self and oozing authority, all looked up to him with much respect. Gorlan represented the Pinns. Chisel, the eldest son of Swiftaxe spoke for the dwarves. Fleck, recalled from the sanctuary of the tunnels, represented Fortown. Gabriel acted as spokesman for the Elves. Meld, Rhys and Michael were also in attendance, as was Yanto Flow, the messenger from the Gates.

All waited for the arrival of Fyros and Ashley. The centaur had insisted on speaking with the Eumor Council before attending the meeting. The meeting members turned to the doorway as it opened and they were finally joined by the pair.

"I am sorry for the delay Farspell. When we opened the link to the council we also opened a link to the White Dwarf. I know not where he is but I do not believe he will live long. He walks through an endless arid desert under a blazing sun. He already lacked the strength to even respond to us when we opened the link. I waited though as I wanted to be sure that it was safe to talk before I commenced our discussion with the Eumor Council."

Gorlan had pricked up his ears at the description of the desert, "Could this be our own Blazing Desert to the south?"

Fyros shrugged, "Possibly, but we have no way of knowing. It could be any desert on any world. It was featureless and looked very, very hot!"

Farspell changed the direction of the discussion, "And what were the findings of the council?" he asked.

Fyros smiled, "As you would expect Farspell. They were delighted with our victory, saddened by the loss of so much life and astounded by the reappearance to our world of yourself and the turncoat, Weldrock. They also recognised your wisdom and authority in these matters and gave me permission to commit the centaur race to whatever this meeting decides."

Farspell nodded, "That is good, but the question as to

what to do next is indeed what we must now focus on." The wizard turned to address the others. "I do not wish to lead you in these matters, only to advise. Each of you have your own leaders and the situation calls for all to work together over the coming years. I feel we have not yet heard the last of Weldrock, he will return and we must make ready."

"Can we not finish him now at his base at Shangorth Towers?" asked Chisel.

Farspell shook his head. "I believe that we will find the tower empty when we arrive. I agree that we should send a force to Shangorth to determine what remains there, but I feel inside that our foe has already flown the nest. He will be licking his wounds and forming new plans of attack. On the hilltop he made reference to a coven. I believe that he may be training others."

"But where do you think he is" asked Gorlan.

Farspell shrugged, "I do not know, but I just feel that he is no longer at the towers. As Chisel suggests though, we should send a force there to determine what remains. The earth youths should accompany that force in case there is an opportunity for them to return home. I fear though that Weldrock will have removed the Runestone key when he closed the portal." Farspell turned to address Gorlan, "What remains of our defences? Do we have sufficient to send on such an expedition whilst still retaining a defensive presence here at Fortown?"

Gorlan called for a review of the casualties. The Fortownians had suffered greatly, only three hundred of their men remained and during the fight with the Graav, many of the women who had stayed to fight had also been slain. Forty fire eagle and riders still survived along with fifty of the Pinn cavalrymen. Fyros reported that only thirty of his one hundred centaurs still lived and half of these had suffered wounds which would prevent them travelling. He also reported the better news that the Eumor Council had already dispatched another fifty centaurs to help defend and restore the town.

Chisel reviewed the dwarf casualties. They had suffered most of their losses during the first melee and only a little over one hundred remained active and, of course, their king, his father, was still missing. The elves had fared the best, most had been protected from the face to face combat but some, their elven shafts expended, had raced to do battle alongside their allies. The elven force was still some seven hundred strong.

The Pinn infantry that had entered the battle from outside the town had been hit the hardest. Initially, unsupported by the elves or the dragon, they had suffered many deaths and their numbers had been reduced to fifty, most of whom were wounded. Gorlan winced as he made his report, five thousand had left Pinn, now only one tenth of that force survived. None knew of the status of the Gates army but Gorlan felt it ominous that Folken had not returned with news.

Farspell pondered the information before speaking. "My head tells me that the town is no longer under threat, but, my heart will not allow me to leave it unguarded. Clearly we do not have enough forces to carry out an assault of Shangorth Towers AND to protect Fortown. So, Gorlan, I would like you to assign to me four fire eagle riders. I will lead this small band to Shangorth Towers and the Earth youths will accompany me. My belief is that we will find it deserted, if not, I will use magic to hide our movements and we will scout the area and return. I suggest we rest tonight and depart tomorrow morning. In the meantime, those that travel with me should take rest. There are others who can clean up the town and bury the dead."

"What of this," asked Meld, holding up the Spider Gem staff.

Farspell looked at the staff. "We cannot use it. It's power is that of deep dark magic and it will corrupt anyone who tries to wield it. Unlike the Capture Orb that held the essence of Michael and myself, this gem is not so easily destroyed." Farspell addressed Fleck, "Fleck, would you secure this in a safe place, a deep vault or similar. When chance allows it should be taken to Pinnhome for storage with the other relics of the dark arts that are buried there."

"I know the very place," answered Fleck, taking the staff from Meld. "There are a number of secret vaults built in the tunnels. I will take care of this."

Meld gave a quick glance towards Ashley, "Farspell, I would ask that you allow me to accompany you to Shangorth," he said, Ashley looked at him and her cheeks blushed when she saw that he was talking to the wizard but looking at her. Farspell smiled too, the gaze of the Meld clearly giving away his reasons for wanting to make the journey with the others. He nodded his assent, "I will allow this providing Fleck agrees."

"Aye, that I do. I feel that it is important that someone from Fortown make the journey," responded the town counsellor.

"What of the forces from the Gates?" questioned Yanto Flow.

"I fear the worst but I will send another fire eagle rider to meet them. If they have not yet reached the Towers then he will instruct them to hold until they hear word from ourselves or from Farspell," Gorlan responded. "I will also send Pinnel back to Pinnhome to report to the OverLord and request that he send additional troops to aid with the defence and the rebuilding of Fortown. I will also ask that volunteers be sent with the troops to help with other activities such as nursing, building and other non military activities."

Fleck added, "I have already instructed a number of the

townsmen to organise the repairs and to assist the families in resettlement. More hands would be welcome though, as would the company that they would bring to those who have lost their loved ones. I have also asked that my people bury the dragon."

"No, don't do that!" exclaimed Farspell but then softened his voice as he realised he had been a little abrupt. "Please, leave the dragon to me. I know a way to return his body to the Peak. It is important that his body rests back at his homeland."

"Very well, I will inform my people. However, we would still like to give honour to the dragon. The battle would not have been won without his aid," replied Fleck.

"What about making this day a holiday each year. It can be known as Fangtor's Day and we could hold street banquet's in his honour," suggested Meld.

Fleck slapped Meld on the shoulder, "An excellent idea, Fangtor's Day it shall be." This decision pleased everyone in the room and all smiled at the idea of having a day to honour the great beast. Only Chisel remained pensive. "What of my father?" he asked.

Farspell looked at the dwarf, his expression changing to match the seriousness of the query. "I do not know Chisel. He leapt into the den of the enemy alone. Not only is Weldrock a formidable foe, even for the great King Swiftaxe, but it is almost certain that the warlock had kept troops back at Shangorth Towers. I hope to find out more about what happened to your father when we reach the Towers but I believe that he may have been captured, or worse."

Chisel's expression did not change, he had already assumed that his father had been lost. "Then I too will accompany you to Shangorth Towers," he replied.

It was not a request, it was a statement.

***

That night the whole town had stopped their activities and moved to surround the hill where Fangtor's body was laid. Farspell approached the dragon and, after a short speech of thanks to the great beast, he used a sharp knife to remove a piece of a claw of the dragon. He then began a complex verbal spell as he used the flat of the blade to crush the fragment.

Rhys had expected another magical light show but this time, as the wizard continued to crush the claw, the dragon appeared to be fading. No auras, no glows or lightning flashes, the dragon was simply ceasing to exist in a solid form. Soon all that remained of the Fangtor was the crushed remnants of the claw which Farspell had removed. In silence the massed crowd gave their last homage and returned to the town as Farspell, shedding tears, formed the claw pieces into a small ball and slipped it into his robes.

CHAPTER TWENTY-FIVE
Searching

H idden from sight by the magic of his cloak, Nexus had followed Farspell and his companions to Shangorth Towers. During the journey, from discussions overheard, he had learned the true identity of the warlock and was not surprised that Weldrock had proven to have been far from truthful with him. Nexus now had to bide his time, waiting to decide what to do next now that the warlock had fled.

They had arrived within site of Towers around mid afternoon. Earlier that day, Green, the Pinn rider sent to meet with the army from the Gates had found them with the sad news of the fate of those forces. Then accompanied by the rider, they had set out once again for the Towers, hurrying their pace and encouraged by information from Green that the area around the Towers appeared to be deserted.

Even so, when they first observed the fortification, it's four corner watchtowers and central keep rising into the sky, Farspell still insisted that they should watch from a distance for a few hours before making any approach. Up until this point the journey had proven uneventful, limited to the spotting of a few lone black eagles which had shown no interest in the passing group.

After a few hours of this vigil, Farspell asked the Pinn riders to approach the town from the air. When there was no defensive response, not even from the half a dozen black eagles that were perched on the battlements, Farspell seemed satisfied and they moved forward once more.

They entered the Towers through the large southern gates that were open to the outside world, a fact in itself that spoke of abandonment. Farspell led them across the courtyard and straight to the main tower, still making tracks through the town cautiously, alive to any sudden trap that may be lurking. As they entered the building, Meld, Green, Carl and Stern stood sentry whilst Kraven and Lloyd followed the wizard. The fire eagles circling overhead provided additional watch.

The wizard was first to climb the stairs and enter the Runestone chamber. As he did he let out a sharp intake of breath at the destruction that had been reaped on the Runestone. Chisel, Rhys, Ashley and Michael followed closely behind and stared at the pile of useless rock.

"Don't tell me that was the Runestone Gate. Please!" uttered Ashley forlornly.

"I am sorry Ashley. I fear that it will be some time before we can find a way for you to return to your own world," replied the wizard.

"Bugger! Bugger! Bugger!" swore Rhys in frustration.

"You can say that again Rhys," added Michael.

Rhys sat down on the disfigured Runestone and held his head in his hands. Looking up he said, "I know that there wasn't much chance of us finding a working Runestone but the closer we got to this tower, the more I felt that we may find a way home. Now we're going to be stuck here forever."

Farspell lowered himself down next to Rhys and placed a supportive arm around his shoulders. "Do not worry Rhys, this is but a delay. We will find another way for you to return home. If not through the Runestones then we will explore your unique skill until we can find a way to control it." The old wizard smiled. Unseen by Rhys and the others the palm of his left hand glowed as it rested on Rhys' shoulder. The wizard had conjured a small spell that would temporarily lift flagging spirits. Almost instantly Rhys perked up.

"You know Farspell, you are right. We'll find another way, I just know it!" responded Rhys.

Rhys high spirits proved infectious and soon they were chatting and teasing each other once again.

"What now Farspell?" asked Kraven.

Farspell responded by requesting that the Pinns search the outer towers whilst he and the youths continue their search of the main tower. "We'll meet back in this chamber once we're done."

The Pinns then descended and in pairs, Stern with Carl, Kraven with Lloyd, they began to scour the outer buildings and towers. They left Green to guard the main tower entrance.

Carl and Stern went towards the North Gate and quickly found the vast underground chamber where the spider army had been housed. It now laid empty. They moved on to find that both of the northern watch towers were completely bare of any furnishing or decoration. From the roof of the first tower they saw the plateau spreading before them with it's channels and pools of lava rock, still glowing red.

Kraven and Lloyd met with similar results, everywhere was stripped bare, there was nothing to be found that gave any indication of the whereabouts of the warlock or of what had happened to Swiftaxe. After a while, Kraven felt so confident that the fortification was abandoned that he began to sing as he and Lloyd searched, the younger Pinn joining in with the choruses of the songs.

In the main tower Farspell, accompanied by Chisel and

the Earth youths, quickly found Shangorth's library but this too had been stripped bare. The bookshelves, now empty were the only thing that indicated the purpose of the room. As they left the library, Ashley kicked a small wooden waste paper bin that had been laying on the floor near the door. It flew high in the air to land upright on the top of the larger shelves.

The youths laughed, "Bet you couldn't do that again Ash!" teased Michael.

"You're on," she replied and she climbed up the shelves to retrieve the bin. As she reached the top she saw that a rolled up scroll sat, hidden from their view on the top shelf.

"Hey look what I've found," she said, picking up the parchment.

"Let me see," replied Chisel as he took the paper from Ashley and unrolled it.

"It is a map of some kind," said the dwarf running his finger over the outline of some objects. "These look like islands." To the right side of the map there was a text written in a strange language.

Farspell, who was looking at the map over the dwarf's shoulder commented, "This is written in a text that I do not know. Although I have seen it before on old documents that are stored in the vaults at Pinnhome. This may be of some relevance as it may show us where the Graav originated. Look here" Farspell pointed to one of the islands on the map, "That mountain looks like a volcano and below it are small sketches of men climbing from the lava." Farspell took the map from Chisel, re-rolled it and stored it away for safe keeping.

After checking the top of the other bookshelves and adjoining storerooms, they returned to the Runestone chamber. Farspell was curious about the closet that still stood in the chamber, it had clearly not been there originally and he wondered at it's purpose. He was inside the closet when Michael entered. The youth stopped as he did so and frowned. "There was magic here?" he said.

Farspell looked at him, "What do you mean?" he asked.

Michael shrugged his shoulders, "I'm not sure and I don't know how I know, but I can sense there was magic here. It's left a mark. I feel the same thing when I touch the Runestone in the chamber, even though it has been destroyed I can still feel the old energy. I can't really explain it."

Farspell nodded, "It is your dragon heart. As I mentioned, you will find that you learn new abilities and that you know things instinctively. Do not be frightened by it or try to understand it, just let the power grow within you and it will seem natural. Now, what else do you feel?"

"Not much. As I said, there was magic here and it was similar to the Runestone magic, but not the same. I think there may have been a portal here, again, I don't know why but it just feels like that was what caused this magic, um, er, 'stain', yes, that's it, a magic stain, that's the best way to describe it."

Farspell smiled, "Then this is how he escaped. Weldrock must have a way of opening portals that are not limited by the Portalia Runestones. Well done Michael, this is of significant importance."

A few minutes later all of the party were back in the main chamber. Disappointed that there were no clues as to the whereabouts of Swiftaxe, Farspell could only make the assumption that the dwarf had either been killed or captured and transported away by their enemy. In his grief Chisel vehemently refused to believe this and decided to carry out his own search of the Towers. He stormed out of the room. Farspell signalled for Kraven to let him go as the Pinn stepped forward to try to console the dwarf, "Let him vent Kraven. He will return shortly."

Kraven obeyed, "And what now Farspell. Do we return to Fortown with this news?"

"Yes, but not all of us!" replied the wizard. "Green, I want you to carry Chisel back to Fortown. He will need to share with his people the news of the loss of Swiftaxe. You yourself need to report the massacre of the Gates army to Gorlan and Yanto Flow." Farspell looked thoughtful for a moment before continuing, "The rest of us, riding with the fire eagles, will go direct to Pinnhome."

"Pinnhome!" exclaimed Rhys, "Why there?"

"Because, Rhys, I believe that in the vaults of that human city lay the key to translating the island map and also documents that may point us towards understanding your ability."

Farspell looked at Rhys, Ashley and Michael, "In short my friends, those vaults may offer us a way to get you back home!"

In the cover of invisibility, Nexus watched silently and listened. *So the wizard is going to reopen the vaults of the Pinns. Then it is time for me to return to my old home too.* With this thought fresh in his mind, he checked that his cloak still concealed him and left Shangorth Towers for the long journey East.

**To be continued in Book 2 of the Portal Chronicles
The Shimmering Gate**

AUTHOR BIOGRAPHY

Taff Lovesey was born in 1959 in the valleys of South Wales, United Kingdom.

Following a period of four years living in Oregon, USA during the late 90s, Lovesey now resides in Lincolnshire, England with his wife and two children.

A fan of all things fantasy and science fiction and inspired by writers such as Garth Nix, Stephen Donaldson, Tolkien, Phillip Pullman and Edgar Rice Burroughs, he recently took time out from his job in the computer services industry to pen his first novel, The Spider Gem.

Weaving together traditional fantasy elements with new thoughts and ideas, Lovesey succeeds in creating a writing style that provides for an entertaining and pleasurable read.

The Spider Gem is the first book of the Portal Chronicle series and Lovesey is currently working on the follow up which should be complete and ready for publishing in 2006.